Teresa So... in Las Vegas, the ... An avid fan of roma... novels, she is delighted to be living out her dream of writing for Mills & Boon.

As a child books took **Robyn Donald** to places far away from her village in Northland, New Zealand. Then, as well as becoming a teacher, marrying and raising two children, she discovered romances and read them voraciously. So much she decided to write one. When her first book was accepted by Mills & Boon she felt she'd arrived home. Robyn still lives in Northland, using the landscape as a setting for her work. Her life is enriched by friends she's made among writers and readers.

National bestselling author **Nancy Robards Thompson** holds a degree in journalism. She worked as a newspaper reporter until she realised reporting 'just the facts' bored her silly. Now that she has much more content to report to her muse, Nancy loves writing women's fiction and romance full-time. Critics have deemed her work 'funny, smart and observant'. She resides in Florida with her husband and daughter. You can reach her at nancyrobardsthompson.com and Facebook.com/nancyrobardsthompsonbooks

The Princes

COLLECTION

Finding
Her Prince

TERESA SOUTHWICK

ROBYN DONALD

NANCY ROBARDS THOMPSON

MILLS & BOON

First Published in Great Britain 2020
By Mills & Boon, an imprint of HarperCollins*Publishers*
1 London Bridge Street, London, SE1 9GF

FINDING HER PRINCE © 2020 Harlequin Books S.A.

Cindy's Doctor Charming © 2011 Teresa Southwick
Rich, Ruthless and Secretly Royal © 2009 Robyn Donald
Accidental Cinderella © 2009 Nancy Robards Thompson

ISBN: 978-0-263-28067-8

0120

Printed and bound in Spain
by CPI, Barcelona

CINDY'S DOCTOR CHARMING

TERESA SOUTHWICK

To all of you who love happy endings
as much as I do.

Chapter One

She was a fake and a fraud.

Cindy Elliott was walking, talking, breathing proof that not only was it possible to make a silk purse from a sow's ear, but you also could take her out in public. So far no one had pointed and laughed at her pretending to be one of the exalted affluent. But the night was young and she was the queen of getting dumped on.

Famous-rich and anonymous-wealthy people were crammed into this ballroom. She was pretty sure that, unlike herself, none of them had won their seat at this thousand-dollar-a-plate fundraiser with a raffle ticket. Any second she expected the riffraff police to see through her disguise and throw her out.

It wouldn't be the worst thing that ever happened to her, but it was not high on her list of things to do. Her plan was to enjoy every moment of this night. Take in every detail and let the memories brighten the daily grind as she dug herself out of the deep financial hole she'd ended up in after trusting a man.

Cindy grew up in Las Vegas but this was the first time she'd ever been to a shindig at Caesar's Palace. Crystal chandeliers glittered overhead and silver light trickled down on white tablecloths and somehow made the fragrant arrangements of fresh, vibrantly colored flowers smell even better. Candles flickered but paled in comparison to the views visible from floor-to-ceiling windows of the neon skyline outside on the Strip.

She wished more people were looking at *it* instead of her, more specifically male people. A lot of the dapper men in dark suits and tuxedos were staring at her as she snaked her way through the crush of bodies. She felt conspicuous and self-conscious in her strapless, champagne-colored cocktail dress. It was knee length, and now was not a good time to wish for more material.

Finally she reached the perimeter of the room and found the table number that corresponded to the one on her invitation. There were eight chairs and all of them were empty. She decided to sit down and take the strain off her borrowed shoes, minding her friend's warning not to test the limits of a Super Glue repair on a four-inch heel.

Moments later someone appeared in her peripheral vision and a familiar deep voice said, "Is this seat taken?"

Cindy looked up. The face matched the voice as she'd feared it would. Nathan Steele, MD. Dr. Charming himself, she thought sarcastically. He always made her think of Hugh Jackman—tall and broad-shouldered, with hazel eyes and dark brown hair. It pained her to admit, even to herself, that his traditional black tuxedo made him look very handsome—for a bad-tempered, arrogant, egotistical physician.

After a couple seconds of him standing there expectantly,

the message translated from her eyes to her brain that he was waiting for an answer. Glancing at the seven empty seats, she briefly thought about saying that her date was sitting there, then abandoned the idea. She might be a pathetic loser who was a really bad judge of men, but she wasn't a liar.

"No," she finally said. "That seat isn't taken."

He smiled, then lowered his excellent butt into the chair beside hers. "Isn't that lucky?"

"You have no idea." She looked at him, waiting for the inevitable moment when he recognized her as the incompetent from Mercy Medical Center's housekeeping department. The same employee he'd chastised earlier that day for something that wasn't her fault. The indignity and unfairness still smarted.

"Would you like a drink?" The tone was pleasant, deep and sexy. Definitely not his icy-cold, all-business hospital voice.

"Yes." It was the least he could do. "A glass of red wine would be lovely."

He stood. "Don't let anyone take this seat."

"I wouldn't dream of it."

Dream being the operative word. Nathan Steele was walking, talking female fantasy. Definite hero material. A handsome doctor whose mission in life was to save babies who came into this world too early. Infants who needed every trick in his medical bag to survive outside a mother's protective womb while their not-ready-to-be born bodies caught up. How could a woman not seriously crush on a man like that?

The answer was simple. Pretty to look at, difficult to get along with. Cindy didn't need the aggravation. She was still paying for the last wrong guy at the wrong time. She was a twenty-seven-year-old college student because she'd lost not only her bank account but money she hadn't even earned yet to a good-looking man masquerading as a hero. She literally couldn't afford another stupid man mistake.

A few minutes later Dr. Charming set a glass of red wine in front of her and a whiskey neat at his own place before settling beside her again.

"I'm Dr. Steele—Nathan." He looked at her, obviously waiting for her to respond with an introduction. When she said nothing, he added, "And you are?"

Surprised and annoyed in equal parts, she thought. The fact that he didn't recognize her was a surprise. It also annoyed her.

"Cindy Elliott," she said, waiting for the "aha" light to shine in his eyes.

"Nice to meet you, Cindy." He held his hand out.

She wanted to tell him they'd already met. More than once their paths had crossed in the hospital. But then she put her fingers into his palm and a ripple of awareness danced up her arm. He held babies weighing hardly more than a pound, tiny little things that easily fit into this hand. It was warm and strong and capable.

Hero worship threatened until she remembered that doing battle for babies barely alive didn't give him license to be a bastard to everyone else.

"Dr. Steele," she said with as much cool reserve as she could muster.

"Call me Nathan."

"All right. Nathan."

He studied her intently and finally said, "Where do I know you from?"

It was on the tip of her tongue to say she saw him almost every day. Granted, the disposable, white "bunny suit" she wore for her housekeeping job in the neonatal intensive care unit made her fairly anonymous. But still...

She was about to tell him, then something stopped her. The devil made her do it. "I look familiar?"

"Yes."

Maybe she'd finally caught a break. "I guess I just have one of those faces."

"Quite a lovely face."

And now it was red. How did she respond to that? "Thank you."

"I can't shake the feeling that we've met." He sipped his drink. "Did you have a baby in the NICU?"

Heaven forbid. A baby was the last thing she needed. Although that would require sex and she hadn't had any for a very long time. "I've never had a baby."

"So you're here at the fundraiser out of the goodness of your heart?"

"I won a seat at the table with a raffle ticket," she said honestly.

"Right." His mouth curved up at the corners.

"I'm not kidding." The amused expression on his face said he didn't believe her. Honesty was always the best policy. "There's no way I could afford to come to something like this otherwise."

"Of course." His gaze lowered to the spot where the champagne-colored piping on her dress criss-crossed over her breasts. For a moment, intensity flared in his eyes and then amusement returned. "Raffle ticket. If I had a nickel for every time I heard that."

"It's the absolute truth."

"Uh huh. Who's your stylist?"

Stylist? She almost laughed. No way could she afford something like that. "Not a stylist. They're called friends. Fairy godmothers."

"So they pulled off a miracle with a magic wand?" One dark eyebrow rose.

"As a matter of fact…" She took a sip of wine and warmed to the subject. "I wasn't going to come, but my friends talked me into it. I borrowed the dress, shoes and bag from Flora, Fauna and Merryweather."

"Who?"

"They're characters from an animated fairy tale. Surely you saw it when you were a kid."

He shook his head and all hint of laughter disappeared. "No."

"You probably don't remember. It's a classic children's movie."

"That explains it. I was never a child."

The sort of lost expression on his face pulled at her heart and she fought the feeling down, mentally stomped the stuffing out of it. Life was hard and then you met someone who made things harder. Not happening to her again. "I don't know what to say to that."

"It doesn't require a response." He shrugged. "Just a fact."

"Sad fact." Those were two words she wanted back. He didn't need her sympathy and she didn't want to feel sorry for him. But tell that to her bleeding heart, which always got her into trouble. *Used* to get her in trouble. Past tense. She was a reformed soft touch.

"What was your childhood like?" he asked.

"There wasn't a lot of money, but my brother and I didn't know anything different." She thought back to the time before her mother died. "We hung out with friends. Had sleepovers. Pizza and movies. Carefree."

He nodded. "Sounds nice."

"It was." She was going to be sorry for asking, but she couldn't stop herself. "What was yours like? You might not have thought you were a child but everyone starts out that way."

"I was more what you'd call an unaccompanied minor." He took a sip from his glass and drained the contents. "On my own a lot."

"Only child?"

He nodded. "You had a brother?"

"Still do. He's in college. In California." And she was struggling to keep him there because it was her fault the money her father had saved for his education was gone. "I miss him."

"And that detour into childhood was really off the subject." His puzzled expression was back.

"What subject would that be?" The question was just a stall. She should just tell him that he knew her from the hospital. She worked in housekeeping. But some perverse part of her wanted a little payback for his earlier temper tantrum.

"Who are you?"

"Cindy Elliott," she answered.

"So you said." He studied her face until shivers of awareness made her want to squirm. Finally he shook his head. "But I still can't figure out why I know you. Where do you work?"

"Mercy Medical Center." That would jog his memory. Again she waited for the "aha" moment.

"Really?" Instead of recognition, his puzzled frown deepened. "What department?"

"Guess." She took a large swallow of wine.

"Nursing."

She shook her head.

"Human Resources?"

"No." She twirled the long stem of the glass on the table in front of her.

"Dietary?"

"You mean Nutritional Services?" she asked.

"That was politically incorrect of me. Yes, that's what I meant."

She shook her head. "Nope, don't work there either."

"Okay. I give up."

"All evidence to the contrary." If he gave up that easily, there were a lot of babies who wouldn't be alive today. Welcome to a classic conundrum. She was invisible to him. In all fairness, at the hospital he was totally focused on his tiny patients and got points for that. But he'd actually talked to her, chastised her really, for something she hadn't done. How could she admire him so much at the same time she found him to be a pain in the neck?

"What does that mean?" he asked.

That she was an idiot. "I've seen you in action in the NICU."

"But you're not a nurse."

"I'm an administrative intern at Mercy Medical Center. In addition to—other things," she said vaguely.

Before he could answer, an announcement was made for everyone to find their tables and the program would begin. Cindy was grateful for the distraction as the seats around them were filled and introductions made. She talked to the people on her right and tried to ignore the man on her left. Not so easy when their shoulders brushed and thighs bumped. Every stroke sent a surge of heat through her.

She smiled politely, laughed when appropriate and planned to slip out at the first opportunity.

Nathan had expected this dinner to be acutely boring speeches and barely edible rubber chicken. A yawn. He'd been wrong. Not about the speeches and chicken. But he'd never felt less like yawning.

That was because of the mysterious Cindy Elliott.

The words from a song came to mind, about seeing a

stranger across a crowded room. The shimmer of her blond hair had first caught his attention. Her slender curves in the strapless, shiny beige dress were sexy and so damn hot he needed about an hour in a subzero shower.

He'd have followed her anywhere, but when she sat at his table, he wondered if somehow the god of luck had finally come down on his side. The certainty that he'd seen her somewhere now seemed less important than getting her attention away from the woman she'd been talking to on her right side. All through the endless meal she'd industriously ignored him and that was about to end. A quartet had set up to play music and people were moving to the wooden dance floor in the center of the room.

Finally there was a break in the gabfest. He leaned close and said near her ear, "Would you like to dance?"

She met his gaze for several moments and finally said, "I don't think so."

It wasn't ego that caused his surprise at the smackdown. It was that women simply didn't do that. He was forever being introduced by matchmaking mothers who were trying to hook up the successful doctor with their daughter or niece. Or a friend's daughter or niece. Or second cousin once removed. Women liked him. And he liked women.

There was never a challenge involved. He rubbed his neck as that sank in. Maybe there *was* a little ego mixed in with the surprise.

"Why?" he finally asked.

"Why what?"

"Don't you want to dance?"

Her eyes narrowed. They were the color of cinnamon and snapping with intelligence. He found himself eagerly anticipating her response.

"I need a reason?"

"It would be polite."

"Not if I had to explain about a prosthetic leg. Or a pronounced limp from a serious childhood soccer injury."

Like almost every other man in the room, he'd watched the sexy sway of her hips as she'd glided gracefully to the table. The only imminent injury was the rising level of testosterone threatening to blow the top of his head off.

"Do you have any physical limitations?" he asked.

"No."

"Okay." Before she made him navigate more speed bumps, he said, "And you know how to dance?"

"See, that's the thing. Mumsy and Daddy begged me to go to cotillion to smooth out my rough edges—"

"Mumsy?"

She smiled. "Yes. My über-wealthy parents desperately wanted to be here tonight but they simply couldn't tear themselves away from the south of France."

"Über-wealthy?" That's not what she'd told him before. "Just exactly how much did you pay for that lucky raffle ticket?"

Amusement curved the corners of her full, tempting lips. "So you actually were paying attention."

"It's part of my charm."

"Oh, please. Do women really fall for that line?"

"Yes. Although usually a line isn't involved."

"It's a darn shame." She eased away, a pitying expression on her face.

"What?"

"You should really do something about your self-confidence. Surgery. Rehab. There must be some treatment. The miracles of modern medicine—"

"Aren't miracles," he finished.

"No?"

"It's science."

"Really?" There was a spark of interest now.

"Absolutely."

"You don't believe in miracles?" She rested her arm on the table as she angled her body toward him.

"I never underestimate the power of the human spirit. But a miracle?" He shook his head. "If I can't see or touch it, I don't believe it exists."

"What about love?"

Oddly enough, he was pretty sure the question wasn't Cindy being flirtatious. If an invitation to his bed was her goal, she'd be in his arms on the dance floor right now. Instead of having her soft curves pressed against him and the scent of her skin snarling his senses, they were having an existential discussion regarding the reality of love.

"I don't believe in it."

"You're kidding, right?" she asked.

"No."

In the NICU he'd seen worried parents who almost literally willed a tiny scrap of humanity born too soon, a being that they'd only just met face to face, to live. Was that love? He didn't know. It hadn't existed in his life. There'd been buckets of money that his father spent copious amounts of time making. His mother got tired of trying to get her husband's attention and turned to her "projects."

Nathan had tried his hand at love. He'd married a woman he liked and respected. But there was no doubt in his mind that if she hadn't died in a car accident, their trial separation would have turned into an amicable divorce. He missed her, as his best friend. Nothing deeper than that existed in his world. He had no frame of reference for love.

Enough with the self-examination, he thought. He was a doctor, trained to act swiftly and decisively in an emergency. Hesitation could cost lives. And as Cindy had pointed out, his self-confidence needed immediate resuscitation.

He stood, then took her hand and pulled her to her feet. "We're wasting a perfectly good waltz."

He'd expected some rebellion in the ranks, but apparently he had surprise on his side. She didn't pull away but followed almost meekly as he led her through the maze of tables littered with half-eaten cheesecake and hastily abandoned cloth napkins.

On the dance floor he slid his arm around her waist and nestled her against him. She wasn't as tall as he'd thought. It was probably that big attitude of hers generating the illusion. He was used to willowy women, but he could rest his chin on the top of Cindy's head and somehow the fit felt just right. Despite her tongue-in-cheek comments about prosthetics and pronounced limps, she was light on her feet and had no problem following his lead. It felt as if they'd been dancing together for years.

Nathan gave brief thought to making conversation, then decided if he kept his mouth shut, he couldn't put his foot in it. The sweet fragrance of her skin filled his head, more intoxicating than any alcohol he'd ever tasted. Thoughts of her in his arms somewhere private, with the sexy, strapless dress on the floor around her feet was temptation with a capital *T*. He was already planning the strategy to make that happen because it had been hard enough to get her in his arms for a dance.

The music ended and he was about to make his pitch when she backed away. The almost stricken expression on her face puzzled him.

"What's wrong?"

"Nothing. I have to go."

"It's not late," he protested.

"It is for me."

"Don't tell me," he said. "Your car turns into a pumpkin at midnight."

"Something like that." She did an about-face, then slipped away through the crush of bodies still on the dance floor.

"Wait." He knew she heard, because she lifted her hand in a wave as she kept going.

The crowd was thinner than when he'd first arrived tonight, but he had trouble maintaining a visual of her. She kept disappearing because almost everyone was taller. Outside the ballroom in the wide, carpeted hall people milled around. Nathan looked left, then right and couldn't see her.

Instinct had him hurrying toward the bank of escalators leading to the ground level. When he reached the bottom, the crush of bodies parted and there she was, one foot bare and holding a high-heeled pump in her hand. The heel dangled at a dangerous angle. Literally a lucky break for him.

"Looks like you could use some help."

She looked up, her expression rueful. "Not unless you can surgically reattach this."

"I could carry you," he suggested.

She made a great show of assessing him from the chest up. "You probably could. And that would be very gallant. But I wouldn't try it if I were you." Despite the spunky words, she put her hand on his arm for balance as she removed the other shoe.

"So you're determined to go?"

"Even more now." The look she turned on him was wry. "I have no shoes."

"Not a problem for me."

"That makes one of us," she said.

"Okay. I'll let you go quietly if you give me your phone number."

She blinked up at him, and for a split second the idea

seemed to tempt her. Then she shook her head. "I don't think that's a very good idea."

"You don't want me to call you?"

"Give the man a gold star." Regret flickered in her eyes although she probably didn't know it was there. "It's not that I don't appreciate the interest, but women like me don't date men like you."

"I have no idea what that means."

"Okay, how about this? My parents aren't in the south of France or even north Las Vegas for that matter. It was the truth when I told you there's no money in my family."

"I believe you. That's not why—"

"Look Dr. Can't-take-no-for-an-answer. I don't want you to call me. You're a jerk at work. You yell at the help. You have a terrible reputation and no one likes you, including me. And everyone thinks you're inflexible."

He laughed. "You're going to have to do better than that."

"No, I really don't."

"If it's not already clear, *I'd* like to see *you* again."

Something flashed in her eyes when she said "Yeah, well, we all want things we can't have."

Before he could stop her, she turned and vanished in the crowd, ending his lucky streak. The most interesting woman he'd ever met had just shut him down.

At least he knew her name. It was a place to start.

Chapter Two

Tired and cranky the morning after her big night, Cindy and her "clean cart" rode the elevator to Mercy Medical Center's second floor. If she'd known her raffle ticket to the ball included a sleepless night because of Dr. Charming, spending the evening at home in her slippers and sweats would have won out over borrowed finery and broken heels. She still couldn't believe that Nathan Steele, the legendary NICU doc, had asked for her phone number. If he'd known she worked in housekeeping at the hospital, the fairy tale would certainly have ended differently.

The elevator arrived at her stop and the doors whispered open. She pushed the cart, holding a mop, trash receptacle and trigger bottles filled with antiseptic spray, down the hall. After rounding the corner, she came to a screeching halt. Nathan was standing right outside the neonatal intensive care unit.

He was looking at his phone, probably a BlackBerry or

whatever was the latest expensive communication technology crammed into a square case barely visible to the naked eye. She wouldn't know. Her cell phone was old, her calling plan the cheapest available on the market, only for emergencies. Which running into Dr. Steele definitely was, but nothing an old, cheap cell phone could handle.

The good news was that he hadn't seen her yet. She could turn around and hide someplace until he was gone, but there was work to do. She was already gowned in the white, paper coverall with the snaps marching up the front that the unit required. Except for the disposable blue booties over her sneakers, she looked like a bunny. If only this uniform included a bag to put over her head, he wouldn't know her because her ID badge was hidden beneath the protective clothing.

Then she got a grip and realized he overlooked her on a daily basis. There was no reason to believe that had changed because the night before he'd flirted with her outrageously and asked a woman he didn't recognize for her number. The dancing had been really nice, too.

With head held high, she walked past him and stopped at the double-door entrance to the NICU. The cart wasn't allowed inside. With all the sensitive equipment, electrical cords and highly skilled personnel hurrying between the isolettes, there wasn't room to spare for the clunky cart. Housekeeping paraphernalia was necessary but not even in the same league with the pricey, sensitive and technical tools that saved the babies.

Cindy picked up one of the trigger bottles and was just about to approach the automatic opening door when she felt someone behind her. The hair at her nape prickled and her skin flushed with heat that had nothing to do with the hot suit. She could be wrong about the awareness, but she was pretty sure she wasn't. The same thing had happened once before. Specifically, last night.

"Cindy?"

It was *him*. Not only that, he'd called her by name and as far as she knew he hadn't looked at her. She turned, bracing for this unprecedented happening. And there was Dr. Charming with his meticulously mussed hair and swoon-worthy square jaw. He was dressed in scrubs, which weren't particularly appealing, except that he was wearing them.

"How did you know it was me?" she asked.

"I recognized your perfume."

Well, damn. Why did he have to be a smooth talker on top of everything else? "I don't know what to say to that."

"Interesting development because last night you had all the answers."

If he really believed that, she'd put on a pretty good performance. "About that—"

"So this is where I know you from."

"Scene of the crime." She'd let him connect whatever dots he saw fit to explain why she'd made him guess her identity.

"Crime being the pertinent word. It wasn't my finest hour. I owe you an apology."

At the speed of light he'd figured out that she was the housekeeper he'd chastised the day before. Pigs must be flying outside the window because this was an unexpected and unprecedented turn of events.

Doctors never apologized to housekeepers, partly because they were the ones who cleaned up after the high and mighty and just disappeared into the landscape.

"Excuse me, but I could have sworn you used the word *apology.*"

"I suppose your hostility is logical."

"Really? You think?" She rested her free hand on her hip. "Maybe because I was found guilty without benefit of a fair trial? I didn't touch that baby in the NICU."

He nodded. "I saw movement. It was a peripheral vision thing—"

"NICU housekeeping 101—never touch the babies. Stifle any rogue maternal instincts and beat them into submission. It was the first thing I was taught and I learned my lesson well."

"There's a good reason for the rule. The babies are incredibly fragile. It's tempting to want to hold them because the heat shield on the Giraffe is up. For a good reason. The neonates need a lot of attention and we need fast and easy access to them."

She knew the Giraffe was the commonly used nickname for the highly specialized isolette that could move up, down and other directions just by pushing a button.

"I know how frail they are," she said. "I understand that the goal is to keep the environment like a mother's womb, warm and quiet. And that begs the question—If calm is what you want, why did you yell at me?"

"Technically, I didn't yell. My tone was moderated. At best, forceful." Her exaggerated eye roll didn't stop him. "And I pulled you aside to the nurse's station, away from the baby."

"And that makes it so much better," she said, lifting the floodgates on her sarcasm. "That way the nurses could really hear you unreasonably humiliate me."

"It was an overreaction." His hazel eyes turned more gold than green and went all puppy dog. "Would it help to explain that the little guy was just born? He weighs a little more than three pounds and it's touch and go. I was worried and took it out on you."

"That's something I never got from the job description

or orientation. Nowhere in my employee handbook does it say that my function is to absorb a physician's deflected tension or anger." She could tell he was listening and letting her vent, but that didn't sit well or turn off the mad. "Housekeepers aren't here to be stress relievers for anyone higher up on the food chain."

He really looked sorry. "That's not fair."

Probably not, but she was weakening and that couldn't happen.

"No one ever said life would be fair, Dr. Steele—"

"Nathan. Remember?"

She was trying not to. "Didn't your mother ever tell you that?"

"She wasn't around much for heart-to-heart chats. I pretty much figured that one out on my own, though." An edgy tone crept into his voice. "Look, Cindy, I said I was sorry—"

"No. You really didn't. I heard the word apology and a detailed justification for why you went off on me for no good reason. Not once, though, did I hear you say the word *sorry*."

"Well, I am." He saw her look and added, "Sorry, that is. I was wrong."

"Wow, the world has gone mad. The *w* word actually passed your lips. As I live and breathe." Her skin started to tingle when she mentioned his lips and it didn't help that he kept staring at her. "I'll be sure not to spread that around. Who'd believe me anyway?"

"While we're setting the record straight, I feel it's only fair to point out that you were wrong, too."

"About what?" Her whole life consisted of being wrong one too many times, so a clarification was necessary.

"Me," he said. "I'll admit sometimes I can be a jerk at work. After all we've established that I did chastise you unjustly. But I take exception to the reputation remark. Mine is impeccable. And I'm not inflexible."

"Okay, then. Color me corrected."

"I'm not finished."

"Right. What else have you got?"

"People *do* like me."

By *people* she was pretty sure he meant women. It would be far too easy to be one of them and that simply couldn't happen. She was too close to getting what she'd worked so hard for. There was light at the end of a long, dark financial and educational tunnel and she couldn't afford *not* to focus on either of those fronts now.

Eyes straight ahead. No distractions; no detours.

"There's probably some truth to that," she agreed. "Someone undoubtedly does like you. File it under 'good to know.' Now, I've got work to do—"

"As do I. It's time to check on Rocky."

"Who?"

"The little guy. From yesterday. How could you possibly forget when you took one for the team?"

"Is that what you call it?"

"My story and I'm sticking to it." He smiled, and the power of it was awesome. "It's what the nurses call him. Somehow the nicknames just seem to stick."

"Rocky. A fighter." That tugged at her heart big time and she needed her space, stat, before she bought into him being a bona fide hero even after yesterday when he'd made her feel like the lowest of the low. He fought for the most defenseless and delicate of God's creatures. How long could she sustain this weak, borderline unjustifiable case of self-righteous indignation? How did she protect herself from him?

"Okay, then," she said, starting to turn away. His hand on her arm froze the movement. She could feel the warmth of his fingers and it had nothing to do with the protective suit keeping in body heat.

"Wait. There's one more thing."

There always was. How many ways did she not need this in her life? She forced herself to meet his gaze and braced to repel the reaction. "What?"

"Your phone number."

"What about it?" That was a stall. By definition one needed a number to dial to contact someone else on a telephone.

What she didn't know was *why* he wanted hers. Surely he didn't really want to call *her*. She'd admit to having the tiniest little crush on him after last night. Sleep had finally come when she'd realized that it wasn't really something to worry about because they were on completely different rungs of the hospital social ladder. But now he knew exactly who she was and had brought up the subject again. What was up with that?

"I'm asking for your phone number," he patiently explained.

"I don't give out that information," she said.

"Why?"

"Why do you want it?"

Now he rolled his eyes. "I'd like to call you sometime."

"So you can yell at me after hours, too?"

"Of course not." His gaze narrowed. "Has anyone ever talked to you about this acute flair you have for the dramatic? *And* holding a grudge?"

"Not recently."

"Look, I'd like your number so I can ask—"

"Don't say it."

He moved in a completely different orbit and she existed in the real world. Under normal circumstances there wasn't a chance in hell that their worlds would collide, but that changed last night and an alternate reality was initiated.

Now he was trying to change the order of the universe. When the last man in her life cleaned out her savings and maxed out her existing credit cards and ones he took out in her name, she learned the hard lesson that men have ulterior motives. The only unknown was how much it would cost her. She absolutely would not be a victim of whatever it was that Nathan Steele was planning.

"Why shouldn't I say it?" There was a charming, confident look on his face.

"Because yesterday you only made me *feel* like an idiot. If I gave you my number now, that would make it true."

She walked into the NICU before he could respond. There was nothing left to do except work through the bittersweet, wistful feeling inside that made her wish a man hadn't screwed up her life. Then she might be tempted to take a chance that another man wasn't going to do the same thing.

Nathan wasn't sure why he cruised the cafeteria at lunchtime instead of going to the doctor's dining room. Then he saw Cindy Elliott sitting by herself and the motivation for his detour became clear. It was an excuse to talk to her. Damage control for his unreasonable behavior, he told himself. But *himself* wasn't quite buying into that story. After her over-the-top reaction to his apology for unreasonable behavior, he'd turned over the unreasonable behavior crown to her. Yet he couldn't stop his own curiosity at her response.

He grabbed a tray and stepped into line, then picked up a ready-made turkey sandwich and a bottle of water. After paying for the items, he looked around, half-expecting her to be gone. She had a way of running out on him. This time she was still sitting alone at a table for two by the wall. Convenient.

"Here goes nothing," he mumbled to himself.

Sunshine leaked through the windows from the hospital's dome tower above this room, allowing the light in. The hum of voices buzzed around him. Balancing the rectangular green tray, he snaked his way through the Formica-topped tables and metal chairs with orange plastic seats.

He stopped beside her and did a replay of what he'd asked last night. "Is this seat taken?"

Her eyes narrowed on him when she looked up. "What if I said I was expecting someone?"

"Are you?"

"No."

Without waiting for permission, he set down his tray and sat in the chair opposite her. He sort of missed the "bunny suit." Now she was wearing the work uniform of cotton pants and dark-blue scrubs top with *Environmental Services* embroidered on the breast. In this light, her eyes were even more interesting—darker brown with flecks of gold. Definitely cinnamon. Spicy. Interesting. Not unlike the lady herself.

"So, how's it going?" He unwrapped the plastic on his sandwich and took a bite.

"Until now there was only one black mark on the day. In the last five seconds that just doubled." She set her spoon down. "Why are you here?"

"I'm hungry?"

"You know that's not what I meant. You could be having lobster, caviar and truffles in the doctor's dining room."

"Actually I think it's pheasant under glass and baked Alaska day. I'm not a big fan of either," he said.

"Again, not my point. You're here with the peasants. Why is that?"

"Maybe I find the environment here more interesting." He finished the first half of his sandwich and glanced at her empty bowl with wrappers piled up in it. "Soup and crackers isn't much for lunch."

"I'm on a diet."

"Why?" Nathan twisted the top off his water bottle and took a drink.

"By definition diet implies trying to drop a few pounds." Her tone was conversational, but mistrust lurked in her eyes.

"Again I ask—why?" He wagged a warning finger when she opened her mouth to answer. "Don't give me the snarky, sarcastic response that I know is on the tip of your tongue. You're not overweight."

"Why else would I go on a diet?" She leaned back and folded her arms over her chest. The classic stubborn, you're-not-getting-anything-out-of-me pose.

"All well and good for someone who needs to shape up, but you don't."

"How do you know?"

"Because I saw you in that dress last night."

The sexy, sensuous image would be imprinted on his mind forever. And he'd held her in his arms. She had curves in all the right places and not one of those places needed to slim down. The memory of her body pressed against his sent a flood of testosterone surging through him. And it wasn't the first time he'd reacted to her that way.

"Why are you really eating this?" he asked.

"Why do you care?"

"Good question. Humor me."

"Would you believe I have irritable bowel syndrome and this is a bland diet?"

"No."

She was irritable, but that wasn't a medical diagnosis.

It had something to do with him personally. Just a feeling, but he was pretty sure this snappish attitude had a lot to do with him not recognizing her, especially after coming down on her for something she hadn't done. And since his apology hadn't produced any discernible softening in her, that cranked up his curiosity.

"Okay." She tapped her lip thoughtfully. "What if I'm still full from last night?"

"Doubtful. You didn't finish the rubber chicken or even touch the prefab cheesecake." He would know. He'd noticed that, along with everything else about her. She was quick-witted, smart and sexy. A triple threat.

She sipped from the straw in her iced tea, then asked, "Are you going to let this go any time soon?"

"That's not my current plan, no."

She sighed. "If you must know, I'm always on a very tight budget the week before payday. Something you probably have no frame of reference for."

"Budgets? Or payday?"

"Either. Both."

"I get the concept, but you're right. It's not something I had to deal with."

"Had?"

"I didn't have a childhood, but not because money was a problem."

He'd had his hands full coping with family issues. And thinking about that could put multiple black marks on his day. Cindy, however, could brighten up an entire room. He'd found that out last night. And she was much more interesting than memories of the clinically dysfunctional Steele family.

"So," he said, rolling the empty plastic from his sandwich into a ball. "The south of France with Mumsy isn't in the budget?"

Her mouth twitched. She wanted to laugh but was holding back. "About that—"

"No need to explain."

"In my small way, I was getting even with you for yelling at me."

"I get that. What's your excuse for being crabby now?" he asked. "Lack of sleep? Staying out too late last night?"

"You got me. Hobnobbing with the rich and famous wore me out. I stayed up way past my bedtime."

And speaking of beds, an image of her in his with twisted sheets tightened a knot of need inside him that had started fewer than twenty-four hours ago when he'd seen her walk like sex in motion across a crowded room. Talking with her, discovering her sharp mind and keen sense of humor had only intensified the feeling. Then she'd really piqued his curiosity by abruptly walking out after cutting short their dance.

"It seemed like you were having fun. Why did you leave the party?" he asked.

"It was time to go." Something in her eyes said that wasn't the whole truth. "Now I've got a question for you— why are you stalking me?"

"That's harsh," he teased. "Take last night—"

"You mean when you didn't have a clue who I was?"

"No offense," he said, "But last night you weren't wearing the NICU jumpsuit."

"It's a legitimate question, Doctor—"

"Nathan, remember?"

The look on her face said she remembered it all and wasn't happy that she did. "My point is that a physician rubbing elbows with the peons here at Mercy Medical Center just isn't deliberately done. So the stalking remark is not out of line."

"It is if I just want to get to know you. And I do. We work

in the same place and it's inevitable that our paths would cross. Which is the reason I'd like your phone number."

"I don't really get the connection." She stood and picked up her tray. Over her shoulder as she was walking away, she said, "And you should just let it go, *Doctor.*"

Nathan knew she was right. He should let it go.

He honestly didn't understand why he couldn't. The average woman would be happy to go out with him. Clearly Cindy wasn't average, which could explain part of her appeal. The other part was curiosity. She wouldn't even give him a chance, and he was pretty sure that wasn't about him chastising her.

Cindy Elliott was quite the mystery and he wasn't finished trying to solve her. He'd see her stubborn and raise her a healthy dose of persistence.

Chapter Three

Cindy had clocked in from lunch after her unexpected encounter with Nathan and was now back to work. The afternoon stop in the NICU was next on her work sheet. Other than Dr. Charming going out of his way to talk to her in the cafeteria, it promised to be an ordinary afternoon. Then everything changed. And it all happened so fast.

One minute Cindy was running a long-handled dusting tool over the linoleum floor, the next Nathan was there with a tiny baby. He was calmly issuing orders like a general in the thick of battle.

The common sense move was to get out of the way even if directions to do just that in the event of a medical crisis hadn't been drilled into her. Cindy had been employed at Mercy Medical Center for nearly two years and had seen her share of medical situations but never one involving Nathan Steele. She knew what he did, had seen his medical practice partner in action, but she had never actually witnessed him saving a little life. And she had a bad feeling that her life was about to change. She couldn't help thinking that darn raffle ticket had somehow altered fate to put her in his orbit.

From her protected position against the wall she could hear the team talking and knew the baby boy was a twenty-five-weeker born just minutes ago by C-section. That made him about four months premature. He was already intubated, and they were using a bag to force air into his lungs. The person bagging the baby was her friend, Harlow Marcelli, who worked in the Respiratory Therapy department.

Cindy couldn't really see what the staff was doing to the baby, but Nathan was taller than everyone and the strain and intensity on his face were clearly visible. When bodies parted, she noticed that he was using two fingers on the tiny chest, compressions for cardiopulmonary resuscitation.

After listening with the stethoscope, he said, "Let's get him on a ventilator. IV line stat and electrodes for EKG. I need to surf him."

She made a mental note to ask what that meant.

Meanwhile, the troops moved to follow his orders, and moments later there were tubes and machines in place. Tracings on the monitors were blue, green and pink—each to distinguish a different function to be watched.

"I need blood gases," Nathan said.

Instantly Harlow moved, like a runner off the block at the sound of the starting pistol. In a few minutes, Nathan looked at the readings and nodded.

"He's a fighter. I think the little gladiator is stable for the moment. Watch him. I want to know if anything changes. I'll be right outside." He looked at the staff who'd fought with him. "Great job, everyone. I'm going to talk to the dad. Mom's still in recovery."

Cindy moved slightly to her right, to see through the double glass doors and out into the hall. The father was probably in his late twenties or early thirties, blonde and blue eyed, with terror all over his face. She couldn't hear what was said, but as Nathan talked some of the fear drained from the man's expression, leaving your garden-variety worry in its wake. When the man glanced over, she could also see love for the tiny little life fighting to survive. The gladiator, Nathan had called him.

Just last night he'd told her that if he couldn't see or touch something, he didn't believe it existed. How could he not see the love in that father's eyes?

"He's pretty awesome, isn't he?"

Cindy jumped at the sound of her friend's voice, then turned. "You startled me. I didn't know you were there."

"Yeah. I can see you're distracted." Harlow Marcelli was a pretty, green-eyed brunette and the fairy godmother who'd loaned her the patched-up pumps for the fundraiser.

"Not preoccupied. Just doing my job," she defended.

"Yeah." Her friend glanced to where the two men were still talking. "If your job is to watch Dr. Hot Stuff."

"Not my day to keep an eye on him." Cindy deliberately turned her back to the doors. "No matter how many times I see you do your thing, it never fails to amaze me. You were pretty awesome just now."

"Thanks." Harlow slid a glance over her shoulder at the isolette surrounded by state-of-the-art equipment. "He's not out of the woods yet. I hope he's a fighter like the doc said."

"Me, too. The gladiator." She smiled.

"The staff usually gives the preemies nicknames," Harlow explained, echoing what Nathan had already told her. "Something inspirational to live up to."

"Live being the operative word. It surprised me coming

from Nathan—" She stopped when the other woman gave her a funny look.

"Since when do you call him by his first name?"

"Oh, that—"

"Yeah, that."

Cindy glanced over her shoulder where he still stood in the hall. "We sat at the same table at the fundraiser last night."

"And?"

"The glue on your shoe didn't hold up."

"Later with the shoes news." Harlow's green eyes snapped with impatience. "When did you start calling Dr. Charming *Nathan?*"

"Last night. When he asked me to."

"Why?" Her friend added, "Did he ask you to, I mean?"

"Probably because he didn't know who I was."

"I need more information than that."

Cindy gripped the long handle of her dusting device. "He sat next to me, bought me a drink and said I looked familiar, but he couldn't place me."

"He didn't recognize you?" Surprise jumped into Harlow's eyes.

"Not even when I made him guess."

"You didn't," her friend scoffed.

"I did." Cindy had her reasons and it had seemed like a good idea at the time.

"Hot damn," Harlow said. "I can't wait to tell Whitney and Mary Frances that we literally transformed you into a mystery woman. That's so cool."

"Not really. When I saw him this morning, he figured it out."

When he smelled her perfume. That memory made her stomach do a funny little shimmy and she told herself it was only because something that sensitive was out of character for Nathan Steele.

"Was he mad?"

It would have been easier if he had been. Then giving him a hard time would have been justified and not just turned her into a roaring witch.

"No. He took it well. Even apologized to me for over-reacting and yelling at me in here yesterday. Then he asked for my phone number again," Cindy explained.

The other woman's jaw dropped. "Again?"

"I refused to give it to him when he asked me last night. After he caught up with me. And he only did because your shoe broke."

"He chased you?" Harlow folded her arms over her chest. "This gets better and better."

"It was time for me to go."

"Apparently he didn't agree."

"That's just because my identity was still in question and that intrigued him," Cindy said. "Sort of like when a superhero assumes an alter ego. It's the whole don't-I-know-her-from-somewhere? thing."

"Then what was his excuse for asking again today?"

"He's one of those guys who can't take no for an answer."

"And why should he? Women in this hospital are taking numbers in the line to snap him up." Warning slid into her friend's eyes. "Let him call. You don't have to commit to anything. And I wouldn't if I were you."

"Preaching to the choir, H," Cindy said. "I don't have time for the games."

Just then Nathan walked back into the unit to check on the baby.

"Gotta go," Harlow said.

Cindy turned away and finished her job in the NICU,

then slipped out the door. Her clean cart was against the wall in the hall. She was still putting away her cleaning supplies when she heard the doors behind her whisper open. It could have been anyone, but not just anyone made the hair at her nape prickle. Only Nathan did that and the development was recent. And, annoyingly enough, recurring.

"Cindy—"

She turned around. "Did I forget to do something in the unit?"

"No. I just—" He ran his fingers through his hair. "I saw you talking to Harlow."

"She's my friend. One of the fairy godmothers, actually."

"Good to know her talents are more than just being one of the best respiratory techs here at Mercy Medical."

"Speaking of that," she said. "I was watching just now, when you were working on the gladiator."

"Don't ask me where that came from," he said sheepishly. The look was too darn cute.

"Okay. But I wanted to ask something else." Anything to take the edge off his appeal. She met his gaze and said, "What did you mean when you said 'surf' him?"

"Surfactin. It's a medication."

"Yeah. I was pretty sure you weren't talking about ocean waves. What does it do?"

"Makes the lungs more flexible. If they're stiff, air can't be pushed in and out," he explained. "One of the problems in neonates is that their lungs are immature. The medication helps them function better until they fully develop."

"I see."

"Good. Now I've got one for you."

"One what?"

"Question. Turnabout is fair play." He leaned a broad shoulder against the wall.

If the inquiry was about how a guy could look so sexy dressed in utilitarian scrubs, she had no answer. On every possible level it was just wrong for him to be so yummy in shapeless cotton material with a drawstring at the waist of the pants. The V-neck shirt at least revealed the hint of chest hair, but really, the ensemble left a lot to be desired. Except the guy in it was more desirable than her favorite chocolate with caramel.

"Okay. You can ask," she said, knowing she was really going to regret giving permission.

"What do you have against giving me your phone number?" he said.

"You'll use it," she answered. "Gotta get back to work now."

She grabbed her cart and pushed it down the hall, feeling his gaze lasering into her back until she rounded the corner. Leaning against the wall, she blew out a long breath.

It was hard work going one on one with a hero. Even harder to remember why she needed to not get sucked into the games. Between work and school, she didn't have the time or energy. Whatever he was selling, she wasn't buying. And even if she were, she'd just blown any chance with him. Like Harlow said, women were waiting in line.

So much for her plan to attend the fundraiser and enjoy every moment. Pulling out those memories of how the beautiful people lived was supposed to brighten her daily grind. She'd made memories, all right, and so much more. She'd snagged the doctor's attention. For all the good that would do.

After today he wouldn't waste any more time on her. Which was just as well because she didn't have the time, energy or emotional reserves to waste on him.

And that made her sad and angry. It made her wish that once upon a time, she hadn't been duped and damaged by a dope.

As Nathan headed down the hall toward administration, he was mentally fine-tuning his case to hire extra staff for the NICU. For the past week things had been nuts. Gladiator, aka Dylan Mason, was the first of some really sick babies. The staff in the unit was working their asses off and he wanted more bodies to care for his patients. Still, it wouldn't be easy to convince the powers-that-be to spend more money, and he braced for the coming battle.

But when he walked into the outer office and saw Cindy at the desk, battles of the sexy sort took center stage. Probably because she'd refused every request to let him call her.

He'd never worked that hard for a phone number and, frankly, the struggle made him even more determined to get to the bottom of her resistance.

Cindy watched warily as he moved closer then settled his hip on the corner of her desk. There were two metal-framed chairs in front of it, but invading her space was more appealing. And this place could use a healthy dose of interesting. The ocean scenes on the beige walls made it generic decorating. With her blond hair and warm brown eyes, she sure brightened up her surroundings.

"Is there any job in this hospital that you don't do?" he asked.

"Brain surgery."

He laughed and that hadn't been his expectation on his way to the administration offices. "So, can I ask what you're doing here?"

"You can *ask.*" The way her full mouth curved up in a

teasing smile finished the implication that she didn't have to answer. "I'm an administrative intern."

"Right. I remember. In addition to your other job?"

She nodded. "After the fall semester, I'll have my degree in hospital administration. This summer was a good time to get the internship part accomplished."

"Busy girl."

She shrugged and the movement did amazing things to her breasts under the pink, silky blouse. By peeking over the desk he could see her black slacks. The business attire was buttoned-down professional. He'd also seen her in plain housekeeping clothes. But by far his favorite look was that short, strapless dress he'd first seen her in. The memory caused a very physical reaction that was a good indication his desire to see her out of it hadn't gone away.

"So," she said, tapping her pen on the desk. "I'm going to take a wild guess that you're here to see Mr. Ryan. And not stalking me."

"You would be correct. I have a staffing issue to discuss with him."

"Specifically?"

"There's a lot of work in the NICU. We're going nuts up there."

"And you want more help," she guessed.

"Right in one."

She swiveled her chair to the right and faced the computer monitor, then clicked away on the keyboard until data scrolled onto the screen. After studying it for a moment, she turned back and looked up.

"Good luck with that."

He stared at her for several moments, then said, "What?"

"I'm pretty sure Mr. Ryan won't give his approval to hire any more people."

"You can tell that by looking at the computer?"

"Yes."

He stood and looked down. "What is it? The great and powerful Oz?"

She grinned. "Pay no attention to the man behind the curtain."

"Seriously? How can a computer tell you we're not up to our necks in alligators?"

"All the productivity information is here. It's about FTEs—"

"No acronyms, please."

"Full time equivalents. Then there are RVUs—" She noticed his frown and her full mouth curved up. "Relative value units."

"Dumb it down for me."

He knew matching personnel to patient load was complicated but had deliberately steered clear of the minutiae because it wasn't his problem. Now avoidance was paying off because she was talking to him.

"There's a formula to determine the percentage of staff hours per patient day for every hospital department. For example, if you're allowed four hours to get the job done and do it in three hours and forty-five minutes, you're over a hundred percent. That's exactly where administration wants it and you're the best thing since sliced bread."

"What if I want two more nurses?"

She turned to the computer, clicked the keys and assimilated the information that popped up. "According to this, NICU productivity is at ninety-four percent."

"That sounds pretty good."

"Not really. It means you have to give up a nurse."

"You're kidding," he said.

"Do I look like I'm kidding?"

No, but she looked like she was enjoying this more than

was absolutely necessary. She also looked like a woman who needed a full-body-contact kiss and he was just the relative value unit to give it to her.

"So, what happens if the NICU is full and the perinatologist sends over a high-risk pregnancy patient who delivers a twenty-four-week baby? How do I get a nurse?"

"The percentages are set at safe staffing levels. But in an extreme case, you contact the on-call nurse. If there's a need for more help, you try to catch someone else at home and ask them to come in."

"And what if we can't find someone?"

"What if a brontosaurus walks in with two eggs and one of them cracks?" She folded her hands on the desk.

He knew what she was getting at, but this spirited back and forth was the most fun he'd had since the last time they'd talked.

"And your point is?" he asked, settling into the chair in front of her desk for a full-on view of her.

"You can't staff for 'what if.' In a perfect world, yes. But we go by averages, then adjust to the reality we're dealing with."

"When I go in to see Ryan, am I going to get a rewind and play of this whole conversation?" It had been much more palatable coming from her, he realized.

"Probably."

"Well, I'm already here." And so was she. He had the testosterone rush to prove it. "Might as well go in and try to grind him down."

"Good luck."

Speaking of luck… It was time to stop talking shop and try again to grind *her* down. Or at least find out what her beef was with him.

"I'm having a NICU meeting today at five o'clock.

Nurses, respiratory therapy. You should come. Everyone who works in the unit is invited."

"I don't work there." Pink crept into her cheeks. "At least not on the babies."

"Consider this part of your administrative internship. Good experience to come and hear the opposing point of view."

"As tempting as that is…"

That was a no without saying *no*. And he knew she really didn't need to be there. Personnel and administration were like Democrats and Republicans. They'd never see eye to eye. He just wanted the opportunity to spend a little time with her.

"I'd really like to see you." He wasn't talking about the meeting, and the way her eyes narrowed told him she knew it. "But this is me *not* using your phone number."

"Look, Nathan, I'm really flattered that you asked. Partly because I thought that ship had sailed last week. But mostly because…" She stopped, clearly weighing how much to say. "Because every single woman younger than fifty who works in this facility, and some who don't, are waiting in line to give you their phone numbers. But I'm not one of them."

"Why is that?"

"Mostly because I can't help wondering why you keep asking."

"You mean am I up to something?" he asked.

"I mean is it just stubbornness? Ego? You being contrary?"

"Is it so hard to believe that I want to get to know you better?"

"Oh, please." She made a scoffing sound. "That's code for hooking up."

He wouldn't say no to a hookup, but that wasn't his

primary objective. "I'd really like to see you outside of work."

"Let me be clear. And honest. You said it yourself. I'm a busy girl. I don't have time in my schedule for a fling."

"Neither do I."

Her eyes flashed with what looked like anger and frustration. "In my experience, guys like you are all about the one who said no."

"Later I'm probably going to be annoyed at being lumped in with the jerks."

She ignored that and continued. "Let's just skip to the end. How about if I just sleep with you? Then I can get you out of my life. It's not even necessary to buy me dinner. It will save us both time. Seven minutes tops."

"Ouch." He'd heard both heat and hurt in her voice, and that took the sting out of the words for him. If only it had canceled out his curiosity, but he wasn't that lucky. "What if I *want* to buy you dinner? No strings."

"Do you?" she asked suspiciously.

"Take a chance. Find out for yourself."

"If I do will you go away quietly?"

"Can we just take this one step at a time?" he asked. "Don't spoil the surprise. That takes all the fun out of it."

"In my experience, there's nothing fun about a surprise."

That was the second time she'd mentioned her experience. It didn't take a mental giant to figure out that whatever happened hadn't been good. If Nathan was as smart as everyone thought, he'd run from Cindy and her emotional baggage. But apparently he wasn't that bright. Because he was inclined to sit here and wait until she agreed to go out with him.

"You know you want to say yes," he coaxed.

"Were you raised by wolves? What part of *no* do you not understand?" She glared at him.

"My parents were incredibly civilized. Just not to each other." He refused to take the bait. It didn't escape his notice that she was pulling out all the stops to get him to give up. That made the challenge of wearing her down all the more stimulating. "Come on, Cindy. It will be fun."

"The *Titanic* was fun, too, if you like freezing cold water and gigantic icebergs opening up the side of your ship like a tuna can."

"I'm not leaving until you agree to have dinner with me tonight." Tonight because he didn't want to give her time to back out.

She thought for several moments and apparently decided he wasn't backing down. After an exaggerated sigh, she said, "All right. But only because I have to eat."

"I'll pick you up at seven."

Chapter Four

Cindy peeked out the window of her tiny three-bedroom home in the old part of Henderson. Nathan wasn't there yet, but it was only six-fifty. She still had ten minutes to fret over and change the sleeveless black cotton sundress that had been her second outfit choice. If only her fairy godmothers were here with borrowed clothes, shoes and much-needed advice because she was running low on clothing options and was fresh out of common sense. A limited budget didn't allow for a large wardrobe. Lack of variety sure cut down on time spent making a decision, but that didn't erase the desperate wish to not care so much about looking her very best.

Because impressing Nathan Steele wasn't the goal for tonight. Men were trouble and she didn't need any more of it. This dinner was all about getting the doctor to back off and leave her alone so she could focus on her internship and the current job that helped pay her mountain of bills.

Cindy paced the living room's wood floor and stayed far away from a mirror that would send her fashion critique impulses into warp drive. The back-and-forth walking lasted for another five minutes before she lifted the edge of the dollar store criss-crossed lace curtains just as a small, sporty silver Mercedes pulled up to the curb. The nerves she'd barely kept under control did a synchronized freak out.

"This is a very bad idea," she muttered.

She grabbed the lightweight black sweater and her purse from the cedar chest that doubled as a coffee table sitting in front of the green floral love seat. Then she waited by the door for his knock. When it came, she whispered one Mississippi, two Mississippi, and continued until she got to ten before opening the door and forcing a bright smile.

"Hi. You're early."

Nathan's gaze slid from the top of her head to her red-painted toes and the casual black and white low-heeled sandals. There was a gleam in his eyes when he smiled. "The rumor is that you're on a tight schedule so wasting time wasn't an option. And you're obviously ready. You look beautiful."

"Thanks."

It was just a line, she told herself. He was only being polite. But all the disclaimers in the world couldn't stop the glow that went nuclear inside her and the tightness in her chest when she looked at him. The sexy scruff on his cheeks and jaw was missing, proof that he'd shaved. For her.

That started more flutters in her stomach, but she managed to say, "You're not so bad yourself."

The truth was that he didn't have a bad look. She'd seen him in scrubs and in a tux. The current crisply pressed khaki slacks and cream-colored sport shirt showed off the tan on his muscular arms with the added benefit of enhancing his broad shoulders and trim waist. It was impossible to pick a favorite Nathan view when he looked like sin-for-the-taking in everything.

Or nothing?

That thought sent hormones surging through her, and she quickly stepped outside on the porch. After locking the door she said, "Let's go."

Nathan followed behind her on the sidewalk so if he found her hurried exit weird, she didn't know, what with not being able to see his expression. At the curb he opened the car, then cupped her elbow in his palm, handing her inside. The touch did nothing to calm her nerves. In fact it started tingles line dancing up and down her arms.

Before there was time to anesthetize them, he was in the driver's seat, starting the car. The interior was small and intimate, not nearly enough space to dissipate the masculine scent of his skin. It surrounded her as surely as if he held her in his arms. Less than two weeks ago he'd done just that, the night he hadn't recognized her. Being that close to him had stirred a fair amount of panic and then she'd made a dash for the exit.

He'd only caught up with her because her shoe broke. Moments later she'd called him a jerk and he'd laughed, then said he wanted to see her again. Turning him down flat hadn't worked so well and here she was, out of the frying pan and into the fire. So to speak.

Speaking of speaking, she wasn't doing any, so she tried to think of something witty to say. All she could come up with was, "So where are you taking me?"

Before turning left onto Lake Mead Boulevard, he glanced over. "Have you ever had a nice surprise?"

She wasn't sure why he'd asked but gave the question

some serious thought. "Probably, but I can't remember one off the top of my head."

"Well, brace yourself. I promise this one will be good."

He turned from Horizon Ridge Parkway onto Eastern Avenue and drove up the hill, then pulled into the parking lot of Capriotti's Italian restaurant. It was dusk and not the optimum time to appreciate the lights across the Vegas Valley, but after the sun set, there would be a spectacular view.

Inside, the muted light made for a romantic atmosphere, and a cozy booth for two in the back corner cranked it up several notches. Their arms touched and Cindy swore she actually heard the crackle of electricity that was anything but static. A little sideways move gave her space but no real breathing room.

The last time a guy had taken her to a restaurant with candles and white tablecloths, he'd sweet-talked his way into her life and her bank account, then proceeded to rob her blind. Nathan probably didn't need her money, but he stirred a need deep inside and she had an uneasy feeling that he could take from her something far more precious than her good credit rating.

A forty-something waiter with salt-and-pepper hair and wearing black pants and a long-sleeved white shirt appeared beside them. "Dr. Steele, it's nice to see you again."

Nathan's smile was friendly. "Hello, Mario. How are you?"

"Very well." He looked at Cindy and bowed slightly. "Welcome to Capriotti's. May I get you something from the bar?"

Dr. Charming met her gaze. "What would you like?"

"Surprise me," she said wryly.

"Mario, I think we'll have a bottle of my favorite wine."

"The pinot noir. Excellent choice. I'll bring it right out." Before leaving, he handed them menus.

When they were alone Cindy opened hers and said, "So they know your favorite wine. Obviously, you come here often."

"The food is really good."

"Do your other women like it?" She was looking at the food choices but not really seeing the words. When she glanced up she saw that he looked more amused than anything else.

"My other women?" he asked. "In spite of what you think and the hospital gossip you base it on, there is no line of women."

Before she could refute that, someone delivered a basket containing warm rolls wrapped in a white cloth. With a flourish, the guy mixed oil and balsamic vinegar on a plate for dipping. Then Mario returned with the bottle of red and skillfully opened it with a corkscrew and twist of the wrist. After Nathan sipped and approved, the waiter poured them each a glass.

"Do you need a moment or are you ready to order?"

"Cindy?"

She saw fettuccine alfredo and pointed, "I'll have that."

"My favorite," Nathan agreed. "Make it two. And two Caesar salads."

"Excellent choice," Mario approved, then quietly left them.

Nathan picked up his wineglass. "Here's to good surprises."

"From your mouth to God's ear." There was a crystal

ring when she touched her glass to his. After taking a drink she said, "That's very nice."

"See? Already something good." He grinned.

She wasn't so sure. The night wasn't over yet and getting through unscathed was a goal in jeopardy when he looked at her like she was dessert. That wouldn't be a problem except she *wanted* to be dessert.

He leaned back against the leather seat and stretched an arm along the back, his fingers nearly brushing her bare shoulder. "So, how are mumsy and daddy?"

"Actually my parents both passed away several years ago. My father nursed mom through cancer. Then a couple of years later, he had a heart attack."

"I'm sorry, Cindy. I didn't mean to bring up—it was a bad joke."

"My fault. I was messing with you that night at the fundraiser." She settled her white cloth napkin in her lap. "It was hard losing them both so close together, but Dad was never the same after Mom died. I think he missed her. Now it's just my brother and me."

"Is he coming home from college for the summer?"

"No. He's taking a class, working and sharing an apartment with some buddies. I'm helping out with expenses." Which wouldn't be necessary if the sweet-talking jerk who'd wined and dined her hadn't cleaned out the money her parents left for their children's education. She took a sip of wine. "You already know about my pathetically normal childhood. I'd like to hear about how you didn't have one."

He frowned, an expression just this side of brooding but no less appealing than his grin. "My father was always working. Because he was never home, Mother had hobbies. She took classes. Painting. Knitting. Needlepoint. Calligraphy. Aura reading." Over the flickering light of the candle, his gaze connected with hers. "Neither of them were around much. I became pretty self-sufficient."

"It sounds to me like your mother was hurt about your father working so much. She was probably hiding in her hobbies." She finished off the wine in her glass. "And I can't decide if you take after her or your father."

"How about neither?"

She shook her head. "You put in a lot of hours at the hospital."

"And you know this—how?"

"While the women wait in your line, they talk about you." The snarky remark made him smile, just as she'd intended. "It's said that you're dedicated. So either you're a workaholic like your father, or you're hiding like your mom."

Just then Mario brought their salads. "Is there anything else I can get you?"

"Not right now," Nathan said.

The light, carefree expression had disappeared and it was her fault. Cindy wished for a filter from her brain to her mouth, but it was too late for that.

They ate in silence for a few minutes. At least he did. She pushed romaine lettuce and croutons around the plate and not much of it got eaten. She wished she'd kept her views to herself.

Finally she couldn't stand the silence. "Look, Nathan, it's just my opinion and worth what you paid for it. About now you're probably regretting this invitation. The offer of sex with no strings attached must look pretty good. Sometimes I don't know when to keep my mouth shut."

His eyes turned even darker with an intensity that was almost tangible as his gaze settled on her mouth. "Let's just say you've given me food for thought. Perspective that's both sincere and sweet."

Yay her. It felt like he'd yelled at her even though he hadn't raised his voice. Unlike that day at the hospital, this time he had a reason to be mad. Amateur psychoanalysis probably wasn't what he'd signed up for tonight in his quest to know her. He'd no doubt learned everything necessary to form the opinion that this night had been a cheap validation for her pronouncement that he should have taken no for an answer.

Two hours later after more to eat and drink and entertaining, idle conversation, they were standing in front of her open door. Cindy was pleasantly full and still rocking a lovely buzz from his favorite red wine.

"Thanks for dinner." She looked up and her breath caught.

The inside light showed the glitter in Nathan's eyes as his knuckles lightly grazed her cheek. "I'm going to kiss you."

"Do you really think that's a good idea—"

"No. But all night I haven't been able to take my eyes off you. I want to see how that sexy, sassy, smart mouth tastes."

Her heart started to pound until she thought it would jump right out of her chest. "Oh, my—"

"I can't help it." He tucked a strand of hair behind her ear with a shaking hand. "I want to feel all the passion you put into being so tough."

Words were trapped in her throat so she started to shake her head. The feel of his lips stopped her as surely as it shut down all rational thought. One moment his mouth was on hers and the next she was plastered against his body, her arms twining around his neck. His big, warm hands restlessly rubbed up and down her back until her skin prickled with awareness and every nerve ending was on fire. Her breasts were crushed to his chest and ached for the touch of his hand.

In an awkward, erotic dance, he maneuvered her inside then closed the door. As he backed her against the wall, the sound of their raspy, ragged breathing filled her small front room and she let her purse fall off her shoulder. When her arms were around his neck again, he slid his palm over her hip then down her thigh before inching up the hem of her dress.

He hooked his finger into the waistband of her panties and drew them down until she stepped out of the restraining prim cotton. Kissing her senseless, he slipped a finger inside her and played until she was mindless with desire. A breathy moan escaped her throat and he groaned.

"Cindy," he breathed against her cheek. "I've wanted you since the night of that damned dinner. But if you don't want this, I'll—"

"No. I want…" Her voice was a wanton whisper. She'd never felt such a powerful need so completely consuming her. There was a very real possibility she would simply implode if he didn't take her in the next ten seconds. "Now. Nathan. Please. Do you have—"

"Yeah."

He dropped his wallet on the floor after pulling out a condom and lowered his pants and briefs before covering himself. Then he lifted her, and as her legs circled his waist, he entered her, bracing his forearm against the wall. The thickness of him filled her and took her breath away at the same time. He drove her higher and higher until she shattered into a thousand points of light and shuddered with the pieces of pleasure surging through her.

Moments later he went still and tightened his arms around her, groaning out his own release. As his breathing slowed, he buried his face in her neck and kissed her gently, tenderly. Finally he let her legs go and they slid down as he wrapped his strong arms around her waist and held her to him.

"Wow." He rested his forehead against hers. "There's no reason you should believe me, but I really didn't mean for that to happen."

"I know." And neither had she. For whatever reason, she believed him and here they were.

"Bathroom?" He was asking where it was. Hard to believe he hadn't been further inside than the front door.

"Down the hall," she said. "First door on the right."

When he was gone, she slipped her panties back on, picked up her purse and tried to figure out what to say when he returned.

It didn't take long. Unlike her with the nerves doing a rumba inside her, he looked as cool as Mount Charleston after the first winter snow. But the expression on his face told her there was a problem. And when had she learned to read him so well?

"What's wrong?" she asked.

"Probably nothing."

"Then why do you look like that?"

"The condom broke," he said.

She blinked at him, trying to make sense of what he was saying. "It broke?"

"That doesn't mean there's anything to worry about. It's probably fine," he assured her. "I just thought you should know even though the odds of pregnancy are slim."

And so it had been the perfect storm of an evening. Dinner. Sex. And a broken condom.

So what else was new? That was the story of her life.

Three weeks later the pregnancy odds went up when Cindy's normally punctual period was late. She'd told herself it could be delayed for any number of reasons and stress was at the top of her list. But just to cover her bases she'd peed on a stick and nearly fainted when the word *pregnant* appeared.

On an ironic note, in the twenty-one days since "seeing" Nathan, he hadn't once badgered her for a phone number or joined her in the cafeteria for lunch. So sleeping with him to get him out of her life had actually worked.

What she hadn't expected was relief and disappointment in equal parts. Then she did the pregnancy test and shock pushed out every other emotion.

She'd just gotten off work and was waiting in the hall outside the NICU for Nathan to be finished with hospital rounds. This wasn't the best place to talk, but she didn't know what else to do. Thanks to her, no phone numbers had been exchanged. And it seemed like forever before he came out of the unit, but that was probably normal when your life was falling apart.

Nathan stopped short when he saw her leaning against the far wall. There was an expression on his face that she couldn't decipher. And it didn't matter anyway.

"We need to talk." Her fingers twisted together as she looked to her left and right, making sure that employees moving in the hall were too far away to hear.

"Hello to you, too."

"Sorry. I'm a little freaked out."

"Ah. So we should go somewhere private?" he asked.

"That would probably be best."

He rubbed a hand across the back of his neck. "How about the Revello Lounge. It's at the M Resort. Do you know it?"

"I'll meet you there."

The one-year-old hotel was on the corner of Mercy Medical Center Parkway and Las Vegas Blvd. Fifteen minutes after leaving the hospital she turned left into the resort lot and found a parking place close to the lobby entrance. She walked inside and took the escalator up, stepping off onto the shiny marble floor. To her right was the gift shop, a café and a pastry place called Baby Cakes. Fate was having a laugh at her expense.

She found the lounge, which was all glass, amber lights and modern glitz. Nathan was waiting in a quiet corner and she took the leather barrel-backed chair across the chrome table from him. They each ordered club soda with lime. She would have preferred something stronger. There was no way to soften the news and she didn't try.

"I'm pregnant."

He was all brooding silence before saying, "I figured."

"I'm pretty sure when you promised me a good surprise at dinner you didn't mean a baby."

"I never planned for anything to happen."

She believed that, and yet he carried a condom. A faulty one.

Just then the cocktail waitress appeared with their drinks and set them down on napkins. "Can I get you anything else?"

Cindy figured she had about all she could stand and shook her head.

"We're good," Nathan said and the woman drifted away.

"You might be good, but I'm pregnant." Cindy picked up her drink and played with the straw. "This is Las Vegas and odds are fickle at best. But I can't believe my luck is this bad."

"Yours?" He was still in his scrubs and checked the pager on his waistband. "What about mine? It appears the planets aligned just right and you were fertile."

"Right back at you, buster," she said.

"I was hoping you were on an alternative method of birth control."

"Since I'm not seeing anyone, there was no reason." She glared at him. "And can we talk about the condom? That was yours so don't even try to make this my fault."

"That's not what I meant. Look, Cindy, I take full responsibility—"

"Don't." She couldn't handle an apology right now.

She'd been a willing participant as soon as his lips touched hers. For God's sake, she'd thought about him naked when he'd picked her up. All through dinner something had been sizzling between them. They'd had sex. Then nothing.

One minute he'd been pestering her for a phone number, the next he completely disappeared. Yet again she'd been fooled. He really was just one of those guys who refused to give up until he got what he wanted. This time he got more than he'd bargained for, but she was also paying a high price.

"This is not part of my plan," she said.

He nodded. "Plans have a way of changing."

Cindy felt a bubble of panic mix with hysteria that was barely held in check. She couldn't handle calm rationality any more than his apology. This was her life. She'd made a bad decision in the past but was working things out. For a short time there had been light at the end of the tunnel, and now it was connected to a speeding locomotive. All because she'd won that stupid raffle ticket and slid into hell when Nathan Steele noticed her.

"You don't understand," she said. "I have another semester of classes. I'm doing my internship, not to mention a full-time job. My bills aren't going to pay themselves.

And I'm putting my brother through college. Harry is my responsibility."

"It doesn't have to be all on you. He can get student loans."

"No. I can't let him do that. The subject of blame keeps coming up. Between you and me the fault for this pregnancy is about equal. But the fact that my brother's college money is gone is all on me." She put her glass back on the table without drinking any of the club soda in it. "I was supposed to take care of his college fund. My father left me in charge of the money. How can I tell him that what our father left for his education isn't there?

"My parents started putting away money for school when each of us was born. One of the last things Dad said to me was to see that my little brother graduated from UCLA. Harry wants to be a lawyer."

"Good for him."

"Not if he can't get his degree." Cindy twisted her fingers together in her lap.

"Why can't he?" Nathan's frown deepened. "What happened?"

"There was a guy." She met his gaze and figured he was thinking that there always was. "Conrad Worthington. At least that's what he said his name was. The cops couldn't find any trace of him."

"What did he do?"

"He charmed me into trusting him, told me he loved me, then cleaned out my bank account." She drew in a shuddering breath. "He maxed out my existing credit cards and all the ones he could get in my name."

"Son of a bitch." Nathan's hands, resting on the arms of the chair, curled into fists.

"Yeah. I called him that, too, and a few things I can't repeat. The banks refused to forgive the debt, but I managed to negotiate payments. I dropped out of school and worked two jobs for a while. When I had better control over the situation, I started taking a few night classes, which is why it's taking so long to get my degree. But I had everything under control and it was going according to plan. The thing is, I'm still paying for that mess. I can't afford another one." Even in the dim light she saw when his expression went from brooding to pity. She could stand just about anything but that. "And then you came along. Dr. Charming. Wanting my phone number and not taking no for an answer."

"I didn't mean for this to happen," he said again.

She believed him, but that didn't help when panic was her go-to emotion. "It's all fun and games until the condom breaks and someone gets pregnant."

Chapter Five

Nathan's head felt like it was ready to explode. It was a sensation that was becoming increasingly familiar where Cindy Elliott was concerned, but this time wasn't about passion. He struggled to process information that was a lot of fact swamped by buckets of emotion.

Fact: The condom broke.

Fact: She was pregnant.

Fact: The odds of this happening were ridiculously low, which put it firmly in the miracle column.

Emotion: He went from *holy crap my boys are badass* to *holy crap I'm going to be a father*.

That was a fact that gave him serious pause since he'd been parented in absentia and had no working model of how to raise a kid.

Cindy was staring at him, then abruptly she stood and slid her purse more firmly on her shoulder. "I just thought you should know about the baby."

"Are you leaving?" He didn't think she could surprise him any more, but somehow she always did.

"We're done here."

"Not by a long shot. Sit down."

"Why should I?"

He met her gaze and the fear there went a long way toward tamping down his irritation. "For one thing this habit you have of running out on me is really getting old."

"And?" She folded her arms over her chest. "You said 'for one thing,' which means there's another reason I should sit."

"We're not even close to being done here."

"What else is there to say?" Her tone oozed suspicion and mistrust, but she sat.

"I'm not sure," he admitted. "This is a shock."

"Tell me about it. At least you told me when—you know." She looked down, suddenly shy. Charmingly so.

Nathan knew she meant he'd warned her about the condom malfunction. He realized something else, too. She didn't trust him to not run out on her like the last bozo who'd robbed her blind then dumped on her and disappeared. If nothing else, being on his own as a kid had taught him to be the soul of responsibility.

He leaned toward her and rested his elbows on his knees as their gazes locked. Her brown eyes were a mixture of gold and cinnamon with a healthy dose of innocence thrown in. The vulnerability there tugged at him, making him want to fold her in his arms, a feeling that came out of nowhere. The things he couldn't explain made him acutely uncomfortable.

"Look, Cindy, you're not in this alone."

"What does that mean?" she asked.

"That we're in this together." How lame was that answer? he thought.

"Oh, so you're going to carry this baby for nine months?"

He hadn't realized doubts about her intentions to do just that were even in his mind until her sarcastic statement indicated otherwise. Relief coursed through him.

"The differences in our anatomy being what they are, I can't really do that—"

"But you would if you could," she finished wryly. "It's easy to promise something when there's no way you can possibly be held accountable for not following through."

Again he felt like he was paying the price for another guy's sin. "I'm not running out on you like the last son of a bitch."

Her gaze jumped to his as anger and hurt gleamed in her eyes. "So you'll be around."

"Yes."

"I see." Primly she folded her hands in her lap. "We already established that you can't take over getting big as a battleship or deal with enough water retention to float it. So what else is there?"

"We'll work it out as we go along," he offered.

"Maybe you could finish up my classes and the internship I need for my degree." She snapped her fingers and shook her head. "Nope. Wrong again. Someone would notice and I'd be out on my backside because of cheating."

"Look, Cindy—"

"Actually, I can probably finish all of that before the baby is born." She tapped her lip thoughtfully, but there was panic around the edges. "Then all I have to do is give birth and find a better job because I have to afford good child care along with having an infant who's depending on me. Piece of cake."

"The martyr act is admirable, but you didn't get like this on your own. I'll help you."

"So in between saving premature babies you're going to watch ours so I can finally get my career on track?"

"Like I said, we'll figure things out."

"I've never experienced a 'we.' There's always just been me. My body, my problem."

"My baby, too," he said quietly.

All the fight drained out of her and she leaned back in the club chair. "Just so you know, *I* know I'm being unreasonable. If it's all right with you, I think I'll blame it on pregnancy hormones."

"That works for me."

As a corner of her full mouth quirked up, he felt an absurd surge of desire. The subdued lighting here in the bar made a sexy shadow of the small dent in her chin and he desperately wanted to explore it with his tongue. Somehow during that brief, passionate encounter when they'd made a baby, he'd missed out on discovering every single inch of her and wanted another opportunity. Not likely now. A good thing because it wasn't rational. And definitely not smart.

He excelled at rational and smart, but somehow Cindy changed the rules on him. She was pregnant with his child and this was uncharted territory. It was also a medical condition and that was someplace to start.

He took a sip of his club soda. "Other than hormones, how are you feeling?"

"A little queasy," she admitted.

He wanted to say something clinically clever, tell her how to fix it, but this wasn't his specialty. "Have you seen an obstetrician?"

Her expression turned wry. "I just barely peed on the stick."

"So that would be a no," he concluded.

"No," she agreed.

"Okay." He nodded thoughtfully. "I can give you a couple of names. But Rebecca Hamilton is at the top of the list. She's very good and I think you'd be comfortable with her."

"I'll see if she's a tier-one doctor on the Mercy Medical insurance plan."

"I'm sure she is because she has medical privileges there. If not, I'll take care of it."

"It? What does that mean?" Tension made her straighten in the club chair.

"I'll take care of the expenses."

"Because?"

"It's my responsibility."

Her eyes narrowed. "Wow, that gave me a warm and fuzzy feeling."

"Is that the hormones talking again?"

"Yeah. Me, my hormones and I." She closed her eyes and shook her head. When she met his gaze again, the hurt was back. "I'm not your responsibility, Nathan. I can take care of myself and this baby."

Apparently, *responsibility* was one of those words that triggered a hormonal response. He tucked the information away and searched for something to say that wouldn't tap into that well of defensiveness she had going on. He was attempting to say and do the right thing without research and training to fall back on. It was like trying to move a canoe with one paddle.

He blew out a long breath. "Look, Cindy, I want you to have the best prenatal care."

"Why?"

The word *responsibility* came to mind yet again but it hadn't gone over well either time. There was no reason to believe that had changed. So he rephrased. "Just so we're clear, I am going to be involved. Because this is my child, too."

She stared at him a long time before saying, "I guess this is a bad time to realize the flaw of sleeping with you to get you out of my life."

And then she really did leave. He sat there for a few minutes as the situation sank in. A baby. It hit him like a meteor dropping out of the sky.

His baby.

Right now his child was growing inside her.

Holy crap.

An hour ago Nathan had been talking to Cindy and now he stood in the NICU at Mercy Medical Center, staring at a baby small enough to fit in the palm of his hand.

An infinitesimal embryo formed from his DNA and Cindy's was actually growing into a baby. He just couldn't wrap his head around the concept and make it real. Especially with the beeps, whooshes and noises of the high-tech sensitive equipment filling the room. This was where babies ended up when there was a problem pregnancy.

"Why are you still here?"

Nathan turned at the sound of the familiar female voice. "Hi, Annie."

The petite, blue-eyed brunette was his medical partner in the neonatology practice. They'd met in school and become friends. She'd introduced him to his late wife and was one of the select few who didn't blame him when the relationship unraveled just before Felicia died. He knew the failures were all his and would carry the burden of that for as long as he lived. This woman's friendship meant a lot to him, especially because he didn't deserve it.

Annie looked up. The pixie haircut suited her small face. "You know I'm on call this week."

"Yeah. I just wanted to come back and check up on this little guy."

She glanced at the gladiator. "I just looked over his latest oxygen saturation levels. The CO_2 and PO_2 results are all in normal range. He's doing pretty well for as small as he is."

"Yeah. I read his chart."

"Respiratory therapy was just here to check the ventilator. It's all good, Nathan."

"I'm worried about a bowel perforation."

"You're always concerned about that. I am, too." She settled her hands on her hips and slanted a puzzled look at him. "But something's up."

"What makes you say that?" Was it tattooed on his forehead? One-night stand? Father-to-be?

"This is me," she said. "Don't even try to pretend I don't know you better than you know yourself."

He was pretty sure she was right about that and felt a little sorry for her. Because she was wasting her time on him. "Nothing's going on."

"Oh, please." She huffed out a breath. "I'll buy you a cup of coffee and we can talk."

"Buy?" He stared at her. "Really?"

"Okay. Technically, I'll pour. Doctor's dining room. Now."

Nathan looked at the infant, the tiny chest moving up and down with help from the ventilator. "I don't know. What if he needs—"

"Don't go there. The 'what-ifs' will make you crazy."

He shook his head. "Maybe we should—"

"Look, Nathan, we'll be right downstairs. If anything happens we can be here in a minute or less. On the really bright side—" She smiled tenderly at the baby who couldn't see her. "This little boy gets two neonatal specialists for the price of one because you're going schizoid on me. You need to talk. I know that look."

"Okay." From knowing her a long time he knew that it was easier to give in than argue and lose.

They headed to the dining room on the first floor of the hospital. It was reserved for the doctor's use and available twenty-four hours a day. The tables were covered with white cloths and there was always one urn with coffee and another containing water for tea. Sodas were packed in ice beside the table with hot drinks. At specific times the steam table held varieties of warm food, but off hours there were only pastries, muffins and fruit.

Annie went to get two cups of coffee while he filled a small plate with sweets. They sat at a table by the floor to ceiling windows that looked out on Mercy Medical Center Parkway and the spectacular lights of the Las Vegas Strip in the distance.

Nathan bit into a brownie and realized he was starving. Lunch had been hours ago, and after Cindy's baby bombshell, food had been the last thing on his mind.

He finished the brownie and scarfed down a muffin, then noticed the expectant expression on his friend's face. "What?"

"Tell me what's going on."

"First you tell me why you're so sure something is."

She tilted her head and gave him an "oh, please" look, then sighed with resignation. "For one thing, you look just like you did when things between you and Felicia were going downhill."

Ironic. Before the baby, there hadn't been anything between him and Cindy except lust, but it felt like more than he'd ever had in his marriage. Felicia was a wonderful woman—pretty, funny, sweet and smart. They'd been friends and got along great. With his career on track, he'd figured it was time to get married. There was no lightning strike, but everything had pointed to them being a good match.

Only when it was too late did he realize that the logic was badly flawed and Felicia had left because he didn't love her. That was the last thing she ever said to him.

"It was a car accident, Nathan." Sympathy swirled in Annie's light-blue eyes. "Some idiot had been drinking and was going too fast. He didn't stop for the red light. That's why she died. It had nothing to do with the fact that the two of you didn't work as a couple."

"I know."

"That's not what the look on your face says." Annie sighed. "But I didn't bring you here to rehash the past. I want to know why you're hovering over that baby in the unit."

"I always hover."

"Not like this. Usually you're cool and clinical. That's not what I just saw." She must have noticed his protest forming because she held up a hand and said, "Don't even waste your breath."

"Okay. Don't say I didn't warn you."

"You didn't." She grinned.

He took a deep breath and said, "Cindy Elliott is pregnant with my child."

"What?" Annie blinked. "Who?"

"She works in housekeeping here at the hospital."

"I didn't know you were seeing anyone."

If just seeing her was all he'd done there wouldn't be a baby. Seeing her had only made him want her. Wanting her had made him determined to have her. He couldn't even say he'd been irresponsible. After seeing her earlier, he *could* say that having her once had definitely not made the wanting disappear. If anything, his hunger for her was stronger.

Nathan took a sip of coffee, then set the cup back on the saucer. "I met her at the hospital fundraiser."

"But you said she works here."

"Right." He dragged his fingers through his hair. "I didn't recognize her in a different environment."

"You mean all dressed up." Annie's look oozed pity. "Bet that didn't go over well."

"You'd win that bet." He laughed, remembering their verbal sparring that night and how clueless he'd been. It wouldn't add anything to this story if he shared that the smell of Cindy's perfume gave away her identity. "I asked for her phone number, but she refused to give it up."

"Ah." Annie held the coffee cup and her eyes sparkled with amusement that escaped him.

"What does that mean?"

"So many things, so little time." Turning serious, she said, "You obviously got together in spite of not being able to call her."

"Because I saw her here, there was no need for the number. I asked her out and we went to dinner."

There was also no need to share that Cindy had agreed to see him in order to get him to back off. Now he knew that was about the jerk who used her. He wondered if having that information would have cooled his jets, then he figured probably not.

"And you're sure the baby is yours?"

"The condom broke," he said.

Perplexed, Annie shook her head. "Isn't it amazing? We can build a space station and put people on it, but no one can manufacture glitch-free birth control."

"Go figure." He stared at the crumbs on his plate.

"So that's the reason you're hovering."

He nodded. "I never looked at what we do from the father side of the fence before."

"I see."

"That makes one of us. The thing is, I'm a doctor. I know all the things that can happen. I know what can go wrong." He pointed at her, then himself. "We see babies every day who don't go full term. The chances of survival go down when they're born too early—"

"Don't think that way," she warned. "There's no reason to assume a healthy woman in her—"

"Twenties," he supplied.

"Right." She nodded. "With good prenatal care a normal pregnancy is the probability."

That didn't seem like enough to ensure a healthy child, he thought. "There must be something more I can do."

"You're going to hate me for saying this," she informed him.

"What?" he asked, bracing himself.

"Support Cindy emotionally."

If he had faith in feelings, Felicia probably would still be alive. Science was what he believed in. He wasn't aware of any scientific study that proved emotional support would guarantee a full-term, healthy child. "You know better than anyone that I don't do emotional."

"Right. If you can't see or touch something, it doesn't exist."

They'd argued this point for hours in medical school and finally agreed to disagree. "There must be something else I can do."

"Other than finding her the best obstetrician in the valley there's only one other thing I can think of."

He waited, but she didn't say more. "Are you going to share?"

"Make sure she has what she needs to minimize her

anxiety," Annie suggested. "Don't let her exert herself. The rest of it will just fall into place if you're supportive of her."

He wasn't so sure. Cindy had been pretty concerned about work, school and the expenses involved in caring for a newborn. "Are you sure that's enough?"

"Positive. Just physically be there."

Okay. He could do that. He was a doctor, after all. *Physical* was what he did. So, it was settled. While Cindy was pregnant with his child, he would be her shadow.

Chapter Six

Peanut butter and jelly had never tasted this good when she was a kid. Now she was going to have one of her own and Cindy figured that was the reason.

She took the last bite of the sandwich she'd brought to work, savoring the sweet grape jelly mixing with the crunchy, salty softness of the peanut butter. She was sitting in the hospital's serenity garden and savored that, too. It was peaceful, and she could use more peace in her life. Ever since she'd won that pesky raffle ticket, peace had been hard to come by.

She pressed the palm of her hand against her still-flat stomach and tried to really grasp the fact that a baby was in there. A baby fathered by Nathan Steele. Life as she'd known it would never be the same.

She was going to be a mom.

Part of her was starting to get excited at the prospect. The other part wondered how in the world she was going to do this on her own. Because, despite what Nathan had said to her about helping, she didn't really believe he'd stick around.

And she was pretty sure she didn't want him to.

At least he was honest, not trying to hide the fact that his birth control had failed. He'd only made a small blip on the blame-game meter when he'd hinted that she should be on the pill.

If only…

Because she'd sworn never to be stupid about a man again, alternative precautions and the resulting bloat and water retention had seemed unnecessary. Now she was looking at about eight months of both. Not to mention figuring out how to do it all and pay the bills.

"Hi, there."

The voice came from behind her. It was deep and familiar and sucked the serenity right out of the garden.

Cindy half-turned just for visual confirmation that thoughts of him just moments ago hadn't conjured him up. The blue scrubs, thick dark hair and serious expression equaled Nathan Steele.

"Hi." She wadded up the plastic sandwich wrap and squeezed it into her palm.

He sat on the wooden bench beside her and glanced around at the shallow pond with the bridge curving over it. Several benches and chairs were scattered around the area. Three sides of the hospital threw the bushes, flowers and grass into shade.

"What are you doing here?"

"I don't think I've ever been here before." His response didn't actually answer the question.

"So your showing up while I'm having lunch is purely coincidence?" If so, she was going to have to burn a candle or something to reverse her continuing bad karma.

"Harlow told me this is where I might find you."

Had he been looking for her? She didn't like the stagger of her heart when she made that wild leap. She couldn't go soft now. It was bad enough that through a horrible twist of fate this man had fathered her baby. One day he'd unjustly yelled at her and the next thing she knew she was pregnant. In between he'd refused to take a negative response regarding her phone number and she hadn't stopped him when he'd kissed her. But kissing him had felt too good and now there were consequences.

Again, it was probably better to confirm. "Why did Harlow tell you where I was?"

"Because I asked," he said simply.

Damn, there was that little heart skip again. She'd like to blame it on the changes of her body from the pregnancy, but that was probably not the case. How could this happen when she wasn't even sure she liked him?

That thought didn't even come close to stopping the pulse in her neck from throbbing, and her voice was just a little breathless. Darn him anyway. "Why did you ask?"

"How are you feeling?" Again he gave her a non-answer.

"Tired," she admitted.

"Still nauseous?"

"A little."

He glanced at the brown bag on the bench between them. "Lunch?"

"Peanut butter and jelly."

He frowned. "Technically you're not really eating for two, but the embryo will take what it needs from you. Nutrition is really important to its development."

How clinical of him. A change from the flash of feeling displayed when he'd said this was his baby, too. That had melted her heart a little. Her bad.

"I did some research online. I know that eating right is the best thing for the baby." She met his gaze. "Protein is important and peanut butter has lots of it."

"Along with fat," he pointed out.

"It's a good fat. Better yet, it doesn't make me want to throw up. And it's not expensive."

"Ah." He nodded. "I just wanted to make sure this wasn't a soup and crackers week."

"You mean just before payday." She refused to be ashamed of her strict budget. It was digging her out of a deep hole. "As it happens, this *is* the lean week."

"Right." He met her gaze. "If you run short, I can help you out. Healthy food is usually more expensive, but right now it isn't an area of your budget that you should be downsizing."

"You're right." She said that because he *was* right, but it didn't constitute agreement to take anything from him.

"Have you made an appointment yet with an obstetrician?"

"Not just an appointment. I've actually seen the doctor, even though it still feels surreal to me," she said. She'd called the day after telling him, and Dr. Hamilton's staff managed to fit her in right away.

"Good. Prenatal care is the first line of defense to prevent premature birth," he calmly pointed out.

"I'm on it," she promised.

"Glad to hear that." He looked around the garden again. "It's nice out here."

"Yeah. Quiet. This is a nice break from work. I've been really busy today."

He frowned. "You have to be careful. Don't overdo. Take it easy."

"I'm pregnant, not an invalid."

The retort was automatic, but for just a moment this

conversation had felt like a fantasy. They could be a couple. He could be a guy sincerely anxious for the woman he cared about who was carrying his child.

Then reality reared its ugly head. She was carrying his child, but they weren't now, nor would they ever be, a couple. The truth was that he didn't care about her any more than she cared about him.

His concern was for this child. His job was saving the lives of babies born too early and that's all this was about. Clinical concern. Still, she could respect that and him. In fact, she respected him very much.

"I'm fine." She smiled up at him. "It's just nice to be outside in the fresh air. In the shade with the breeze blowing it's still cool enough to come out here."

"Pretty soon it won't be."

"I know." She took the tangerine from her bag and started to peel it. "It's probably a good thing that I won't get too big while it's hot."

He nodded. "The first trimester will be over before fall. That will be easier on you."

"Yeah." That sounded like a concern more personally focused on her. He got points.

"You need to get in a lot of fluids. Water primarily. To flush the amniotic fluid."

Again clinical. And cute. As they stretched out the topic of weather in Las Vegas she ate the segments of her fruit, grateful to have something to keep her hands busy. She was much more comfortable with him when he was in doctor mode or chastising her for something not her fault. When Nathan was nice and charming, it made her nervous.

She glanced at the watch on her wrist. "I have to get back to work."

"Me, too."

They walked back into the hospital and the coolness felt good.

"Where are you headed?" he asked.

"I have to get my cart, then the NICU is next on my assignment sheet."

He fell into step beside her as she moved down the first-floor hall on the way to Central Supply. All equipment had to be put away during employee breaks. Besides the liability of leaving cleaning products out in the open, there was the problem of obstruction in the halls and impairing movement of equipment and patients on gurneys.

Environmental Services was located next to Central Supply on the first floor. Cindy opened the door, then turned to Nathan. "Thanks for checking up on me."

"You're welcome." He pushed the door wider. "Which cart is yours?"

She pointed it out, then was surprised when he grabbed it for her. "What are you doing?"

"I'll take it upstairs for you."

"You don't have to do that," she protested.

"You're going my way. I'll drive."

There it goes again, she thought when her heart skipped. Three times since he'd shown up in the garden. Could it be she was actually starting to like him?

The glow lasted until they entered the elevator. Two of the nurses from the NICU got in behind them and noticed Nathan helping her. Hostility, like an invisible force field, backed her up against the wall beside Nathan.

"Are you on your way to the unit, doctor?" Barbara Kelly asked. She was a slim blonde, very pretty.

"Yes," he said, and the nurse pushed the appropriate button on the elevator's control panel.

Cindy felt as if she'd been caught cheating with another woman's husband, and it brought her down to earth with a thud. Lowly housekeepers didn't mix with medical royalty.

Nathan tested the weight of the cleaning cart and said, "This thing is heavier than it looks."

Cindy decided not answering would be best because she didn't want to give the nursing staff any personal information. Gossip spread through the hospital faster than the flu and the facts of whatever story was spreading were usually wrong.

"You need to be careful while you're pushing it," the clueless doctor continued.

Apparently he didn't get her *"silence is golden"* vibe. Fortunately, before he could say more, the elevator stopped at their floor.

The two nurses got off first. One whispered something to the other. Cindy couldn't hear what was said, but she could definitely translate the bitchy looks both of the women lobbed in her direction. The message in the toxic glances said more clearly than words that she had a lot of nerve violating the unwritten hospital social code and consequences would follow quickly and without mercy.

Wrestling the cart off the elevator, Nathan missed the communication.

Before he could go any farther with her cleaning stuff, she put her hand on his arm. "I'll take it from here."

"We're almost there. That's okay."

"It's really not. Please, just let me do my job or I'm afraid I won't have one."

"What are you talking about?" He stared down at her, obviously confused.

Cindy glanced down the hall where the two nurses had disappeared. "By now it's all over the hospital that you were slumming with one of the housekeepers."

"What? Just because I gave you a hand?"

"And showed concern," she agreed.

"For that they're going to take me out back and shoot me?"

"Not you. Me," she clarified.

"You're joking."

"If only."

It wasn't pretty, but that didn't make the reality any less true. Bullies grew up but they didn't always lose their pick-on-the-peons mentality.

"The thing is," she said, "you can do anything and no one will say squat. But I have the audacity of letting you push my cleaning cart and the you-know-what is going to hit the fan."

"I'll make sure that doesn't happen," he said grimly.

The fact that he didn't even attempt to convince her she was wrong proved that he understood the hospital's insular social environment, at least on some level.

"If you really want to fix this, just back off."

"That doesn't work for me." He shook his head. "Like I said, I'm going to be there for you."

She put her hands on the cart and met his gaze. "I appreciate that you would want to, but please don't. I'm serious. It could cost me my job."

She walked away and felt his gaze on her back. Right this minute his attitude might be completely sincere. And that was extraordinarily sweet, but it wouldn't last. She didn't have the best judgment where men were concerned, which meant that he must have a flaw that would surface when she was most vulnerable. With a baby on the way she couldn't afford to jeopardize her employment and medical insurance benefits.

She needed her own space, no matter how much she was tempted to take a chance that he was different from the last jerk.

* * *

Twenty-four hours later Cindy was sitting in her supervisor's outer office. She'd been summoned and there was little doubt in her mind that it was somehow connected to her being sighted hanging out with Nathan—Dr. Steele—yesterday. There were so many rules, regulations and laws in this work environment, not to mention an anonymous hotline for grievances, that complications and intimidation were fairly easy to pull off.

If it got to be too much, quitting was an option for some. But not for Cindy. The nausea grinding through her wasn't just on account of the nerves about facing her boss.

The door opened and there stood Dina Garrett. She was somewhere in her late thirties or early forties with sun-streaked brown hair framing her pretty face in a stylish bob. A tailored navy-blue suit showed off her slender, petite frame.

"Hi, Cindy. Sorry to keep you waiting. Come on in."

Cindy stood and followed her, then stopped in front of the desk. "What's up?"

"Have a seat." Her boss indicated the two empty chairs.

"Thanks." Cindy tried to look relaxed and composed, but that wasn't easy when it felt like there was a scarlet letter embroidered on her chest.

"So how's everything?" Dina folded her hands, then rested them on the desk.

Cindy considered this woman a friend. They'd socialized occasionally, and she'd had dinner with Dina, her husband Ted and their two daughters. She'd even attended a piano recital for one of the girls. A family picture was prominently displayed on the desk, and she felt a stab of envy at the smiling faces, the close-knit family.

That was what she wanted someday, but the dream

seemed doomed from where she was sitting. It was on the tip of her tongue to reveal everything, but she decided to proceed cautiously. Once this was out of the bag, there wouldn't be a way to stuff it back in.

"Oh, everything is fine," Cindy said shrugging. "You know. How are Ted and the girls?"

Dina glanced at the picture and smiled. "Doing great. Summer camp. Swimming. Friends over. When school is out it's always harder for a working mom to juggle everything."

Cindy was already afraid of what her future held and didn't really need to hear that. "Tell them I said hello."

"I will." Dina smiled and when it faded she went into supervisor mode. "So, I wanted to see you because I received a complaint about your work."

"Anyone I know?"

"It was anonymous," she explained. "But I'm required to investigate and wanted to hear your side of things before proceeding."

That wasn't a surprise. Her boss bent over backward to be fair and that required more time, energy and work hours than simply jumping to conclusions.

"I don't know what to tell you." Cindy gripped her hands together in her lap. "I'm doing my work the same as I always have." When there are no complaints, she wanted to add. Nathan was the only variable. "Was the accusation specific?"

"No." Dina leaned back in her chair. "Because this is you and your record is spotless, I'm inclined to believe there's no substance to the accusation."

Cindy's grip on her hands loosened and blood flow returned to her fingers. "That's good."

"But there's another reason I think it's without merit."

Dina met her gaze. "I've heard rumors. Specifically, gossip regarding you and Dr. Steele having a relationship."

"There's nothing—"

Her boss held up a hand to stop the protest. "I don't need details. Your personal life is just that. Personal. But it's my job to see that work isn't affected."

"It's not," Cindy assured her. "Nathan and I—what I mean to say is, Dr. Steele—there is no relationship between us."

"Okay. Your work has been exemplary from the first day you started here at Mercy Medical Center." Dina studied her and, going by past experiences, she didn't miss much. "I'm your supervisor, but you need to remember that I'm also your friend. It's a fine line to walk and I work very hard at not showing favoritism. But if you need someone to talk to, I'm there for you."

The sympathetic expression and the invitation for a confidence seemed to unleash the dammed-up feelings Cindy had been struggling to hold back.

"I'm pregnant," she blurted out.

"I see." Shock mixed with curiosity in the other woman's expression. Curiosity won. "Do I know the father?"

"Do you know Nathan Steele?"

"Really?" This time shock squeezed everything else out of her face. "He's the father?"

"I don't know quite how it happened," she hurried to explain.

Dina's expression was wry. "Then you and I need to have a conversation about the birds and bees. It'll be good practice for *'The Talk'* with my girls."

"I *know* how *it* happened." Cindy felt the heat in her cheeks. "What I meant was that I've seen him in the NICU, but he never saw me. Not until the night of the hospital fundraiser."

"I heard you won the raffle."

"*Won* is a relative term. I couldn't resist messing with him when he said I looked familiar, but he didn't have any idea who I was."

"Apparently you clean up pretty good, or at work you look like something the cat yakked up."

"There's a visual." Cindy squirmed in the chair. "He recognized me the next day at work. By my perfume."

Dina looked more surprised about that than the pregnancy. "Obviously that line worked for him."

"Not really." It was only a small lie. "He asked more than once for my phone number, but I turned him down."

"Something changed your mind because you're not the sex-in-the-supply-closet type."

Cindy was grateful for that unwavering faith in her. "I happened to see him in action saving a baby."

"Ah. The hero factor worked in his favor. It's very powerful female fantasy material."

"I still said 'no,' but he wouldn't give up. So finally I gave in to a dinner invitation." She decided to leave out the portion of the conversation where she offered sex to get him out of her life. That had not worked out as planned.

At least not yet.

"If I had to guess, I'd say dinner went well?"

Cindy nodded. "He's more charming when he's away from the hospital."

"No kidding," Dina said.

"It wasn't like that." Cindy didn't want her boss to get the wrong idea about him. "He just kissed me good night."

She also decided to leave out the part about him saying he wanted her sexy, sassy, smart mouth. And the part where he wanted to taste the passion she put into being so tough. It had surprised her that he understood her so well. Maybe that's what had pushed her over the edge into mindless passion, but she didn't believe he'd planned to seduce her. Although she'd been very wrong about a man once before.

"Neither of us planned for this to happen," Cindy added. "Precautions were…problematic. It's just one of those things. But I want to clarify that there is no relationship between the two of us."

"Okay." Dina didn't look away.

"I'm aware that the staff is gossiping. For what it's worth, I believe the complaint about my work has more to do with the social differences between us. Although on the surface the two aren't connected."

"Just someone lashing out," Dina agreed.

Cindy leaned forward in her eagerness to dispel any lingering doubts. "It's just talk. I told him to back off, so that should be the end of it."

"Don't be too sure." The other woman looked skeptical.

"If not, I can deal with this. I have to," she added. "I need this job. Looking for another one isn't an option because of the medical insurance. Pregnancy would be a pre-existing condition and excluded from another employee plan. I'm just barely scraping by now. I couldn't handle it if medical bills were added to everything else—"

Dina held up her hands. "Don't borrow trouble. Not yet anyway."

Cindy got the subtext. "Yeah. When the baby starts to show, I won't have to do anything but waddle down the hall to stir up trouble and start talk."

"Okay, let's hope this is the end of it. Probably whoever called the hotline is just an anonymous whiner," Dina said. "If there's anything else I can do for you, let me know."

"Thanks." Gratitude for her friend's understanding and

support brought a lump to her throat and Cindy swallowed hard before saying, "You've already done it."

Dina shook her head, an indication that boss-mode was gone for now. "Wow. A baby. How do you feel?"

"Not too bad."

"Have you seen the doctor?"

"Rebecca Hamilton," Cindy said.

"Excellent choice. That's who I would have recommended."

What a relief that someone besides Nathan knew and she could talk about what she was going through. For another few minutes Cindy shared the changes already starting in her body, the emotions so close to the surface, the fears for the future. Dina talked about her own experiences and the joys of being a mom.

When Cindy left the office, she was relieved about her job status but not much else. The last time she'd been involved with a man, he'd taken her confidence along with her money. Yet again her life had been complicated by a man and she had the nagging feeling that Nathan Steele could take more than her bank account.

But that wasn't going to happen.

Just talking to him could cause trouble and cost her what little she had left. To keep peace in the workplace, she needed to become as invisible as she'd been before that darn dinner where she'd caught Dr. Charming's attention.

Somehow she had to rewind and delete.

Chapter Seven

Cindy was in the kitchen looking in the nearly empty refrigerator for dinner inspiration when she heard someone at the door. It was rare for her doorbell to ring, especially in the evening like this. Uneasiness crept over her. After peeking out the window to see who was there, her uneasy feeling was validated.

"Nathan," she whispered.

For a nanosecond, she debated whether to answer, but her car was in the driveway. He knew she was there.

After a deep, bracing breath, she opened the door. "What part of 'back off' did you not get?"

Resting his hands on lean hips he answered, "And what part of 'that doesn't work for me' did *you* not get?" One dark eyebrow lifted as he looked down at her. "Do you always answer the door like that? Hello to you, too."

"Hi. Why are you here?"

"We need to talk."

Cindy folded her arms over her chest and wished her hair didn't look like rats had nested there and her cotton shorts weren't quite so short. And quite so cotton. They were practically see-through.

"I have nothing to say."

"Then you can just listen."

She wished he didn't look quite so yummy and tempting in his worn jeans and white cotton shirt. The long sleeves were rolled up to his elbows, revealing wide wrists and strong forearms. Since when had cotton become the sexiest fabric on the planet? In his case, if it was just a little more see-through she might catch a glimpse of his broad chest, and that would be really nice.

Pulling herself together with an effort, she said, "I don't want to listen. Go away. I'm looking for something to eat."

She started to shut the door, but his hand shot out and he flattened his palm against it.

"Let me take you out," he offered.

She glanced down at her no-one-should-see-this-in-public attire. "Do I look like I'm ready to go out?"

Something hot and primitive flashed through his eyes as his gaze lazily drifted over her. "Then we can stay here."

"I'm not prepared to feed company." Did her voice sound as breathless and needy to him as it did to her?

"That's code for you're broke, right?"

"It's the week before payday." Her whole life felt like the week before she got paid.

"So we'll order pizza. I'll buy," he added.

That was a really bad idea. The last time he'd been in her house they'd had sex and now she was pregnant. She wasn't sure if something worse could happen, but she wasn't willing to take the risk.

Before she could figure out a way to turn him down, he

said, "I can see the wheels in your head turning and before you use up any more mental energy, you should know that I'm not taking no for an answer. Just look at it as a meal you don't have to pick up the tab for. My treat."

He was a treat, all right. That's what worried her the most. But it didn't look like he was going away without getting what he wanted. She wasn't sure if his persistence was endearing or annoying, but at least she'd get a free meal out of it.

"Okay. I'll change my clothes and we'll go out."

"While you're at it, how about changing your attitude?" he called after her.

She heard the humor in his voice and couldn't help smiling. He wasn't giving her much of a choice, so she might as well make the best of it. The prospect of not sitting home all by herself and fretting about how she was going to make this baby thing work did lift her spirits.

Besides, what could happen in public?

Nathan sat across from Cindy in a diner near the hospital and watched her hide behind a large menu the waitress had delivered when taking their drink orders. If it wasn't the week before payday, there was a better than even chance Cindy would have told him to stuff a sock in his dinner invitation. He hadn't worked that hard for anything since his internship.

Determination had served him well then, but he'd need more than that to deal with this woman. She had a chip on her shoulder as big as Nevada and somehow he had to separate her from it. The challenge got his juices going.

Sooner or later she would figure out that he wasn't going away.

"Have you been here before?" he asked.

"No. Have you?"

"Yes." It was handy when he was working.

The restaurant had a black and white tiled floor, red Formica tables and matching upholstery on the chrome stools at the counter. Waitresses wore red and white pinstriped uniforms to go with the retro look. It wasn't Capriotti's, which was kind of the point. That romantic atmosphere had landed him in this complicated mess. Now that he thought about it, he'd worked pretty hard to get her to have dinner with him that night, too.

And now she was pregnant.

Wrapping his head around the reality wasn't easy, especially when she looked as slender as the night he'd held her in his arms. She'd changed into a pair of denim capris, but he really missed the shorts that left her legs bare. And the short, knit top that let him have flashes of the naked flesh beneath. Neither outfit gave a clue about her condition, yet he didn't doubt that she was telling the truth. Funny, but her prickly attitude and the order to back off landed squarely in the confirmation column. She wouldn't do that if she were trying to pull a fast one.

There was zero romance here in this diner, but he could still smell the intoxicating scent of her perfume, and that cranked up a yearning in his gut that had nothing to do with food.

He blew out a long breath. "So, what are you going to have?"

"I don't see peanut butter and jelly," she grumbled from behind the menu.

"How about a cobb salad?"

She peeked around the tall plastic and met his gaze. "Really? Salad? You promised me dinner, not gerbil food."

"PB&J is dinner?"

"In my world." She ducked back into hiding.

"Okay," he said patiently. "What looks good to you?"

"Banana cream pie. With a pickle," she added.

"If that's representative of your current dietary choices, no wonder you're nauseous."

Again, she peeked out from behind the menu and gave him a sassy look. "Just wanted to see if you were paying attention."

Ignoring her seemed to be a challenge he was unable to meet no matter how determined he might be. "I guess I passed the test."

"Yeah. But I was serious about the pie."

"That's a lot of empty calories," he warned.

"Don't get your stethoscope in a twist." She put the menu down on the table. "It just sounds good. That's not what I'm getting. The doctor told me about the pregnancy weight parameters. Twenty-five pounds or so."

The perky waitress—Jayne her name tag said—returned with their drinks. Coffee for him. Water for Cindy. "So what can I get for you two?"

"Club sandwich. Wheat bread. No cheese. Side salad with oil and vinegar." She handed over her menu.

"Hamburger and fries," Nathan ordered, doing the same.

"You're going to hell," Cindy muttered.

Jayne wrote on her pad and smiled brightly. "Coming right up. Let me know if there's anything else you need."

He needed to let Cindy know he had her back. Unlike his father, he was someone a woman could depend on. If the waitress could rustle up an order of trust, there'd be a really good tip in it for her.

When they were alone again, he looked across the table. "So, how do you like Rebecca Hamilton?"

"She seems like a good doctor." Cindy removed the paper from her straw. "I like her a lot. She's young, smart. Easy to talk to."

He agreed. They had worked together from time to time. Every once in a while Rebecca called him in to consult when one of her patients delivered a baby too early.

"She's thorough, too. So she probably told you that staying in shape is important for both you and the baby."

"She did," Cindy confirmed. "And isn't it fortunate that I have a job that affords me the opportunity to move around a lot?"

And she couldn't afford much else, he thought. Thanks to the jerk who used her and disappeared. Nathan was furious every time he thought about that. And he didn't like the idea of her pushing around the housekeeping cart.

"Aren't there exercise classes specifically for expectant mothers?" he asked.

"There are. And I'll do that in my copious free time, right between my job and administrative internship responsibilities."

"How about on the weekend?" he suggested.

"Right." She took a sip of her water. "I can do that because money grows on trees."

"I'll pay for it."

The words just came out of his mouth. What was it about this woman that made him want to fix things for her? It wasn't the pregnancy because the protective feeling had simmered inside him from the moment he'd seen her cross that crowded ballroom.

"No, thanks." She smiled, and for the first time since he'd asked her to dinner there was warmth in the expression.

"I'm only trying to help."

"Believe me, I noticed." She dragged her finger through the condensation on her glass. "And I appreciate the gesture. But I don't care for feeling pathetic, that my life is a bad B movie. And if this were a romantic comedy, you'd have proposed to me by now. But we both know *that* kind of offer would be out of character for you."

There was nothing wrong with his character. He paid his bills, didn't use women and never made promises he didn't intend to keep. "How do we know that?"

"It's common knowledge," she said with a knowing look.

Not to him. *"It?"*

"You're a serial dater, which by definition means anti-matrimony."

"So that's the current rumor at the hospital?"

She nodded. "Is it wrong?"

Damn right. Partly. He dated because he hadn't been very good at settling down.

"Yeah, it's wrong. Imagine that. A rumor making the rounds at Mercy Medical Center that's been twisted and sensationalized."

"Which part?" Cindy asked.

"I'm not anti-matrimony. In fact, I was married once." He saw her glance at his left ring finger, which was bare.

It always had been. After the formal ceremony when he and Felicia had taken their vows, he hadn't worn a wedding band. He'd given his wife a host of excuses about it getting in the way when he was working. Gloving up. Sterile procedure. But she'd seen through all the crap and realized the truth about him.

"You said *was*." Cindy frowned. "Past tense. You're divorced?"

"No." He saw the look of surprise and clarified. "My wife died in a car accident."

Not long after she'd left him because he didn't love her.

She'd been right, but it wasn't about her. Love was something he couldn't make himself believe in.

"Oh, Nathan—" Cindy's eyes widened with distress. "I didn't know."

"Not many people do."

"That's awful. I'm so sorry."

"Don't be." The fault was his and so was the guilt.

"I can't help it. That's what happens when you hear rumors and believe them without question. I should know better than to listen to that stuff. There's so much talk and every time a story is told it gets—"

The words stopped as she focused on something behind him.

"What's wrong?"

"Two of the NICU nurses just walked in," she whispered.

"So?"

"Isn't it ironic that we were just talking about gossip?"

Her expression took on the same wariness the day he'd tried to help her out. She'd told him to back off or it could cost her job.

"I have no idea what you're talking about," he said.

"Rumors will spread like the plague. You. Me. Here. Alone." She put her elbow on the table, then settled a hand on her forehead, trying to shield her face. "Where's a really big menu when you need one?" she mumbled.

"It's no one's business but ours why we're here."

"In a perfect world that would be true. But, trust me on this, there will be talk."

Nathan looked up when the two hospital employees walked by. He recognized the nurses—Barbara Kelly and Lenore Fusano. The first was pretty, blonde and blue eyed. The other woman had dark eyes and hair. Also attractive. He nodded a greeting and they both smiled and said hello, then kept moving without acknowledging Cindy in any way.

"This is just great," she said. "And the timing couldn't be worse. I told my supervisor that everything was under control."

"What does this have to do with your boss?"

She met his gaze. "I met with her because there was a complaint about me. Anonymous. On the hospital's hotline."

Nathan glanced at the two nurses and saw them look quickly away. "What was the complaint?"

"Supposedly about my work."

He remembered what she'd said about her life getting more difficult when word got out that he was "slumming" with one of the housekeepers. Then she'd told him to leave her alone because it could cost her job. That remark was one of the reasons he'd felt compelled to talk to her. To reassure her that she had nothing to worry about.

"Someone complained because you talked to me?" he asked.

"No. Because *you* talked to *me*."

He hadn't really bought into what she'd said about all the social hierarchy stuff affecting her employment. But someone had gone on record and the paperwork trail had started. "You should have told me."

"Why? What can you do?" she protested. "I already asked you to leave me alone, and we can see how well that worked out."

He wasn't walking away and everyone should just get over it. Including Cindy. "Backing off isn't exactly my style."

"Then you're the exception."

"I take pride in staying friends with the women I've taken out," he said.

Cindy blinked at him. "Don't tell me. The serial dater rumors are true."

"I object to the 'serial' label." He rested his forearms on the table. "I go out. In fact, I went out with one of those nurses for a while. We're still friends."

Cindy glanced over her shoulder and tensed before meeting his gaze again. "Don't tell me. You dated the one glaring a hole through my back."

"I don't see anyone scowling in your direction. Barbara Kelly and I went out a few times. No big deal."

"For you," she said pointedly. "But this is going to be trouble for me. And it's not like I don't have enough on my plate already."

"You're being overly dramatic."

She shook her head. "Must be nice to live in fantasy land."

On the contrary. He was a realist. The reality was that the child she carried was his responsibility and he would take care of it. And her.

Whether she wanted him to or not.

The day after dinner with Nathan, Cindy dreaded her work assignment in the NICU. Facing the two nurses after being caught "red-handed" with a doctor wasn't something that would make for a relaxed atmosphere. There were no written rules, nothing in the employee handbook, but that didn't make it any less true. Anyone who crossed the line did so at her own peril.

There was only one thing she could do. Her job. And she did it to the best of her ability, ignoring the hostile looks from Barbara, who watched like a prison guard from her nurse's station fortress in the center of the large room. The unit was full of tiny babies, but all was normal and quiet. Nathan was nowhere in sight.

A small thread of disappointment told her she'd started to look forward to seeing him, which was a much-needed wake-up call. Her pregnancy was the only reason he acknowledged her at all. He'd all but confessed to being a serial dater. And to losing his wife, which could explain why he *was* a serial dater. Heartbreak could make a guy unwilling to commit.

But understanding didn't change the facts. By definition, seeing a lot of women meant that he had a short attention span and sooner or later he would disappear.

One thing about having lots to think about was how fast she got her work finished. She glanced around to make sure everything was taken care of and all her paraphernalia was picked up. That was when she caught Barbara's toxic look with the three Ds—disapproval, disdain and distaste.

"Ignore it," she muttered, turning away. "Be Switzerland."

The resentment would blow over when Nathan reverted to typical male behavior and showed more interest in a ventilator than her. Until then, she'd do her job and keep a low profile.

She walked out into the hall and replaced her supplies on the cart before unsnapping her "bunny suit." Just as she was stepping out of it, the NICU door opened and Barbara walked out.

Cindy's stomach knotted because her luck wasn't good enough for this to be a coincidence. She turned away and set the disposable suit on the handle of her cart, then picked up her clipboard and pretended to study her next assignment.

"I want to talk to you." The nurse's voice vibrated with antagonism.

Cindy took a deep breath and faced the woman, faking a calm she didn't feel. "Is there something you needed?"

"I need for you to concentrate on your job instead of your social life."

She'd always thought the nurse was beautiful. Not anymore. The woman's mouth pulled tight, making her chin, cheeks and nose sharper, more Wicked Witch of the West. The coldness rolling off her made Cindy wish for wool socks and a parka. But a confrontation required at least two, and she was determined not to take the bait. That meant bottling up a whole lot of outrage and indignation.

"I'm sorry. I thought I was thorough in the unit. Did I miss something?"

"Yeah." Barbara folded her arms over her chest. "You missed the part where you keep your nose out of other people's business."

Cindy knew that "business" meant Nathan Steele. She decided to play as dumb as this woman desperately wanted her to be. "I don't know what you mean."

"Oh, please. Since when does a neonatologist push a housekeeping cart?" she asked sarcastically. "And take you to dinner. Isn't he a little out of your league?"

The knots in Cindy's stomach tightened, then cramps started in her lower abdomen. She resisted giving in to it. Show no weakness.

"Dr. Steele and I are nothing more than friends." And parents-to-be, she thought. But that "business" she was keeping to herself for as long as possible.

"Right. And next you'll be trying to sell me beachfront property in Arizona."

Cindy shrugged. "Ask him if you don't believe me."

Anger flared hot in the other woman's eyes because they both knew she couldn't and wouldn't do that. Barbara jabbed her index finger in the air. "Look, just because you won a seat at the big table, don't go shining up your glass slippers for a walk down the aisle with Nathan Steele."

Cindy wanted so badly to ask if this was junior high and Barbara had dibs on him, but that would just prolong this awful scene and the pain in her stomach was getting worse.

"I've heard he goes through women at the speed of light. It's really nice of you to warn me."

Barbara's fingers curled into her palms and the frustration seemed to roll off her in waves before she turned without another word and went back into the unit. Chalk one up for the peon, Cindy thought.

But the brief feeling of triumph was cut short by a cramping pain that had her sucking in air before leaning against the wall. She took deep breaths and waited for it to pass. The discomfort eased but didn't disappear and she very much needed to sit down.

She made sure her cart was flush against the wall and not impeding the flow of traffic in the hall. Slowly she walked around the corner to the empty NICU waiting room and tentatively lowered herself into a chair, folding her arms protectively over her abdomen.

She'd never felt more alone or scared, not even after losing her father. Something wasn't right, but she didn't know what to do. Finally she took out her cell phone and called her supervisor. A few minutes later, Dina hurried around the corner.

"What's wrong?" she asked.

"This is Mercy Medical Center. I figured by the time you got here you'd already know," Cindy answered, trying to joke her way into being brave.

Dina sat down beside her. "Did something happen?"

"Before or after Barbara Kelly got on my case?"

The other woman angrily shook her head. "She's not happy unless she's complaining about something. Or someone."

"Then she must be ecstatic right now." Cindy winced.

Concern went up a notch in Dina's eyes. "Tell me what's going on. You're white as a sheet."

"I think—" Cindy's voice caught and she bit her lip. "I have cramps. I'm just sitting here until they go away. I thought you should know in case someone says something about it."

"How long?"

"Just until the pain stops."

"No." Dina shook her head impatiently. "When did the pains start?"

"About fifteen minutes ago."

"It could be nothing," Dina said. "And probably is. But that's a chance you don't want to take. You need to call your doctor."

"I will," she said, nodding. "But it's getting better. When my shift is over, I'll—"

"Don't worry about that." Dina waved a hand dismissively. "You need to find out right away whether or not there's something to be concerned about. We're talking about your child's welfare."

Her child.

Her baby.

Cindy rested her hand on her stomach. There was a life in there. A life that could be in jeopardy. Fear rolled through her and cleared away the doubts.

In that instant, what had been a surreal, intangible, complicated problem became crystal clear.

There was nothing more important than her child. There was nothing she wanted more than this baby.

Nothing.

She would do whatever was necessary and everything in her power to protect it.

Chapter Eight

Nathan rang Cindy's doorbell for the third time. He knew she was in there; her car was in the driveway. If she didn't answer in the next thirty seconds, he would break in.

Finally the door opened and she stood there in shorts and an oversize T-shirt. Her eyes were red-rimmed, as if she'd been crying.

"What's wrong?" he asked.

"This showing up unannounced is getting to be a bad habit," she said, not actually answering the question.

"So is not calling me."

"Why are you here?"

"Dina Garrett told me you left work early. And why." He'd broken speeding laws getting over here after hearing.

"You went to my supervisor?"

"Because I couldn't find you and no one had seen you. It wasn't time for your shift to be over and you're not the irresponsible type. I figured your immediate boss would know what was going on."

"Oh."

Yeah. The woman had looked at him as if he were an ax murderer. Dina was very protective. Apparently Cindy inspired that feeling in someone besides him.

"So... Did you see the doctor?"

Tears welled in her eyes as she nodded without embellishing.

"And?" he prompted.

"I was cramping. She was concerned. I'm on bed rest for a few weeks."

That meant the pregnancy was still viable and the baby was okay. Relief washed through him, followed by anger.

"Why didn't you call me?" he demanded. "I'm a doctor."

"Not mine," she countered.

"I have every right to know what's going on." He would have driven her to the office. Been there to support her. But she kept shutting him out and that pissed him off.

"If there had been anything to tell you, I would have. Now, if you don't mind, I'm supposed to stay off my feet. And not worry about anything—" Her voice caught and she put a hand over her mouth.

Nathan swore under his breath as he lifted her into his arms and shouldered the door closed.

"What are you doing?" she demanded.

"Getting you off your feet." He looked around the room. There was a small sofa, a wooden rocking chair and not much else. "I'm taking you to bed."

"Put me down." There was an edge to her voice.

"I didn't mean that." Not really. Not now that the pregnancy had turned risky. But before this, the thought had crossed his mind more than once. "That didn't come out right. I'm going to put you in bed."

"The love seat is fine."

He glanced at it, a green overstuffed little sofa with tiny yellow and coral flowers. The first time he'd been here, having Cindy had been his only focus. Then he found out the condom broke and other details about the room disappeared. Now he took it all in.

The floor was wood, a medium-tone pine. A stand in the corner of the room held a small old TV. By the front door was a tiny mahogany occasional table with a mirror above it, right next to where he'd backed her against the wall and taken her. A bed would have been nice, but he couldn't wait. And he couldn't regret the most mind-blowing sex ever. Now there was going to be a baby. His responsibility was to take care of the mother in his arms.

That was why he was here. Because of the child.

In front of the love seat there was a cedar chest with a coaster and a glass of water. Five wadded-up tissues were scattered over the scratched and scarred top of the wood. She *had* been crying.

He walked over to the love seat and gently set her down. Now he felt the need to do more. To fix something. "Are you hungry?"

"No."

"Did you eat lunch?"

"A little."

That didn't sound good. "I'll fix you something."

"I haven't been to the grocery store." Her eyes filled with tears again.

Nathan moved the glass out of the way, handed her a tissue, then sat on the cedar chest across from her. "Talk to me, Cindy."

She dabbed at her eyes with the tissue. "I'd just finished my assignment in the NICU and started cramping."

He knew from Dina that there'd been a confrontation with one of the NICU nurses just before Cindy doubled over. That made him want to put his fist through the wall. She had tried to tell him, but he'd blown her off.

"Go on."

"The pains wouldn't go away and I got scared and called the doctor. She did a thorough exam and said everything looks okay. That probably extreme tension caused the episode. Then she said to be on the safe side I should stay off my feet for a few weeks. Then we'll reevaluate after the pregnancy stabilizes."

He nodded. All good advice. Err on the side of caution. Every doctor takes an oath and vows to "first do no harm."

"Then rest is what you should do."

"In a perfect world," she cried.

"You're not seriously thinking about ignoring her advice."

"No, but—"

"What?" he demanded.

"The Family Medical Leave Act will preserve my job, but if I don't work, I don't get paid. Without money I can't pay my bills. I'm terrified for the baby, but what am I going to do?"

"First, you're going to calm down," he said, concerned that she was working herself up. "Then you're going to let me help you."

"I can't let you do that."

"I can afford it." Chump change for him.

"This isn't your problem. It's mine," she protested.

"You didn't get pregnant by yourself. I want to do something."

"I'll figure it out. But I appreciate the offer. Really." She reached over and touched his hand.

His skin burned where her fingers squeezed, and the contact threatened to fry his concentration. He shook his head and struggled to focus. She needed his help. Because not working would give her lots of time to stress over everything she couldn't pay. But if he'd learned anything since getting to know her it was that stubborn was her middle name. Picking a fight over how he could help wouldn't be following her doctor's orders. So he had a better idea.

"You'll move in with me," he said. "The pantry, fridge and freezer are full. You can eat pickles and ice cream to your heart's content. I'm in and out, but I can monitor your condition—"

"No."

Nathan waited for more and when she didn't elaborate, he tried to figure out what was going through her mind. "I have lots of room."

"It's not about that." She folded her hands in her lap.

"Then what's wrong with the plan?"

"So many things, so little time." Her answer was no answer at all.

Nathan stared at her—the big, beautiful eyes looked bruised and battered. Her full mouth with its defined upper lip trembled. The escalating need to pull her into his arms made him increasingly uncomfortable. But it wasn't just because he wanted to comfort her. The truth was that if she wasn't on doctor-ordered bed rest, he might have carried her to bed and made love to her properly.

Her spirit and courage in the face of adversity were admirable and he should be grateful that she was giving him an out. Every instinct he had urged him to take it and run like hell, but he wouldn't turn his back on his kid, like his parents had with him. He was determined to be there and make the environment safe for his child.

To do that, he had to first of all not argue with the woman carrying that child. She'd drawn a line in the sand, so he had to find a way around it.

"Okay. We'll stay here then."

Some of the bruising left her eyes when suspicion replaced it. "We?"

"You won't come to my house and I'm not leaving you alone. That means I'm not leaving."

"You can't do that."

"Why?"

"I didn't invite you," she said.

"With all due respect," he answered, "how are you planning to stop me?"

"Logistics for one thing." She folded her arms over her chest. "There's nowhere for you to sleep. Certainly not in my room."

"Never crossed my mind," he lied.

"And the other two bedrooms are set up for an office and storage."

He shrugged. "Don't worry about me. I'm a big boy. Been taking care of myself for a long time."

"Nathan, no—"

He shushed her with a finger to her lips, and the touch seemed to shock her into silence. "You're not supposed to worry. So, forgive my bluntness, but shut up and relax."

Three days later Cindy wasn't exactly relaxed, but that was less about pregnancy and more about Nathan invading her space. It was early in the morning and she was still in bed, putting off getting up because she knew he was still there. Nathan had spent every moment he wasn't at the hospital in her house. Every morning since he'd refused to go away she'd walked out of her bedroom and peeked into the living room expecting him to be gone. And every day he wasn't.

Yet she knew he couldn't keep this up. He was a guy. Sooner or later he'd get bored with her as his latest charity case and bail. She wished he would get it over with—before she got used to him. Before it would hurt like crazy when she found out she'd been right, before she was alone again and less prepared to be that way.

Maybe she was borrowing trouble. Maybe today was the day he'd be gone. Today would be okay because she was ready for it, expecting him to disappear.

She threw the sheet off and slid out of the queen-size bed. After stopping in the bathroom, she tiptoed down the hall and through the kitchen. Peeking around the corner, she first saw his feet, then the rest of him dressed only in boxers. There was a sheet on the couch and he was still asleep, but probably that was from complete exhaustion. The sofa wasn't anywhere big enough to accommodate him, yet there he still was.

He looked a little dangerous, she thought, and a lot dashing with the shadow of stubble on his jaw. He was all rumpled, sleepy, sex appeal, and an unmistakable tug on her heart made her hope this was the last time she would find him here.

His eyelids flickered and he stretched, then suddenly sat up when he saw her. "Are you okay?"

"Fine." In the physical sense that was true because there was no more cramping. But emotionally she was a mess.

"You're not supposed to be on your feet. Are you hungry?"

"Yes," she admitted, admiring the expanse of broad male chest covered with a dusting of dark hair.

"I'll make breakfast. Go back to bed," he ordered.

After three days she knew resistance was futile, so she went back to bed. Before long the smell of eggs, turkey sausage, potatoes and toast drifted to her. Over her protests he'd grocery shopped and stocked her pantry. She had to admit the delicious aromas made her mouth water.

Then Nathan appeared in her doorway. He'd dressed in jeans and a T-shirt, but his feet were still bare, his hair rumpled and the stubble unshaved. He held a food-filled tray, and she held in an appreciative sigh. Her mouth was watering, but it had nothing to do with the food.

"Breakfast is served." He set the tray on her legs and started to leave.

"Can I talk to you, Nathan?"

"Sure." The bed dipped from his weight when he sat on the edge, just inches from her leg. "What's up?"

"This isn't working."

He frowned. "I can make something else for breakfast—"

"No. I mean this arrangement. You have to be exhausted from not having a bed to sleep in."

"I have to admit I'm not lovin' the love seat."

"That's what I'm talking about." Sort of. She had to convince him to go away. "And I don't need you hovering over me. I haven't had any more cramping. So, really, you can go back to your place."

"I'd like that," he agreed. Much too easily. "On one condition."

"Anything."

"You come, too." He must have seen her start to protest because he held up a hand. "It has more room and everyone would have an actual bed to sleep in."

"Don't think I'm not appreciative because I am." Except for her family and three best friends, no one had ever been there for her like this. "But this is my home."

"Okay. No problem." He rubbed a hand across his chin. "Maybe I'll pick up an air mattress. My mother will understand why I'm not at the house."

"Your mother?"

"She dropped in unexpectedly. She does that sometimes," he said.

"You should go be with her. No need to babysit me."

A gleam slid into his eyes. "Actually, you'd be doing me a big favor if you moved in. Mom and I could use a buffer."

"You're not close?"

His mouth pulled tight. "She has her own interests."

Shouldn't her interests include being with her son? None of her business, Cindy thought. "I wouldn't want to intrude. It would be such an inconvenience."

"Look, Cindy, I'm serious about Mom and me needing someone to take the edge off. But here's the bottom line. You and I both want the baby to be healthy. That depends on your ability to stay off your feet and reduce your stress level. I intend to make that happen. Where it happens is up to you."

She knew when to say when. Stalemate. Impasse. Someone had to blink, and apparently it would be her. She couldn't stand the thought of him being completely exhausted because she was too stubborn to compromise. There were other babies and parents depending on him.

"All right," she said. "Your place it is."

Nathan pulled into the driveway of his really big house before Cindy had time to process that she'd actually agreed to move in with him. He'd packed her things and wouldn't let her lift a finger, which was seven different kinds of sweet.

Now here they were. Parked beside a BMW SUV in his

driveway. It was a reminder that he already had a guest. Her stomach clenched.

"Did you tell your mother about the baby? Does she know you're bringing me here?"

"Yes." He pulled the keys from the ignition, then looked at her. "And yes."

"Good." At least there wouldn't be that awkward moment where she had to stand quietly by while he explained the unexplainable.

When she started to get out of the car, he said, "Stay put. You're not supposed to be on your feet."

"Then how am I going to get inside?"

A shimmy of anticipation danced up her spine when she remembered him sweeping her into his arms to carry her inside at her house. But the romantic notion dissolved when he emerged from the front door pushing a wheelchair.

"Be still my heart." Cindy wondered what kind of damage was done when a romantic fool dropped back to earth. But she sat in the chair.

It was a beautiful June day and already getting hot, so the cool air that washed over her when he pushed her inside felt good. When her eyes adjusted from bright sun to the dim interior, she saw that travertine tile went on forever in the entryway. There were high ceilings with crown molding and pale wheat-colored walls.

An older but very attractive woman walked into the entryway. She was tall and slender with a short brunette bob. Her eyes were hazel, and it was obvious that Nathan got his coloring from his mother. And his fashion sense. Her white capris were crisp and spotless. The black and white striped silk blouse was trendy and fitted. Even her sandals coordinated with the summer ensemble.

"So here you are," she said, her eyes narrowing on Cindy.

Nathan's voice came from behind the wheelchair. "Shirley, this is Cindy Elliott. Cindy, Shirley Steele, my mother."

They shook hands and Cindy felt at a disadvantage in the chair. Even standing she would be shorter, but at least she wouldn't have been loomed over.

Nathan leaned down. "I'm going to get your things out of the car and put them in the guest room."

Moments later he walked inside with her two suitcases then disappeared down the hall. He returned and glanced at his watch. "I have to get to the hospital. Shirley, will you get Cindy settled?"

"Of course."

"I'll be back later." He looked down at her with a warning expression on his face. "Take it easy."

Nothing about this was easy to take, especially being left alone with his mother. But he walked out the door and it was just the two of them.

Cindy didn't know how to be anything but direct. She got up from the chair and met the other woman's gaze. "This pregnancy was an accident."

"So I've been told."

"I didn't even want to go out with him."

"Technically one doesn't have to actually go out for something like this to happen," Shirley commented, her tone guarded. "But why did you? Go out with him."

"He was relentless and I said yes to get him out of my life."

"Yet here you are in his home. So we can see how well that worked."

"I didn't want to move in." Cindy refused to look away, even though that's what she desperately wanted to do. "But he's so darn stubborn and he wouldn't leave me alone. He's exhausted and the only way he's going to get any rest is for me to stay here. That's the truth."

"All right then. Nathan is a grown man and knows what he's doing." Shirley glanced over her shoulder. "I take it you know your way around?"

"Actually, I've never been here before." Cindy stopped there, not wanting to explain the one-night stand at her house.

The older woman looked just the tiniest bit surprised when she asked, "Would you like a tour?"

"Are you going to make me use that stupid chair?" Cindy glared at the thing.

"I think that's about my son being overly cautious. Stay off your feet means don't do the trampoline or go bungee jumping, not be an invalid."

Cindy nodded. "I think so, too."

"All right then. Follow me." Shirley turned and started walking away. "This place has five bedrooms and a guest house. That's where I stay."

Interesting. Nathan didn't really need her to be a buffer between him and his mom. There was plenty of space for the two to peacefully coexist. This house was big enough for its own zip code.

Cindy noted that the living and dining rooms were separated by the wide entryway and filled with dark cherry wood furniture and fabrics in earth tones. White plantation shutters covered the windows. The family room was right off the kitchen and had a fireplace on one wall. A huge leather corner group sat in front of a gigantic flat-screen TV.

"My whole house would fit in this room," Cindy said, still in awe.

"The bedrooms are down this hall," Shirley said.

She pointed out the master bedroom at the back of the

house, and Cindy politely glanced through the doorway, although it felt like invading Nathan's privacy. The room was huge, with a king-size bed across from a sunken conversation area and fireplace. A little twinge that could be jealousy told her it was best not to think about all the women who'd no doubt "conversed" in here with him.

Across the hall there were two more bedrooms connected by a bath. Her suitcases were visible in the first room.

"This is where you'll stay." Shirley walked through the bathroom into the connecting bedroom. "This gets the morning sun. And there's that charming window seat. I think this would make a wonderful nursery."

Cindy glanced at the L-shaped desk with the computer on top. There was an eight-foot couch and a wing chair in another corner. Clearly it was set up as an office.

"It would certainly work. But I'm not staying here permanently," Cindy protested.

"But you and Nathan will share custody."

It wasn't a question except in Cindy's mind. If she had to judge by her experience, Nathan wouldn't be around long enough to share custody or anything else. But telling his mother that didn't seem appropriate.

"I believe children should know both of their parents," Cindy said diplomatically. "If at all possible."

"I'm glad you feel that way because I've jotted down some ideas for a mural in here." Shirley picked up a sketch pad from the desk. "Would you like to see?"

It felt a little weird, but, "Okay." She looked at the drawings of cuddly zoo animals on the first page. "These are too cute."

"Those are generic," Shirley explained. "The next page is cars, fire trucks, airplanes. Boy stuff. Then there's the sports-themed sketches. Followed by fairy tale characters and princess pictures. Nathan can make a decision when he finds out the sex of the baby."

"These are really good." Pretty amazing, really.

She flipped through the pages, each set of sketches more impressive than the last. Knowing whether the child was a boy or girl would narrow down themes, but they were all so adorable, making a decision wouldn't be easy.

"You're incredibly artistic," she said.

"Not really. I just had lots of time to practice." Shirley's pleased expression instantly disappeared.

Cindy felt guilty because it was the first time the other woman had smiled and something she'd said had made the warmth dissolve. "You have a lot of natural talent. I don't think practice alone would be enough to do this."

"It is if you have the time. My husband left me." She shrugged. "Because I wasn't being a wife, I had a lot of time to work on other, creative endeavors."

But you were a mother, Cindy wanted to say. If the marriage wasn't working, why didn't this woman's time and energy get channeled into the young son who must have been hurt and confused about his deteriorating family? She'd never understood before how priceless her carefree childhood had been but kept the revelation to herself. In fact, she didn't know what to say.

But not saying anything made this more awkward than watching Nathan explain their complicated association to his mother.

Shirley must have felt it, too. "I've kept you on your feet too long. You should rest."

Alone, Cindy walked back into the room where she'd be staying. The bed was queen-size, covered with a floral quilt and a striped bed skirt in green and white. A tufted bench sat at the foot with her suitcases resting on top. There was an oak dresser with a mirror over it and matching nightstands. Very comfortable and should have been cheerful.

Cindy remembered what Nathan had said about being an unaccompanied minor. She'd assumed both of his parents had demanding careers, but that wasn't the case. He was a handsome doctor, brilliant and wealthy. Yet she felt sorry for him. And that was stupid. It could potentially weaken the hard crust around her feelings. And that would be a disaster.

If she made it through this pregnancy and delivered a healthy baby, it would be in no small part because of Nathan's support at this traumatic time. She would be forever grateful to him, but they were having a baby, not a relationship. That's the only reason she was living in his house.

The emotional health of her heart depended on remembering that.

Chapter Nine

Cindy had always thought that leather belonged on animals, not furniture, but that was before she'd experienced Nathan's decor. All afternoon she'd been relaxing on his family room corner group. The cushy feel of the soft leather had changed her opinion. And the TV wasn't bad either. It had to be at least a seventy-five-inch screen. In her tiny house it would be too big, but this room accommodated it perfectly.

"So size *does* matter," she said to herself.

She was watching an old chick flick starring Steve McQueen and Natalie Wood. The TV was so big and clear she could see practically every pore in the actress's flawless face.

Glancing at her watch, she realized it was after seven. Shirley was out and Nathan hadn't returned from the hospital. She was getting hungry and wondered whether to go digging into his provisions. *Mi casa, su casa,* he had said.

Before she could decide, the front door opened and closed, then he walked in lugging plastic bags of groceries in both hands.

"Hi," she said. "Need some help?"

"This is everything." His eyes narrowed on her. "And you're here because of questions like that. Your job right now is to carry nothing heavier than the TV remote."

"Then you should be proud because today I totally rocked this remote control. It got an excellent workout."

He carried the bags into the kitchen and set them on the granite-covered island in the center. While he unloaded them, he asked, "How do you feel?"

She muted the TV sound before answering. "Good. Normal. No more pains. Not even a hint of a cramp."

"Excellent."

"I'm thinking it's okay to go back to work."

He was putting a box into the pantry and turned to stare at her. "Your doctor advised you to rest for several weeks."

"But I feel fine."

"That's great. And we want to keep it that way. So just relax and go with it." He closed the cupboard door. "Where's Shirley?"

"Astrology class. She was going to skip it and stay with me, but I talked her into going." He didn't respond and she added, "You don't seem surprised."

"I'm not. Shirley keeps busy."

"She showed me some sketches for a mural in the baby's room."

"Oh?" He put bananas in a cobalt blue pottery bowl on the island.

"They're really good ideas—for either a boy or girl. She's quite an artist."

"Shirley's had a lot of practice."

"That's exactly what she said," Cindy informed him.

She was looking for some kind of clue as to how he felt about that, but he gave her no reaction, as if he'd perfected not reacting. And really that information was need-to-know. She didn't need to. Nathan's relationship with his mother was none of her business. But the fact that he called her Shirley spoke volumes.

When the silence stretched between them, she asked, "So what's in the bags?"

He wadded up the empty ones and threw them in the trash. "Nothing now. But I got you peanut butter and jelly."

She wanted to go all mushy inside from the gesture but held back. "What kind?"

"Crunchy. I wasn't sure what kind you liked, but how can anyone not like crunchy?"

"Sound logic," she approved. "And jelly?"

"That was a tougher decision. I fell back on personality."

"How so?" She sat up straighter and tucked her legs to the side.

"Strawberry seemed way too cheerful, so I went with grape."

"You think I'm more sour grapes?"

He rested his hands on the counter separating the two rooms. "Am I wrong?"

"I think I'm a peach of a person," she said.

"If you don't like grape, I'll go back to the store and get peach."

"No. Grape's my favorite."

But how gallant of him to make another trip. Her heart gave an odd little skip that she hoped was about her "delicate condition." The warm, fluttery feeling in the pit of her stomach could be nothing more than normal for a pregnant woman. One could hope, anyway.

"What else did you get at the store?" she asked.

"Lots of healthy stuff. Fruit. Vegetables."

"I don't like broccoli." She rested an elbow on the arm of the sofa.

"Then you don't have to eat any. And in case you weren't kidding about the cravings, I got pickles and ice cream."

She'd never been much of an ice cream addict, but suddenly the idea of it made her mouth water. "What kind of ice cream? And please don't say Rocky Road to complement my difficult personality."

He grinned. "Cookies and cream."

"Sounds yummy."

"I'm sensing symptoms of hunger. What else tempts your appetite?" he asked.

"Peanut butter and banana."

"Coming right up," he said without hesitation or editorializing.

She watched him work, pulling out plates, bread, the jar of crunchy peanut butter and the bananas. A warmth trickled through her that had nothing to do with the baby growing inside her. If she had to describe the feeling, the first word that popped into her head was *pampered*.

And perturbed.

He looked so cute moving around the kitchen making sandwiches. A feast for the eyes as she watched the muscles in his biceps bunch and his broad shoulders square off on the task. She was uneasy because when she'd agreed to temporarily move in with him, her concern had been mostly for the baby but partly about him being exhausted. She'd never considered him hanging around with her and unleashing a siege on her senses.

"How was work?" she asked. Anything to get her mind off this personal turn her thoughts had taken.

"The gladiator is holding his own against the lions and tigers. But his prognosis is still guarded."

"Why?"

He walked over to her with a plate in each hand before handing her one and setting the other on the coffee table. "Because he's fragile and anything can happen. Do you want milk with dinner?"

"What are you having?"

"A beer since I'm officially off call." He rested his hands on lean hips. "But I don't think you'd better have one."

"It doesn't even sound good and probably wouldn't be the best choice for the baby." Talk about his work reminded her that he knew better than anyone the need for prenatal caution. That's why she was here. "Milk it is."

He nodded, then fetched and delivered the drinks before sitting down beside her. He was staring at the muted movie on TV as he took a bite of the sandwich identical to hers. To his credit, he didn't choke or spit it out. Also to his credit, he'd put apple slices and baby carrot sticks on each plate.

Cindy stared at her food. "Do you always eat like this?"

"Like what?" He took another bite.

"Peanut butter and banana. Healthy and nutritious."

"Never had this before. It's pretty good," he admitted.

Suddenly she was really curious about his usual habits. "What's a normal dinner for you?"

"I grab takeout on the way home from the hospital. If forced to cook, it's a steak on the barbecue."

"So you're doing this for me," she said, indicating the fresh fruit and veggies.

"Yeah." He crunched on a carrot. "It's the right thing to do."

To some men "the right thing" in this situation would be marriage, but he'd never brought it up. Maybe because his wife had died. Was that why he didn't believe in love? Because it hurt when you lost that special person?

At least he was honest, and that was refreshing after the jerk who'd done nothing but lie to her. And Nathan was a nice man. It was incredibly difficult to work up a heart-healthy amount of resistance to him when he was nice.

"What are you watching?" He took a sip from the long-neck bottle of beer.

"I was channel surfing." She wasn't sure why, but she felt the need to explain stumbling onto this old movie. "Came across this Steve McQueen, Natalie Wood picture. *Love with the Proper Stranger.*"

"What's it about?"

She took a big bite of her sandwich and savored the flavors mixing together. But the truth was that peanut butter did stick to the roof of your mouth and it took her a minute before she could answer the question. Long enough for the parallel between her life imitating movie art to become clear.

"It's a chick flick." That should put an end to his curiosity.

"Steve McQueen usually plays a tough guy. Guns and car chases. Why is he standing in the middle of a crowd holding bells and a banjo with a sign around his neck that says, 'Better wed than dead'?"

"You don't really want to know."

"If I didn't, I wouldn't have asked."

"Okay." She looked at the happy ending silently playing out on seventy-five inches of screen. "They had a one-night stand and she got pregnant."

"Really?" His expression said that he got the parallel.

"He's not the marrying kind but asks her anyway because

it's the right thing. And in the olden days it was quite the stigma for a woman to be unmarried and pregnant."

"I actually know that."

"She turns down the proposal. Stuff happens and when he gets to know her, he discovers that he can't live without her, but he's blown it big time. The bells, banjo and sign are very public, his grand gesture to prove he really wants to be with her. That he loves her. Very romantic."

"I guess." He set his empty plate on the coffee table. "If you believe in that sort of thing."

"Someone must because romance is a moneymaker at the movies."

"Oh?"

"Yeah. *Titanic* was the highest grossing movie ever. Until recently."

"The boat sinks. So what's your point?"

"Exactly that. Everyone knows the boat sinks. The only reason that movie was so successful is because there was a love story at the heart of it. No pun intended."

"Is it possible that the special effects pulled in the public?"

"Some," she admitted. "Did you see it?"

"Yeah."

"Why do you suppose Rose as an old woman threw that expensive necklace in the ocean?"

"Dementia brought on by advancing age."

She laughed. "That works. I just kept thinking if she didn't want it, she should give it to me. I could really use the money."

"But if romance is the heart of the movie, that scene is symbolic. One could deduce that love makes no sense."

"If you don't believe in love, far be it from me to try and convince you otherwise. It's not worth the argument."

"Good. Do you mind if I put on a ball game?"

"It's your TV."

And house. Love had no place in his life. She was grateful for the reminder because hanging out with him was fun but a bad idea. After what felt like an eternity of digging herself out of debt by herself, leaning on him would be too easy. It would also leave her vulnerable and with nowhere to hide.

However, since their one-night stand he hadn't made a single move on her. Maybe because she was pregnant, but more likely because he was so over her. That meant the attraction getting stronger for her was one-sided and made the obsession to fortify her heart just silly.

His lack of attention proved she'd been right about him losing interest when he got what he wanted.

Sometimes she hated being right.

Cindy sat in Nathan's family room with her feet up and looked at two of her three best friends, Harlow Marcelli and Mary Frances Bird. Whitney Davenport, a medical technician at the hospital, had to work because the lab was short-staffed. She was counting on her friends to fill her in on what the heck was going on.

The two who were present hadn't told her that, but Cindy knew. The four of them had met at the hospital's new-hire orientation. Though they all worked in completely different departments, the click of friendship had been instant. Since then, the other three women had pulled Cindy through heartbreak and the financial fiasco that followed. She'd been there for the others during crises of dating, declining parent health and anything else they needed. Now she had to explain to them the unexplainable—how she'd gotten pregnant and why she'd kept it to herself.

This morning Mary Frances had called Cindy's cell and demanded to know why she hadn't been at work. She and Harlow had gone to her house, which, of course, was empty. They were worried. Cindy had given her Nathan's address and invited them over for in-person details. This wasn't a quick, cell-call kind of conversation. Nathan was at work and Shirley had gone to a candle-making class at the astrology store.

The time had come to confess all.

Cindy sat in the corner of the big, L-shaped sofa with her friends on either side of her. "So, how have you guys been? What's new?"

"That's what I'd like to know." Mary Frances was a petite, auburn-haired Labor and Delivery nurse at the hospital. She and Cindy were the same size, and the fundraiser dress had been borrowed from her.

"Okay. Before we start, anyone want water, soda, juice or coffee? You guys hungry?"

"Yeah. For information. What is going on? Whose house is this? And when can I move in, too?" Mary Frances's blue eyes held equal parts of humor and confusion.

Harlow tucked a shoulder-length strand of shiny brown hair behind her ear. Green eyes that missed nothing were narrowed. "I think I can answer the who question. But the why is still a mystery."

Mary Frances slid forward. The seat of the couch was so deep, if she scooted back, her legs stuck straight out in front of her. She lifted her hands in a helpless gesture. "Someone please start filling in the blanks because I'm clueless here."

"This is Dr. Steele's house, isn't it?" Harlow tapped her lip. "Oh, wait, he asked you to call him Nathan."

"What? When did this happen? How come you know and I don't?" Mary Frances glared at both of them. In spite of her small size, she looked fierce enough to do great bodily harm.

"Harlow knows because she was in the NICU working on a baby and picked up on some vibes," Cindy explained.

"So, she's right? This is Nathan Steele's house? You didn't win ten million dollars playing Megabucks?"

"No, I didn't win money. Yes, it's his house."

"How come you didn't tell me about this?"

Harlow shrugged at the accusing look. "You've been busy. I've been busy. And I didn't know Cindy moved in with him. What's up with that, anyway? I guess you finally gave him your phone number. Or went out with him. Or both." She looked around the beautiful, spacious room that could be from a photo shoot in *Decorator's Digest*. "I'd say he got both."

"Please tell me her imagination is on crack and she's gone to the bad place for no good reason."

"I can't." Cindy glanced at both her friends. "I'm pregnant and he's the father."

Harlow didn't shock easily, but she was now. "That's a place my imagination didn't even consider."

"No way." Mary Frances shook her head. "It's a joke, right? You guys think I'm gullible, but I'm not falling for it. You know better than to do something like that."

"I'm not kidding," Cindy confirmed. "And you both are a little bit to blame."

"Someone needs to learn how to take responsibility for her own actions." Harlow tsk-tsked.

Mary Frances stared at her. "How do you figure this is our fault?"

"You guys did too good a job styling me for that dinner I won the raffle ticket for."

"What?"

"Steele didn't recognize her," Harlow explained. "She made him guess where he'd seen her before, but he drew a blank. Then she ran out of the ball and he only caught up with her because the heel on my shoe broke."

Mary Frances pointed at them. "Do either of you see the parallel here?"

"What are you talking about?" Harlow demanded.

"Fairy tales. Cinderella." She nodded emphatically. "Am I right?"

"He's a doctor, not Prince Charming," Cindy said. "And he doesn't believe in love, so that ball had nothing to do with him finding a wife."

"But we digress." Harlow looked at each of them to get their attention. "He bugged her for her phone number and I advised her to let him call but dodge everything else. Bob and weave until he got bored and turned his attention elsewhere. Clearly that didn't happen. Which begs the question. How did you get from giving him your phone number to... You know."

"Sex?" Cindy clarified.

"Yeah," they both answered.

"It started with dinner at an Italian place—"

"Not Capriotti's." Mary Frances slid a knowing look to their friend.

"Yes. How did you know?"

"Doesn't matter. Go on."

What did they know that she didn't? Cindy wondered. Although it wasn't really important because the final outcome was the same. "There was candlelight, flowers, wine and food."

"Isn't that always the way?" Harlow was their token skeptic.

"So you got swept away. I understand that. But what about birth control?" So spoke the Labor and Delivery nurse who every day saw the result of planned and unplanned pregnancies.

"The condom malfunctioned." Cindy shrugged.

"That explains getting pregnant," Harlow said. "But why are you here in his house?"

"I had cramps and some spotting. The obstetrician said stress can sometimes be a factor. She ordered me to stay off my feet for a few weeks."

"You have a bed at your house," Mary Frances reminded her.

"Nathan watched over me and refused to leave. He's too big to throw out and there was no bed for him. So I agreed to move in here temporarily. It's really sweet when you think about it."

"Don't go there," Harlow warned. "I know that look."

"She's right. It's the soft and gooey expression. The one that happens just before you throw caution to the wind," Mary Frances said knowingly.

"I'm not throwing caution anywhere." Cindy folded her arms over her chest.

"Oh, really?" Mary Frances lifted one auburn eyebrow. "You're not the first woman he's taken to Capriotti's."

"I never said I was. That was obvious when he was on a first-name basis with the waiter. Who also knew his favorite wine." Cindy blew out a breath. "Look, you guys. I appreciate your concern. Really. But it happened. It was an accident and he's taking responsibility. That's all this is about. He's helping out. For now."

She didn't need her friends to warn her not to count on anything but today. She warned herself enough for both of them.

"Why is it that you didn't come to us for help?" There was challenge and a little hurt in Mary Frances's blue eyes.

It was a very good question. Cindy wasn't sure she had an answer. She shrugged. "It happened fast. I knew there was a chance of pregnancy, but really what were the odds? Then I did the test and figured Nathan should be the first to know. And I was pretty freaked out. I guess I felt stupid about it all. Please say I'm forgiven."

"Of course." Harlow patted Cindy's knee. "What are friends for? Show me a woman and I'll show you someone who's made a big mistake with a man at one time or another."

"Doesn't mean you have to compound the situation by falling for him." Mary Frances patted her other knee. "Don't go gooey. Stay tough. Get an attorney."

"She's right," Harlow agreed. "It's a well-known fact that Nathan Steele is a good doctor but a bad boyfriend."

Cindy nodded. "I'm well aware of his flaws."

"Then our work here is done." Mary Frances looked at her tummy and smiled, a soft and tender expression on her elfin face. "So we're going to be aunts?"

"Yeah." Cindy put a hand on her abdomen. "Can you believe there's a little someone in here?"

"We'll throw you a baby shower," her friend said.

And talk turned to babies, night feedings, dirty diapers and how her life was going to change. As if she needed the reminder. Everything had turned upside down the night Nathan noticed her.

As they chatted, Cindy figured out why she'd kept this to herself for as long as possible. She knew her friends would give her a reality check, bring her down to earth. Part of her didn't want to feel the thud. The same part that wanted to stay in the land of denial. But she couldn't hang out there anymore. Past mistakes had taught her she could take care of herself, but it was comforting to know her friends cared. It had been stupid to hold back, and they'd forgiven her without question. They would be there for her.

Their loyalty included reminding her of the truth:

Nathan was an exceptional and brilliant doctor. He was also a bad boyfriend. It was up to Cindy to get over the if-only-that-could-be-different feeling.

Chapter Ten

"I don't cook and Nathan would not be happy if I let you do it." Shirley sat down on the family room sofa and set a big, fat Las Vegas directory on her lap. "I can, however, dial the phone. What kind of food are you craving?"

"Don't go to any trouble. I'm happy with a peanut butter and banana sandwich," Cindy protested.

In spite of the resolve her friends had instigated just yesterday, she realized a lot of that sandwich appeal had to do with Nathan making and eating it with her. She needed a refresher course in not setting herself up for a letdown.

"I had a thing for peanut butter and pickles during my pregnancy with Nathan." Shirley's smile was small and sad. "But as delicious as that all sounds, I think a meal is the way to go. What about Chinese?"

"I like it." Although not right now, she thought.

"That was distinctly lacking in enthusiasm." The other

woman studied her. "I don't have to read your astrological chart to know you're humoring me. Mexican?"

Just the mention of spicy made her stomach lurch. She put a hand on her abdomen. "Probably not."

"Italian?"

That brought back images of candlelight and atmosphere the night this baby was conceived. Whatever happened, it would always be a lovely memory.

Before she could respond, Shirley said, "We have a winner."

"How did you know?"

The older woman tilted her head and tapped her lip, never taking her eyes off Cindy. "You just got this look on your face. All soft and sort of glowy."

If she was that easy to read, The World Series of Poker was out of the question.

"What would you like?" Shirley was flipping through the phone book.

"I guess fettuccine alfredo."

"Coming right up. I'll make the call. There's a place not far away that delivers." Shirley stood and started to walk away, then stopped. "When Nathan called, he said he'd be home in a little while. I'll get something for him, too. What does he like?"

Apparently he hadn't shared that they'd had exactly two meals together before conceiving this baby. One was rubber chicken at the fundraiser. The other had been Capriotti's.

"He likes fettuccine alfredo, too. And caesar salad."

Shirley nodded. "Okay."

Pretending to read her book, Cindy heard the other woman on the phone in the kitchen, placing the order. Then there was the sound of glasses set on the counter and the refrigerator opening and closing. Shirley brought wine for herself and a glass of water for Cindy.

After handing it over, the older woman sat on the end of the sofa. "So, what do you do, Cindy?"

There was a whole lot more that Nathan hadn't shared. Cindy should have expected the question, but she hadn't. She wondered if he talked with his mom about anything. It was possible he only told her about the baby because the pregnancy had turned risky at the same time Shirley showed up.

"I work in the housekeeping department at the hospital," she said. "I'm also doing an administrative internship for my degree in hospital administration."

"Aren't you a little old to still be in school?"

Way to find the exposed nerve, Cindy thought. But she was only ashamed that being a fool had cost her time in getting an education, not that she was still pursuing the goal. "Personal problems delayed me. But I'm almost there."

"Ambition. Good for you." Shirley sipped her wine.

"It definitely keeps me busy."

"You'll be even busier after the baby is born." The other woman's comment held more question than statement.

How was she going to juggle her career and child care? Pay for it all? And a lot more things that Cindy could only guess at. Curiosity mixed with suspicion in Shirley's expression. That was understandable. On some level she must be concerned about her son.

"To tell you the truth, I haven't really thought that far ahead." She turned down the page of her book to mark the place then set it beside her. "I'll be able to finish up my degree before the baby is born. And I have medical insurance through my job at the hospital. I have a tight-knit group of friends for support."

"Your parents?"

"Both passed away," she said. It wasn't a fresh loss, but a wave of sadness washed through her that her folks would never see this grandchild. "I have a brother in school at UCLA."

"So, you're basically on your own."

"Yes. And I'll deal with decisions as necessary and make the best ones I can make."

"What about Nathan?"

"What about him?"

"How do you see his role in this?" his mother asked.

"Whatever he wants it to be." Cindy hadn't expected him to do as much as he already had. She also refused to picture the three of them as a happy little family.

"So, the two of you haven't discussed marriage?" Shirley swirled the wine in her glass.

They had but only in jest or sarcasm. In one of her least shining moments, Cindy had said if her life was a romantic comedy, Nathan would have proposed to her. But she knew what his mother was asking.

"No. We're not getting married."

Shirley's expression gave no clue about her reaction to that—either positive or negative. She nodded and said, "That's very progressive of you not to feel the need to marry because of the baby."

Cindy recalled the old movie they'd watched, filmed at a time when a baby out of wedlock ruined a woman's reputation. But men got a free pass, even then. The old double standard. If there was any silver lining in this situation, it was that no stigma would be attached to her or the baby. She would be raising this child as a single mother. But the question reminded her about his revelation that he'd been married before.

"From what he's said, Nathan shows no inclination to get married again."

Shirley's gaze jumped to hers. "He told you about Felicia?"

"Not much. Just that he'd been married." The information had been offered only to validate his claim of not being anti-matrimony. "And that she died in a car accident."

"Such a tragedy."

"Losing someone so young is just horrible."

"It was awful. They'd only been together a little over a year." Shirley set her glass on top of the table, then reached down and picked up an album on the shelf below. "Their wedding was just perfect. And so beautiful."

"May I see the pictures?" Cindy wasn't sure what made her ask. Maybe it was like the all-too-human reaction to gawk at a car accident or stare at a train wreck.

"Of course." The older woman stood, then settled the heavy book of photos on her lap.

Cindy opened the cover. There on the first page was Nathan looking ecstatically happy and incredibly handsome in his traditional black tuxedo. She'd personally experienced him in a tux, including the dance that had started her world rocking. Her heart had been beating so hard she could barely breathe.

What would it be like seeing him so tall and strong while he waited impatiently at the front of a church while you walked down the aisle in a white dress and veil?

Cindy turned the page and saw his bride. Her big dark eyes sparkled with excitement. Long black hair fell past her bare shoulders in the strapless, beaded wedding gown. The veil was attached to a three-banded, crystal-studded headpiece. She'd been a beautiful woman and was absolutely stunning in the photographs.

As she flipped through, there were countless images of the blissful couple at their reception. The white tent was situated on an estate with a bricked-in patio, a crystal-clear pool and an endless expanse of grass. Table settings of delicate china and crystal glasses were set up on white tablecloths. A photo showed the first dance as man and wife, cutting the cake, the happy bride and groom chatting with friends and family.

And just over a year later his wife was dead.

"Have you ever seen a more fabulous wedding?" Shirley asked.

"No."

"Or two people more in love?"

"They look very happy," Cindy answered, closing the book.

"When she died, Nathan blamed himself."

"Why?" She looked up and saw the sadness in Shirley's eyes. Obviously his mother had cared a lot about the woman her son married. Would anyone ever be able to fill that void?

"I've heard people say that it happens when you lose the love of your life. Although I wouldn't know about that since my husband walked out because he *didn't* love me." Shirley rubbed a finger beneath her nose. "Felicia was like the daughter I didn't have."

What about the son you *did* have?

Piecing together the little Nathan had said, she knew Shirley had buried herself in projects to get through a hard time in her life. Cindy couldn't help wondering how that affected Nathan. But it wasn't her place to judge.

The pain of losing someone you love could do funny things to a person. Some ran away from life. Others ran away from love. She knew which category Nathan fell into after seeing how happy he looked in his wedding pictures.

So the question had to be asked. Did Nathan not believe in love? Or was denying it existed at all his way of hiding from an unimaginable loss?

Either way, this little stroll down memory lane confirmed

that she was wise to guard her heart. It was unlikely that he was open to caring about someone no matter how much Cindy might wish he could care just a little bit about her.

Nathan had driven Cindy to Rebecca Hamilton's office and now sat nervously in the waiting room while the obstetrician examined her. Over the last few weeks, his initial fear for her and the baby had receded when there were no further symptoms. And without further symptoms it got harder and harder to keep her quiet and resting as the days passed. When he wasn't working, he was home with her, making sure she ate right and got enough sleep. The rest of the time they watched movies and played quiet board games.

Although quiet was a relative term. Cindy was a ferociously competitive Scrabble player and pretty darn good at gin rummy. She was anything but quiet when she beat him badly at whatever game they were playing. It had both amused and entertained him. Mostly he hoped that she was entertained and the enforced R&R had done the trick.

Sitting by the door that led to the back office, Nathan looked around the waiting area feeling like a fly in a glass of milk. He was the only guy, caught in some gray area of this crazy journey to fatherhood. Though he'd never experienced it himself, he figured husbands probably accompanied their wives into the exam room. Even men in a committed, intimate relationship would be allowed in with the woman carrying their baby.

He felt like a sperm donor, relegated to benchwarmer. It was damn disconcerting because he was normally elbow deep in the action and calling the shots. The urge to pace was pretty overwhelming, but he wouldn't give in to it. If Cindy didn't emerge from the back office bastion of femaleness, he would take the necessary steps to get any answers he deemed appropriate to his involvement in this adventure. Ten more minutes, he decided, looking at his watch to start the clock ticking on his plan.

Eight minutes and forty-five seconds later the door opened. Every woman in the waiting area looked up and so did he. Cindy walked out, and he studied her expression for elation or agitation. If she'd just bested him at Scrabble, she'd have pumped her arm and shouted "yes" as a victorious gleam sparkled in her brown eyes. When he beat her at anything, the gold flecks disappeared. Before he could decode the current color, she slid her sunglasses on and stopped at the reception desk a few steps from where he was sitting.

Nathan joined her there while she made another appointment, then settled his hand at the small of her back to escort her out. It jolted him how strong and instinctive the inclination was to slide his arm around her. But he stopped just in time.

When the office door closed after them he asked, "Well? What did she say?"

"Everything's fine with the baby. There's no reason to assume there will be any more problems. It just happens sometimes. All is currently well and I have her dispensation to resume all normal activities."

Nathan's mind went immediately to sex, not that it was a normal activity for the two of them. But the need was more than he wanted it to be.

She let out a long breath. "What a relief."

Yes. And no.

He was incredibly grateful that the baby was okay, but the risky pregnancy had effectively kept his mind off ideas he had no business having. Their situation already defied reason, and factoring in sex made it off the chart in terms of complicated.

The sun was hot when they left the medical building's courtyard, but visions of getting Cindy naked made his skin burn for reasons that had nothing to do with the UVA index. In the June heat, she wasn't wearing all that much— a little yellow cotton sundress and white sandals. He could put the flat of his palm on her belly and feel the way his baby was already changing the feminine curves of her body.

That was about the sexiest thought he'd ever had. The wanting that he'd been suppressing for weeks broke free and the only thing preventing him from pulling her into his arms and kissing the living daylights out of her was the way her lips pulled tight.

Something was wrong.

They walked through the parking lot and found the car. He opened the door, then handed her inside without exchanging a word. After he got in, he turned the key in the ignition to give it just enough juice to get the cool air going, but he made no move to drive anywhere.

"What aren't you telling me?" he demanded.

Cindy glanced sideways. "Nothing."

"Then what's bothering you?" He knew her moods pretty well now and something wasn't right.

"It's nothing really."

"Nothing really means it's really something. Tell me," he urged.

"It's just—" She caught the edge of her bottom lip between her teeth. "Resuming normal activity means going back to work."

"Right."

Right. Of course she would go back. He should have realized that, but when testosterone got the upper hand, rational thought didn't stand much of a chance. Tension from rumors and talk at the hospital could very well have caused her original symptoms in the first place.

"You know, Cindy, if you want to resign from your job, I'll support you through the pregnancy."

"What about after?" She was thoughtful for a few moments, then shook her head. "There's still my internship at the hospital. They gave me a short leave of absence, but the health of my future career is there, too. And, as generous as your offer is, I need a career to take care of myself and the baby."

"You don't have to worry about—"

"Yeah," she interrupted. "I do have to worry. I need to go back to my house and my job. I have to take care of myself."

"You're not alone."

"If you say so." Cool air from the dashboard vents blew the hair off her forehead.

It was probably his imagination, but he could swear there were shadows on the half of her face he could see. She looked small and scared. Nathan wanted badly to pull her against him, fold her in his arms and convince her it was okay to trust him. So the fact that this car was a small two-seater without room to act rashly was probably for the best. The only tools in his arsenal were words and logic.

"There's no need to be afraid of going back to work. I'm sure all the rumors have blown over by now."

"You don't really believe that, do you?"

"Yeah, I do. It's been a few weeks. Everyone's no doubt moved on to other, more interesting topics."

She shook her head ruefully. "No one questions your IQ creds, but street smarts are a different story."

"What does that mean?"

"You don't live in the real world. You're so many levels

removed from the rank and file that you have no idea how the pecking order operates."

"Okay. So explain it to me." He didn't walk in her shoes, but he wasn't completely oblivious.

"When I show up back to work, talk will start up all over again about why I was gone."

"Because you didn't feel well." He shrugged. "It's not a lie."

"Without details there will be theories from swine flu to shingles. Either or both will be taken as fact."

"So ignore them."

"I plan to. And hope it blows over and talk goes back to politics and how the new healthcare legislation will change things at the hospital."

"That's the spirit."

"Yeah, one can fantasize. But if the best-case scenario doesn't pan out—"

Before she could finish the negative thought, he said, "I've got your back."

"Absolutely, positively no." Her full lips compressed to a thin line as she shook her head.

Talking to her was old news. Coworkers did it all the time. "What's wrong with me being your friend?"

"You're a doctor and I work in housekeeping—"

"Environmental Services," he corrected.

"Whatever. If you acknowledge me in any way, or exhibit sympathetic behavior, anything that even hints of preferential treatment, I promise you it will get ugly. And I can't afford to get fired. On top of providing for this baby, I'm still digging myself out of debt from my last mistake."

Meaning that he was her current mistake.

Instead of responding to that, Nathan started the car and backed out of the parking space. Then he turned right onto Horizon Ridge Parkway. The second light was Eastern

Avenue and he turned left, heading for the 215 Beltway. Traffic congestion meant he had to concentrate on driving and couldn't lose his temper, which he really wanted to do.

But that wasn't fair to Cindy. She'd already been used and abused by a back-stabbing son of a bitch and Nathan fervently wished for five minutes alone with the jerk who'd swiped more than her credit. The bastard had stolen her trust and it made Nathan furious.

He was paying the price at a time when Cindy needed to believe in him the most. It fried him big time that she couldn't let herself count on him to protect her.

"Nathan?"

"What?" he snapped.

He'd turned onto the beltway and merged into traffic then pressed on the gas as the sporty luxury car smoothly took off and left the rest of the clunkers in his dust. This time of day there was very little traffic on this road and lots of open road in front of him.

"Nathan?"

"What?" he said again.

"You might want to slow it down a little." She glanced over at him. "You could probably talk your way out of a speeding ticket on account of being a doctor except for two things."

"Which are?"

"You're headed away from the hospital and I'm in the car. No cop would believe you've got an emergency with a patient."

He wasn't going that much over the legal limit, but he slowed down and set the cruise control. If only he could do that to the fury raging inside him. Losing focus wasn't his style. He didn't normally get this angry, let alone give in to the primal, passionate feelings.

Not until Cindy.

Nathan wanted her to let him help, to allow him to take some of the stress off her, but because of what that one moron had done, she was pushing back. Telling her he wouldn't let her down wasn't going to convince her that he meant the words, even though he'd never been more sincere about anything in his life.

He knew how it felt to be abandoned by the very people who should have cared the most. Now he was going to be a parent. He intended to step up even before the baby was born.

That meant he had no intention of abandoning Cindy.

Correction: He wouldn't abandon his child and she was the child's mother. Therefore he would be there for her.

It wasn't her fault that he couldn't stop wanting her. That was a perplexing footnote about this whole complicated situation because that had never happened to him before.

He always lost interest. To his way of thinking, that was significant data proving that love didn't exist. But Cindy continually surprised him, and sex was at the top of his interest list. Both did a number on his peace of mind, and neither were beneficial to him in the long term. When feelings started to get complicated in a relationship, he left. Because of the baby he couldn't do that now.

So, he had to keep things from getting complicated. He would have to prove he wasn't going away and at the same time keep Cindy from knowing how much he wanted her.

No pressure there.

Chapter Eleven

It was her first day back to work after Dr. Hamilton had green lighted her to return. Cindy was ecstatic about that *and* about returning to her home. Normal was good. Having her own Nathan-free zone was awesome. Earning a paycheck again gave her peace of mind.

At least that's what she told herself.

The morning at the hospital had been uneventful, if you didn't count her tense, awkward bathroom run-in with the two NICU nurses who'd made it their mission in life to keep her from getting uppity. Cindy had been the model of serenity. She'd smiled politely, taken a deep breath, then imagined herself enveloped in a force field that repelled everything, including the hostile glares.

Now it was lunch time and the first half of her first day was over. Without incident. Of course, she hadn't been to the NICU yet or seen Nathan. She could only hope that the seed of her warning to not acknowledge her in any way, and not give her a hint of preferential treatment, had fallen on fertile ground. He hadn't been happy, and she was sorry about that, but it couldn't be helped.

"May I join you?"

Cindy had been so wrapped up in her own thoughts, she hadn't noticed the woman stop beside her table in the back corner of the cafeteria. Dr. Annie Daniels patiently waited for her response with a tray of food in her hands. If she was here at the hospital, that would explain why Nathan wasn't. They were medical partners.

"Cindy?"

Hearing her name was like a shot of adrenaline to snap her out of it. "I'm sorry. Of course you can sit. If you want to."

"If I didn't want to, I wouldn't have asked."

Shocked into a response didn't mean Cindy wasn't still shocked. This doctor was a brainy, beautiful brunette with a stylish pixie haircut that made her blue eyes look enormous in her small face. The hospital had a special dining room for doctors so they weren't forced to mingle with the employees. Yet this doctor was voluntarily mingling. What was up with that?

Dr. Daniels had always been friendly, but she was that way to everyone. Never condescending or abrasive. But it didn't answer the question of the day: Why in the world would this elite female physician want to join her?

The doctor set her tray on the table and sat. "How are you feeling?"

"Fine." Feeling? That seemed kind of specific. Most people just said a generic how are you. And that's what she did now. "How are you?"

"Really good." She mixed dressing into her cobb salad. "But I'm not pregnant."

And that answered the question of whether she knew

about the baby. She was also Nathan's medical partner. Did she know he was the father?

There was nothing but kindness in her blue eyes. "And I didn't just return from a leave of absence taken because my pregnancy turned risky."

"Look, Dr. Daniels—"

"Call me Annie. If I'm going to butt into your business, the least you can do is call me by my first name." She smiled, then took a bite of salad.

Cindy chose to believe she meant that and said, "Annie, I don't mean to sound suspicious and ungrateful, but why are you butting into my business?"

"I feel responsible for some of the crap you're dealing with."

Color her shocked. Again. "Why?"

"The thing is, Mercy Medical Center is like a family." The doctor smiled at her skeptical look. "Don't get me wrong. I know it's a big, messy, dysfunctional one, but still a family. There are very few secrets."

"Meaning?" Cindy kept her hands busy peeling a tangerine and pulling off all the little strings.

"Nathan told me he's the father of your baby."

"I see." That was a big, fat lie. She didn't see anything. There was nothing hostile or toxic in the other woman's expression, but that didn't mean a zinger wasn't coming. "Why would he tell you that?"

"I don't think he planned to. But apparently he'd just found out." Annie speared a piece of egg with her fork. "It was my shift in the NICU, but he came back to check on a baby."

"Is that unusual?"

Annie shook her head. "But something was different and I sensed that. After a little nagging on my part, he admitted that he was going to be a father. And that he'd never looked at what we do from the dad side of the fence before."

"Okay."

"He told me about you. How you'd met. That he didn't recognize you all dressed up. And that didn't land him on your good side."

Cindy smiled at the memory. "I gave him a pretty hard time about it."

"Good for you. He needs someone to take him down a peg or two and keep him grounded in the real world."

"My world is all too real," Cindy said grimly.

"I feel responsible for what you're going through here at the hospital," she said again.

"What do you mean?" She stared across the small table.

"The tension and resentment other employees are exhibiting toward you."

Interesting that someone else had noticed, Cindy thought. That made it easier somehow. "But why do you feel responsible?"

"I overheard a couple nurses in the NICU talking and I decided to chat with you."

"I don't understand."

Annie poured sugar into her iced tea and stirred with her straw. "It all goes back to that night Nathan came back to hover over the baby. It's what he does. His job. Our job. We take care of babies who aren't big enough, strong enough or mature enough to survive without medical intervention."

Cindy pressed a hand to her abdomen. "It's a scary thing."

"Not just for you." Annie met her gaze. "A little knowledge is a dangerous thing because Nathan and I know all the things that can happen. The problem is he's a guy."

Not a newsflash, Cindy thought. He had the broad

shoulders and muscles in all the right places to prove that. If he weren't quite so mouthwateringly masculine, she wouldn't be in this fix in the first place. And worse, spending time with him at his house had not taken away any of his appeal. But she was pretty sure that's not what Annie meant.

"Why is that a problem?" she asked.

"Guys want to fix things. He's also a doctor. So when he was feeling the need to do something for his child, I had to talk him down."

"How?"

"I advised him to support you emotionally."

"He's not into that." Cindy popped a tangerine segment into her mouth and chewed for a moment. "When we met, he said that if he can't see and touch something, he doesn't believe it exists."

"So, you've heard his company line. He's a man of science. Facts and results. That's such a lame excuse and on some level he knows it." Annie sighed. "At any rate, I advised him to be there for you. Make sure you have everything you need to minimize any anxiety."

"It's good advice. I don't understand why you feel responsible for anyone else's behavior."

"I also told him not to let you exert yourself." Annie watched carefully and nodded when the truth sank in.

"He was taking your advice to heart. Trying to keep me from overdoing it here at work," Cindy said.

A man who actually listened. It also proved the saying "no good deed goes unpunished." Unfortunately, she was paying the price for his chivalry.

"That's right," Annie agreed. "The down side is that people noticed."

By *people* she meant a certain nurse who just happened

to be an ex-girlfriend. Scenarios didn't come more volatile than that.

"Noticing isn't the problem. But I could do without the ugly comments."

"I'm really sorry about that," Annie sympathized.

"Unless you wrote the script, you have nothing to apologize for," Cindy assured her. "There will be more talk when the pregnancy starts to show."

"Thanks to me and the ideas I gave Nathan, it won't be hard to put two and two together and figure out he's the father."

"Yeah." This wasn't the first time Cindy had thought about that. "It'll be fun to hear the creative ways they'll say how I'd do anything to trade up from housekeeping."

Annie pointed with the business end of her fork and forcefully said, "Ignore the small-minded…witches and their rumors. Whatever is between you and Nathan is no one's business but yours. And his."

"And yours?"

"I've known him since medical school." The lady doctor shrugged. "It's hard to ignore how well I know him."

"He's lucky to have a friend like you."

"I'm the lucky one." Her expression turned introspective and a little sad. "He was there for me when I lost my baby. It was a double whammy because to save my life, they had to do a hysterectomy."

"Oh, no—" Cindy reached out and squeezed the other woman's hand. The gesture was automatic, generated by a profound sympathy. One woman to another. She'd thought her problems were big and had to admit that all things considered the ability to have a baby was a blessing. "I don't know what to say."

"Thanks for not saying you're sorry. For some reason that response makes me want to scream. And I have no idea why I told you that." Annie shook her head. "Don't fret on my account. Thanks to science and other options my husband and I are exploring ways to be parents that do work for us."

"Your husband sounds like quite a guy," Cindy said.

"I won't argue that. Ryan is the best." Annie's eyes glowed. "And so is Nathan. Quite a guy, I mean. For what it's worth, the weird and wonderful chemistry that men and women feel for each other knows no boundaries—not caste, class or career. Take it from someone who knows—your energy is better spent taking care of you and your baby. To hell with the rest of the crap."

"No wonder Nathan talks to you." Cindy smiled. "Not only do you have a way with words, you give very good advice."

Annie laughed. "Nathan has been through a lot. Just remember that underneath all the geek and science stuff he preaches, he's a good man."

Annie suddenly pulled a pager from the waistband of her scrubs and glanced at the display. "Gotta go."

"Thanks for sitting with me."

"Let's do it again sometime soon." And then she hurried away.

Cindy had always liked Annie Daniels and the feeling was even stronger now. She was a good doctor and a warm human being who had little tolerance for small-minded people. From the moment Cindy had peed on the stick and discovered she was pregnant, her life had been in free fall. She'd never considered how it would feel to lose a baby and never be able to have another one.

Nathan had supported his friend through the nightmare. Actions like that and the friends in his corner spoke to the kind of man he was. The information troubled her because it would be so much easier if he had the decency to live up to his reputation of good doctor, bad boyfriend. Then her feelings could be black and white. She could dislike him. Dr. Daniels had just confirmed what Cindy had been suspecting for a while.

It was impossible to dislike Nathan Steele.

And what if she couldn't stop with just liking him?

Cindy walked barefoot to the kitchen after changing into shorts and a skinny-strapped tank top. She and the baby had survived the first day back at work. If you didn't count her conversation with Annie, it had been ordinary and nothing to write home about.

She wasn't sure what to do with the doctor's independent confirmation that Nathan was a nice guy. Theoretically the information shouldn't change anything. This baby was his and he was merely taking responsibility. The form that responsibility would take was yet to be determined. That being the case, she needed to move forward expecting nothing from anyone and relying only on herself. If she stuck to that—her standard operating procedure—she would be fine and dandy.

"Okay." She nodded with satisfaction and opened the refrigerator door, disappointment growing as the situation became clear. "Crash and burn."

There wasn't much in the way of edible, nutritious food. Ketchup. Mustard. Mayo. Diet soda. Grapes that were well on their way to spontaneous fermentation. She'd been at Nathan's house, where provisions that she didn't have to hunt and gather were plentiful. Note to self: Go to the grocery store. And while you're at it, she thought, look for an antidote to pining for peanut butter and banana sandwiches and his seventy-five-inch flat-screen TV.

She managed to find a frozen dinner and was just about to put it in the microwave when the doorbell rang. Her heart did a little skip, then sped up in a way that always signalled her expectation to see Nathan. It was proof that she'd resumed her normally scheduled life just in the nick of time. Expectations were a precursor to disappointment and heartache. She couldn't afford either.

After a stern talking-to, she walked into the living room and peeked out the window to see who was there. Her heart went back to accelerated rhythm, which was standard Nathan mode. That was acceptable because he was actually standing on the porch.

She turned the deadbolt and opened the door, ridiculously glad to see him. "Hi."

"Hi." He held up a bag. "I brought rotisserie chicken. Potatoes to bake. And salad. Are you interested? Or have you already—"

"I could kiss you—" She grabbed his arm and pulled him inside. "Not really. It's just an expression."

And that was just an excuse for the slip of the tongue. She would have wanted to kiss him even if he had nothing in his hand.

"The cupboard is bare?" he guessed.

"Pretty much."

Cindy closed the door behind him and ignored the happy little bubble expanding inside her as she led the way to the kitchen.

"What can I do?" he asked.

Just his presence was enough, but she couldn't say that. "How about setting the table?"

While he did that, she microwaved potatoes instead of the frozen dinner that probably tasted worse than the military's ready-to-eat meals.

Within ten minutes they were sitting across from each other at her small table. She looked at the whole chicken he'd neatly carved into recognizable parts.

"You should have been a surgeon," she said.

"Not my field of interest." He sliced off a piece of meat and chewed. "How was your first day back?"

"Good. Normal. Nothing much to report."

"That's a relief."

She glanced up at him. "Were you worried? Is that why you stopped by?"

He shrugged. "I wanted to check up on you. And the baby. Just make sure everything was okay."

"It was nice of you to bring food." It was nice, period, but she kept that to herself. She took a bite and sighed with pleasure. "I can't believe how good this tastes."

"You must be hungry." He frowned. "Did you eat lunch today?"

"As a matter of fact I did. With Annie Daniels."

He looked surprised. "Really?"

"I know. Shocked the heck out of me, too, when she came in the cafeteria and sat down at my table."

"She's good people," he said.

"Agreed. She advised me to put my energy into taking care of me and the baby. And I quote, 'to hell with the rest of the crap.'" There was no point in mentioning what his partner had said about the weird and wonderful chemistry between men and women.

He grinned. "Gotta love Annie."

Speaking of chemistry, Cindy felt a ridiculous tug of jealousy. She wasn't proud of it, but that didn't change the feeling. And there was no reason for it. Nathan's medical partner was married. The couple was looking into having children. Unlike them, she and Nathan weren't a couple, but they were definitely having a child. And they hadn't discussed any legalities or logistics. Maybe it was time to dip a toe into that water.

"So, did your mother tell you she wants to turn your home office into a nursery?"

He looked up quickly. "What?"

"Yeah. She showed me sketches for a wall mural—generic baby, boy and girl themes. She's going to let you make the final decision."

"Big of her," he mumbled, "what with me paying the mortgage and all."

"They're really good, the sketches, I mean." She met his gaze. "She claimed it's not talent, but practice because she had lots of time on her hands after your dad left."

"She was only deserted once. I got it twice." He put down his fork. "Three times if you count getting uprooted from home against my will and dumped in boarding school."

"Oh, my—" Cindy didn't think. She just needed to touch him. Reaching across the table, she put her hand on his arm. The warm strength there was vivid contrast to the stark vulnerability in his expression. "How old were you?"

"Eight or nine."

"Oh, Nathan—how awful. That's why you didn't have a childhood."

He shrugged but didn't slide his arm away from her touch. "I got used to it."

"Still—"

"It was hard. Eventually I realized they did me a favor. I made friends. Learned to be self-reliant. Independent. I got good grades and became a doctor."

He learned about everything but love. The one time he gave it a try, fate kicked him in the teeth when his wife died. No wonder he couldn't reach out now. She could hardly blame him. But it made her so sad.

"Cindy?"

"Hmm?"

"Are you all right?"

"Sure." She met his worried gaze. "Why?"

He turned his hand over and closed his fingers around hers. "You look like someone edited out the happy ending of one of your chick flicks."

In a way, someone had. But that wasn't a place she wanted to go.

"No," she said. "I was just thinking."

"Uh oh. Scary."

"I know, right?" She saw the expectant expression in his eyes and knew he was waiting for her to explain.

"What were you thinking about?"

"Life." She shrugged. "It's pretty unfair sometimes."

"How do you mean?"

"Your parents were so lucky to have you and they didn't appreciate the amazing gift of a child."

He frowned, clearly not getting her drift. "Like I said, I'm okay. Boarding school didn't really turn me to the dark side or anything."

"Right. I was actually thinking about Annie. She told me about losing her baby. And not being able to have another one. That had to be devastating."

"Yeah. It sucks. She really wants kids."

"That's what I mean. Your parents had a brilliant, hand-some child—"

"Thank you." His mouth curved up as humor pushed the darkness from his expression.

"That was simply the truth and not a comment made to inflate your already bloated ego." She smiled. "But why does that happen? Your parents didn't appreciate the gift. And someone like Annie who would embrace the whole exciting and magical experience can't have it."

"She's looking at surrogacy or adoption," he said.

"That's what she told me." Then a thought occurred to her. "Maybe that's the bigger plan."

"What?" His gaze never wavered as he threaded his fingers with hers instead of releasing her hand.

Tingles danced through her, making it difficult to form a coherent thought. But she hunkered down and forced herself to concentrate. "There are so many children in this world who don't have homes and parents. Maybe she's meant to be a mom to a baby who doesn't have one."

"That's a very rose-colored-glasses take on a lousy situation."

"I guess I'm just a rose-colored-glasses kind of gal," she said. "It beats doom and gloom."

"And I don't believe in fate, destiny and a grand plan. Give me science, data. Hard evidence. I'll take that over mysticism and conjecture any day of the week."

"Don't you ever make a guess in practicing medicine?" she asked.

"It's an *educated* guess, based on scientific studies and verification."

He'd said up front that he put facts over love, but part of her had been hoping it wasn't true. Now she knew he really needed to see and touch something to know it was real. Part of her wanted to shake some sense into him. The other part finally understood why he felt that way. And again sadness overwhelmed her.

His career was all about giving life a fighting chance, but in his life he wouldn't give love a chance. To her, that wasn't really living.

Cindy had grown up surrounded by love. She'd seen her parents pack a whole lot of living into life even when a cancer diagnosis cut their time together short. Her father had tenderly and with dedicated devotion nursed his wife until she took her last breath.

That's the kind of love she wanted.

It meant her problem was the exact opposite of Nathan's. She'd seen how good love could be and tended to jump into a relationship with both feet. But her eyes were wide open now. No matter how good it felt to have Nathan watching over her, she needed to resist her pattern. The jerk who'd put her in debt had just stolen her money and trust.

With Nathan, going all in could be a bigger disaster. Repairing bad credit was a walk in the park compared to the impossibility of putting a broken heart back together.

Chapter Twelve

Nathan watched the taillights of Cindy's aging compact brighten as she braked for the light on Water Street and Lake Mead Boulevard. Her right signal light went on and when traffic permitted, she made the turn. He did the same when it was safe to do so. Just as he'd been doing for weeks now. He knew the way to her house like the back of his hand.

They'd fallen into this routine since she'd gone back to work after the pregnancy scare. He either followed her home or, if he was tied up with a patient, he stopped by later when he was free. The official excuse, if anyone asked, was to make sure she was okay. But no one asked because he was careful not to draw attention to her, as she'd requested.

Privately, on some level, he knew this time was the best part of his day and he looked forward to it. If anyone demanded an explanation, he would swear on a stack of Bibles that this was about avoiding his mother.

Shirley was in a holding pattern, too. For some reason she hadn't returned to her condo in LA and was sticking around longer than usual. She claimed it was about her astrology class and the genius teacher who was tutoring her about the alignment of stars and planets. But Nathan suspected it had more to do with Cindy and the baby. Apparently making excuses to cover a certain behavior was a Steele family trait.

But the fact was, he wasn't the only Steele who dropped in on Cindy. Originally skeptical of her motives, Shirley had stopped by on the pretext of getting to know the woman who would be the mother of her first grandchild. She was nothing if not cynical and eventually had been won over. His baby mama's sweet nature had made his mother a fan.

That didn't run in the family. He was simply doing his duty.

He parked at the curb in front of her house just as she stepped out of her car. Obviously she'd made it just fine and he could have waved and driven away. But that's not what he did. After exiting the driver's side, he met her and together they walked to the front door.

"Want to come in for dinner?" she asked.

"What's on the menu?" It didn't really matter because he wasn't planning to leave even if she was serving slop.

"Tacos. I put a chuck roast in the crock pot before leaving for work this morning. It should be stringy by now. All I have to do is assemble everything else."

"I'll give you a hand."

"Thanks."

The porch light turned the honey color of her hair into a halo and the smile on her lips was nearly painful in its sweetness and beauty. Who died and made him a poet? The poetic turn of his thoughts made him feel sheepish. Fortunately she wasn't a mind reader.

After opening the door, she flipped on the living room light and started inside. She stopped so suddenly that he ran into her. Either that or he was following too closely, just to stay within arm's reach of her warmth. Either way the result was the same. He wanted to wrap his arms around her.

"Sorry," he mumbled.

That was pretty much a lie. The only thing he was sorry about was that the contact was too brief. He wanted to pull her against him while he breathed in the fresh, floral fragrance of her hair. He wouldn't have to lower his head all that much to touch his mouth to her neck.

"I forgot to get the mail," she said, starting to move around him.

"I'll get it."

"That's okay, I'll just run back out."

"No running. Let me."

"Okay. Thanks."

A few minutes outside to regroup was a good idea. It was summer and still over a hundred degrees, even though the sun would be going down soon. But a brief break was just the prescription to remind himself of all the reasons why kissing her neck was not the smartest move to make.

He walked out to the mailbox at the curb. Before reaching inside, he took a deep breath. She'd accepted his original dinner invitation just to get him off her back and now they were having a baby. Those were the facts. It was harder to quantify anything else. This compulsion to see her every night, to make sure she was okay, were actions firmly under the responsibility umbrella, but it didn't quite wash. Fortunately he didn't have to figure it out today.

He opened the door on her mailbox that looked like a miniature Quonset hut, then reached inside. There was quite a stack of envelopes, most of them official-looking and not of the junk mail variety. As he walked back to the front door, bright rays of light from the setting sun hit him full in the face until Cindy's house blocked it out. Sort of reminded him how she obstructed rational thought.

Inside, the coolness from the air conditioner felt good. He dropped her mail on the cedar chest coffee table, then joined her in the kitchen. She'd changed into white shorts and a black tank top. Her feet were bare and the sexy, domestic picture she made just cutting up lettuce and to-mato made him want to swallow his tongue. Heat slammed through him as though his time-out to regroup had never happened.

"What can I do?" He hoped his tone didn't sound as pathetic as it felt. Guidance would definitely be in order, but it probably needed to come from a shrink.

She glanced over her shoulder and smiled. "The usual—

"Set the table," he finished along with her.

Five minutes later they were sitting across from each other with taco shells, meat, beans, cheese, lettuce and tomatoes in containers between them. Nathan fixed one with everything, then wolfed it down, surprised at how hungry he was. Cindy did the same, but she ate at a more ladylike pace.

He needed to distract himself from watching her mouth. Food wasn't all he was hungry for, but it was all he'd let himself have.

"So, it's about time you gave me another shopping list," he said. "There must be some things you need."

She wiped her mouth with a napkin. "You really don't have to do my shopping, Nathan. I'm well past the first trimester and the doctor says there's no reason to believe I'll have any more problems."

"Good to know. And I intend to keep it that way."

"By shopping for me?"

If only that's all it would take to ensure that the rest of her pregnancy was healthy. "That and carrying it all. You can't be too careful."

Her eyes gleamed with mischief. "Okay, burly boy. What if I told you there was a sale on canned vegetables and I bought a case? *And* carried it in the house without assistance?"

One of his eyebrows went up. "Burly boy?"

"That would be you."

"I've been called science geek and math nerd, but never burly boy."

She laughed, such a merry and bright sound that it lighted a dark place deep inside him and took away some of the shadows.

"I appreciate you helping out," she said, "but it's really not necessary."

"Maybe not." But he remembered what Annie had said about not letting her physically exert herself. And that was before she'd had a problem. "Either make me a new list or I'll go by the old one."

"No, please, anything but that." Her expression was rueful. "I have enough paper towels to clean up a toxic waste dump. If I have to store more, there won't be any room for me."

He barely held back the words on the tip of his tongue, which were to the effect that she should move back in with him. Instead he said, "I have one word. *List.*"

She held up her hands in surrender. "Okay. You win."

"That works for me."

When they'd both finished eating, he helped her put the

leftovers away and clean up the dishes. It was time for him to go and the shadows that had disappeared a little while ago were creeping back. He was trying to figure out how to put off leaving when she gave him a way.

"Would you like some coffee?"

"Yeah," he said. "I would. But I'll make it. You go sit in the living room and put your feet up. That's an order."

She must have been tired because there was no argument. Just a sassy salute. After all these weeks he knew his way around her tiny kitchen and fixed himself a cup of instant coffee, then joined her in the other room. Not only were her feet still on the floor, she was staring at the stack of mail and frowning.

He set down his mug on the cedar chest, then lowered himself to the sofa beside her. "I'm not used to having my orders disobeyed."

"Hmm?" She glanced at him.

"Your feet aren't up."

This time when she smiled there was sadness around the edges. "You sound like my dad."

He preferred *burly boy*. "Why?"

"I was about nine when my mom was pregnant with my brother. So I remember a lot. My dad would make her sit down and then he rubbed her feet." There was a suspicious brightness in her eyes when she looked at him.

"What's wrong, Cindy?"

"They'd be so disappointed in me." She flicked the stack of mail, and it toppled to the floor on the other side of the chest. "My bills rival the national debt. And that's not what they would have wanted. I've made some really bad choices."

Nathan was in the business of fixing things and badly wanted to now. But this wasn't a science-based problem with formulas and solutions. Mostly he couldn't stand to see her upset. He didn't know how to fix what was wrong, but he had to try.

"Everyone has done something they'd like to take back." For him it would be asking Felicia to marry him. A man who didn't believe in love had no business making promises he couldn't keep. "It's not your fault the guy conned you. And if your mother and father were here they'd tell you the same thing. It's a parent's duty to make sure their kids can function independently. Mine did an exemplary job on that score," he said wryly. The rest of it was a dismal failure, but that wasn't pertinent to this conversation. "The point is that you didn't give up. You didn't ask for help. You simply picked up the pieces and moved on. You're putting your brother through college and working to pay your bills. It seems to me that your parents would be extraordinarily proud of you."

"Thanks for that, Nathan," she whispered.

"You're welcome." He didn't usually make speeches and was disconcerted that he'd done it now. "Okay, moving on. Put your feet in my lap."

"What?"

"Just do it. That's an order. I'm going to take care of you."

Without another word, she swung her legs onto his thighs and leaned back against the arm of the love seat. He took one of her slender ankles in his hand and with the other he pressed a thumb into the arch of her foot.

"How does that feel?"

"Heavenly."

The sound that came from her throat was somewhere between a moan and a groan, as if she were in the throes of passion. In a nanosecond, the blood drained from his head and raced south of his belt.

"Good." He could only manage the single word and it

came out more rasp than anything else. The wanting was getting worse every day, proof that his character was in serious trouble.

"Now I know why my mom liked this so much." When she met his gaze, her eyes were filled with tears again. "I w-wish they were here to see their grandchild—"

Cindy stopped, unable to get any more words past the lump in her throat. She hated the pregnancy hormones that made her so emotional. But she had a feeling this would have gotten to her even if she wasn't having a baby. This gesture reminded her of the loving relationship her parents had. The way her father had cared for her mother all through their marriage, right up until the day she'd died.

And that's when the tears went rolling down her cheeks and she put her hands over her face.

"What is it?" Nathan's deep voice was laced with concern.

"I'm pregnant," she managed to say.

"Not a newsflash." Now there was just a hint of humor in his tone. "Why are you crying? Although it makes no sense to me, don't women sometimes cry when they're happy? Is it possible this is one of those times?"

How could she tell him that he was the problem? That she wanted what her parents had and she wanted it from him. Whatever his hang-ups were, he was still a good man. He hadn't disappeared as expected; he'd been there from the moment she'd told him about the baby. How could he understand that it wasn't enough, would never be enough?

She brushed at the moisture on her cheeks and tried to smile with mixed results. "You got me. Happy tears."

His expression was skeptical. "Really?"

"Yeah." But another tear leaked out. "I think I n-need to be alone."

She pulled her legs off his thighs and straightened away

from the sofa arm, turning beside him to put her feet on the floor. Before she could stand up, he put one arm behind her back and the other beneath her legs, then scooped her into his arms and onto his lap.

"Not so fast."

"Please—I feel so silly."

"And I hate to see you cry. So if there's anything I can do to fix it, I'm going to. Now talk to me."

Through a shimmery blur of tears she looked at him, his face just inches from her own. Concern was etched in his eyes and there was tension in his lean jaw. The steady determination in his gaze was proof that he was dead serious about making it better. The utter sweetness of the gesture brought on a fresh wave of waterworks.

"Sorry. I just can't help it. I'm in hormone hell."

When he gathered her into his arms, she buried her face against his neck.

"I can't fix hormones. That's chemistry. Your body's taking care of the baby."

The words were a gentle, reassuring whisper as his breath stirred her hair. Shivers danced down her neck and put a hitch in her breathing. Body chemistry was going on, but suddenly this had nothing to do with the baby and everything to do with repeating the act that had created it in the first place.

When she lifted her head, their gazes collided and Cindy saw in his eyes a yearning that mirrored her own. It wasn't clear if he moved first or she did, but suddenly their mouths were locked together in a hungry fusing of mutual need.

She slid her arms around his neck and pressed against the solid wall of his chest. Breasts sensitive from pregnancy tingled from the contact and she yearned to know how it would feel without clothes blocking the sensation. Nathan's hands alternately rubbed up her back and curved around her waist, his thumbs skimming the undersides of her breasts. He kissed and nipped her mouth and chin, cheek and jaw.

When he traced her lips with his tongue, she opened her mouth to him, eagerly inviting him inside. He entered and took over, boldly laying a claim that she gratefully turned over to him. She welcomed the invasion, the invitation into the dark and dangerous. There was no fear or hesitation as her tongue dueled with his. The sound of his quickened breathing was like an echo of thunder announcing the coming storm. And she welcomed that, too.

With the flat of her hand she touched his broad shoulders and strong back, savoring the masculine feel of him. She leaned back against his arm and tried to tug him down on the love seat.

"No—"

Every part of her cried out in protest at being denied the pleasure his body had promised.

She forced out words in spite of her labored breathing. "But I thought you wanted—"

He nodded. "Not here. This time it's going to be good."

"Last time was pretty amazing." She could tease now that she knew he hadn't changed his mind.

"Not what I meant. I want to do it right." He put a finger on her mouth to shut off the smart-ass comment he knew was coming. "This time I want it right, with you in bed."

Her heart melted. She could feel the warmth trickling through her.

She smiled. "Why didn't I think of that?"

"Because I have the superior IQ and skills to—"

This time she silenced him with a quick kiss before saying, "That was a rhetorical question."

"I'll show you rhetorical." His voice was a sexy growl as he stood with her in his arms.

Her heart did that melty thing again and she barely held in a sigh. "You should put me down before you hurt yourself."

He settled her more firmly in his arms as he said, "You know, the density of peanut butter and banana is definitely evident."

"Watch it, buster."

"You hardly weigh anything," he said, already moving down the hall toward her bedroom.

"Much more politically correct," she approved.

When he stopped beside her bed, he gently set her on her feet next to it. "Someone was in a hurry this morning."

She glanced over her shoulder at the jumble of sea foam green sheets, blanket and floral-patterned quilt on the unmade, queen-size bed. "Are you going to dock my allowance for not completing my chores?"

"Actually I was thinking more in terms of a bonus for exemplary time-management skills. Now I don't have to unmake the bed."

The teasing in his eyes mixed with something bright and hot that set her skin on fire. She slid her hands up underneath his black T-shirt and settled her palms on his bare flesh. He grabbed the hem and pulled it off in one fast, fluid, ever-so-manly motion.

Cindy did the same with her tank top before he reached behind her and unhooked her bra. She felt it release and he took the straps, sliding them down her arms. The scrap of lingerie fell to the floor between them.

The snap on her shorts was already undone, a concession to her expanding waistline. When Nathan noticed, a slow sexy smile curved up the corners of his mouth. He unzipped her pants and she pushed them over her hips and stepped out. Nathan settled his palm on her belly, now rounding with the baby bump.

His hand was warm and all he said was, "Wow."

"Yeah, huh? Overnight I just got fat—"

"No." He shook his head. "It's perfectly natural. And you look incredibly beautiful."

"My fragile ego chooses to believe you even though that's a bald-faced lie."

"I've never meant anything more. You're beautiful, Cindy. So beautiful…"

His voice trailed off as he leaned down and settled his mouth on hers. It was the barest brush of his lips, but still the breath backed up in her chest. That kiss was the only place their bodies touched and yet it was like a flashpoint, sending heat burning back and forth between them. He removed his shorts and boxers and was now magnificently naked.

He pulled back and eyed her panties. "One of us is over-dressed."

She looked at him, so ready that her heart lurched and her legs felt weak. "And one of us is an overachiever."

He laughed before backing her up against the mattress, then gently lowering her to the cool sheets. He slid one finger beneath the waistband of her underwear and into her waiting warmth. She sucked in air even as she wiggled out of the last of her clothes.

Anticipation knotted inside her as he brushed his thumb across the bundle of nerve endings at her center. The touch was driving her closer to the edge, making her crazy with wanting. She nearly whimpered when he stopped.

Before she could protest, he rolled on top of her and nudged her thighs apart. Taking most of his weight on his elbows, he slipped inside her and she felt him catch his breath at the same time hers caught. Then he stroked in and out, slowly building the storm inside her until she was swamped with sensation.

He drove her crazy, took her to the top of the swell, then groaned as they both rode the wave over the crest and down, drowning in the pleasure that washed through them.

Nathan held her until the quaking stopped and she could breathe again. She expected him to let her go then, but he didn't. With a satisfied sigh, he gathered her closer and she rested her palm on his chest. Feeling the strong and steady beat of his heart, hope swelled inside her.

He hadn't said the words, but maybe, just maybe he was beginning to feel something warm and deep for her. The tenderest of emotions flooded her heart and this wasn't about hormones. He'd been right about taking her to the bedroom and he didn't really understand how much.

Her parents had spent their lives together in this house, this room. They'd raised two children, lived, argued, made up and loved here. She felt their presence, the two loving spirits watching over her, and knew they weren't disappointed. Just the opposite.

The sensation made her believe in possibilities. Nathan was a show-don't-tell kind of guy. The fact was that he'd shown her with his hands, mouth and body that he was tender and protective. It was just possible that was his way of showing what was in his heart. Wasn't it possible that the affectionate and adoring spirit of love that permeated this place might have just rubbed off on him?

Maybe he actually *could* love her.

Chapter Thirteen

Nathan put his hand on Cindy's arm to stop her from getting out of the car. "You can't hide your pregnancy much longer."

"I know."

Shadows drifted through her eyes and he hated himself for putting them there. He'd picked her up and brought her to Dr. Hamilton's office for her ultrasound. It was hard to believe, but she was already in her fifth month of pregnancy. Loose-fitting tops and big sweaters with excuses about the air-conditioning making her cold weren't going to conceal her condition for much longer.

The days and weeks had turned into months that passed in a blur. His mother was still in his guest house, which was probably a world record, but he didn't want to know why and she didn't say. Nathan had enough trouble figuring out what this thing was with Cindy.

He saw her nearly every day, but his story for the pattern

of behavior was wearing thin. After the problem in the first few weeks, the pregnancy had been textbook normal. How much longer could he claim that he was checking up on her because of the baby? Or making sure she ate right for the baby?

He sure hadn't slept with her again because of the baby.

That had only confused the issue more, so he'd been careful not to make the mistake again. His reaction to her was so powerful, it was entirely possible that he couldn't do without her. And he would never let himself depend on anyone that completely.

There was only one problem with abstinence. Wanting her again was eating him up inside. They didn't live together, but they might as well. Either he was at her place or she was at his. And the hell of it was that when he wasn't with her, he wanted to be. He worried about her and couldn't completely blame that on the fact that she was pregnant with his child.

Her hand was resting on the car's console between them and he covered it with his own. "Have you thought about what you're going to say to people?"

"You don't think they'll swallow the story of too many cheeseburgers and fries?"

He remembered her saying she was fat the night he'd taken her to bed. It had ticked him off more than a little. The sight of her—honey-blond hair tumbled around her face, the gentle swell of her belly that was his baby growing inside her—was the most profoundly beautiful thing he'd ever seen. And sexy as hell. If he'd had a prayer of not sleeping with her, it disappeared in that second.

Nathan shook his head. "No one will believe you're getting fat."

She smiled a smile that was mischievous around the

edges. "The speculation will drive them crazy. Is she or isn't she?"

By "them" he knew she meant the nurses at the hospital who'd given her a hard time. And that was the reason he'd brought this up in the first place. When the news broke, he didn't want Cindy stressed out by anything.

He raised an eyebrow. "This is a side of you that I've never seen before."

"What?"

"Kind of wicked."

"Gotta take the victories where you find 'em." She shrugged. "If those witches in the NICU want to know for sure, they'll actually have to speak to me and not make snide comments behind my back."

It was frustrating that she wouldn't let him run interference to make sure no one upset her. "And you'll tell them too many cheeseburgers?"

"Maybe they'd believe I swallowed a watermelon seed."

"They're nothing if not narrow-minded, but they were smart enough to pass anatomy and physiology classes. I'm not sure that explanation would fly."

"Then I'll just let them make their own assumptions."

"And when they want to know who the father is?" he asked.

"Immaculate conception?"

It was definitely conception, but nothing about it had been immaculate. Sex had been messy, sweaty, spontaneous, passionate and completely mind-blowing. Cindy made him feel that way again every time he was with her.

He took a breath to steady his elevated pulse. "No one will go for that any more than the fruit story."

She tilted her head and studied him closely. "Are you afraid that I'll rat you out, Doctor?"

"What?"

"Don't worry. I won't spill your secret. No one will know you've been slumming with the housekeeper."

"You may or may not be kidding, but stop right there." This could be pregnancy hormones or just her personal peeve but he wasn't letting it go. "I've been ready to support you from day one. I don't give a damn what anyone says. Apparently that's your thing. You told me to back off—"

"I know." She held up a hand. "You're right. I'm sorry. That was completely unfair. I guess you just caught me off guard when you pointed out that very soon it will be obvious that I'm pregnant."

"I apologize—"

"No. You're right. It's crossed my mind, but I've been burying my head in the sand."

"You know what happens then, right?" he asked.

She met his gaze and the corners of her full mouth curved up. "I leave my backside exposed?"

"Pretty much."

"What do you think I should say?" she asked seriously.

"Probably that you don't believe—"

"Whoa," she interrupted, glancing at her wristwatch. "We're late for the ultrasound. That's pretty bad when we've been sitting here in the parking lot for fifteen minutes."

"Let's go."

It was a conversation they needed to have but not in an obstetrician's waiting room full of women. The reality was that the doctor would probably be running late and wouldn't notice they were a few minutes behind schedule.

As they walked through the parking lot and the medical building's desert landscaped courtyard, Nathan settled his palm at the small of Cindy's back. He'd almost taken her hand, an intimate, automatic gesture that came out of nowhere.

Intimate gestures didn't come automatically to him.

That was one of the things his wife had called him out on. During an ugly scene, she'd accused him of being a clone of his father. Then she'd walked out on him just like everyone else.

The interior of Rebecca Hamilton's office was dim and cool after the heat outside. Summer was almost over, but the Las Vegas Valley wouldn't give up its warm days for a while yet. He remembered Cindy's remark about not having to go through being big as a battleship while it was hot. Now she was big enough to have an ultrasound.

She signed in at the reception desk, but before they could take a seat, the back office door opened.

The dark-haired young woman wore blue scrubs and held a chart in her hands. "Cindy Elliott?"

"Here," she answered, raising her hand as if someone were taking attendance.

"Come on back."

"I feel like a game show contestant," she confessed nervously.

When he started to sit down, the office assistant said, "Your husband can come with you if you'd like."

Cindy looked at him and faltered. He could almost read her mind. Should she set the record straight about their relationship? Let the error ride? Or was she hesitating about whether to invite him into the experience?

Cindy looked at him. "I'd like you to be there."

"Okay."

Her reasoning might have been about nerves, even though she'd already had the test once. She knew the procedure was noninvasive. This time he wanted to be in the room with her, but he hadn't pushed. There were privacy laws in place and because they weren't married, any of her medical information wouldn't automatically be revealed to him without Cindy's permission.

He understood the need for rules, and it had never bothered him before. But it did now. He had a personal interest; this was his baby. That lame excuse again. It was the best he could do.

After the assistant weighed Cindy and took her blood pressure, she got her settled on an exam table with the ultrasound machine beside it. Nathan pulled up a chair and prepared for a lengthy wait. But moments later the doctor walked in.

"Hi, Cindy." She looked at him. "Nathan. How are you?"

"Fine."

"Congratulations, by the way."

"Thanks."

The doctor looked at him. "Are you ready to meet your baby for the first time?"

"Yes," he said, as excitement rippled through him.

Cindy smiled radiantly at him and that sent a different sort of ripple through his system.

The doctor pulled down the sheet and lifted Cindy's shirt to squirt warm gel on her gently rounded belly. She moved the transducer and turned dials on the machine to improve resolution and get optimum views.

And then he could see the image. That was his baby! He'd known the fetus was real, but now he really understood what Rebecca had meant about meeting his child. He'd never felt anything like this and was moved beyond words.

"See the pulsing, Cindy?" Rebecca pointed to the screen. "That's your baby's heart. It looks strong. Normal. Here are the arms and legs."

"Oh, my goodness," Cindy breathed. "Nathan, do you see?"

"Yeah."

The doctor glanced at them. "Do you want to know your baby's sex?"

"Yes."

They both said it at the same time even though the topic had never come up for discussion. The fact they agreed sent a warm feeling through him.

"Are you sure you want to know?" he asked.

"Very sure." Cindy grinned. "Then Shirley can get started on the mural."

He'd forgotten about that, but it would explain why his mom was sticking around. Still, it was out of character for her to be there for a kid, even if it was her first grandchild.

"Okay," he said to the doc. "We're in total agreement. If you can get a good view."

She studied the screen for a while. Frustrated she said, "Move your leg, little one." A few moments later she smiled. "We have a boy."

Without thinking Nathan took Cindy's hand and squeezed gently. He stared hard at his son moving in her womb. A powerful feeling of protectiveness moved through him. They were having a boy, a tiny perfect son who would need them to be there for him. Both of them. Together.

Nathan had no blueprint for successful parenting. His childhood had pretty much sucked. But he'd had one thing his son didn't. A father and mother who were legally married when he was born.

That was something easily fixed.

"So, thanks for dinner." Cindy looked up at Nathan, tall and handsome in the moonlight, and wished he would kiss her.

She was standing on her front porch, so close to him the heat from his body warmed her skin. After the ultrasound he'd taken her to celebrate at Capriotti's where he showed off the ultrasound picture of his son. Now they were awfully close to the exact spot where their son had been conceived.

She wanted a repeat of that impulsive, explosive, out-of-control sex. Or even sweet, slow bedroom sex. Any sex, really, because they'd been drifting along in limbo and she needed a sign that there was reason to hope he could care as much for her as she did for him.

Nathan rubbed a hand across the back of his neck. "Would you mind if I came in? There's something I'd like to talk to you about."

Talk didn't really thrill her. He was looking very serious about something and that was never a good thing. She could think of a much better use for their mouths than conversation. But, again, hope deflated like a leaky balloon because his mood was leaning more toward serious than sexy. She needed to concentrate on the baby.

A boy!

Maybe a rough-and-tumble little guy. Or possibly a brilliant, quiet heartbreaker like his father.

"I'm awfully tired, Nathan. It's been a big day. Exciting," she added, "But really exhausting."

"What I have to say is pretty important. I promise it won't take long," he said. "There's just something I'd like to settle between us."

Cindy studied him and would swear he actually looked a little nervous. It was a side to him she'd never seen. He'd been concerned when the doctor put her on bed rest, but this was different. The always unflappable Dr. Nathan Steele actually looked—flappable.

"Okay." She fit her key into the lock, then opened the door. "Come in."

"Thanks."

She set her purse on the cedar chest. "Do you want something to drink?"

"No."

Studying the solemn expression on his face, she asked, "Is this a standing-up sort of conversation, or something I should sit down for?"

"That depends."

"On what?"

"How surprised you're going to be."

He'd said they needed to settle something, which probably meant this was about the baby. His reaction to the ultrasound had been clear to anyone within visual range of his face. Quite literally he'd been beaming. Such a guy, pleased this was a boy child to carry on his name.

His name?

She suddenly went cold all over. "You want to take the baby away from me?" Another thought struck her, and she didn't have the financial resources to fight him. "You're going to sue me for custody?"

"No." He looked horrified. "God, no."

She'd been holding her breath and finally let it out. "Okay. Sorry. Sometimes I go to the bad place."

"That's an understatement. You don't even slow down for stop signs when you go there."

"It's easier that way." She shrugged. "Get the very worst out of the way and the rest isn't so bad."

He ran his fingers through his hair. "Well, I'm sort of hoping this isn't something even in the same neighborhood with the bad place."

She walked over to the love seat and sat. "Maybe this is

a sit-down talk after all. If nothing else, I can take a load off while you get to the point."

"I think you should marry me."

She blinked up at him. "What did you say?"

"We need to get married."

"That's what I thought you said. Way to get to the point."

Cindy knew she'd chosen wisely in sitting down. The shock of his point would have dropped her like a stone.

Married?

He wanted to marry her? Happiness expanded inside her. This was something she hadn't dared to let herself hope for.

His gaze never left hers as the silence grew. Finally he said, "Please say something. What are you thinking?"

"Wow. I'm thinking a proposal, really?"

"Yes, really." He sat on the cedar chest in front of her. "Seeing our baby really put things in perspective for me."

"Such as?" She really wanted him to touch her. When a guy proposed marriage, didn't he at least take her hand?

"A kid needs a mother and father."

"Check." She pointed to herself, then him. "Both present and accounted for."

"And a stable environment. That means both parents under the same roof."

"We've kind of been doing that already."

"I don't want 'kind of.' I think we need to officially be under the same roof to make a family."

Why did he want to get married now? Something didn't feel right.

"This is important to you?" she asked.

"It is. I never want my son to feel different, out-of-step, that he doesn't fit—"

"Because his parents aren't legally married?"

"Yes," he said, as if she'd come up with the elusive answer to the riddle of the day.

He'd listed logical reasons to take the step, but not one of them was about loving her. He'd said "We need to get married," not "I want to marry you."

Silence stretched to the breaking point between them before he finally said again, "Please say something. Tell me what you're thinking."

"Honestly?"

"That would be good."

Cindy blew out a long breath. "Because we both know life isn't a romantic comedy and you just asked me to marry you, I'm honestly wondering why."

"I told you why," he protested.

"You listed legal and logistical reasons, but not one of them was the most important one."

"I don't understand."

The endearingly clueless expression on his face tugged at her heart. "Then I'll explain it to you."

"Please."

"During our very first conversation you told me that you don't believe in something if you can't see or touch it."

"I remember. You're talking about love." His expression shuttered.

"Yes." She gripped her hands together in her lap. "But your mother told me you and your wife were completely in love. That you were inconsolable when she died and blamed yourself. To me, that doesn't sound like a man who doesn't believe love exists."

"The only part of what my mother said that's true is I do blame myself for everything that went wrong." His voice was harsh and cold.

"Meaning what?"

"I liked and respected my wife. That should have been enough, but it wasn't. She left me." He ran his fingers through his hair. "In all fairness, I was never there for her. Work always came first."

That was hard to believe. He'd been there for her, Cindy, from the beginning. Asking for her phone number. Persistently. Then when she found out she was pregnant, he'd had to wear down her resistance because she kept waiting for him to not be there. When had she started to trust him? It was all a blur, but she realized she did have faith that he wouldn't run out on her. But that was only now because she and the baby were one.

"Shirley didn't say anything about that," she accused.

"Because she doesn't know. You may have noticed that Shirley and I don't really communicate all that much."

"But still… That was a life-changing event in your life. You're her son."

"There was no point. Felicia and I had just separated when she was killed in the accident. Shirley didn't need to know we were getting a divorce." Sadness and anger fused together in his grim expression. "If I'd been capable of loving her the way she deserved to be loved, she would still be alive."

So he hadn't been in love. She'd truly thought he was capable of the emotion because he'd been married. The truth made it hard to breathe.

"You don't know that things would have been different if your feelings were deeper," she said, trying to be rational when she just wanted to fall apart.

"Yeah. I do." His mind was made up about that. "I missed my best friend, but she was never the love of my life. I don't even know what that means."

Because he'd never seen what love looked like. Cindy knew something else, too. His greatest strength was also his biggest flaw. Scrupulous honesty. He'd told her straight up that he didn't believe in love and was now proving it wasn't a lie.

But Cindy had been lying to herself.

She'd thought her heart was protected by scar tissue from her last disastrous relationship. Now she realized the foolishness of that strategy. She was the kind of person who led with her heart. And she'd always known she wanted to be someone's great love. As her trust in Nathan grew, she'd yearned for that someone to be him.

She was completely and hopelessly in love with him.

But he'd just told her that he couldn't be in love with anyone. It wasn't a good plan to propose marriage, then declare love didn't exist in your world.

"You're right about one thing," she said. "Shirley doesn't need to know the truth. And yet, as dysfunctional as your relationship is with her, you kept that information to yourself to protect her."

"Not really."

She didn't have the strength to argue with him. Holding back tears that desperately wanted release took all her energy. He'd asked to come in so they could settle this business of marriage. The least she could do was give him an answer.

"Thank you, no."

His eyes narrowed. "No what?"

"I can't marry you. But I appreciate that you're trying to do the right thing for our son."

"You don't even want to think it over?"

"There's nothing to think about. My mind is made up just as surely as yours is." She stood and walked over to the door, then opened it. "Goodbye, Nathan."

Cindy didn't think it was possible that hope had survived the beating it had just taken, but she was wrong again. Hope didn't really breathe its last until he was gone without even trying to convince her she was wrong.

After her heart cracked in two, the last sound she heard was the squeal of tires as he drove away.

Chapter Fourteen

"**D**amn these pregnancy hormones—" Cindy sniffled as she set a single place at the table.

It always seemed so small when Nathan sat across from her. Now it felt big enough to land a jumbo jet, and had for the last week. That's how long it had been since the night he'd proposed. A short time and yet being alone made it feel like forever.

She'd seen him briefly at work but hadn't talked to him. And every night, right about the time he usually rang her doorbell, the tears started when no one came.

"Stop it," she ordered herself.

She was preparing to cut up vegetables for a salad and actually being able to see would be good. She needed all her fingers. An appetite would come in handy, too, but that had been missing for the past seven days.

Maybe turning him down had been a mistake. She might be in love by herself, but at least she wouldn't be alone.

"That didn't work out so well for Felicia. Or his mother." Now she was talking to herself.

She'd existed in a world where she desperately missed Nathan's warmth, humor and caring, but in her heart she knew it was the right thing. Alone was better than watching the man you loved not love you back. But she had to admit that walking by herself on the high road didn't make her feel less lonely.

She sprinkled extra-virgin olive oil and balsamic vinegar on the lettuce, tomato, cucumber and avocado in her salad bowl. Then she put in some cold diced chicken and grated cheddar cheese and placed it on the table. After adding ice to a glass, she was filling it with filtered water from the refrigerator when the doorbell rang.

Her hand jerked and water sloshed over her wrist. "Nathan?" she whispered.

She ran to the front door and peeked out the window, reminded once again how incredibly cruel hope could be. One minute on top of the world, anticipating what you wanted more than anything else. The next you were lower than you'd ever been before. There was a Steele standing outside, but it was not Nathan.

Cindy unlocked the deadbolt and opened the door. "Hi, Shirley."

"Cindy." She looked closer. "Are you all right?"

No. But she would be. When her eyes stopped feeling ten sizes too small from crying.

"I'm fine. But this isn't a very good time for me. It hasn't been a good week."

"Tell me about it." She looked upset. "This won't take long, but I really need to talk to you. It's about Nathan."

"Is he all right?" Cindy opened the door wider and let the other woman walk inside.

"He's not hurt." Shirley turned when the door closed. "At least not physically, if that's what you mean."

"What a relief." She couldn't stand the thought of anything happening to him. "I was just going to eat a salad. Can I make something for you?"

"No, thanks. I've had dinner. But you need to eat. Would you mind if I kept you company?"

"Okay." Although she didn't think her company would be very good, to talk to an actual person would be a welcome change from talking to herself. "I'd like that."

Shirley sat across the table from her in the chair Nathan usually occupied. "That's a nutritious dinner."

"I'm trying to eat healthy for the little guy."

"A boy?"

"Yes." Cindy smiled before noticing the look of awe, then stark and genuine surprise on the other woman's face. "Nathan didn't tell you."

"No."

"We found out last week at the doctor's appointment. She did an ultrasound."

The same day Nathan proposed so the son he'd just found out about wouldn't ever feel bad because his parents weren't married. There was no way to explain to him that saying "I do" was not an inoculation against dysfunctional. The queen of screwed-up relationships was sitting right across from her.

"I can't believe he didn't say anything." Shirley slid the Coach purse off her shoulder and set it on the floor beside her. "But then he hasn't been acting like himself. That's why I came to see you."

"Oh?" Cindy took a bite of salad, but couldn't taste anything.

"Yes. He's been short-tempered and moody. That's so unlike him." She linked her fingers. "I asked him about painting a bedroom for the baby and he walked away without answering. Is there something wrong with the baby?"

"No." She rested her hand protectively on her growing belly. "He's doing great."

"Thank goodness." In the next instant, the relief in her face gave way to worry. "I don't understand why he didn't tell me you were having a boy. Nathan has always been so steady, so even. There's something wrong with him. I just know it. He wouldn't talk about anything, which isn't new. But he's been acting so strangely and that is different. I was so hoping you could enlighten me."

Cindy choked down more salad before setting her fork in the bowl of half-eaten greens. She sipped some water, then took a deep breath. "Nathan proposed to me."

Shirley blinked several times, then smiled. "That's wonderful. Congratulations. I know what I said about you two being very modern and not feeling as if you had to marry for the sake of the baby. But I've gotten to know you and I think you're very good for him."

"I turned him down."

"But why?" Her smile disappeared, replaced by shock. "I don't understand. Any fool can see that you're completely in love with him."

"I am," Cindy agreed, more calmly than she felt. Especially when her heart cracked just a little bit more. "But marrying him would set a new record for foolish. It would be too painful knowing he can't love me back."

"I don't think that's true. They say a man who loved once is more likely to love again. Felicia has been gone—"

"He didn't love her." Cindy felt a pang of guilt at being the one to reveal this information. But, in spite of her faults, this woman meant well and needed to understand why there would be no wedding for her grandson's parents.

"That's not true. He was inconsolable when she died."

"Because he blamed himself for the marriage not working. When Felicia died in the accident they were separated. That being the case, he felt there was no point in revealing that to you. He understands that you were very fond of his wife."

"He was protecting me?"

"Ironic, but true," Cindy said. "Apparently Felicia walked out when she realized he didn't love her the way a husband should love his wife."

"I can't believe this." Her hazel eyes grew even wider.

"It's true." Cindy had just revealed Nathan's secret, but to make it count for something she needed to get another concern off her chest. "Nathan doesn't believe in love, Shirley. And you bear some responsibility for that."

"Me?" The older woman recoiled as if she'd been slapped. "I don't know what you mean."

"Think about it for a minute. When the going gets tough, the tough don't take art classes. But that's what you did." Cindy expected an angry, defensive reaction to her words, but there was only silence. And sadness in Shirley's expression. "You and Nathan's father had problems and neither one of you talked to him about what was going on. Neither one of you bothered to say you stopped loving each other but still loved him. You handled the situation by hiding, and that's the coping skill your little boy learned."

Shirley sighed and eyes so like her son's filled with misery and self-recrimination. "I was in no condition to be a good mother to him. You may choose to believe I'm simply making excuses for my shortcomings, but I sincerely believed that and was afraid that me being in such an emotionally damaged state, I would hurt Nathan more."

"You were wrong." Cindy couldn't hold back the words, but it wasn't her intention to hurt. Just to clear the air.

"I see that now. Obviously I've made mistakes. If I could take them back, I would do it in an instant. But if you believe nothing else, believe this—I love my son with all my heart."

Cindy could see that. "I know you do."

"This is no excuse for my behavior, but I'm not the only parent he had."

Cindy remembered Nathan saying he was abandoned by both of them and then shipped off to boarding school. Unfortunately, knowing why he was the way he was didn't flip the switch to turn on his ability to love her back.

"You're right, Shirley. His father didn't help. Nathan's whole world was falling down around him and he had no support system in place to handle what was going on."

"I wish there was something I could do to change the past." Regret shimmered in her eyes. "That's not possible. But if there's anything I can do for you, just ask."

The absolute sincerity in the other woman's expression convinced Cindy that she meant what she said. But the harm was already done and her own broken heart was collateral damage.

"Thanks, but I don't think there's anything. He won't let himself take a leap of faith that love exists and I won't tie myself to a man who can't let me be his great love. I won't settle for less. More important, my baby won't get caught up in the fallout from a mistake."

Shirley nodded but looked uneasy. "Still, don't forget that this is his child, too."

"I won't."

Cindy had thought about that a lot. He was committed to his son, so much so that he'd gone against his beliefs and proposed marriage. He cared deeply, a father's love, whether or not he thought about his feelings in those terms.

And because he cared, they would be tied together forever by this child.

"You wouldn't punish him for the sins of the parents, would you? Keep him from seeing the baby?"

"Never," Cindy vowed. "My baby deserves to know his father. Having both of us in his life is the best thing for him."

And the worst thing for her because it would hurt every time she saw him and was reminded that she was in love all by herself.

"Thank you, Cindy. You're a better mother to your son than I ever was to mine." She sighed again. "I'm sorry."

"I'm not the one you should be apologizing to."

"You're right." A determined look slid into the older woman's eyes. It was the same expression Nathan had worn when asking for Cindy's phone number. Shirley nodded resolutely, then stood. "I've taken up enough of your time."

Cindy stood and followed her to the front door. "You don't have to go."

"I have a lot to think about." She leaned over and pulled Cindy into a quick, hard hug. "You're a remarkable woman, Cindy Elliott. Honest and straightforward. My grandson is a lucky little guy to have you for his mother."

Shirley left before Cindy's tears started up again.

Sniffling, she leaned back against the door. "Damn hormones."

It was his day off, but Nathan didn't know what to do with himself. He paced his house until he wanted to put his fist through a wall. Every square inch of the five thousand plus square feet reminded him of Cindy. In fact, everything and nothing reminded him that she'd turned him down. The feelings running through him were strangely like the abandonment he'd experienced when he'd been dumped at boarding school.

Finally, he decided to channel his energy in a more productive way and drove to Mercy Medical Center. He took the elevator to the second floor and walked into the NICU. Annie was standing by the nurse's station writing in a chart. She glanced up at him, then did a double take and frowned.

After handing the chart to the charge nurse, she walked over to him and slid her hands into the pockets of her white lab coat. "It's not like you to read our schedule wrong."

"Meaning?"

"You're off today."

"I just wanted to check in on the thirty-two weeker we got yesterday."

Annie stared at him. "Buffy?"

"Please tell me that's not her legal name."

"No. That would be Alexandria Michelle Morrison. I named her Buffy—as in the vampire slayer." She tipped her head to the side. "The blank expression on your face suggests that you have no idea what I'm talking about."

"I don't."

"It's a TV show, a cultural phenomenon. The chick can kick some serious vampire ass."

"I'll take your word for it." He glanced over to where the tiny baby was sleeping. "How's Buffy doing?"

"Kicking some serious preemie problems," she said with a grin. "She's one tough little chick. Her oxygen saturation is good and the blood chemistries are within normal range. Holding her own and all signs are positive."

"Good." He looked around and noted the unit was unusually quiet. "Do you need any help?"

"You're kidding, right?"

"No." Nathan just wanted to do something, anything to keep himself from thinking about Cindy.

He'd made her a good proposition, but the cost of her counteroffer was too high. They got along great. Why mess that up by putting a label on it? That all made sense in his head, but it didn't stop him from missing her smile. The need to be with her never went away. Every night for the last week he'd left work and turned toward her house before he remembered she didn't want to see him.

"So you don't trust me to do my job?" Annie asked.

"Of course I do."

"This unscheduled drop-in says something different. It's going to start rumors about the stability of our medical practice."

"That's ridiculous. You're the best neonatologist I know. Besides me, of course."

"Of course." Her voice dripped sarcasm before she turned serious. "Then I don't get it, Nathan. Surely you have something better to do than hang around the hospital."

"Not really." He folded his arms over his chest.

"What's Cindy doing? Working today?"

He barely suppressed the wince from hearing her name out loud. "No idea."

"You two are having a baby." She glanced over her shoulder to make sure no one was eavesdropping. "Don't you have stuff to do to get ready?"

"There was one thing I wanted to do, but she blew me off."

Annie's gaze narrowed. "I could use a cup of coffee. And I strongly suggest that you join me."

"Why?"

"It's suddenly clear to me why you came to help me out."

"Enlighten me."

"You're feeling an overwhelming urge to unburden yourself. And I'm willing to listen." She nodded emphatically. "You know the drill."

"Doctor's dining room," he said with a sigh.

Annie looked over at the charge nurse, pointed to the door and mouthed the word coffee. The nurse gave her a thumbs-up and a goodbye wave. He fell into step beside her and they rode the elevator down to the hospital's first floor. After walking past the lobby and outpatient registration desk, they turned left and opened the door to the dining room. He was relieved to see it was empty.

"You pour the coffee. I'll get the carbs." She grabbed a couple small plates and put a token slice of cantaloupe beside cookies, coffee cake and muffins.

Nathan wondered how she could put away that much food and still stay so petite. That was simpler than trying to figure out why he felt so screwed up.

Annie picked a table by the window and sat. "I love the cookies. Want one?"

Nathan set two cups of coffee on the pristine white tablecloth, then took the chair across from her. Food was the last thing he wanted. "I'd rather chew off my arm."

"That response to a simple and courteous question contains a disproportionate level of hostility. Want to tell me what's going on with you?" She held up a hand. "And before you try to say no and brush me off, let me remind you—this is me. You can run, but you can't hide."

Her directness was one of the things he liked best about her. So he'd see that and raise her. "I found out that I'm having a son."

"Oh, wow." A soft expression turned Annie's blue eyes tender. "A little Nathan."

"Yeah." He grinned and for just a moment all the other complicated crap was pushed to the background.

"Someone to carry on your name."

And just like that it all came rushing back. "Maybe."

"What maybe? There's no question that Cindy is having your baby. The right of succession has been secured. No?"

"I asked her to marry me."

Annie stared at him, the coffee cup frozen in midair halfway to her mouth. She set it down. "So that's what you wanted to do to get ready for the baby. And she blew you off."

"Pretty much." It was actually a relief to get that off his chest. Maybe confession really was good for the soul.

"So what did you do wrong?" His partner narrowed her gaze on him.

And just like that confession didn't feel quite so self-righteous or satisfying. "Why would you automatically assume it's my fault that she said no?"

"This is me. I know you—the good, bad and ugly. It's not a newsflash that you're not the brightest bulb in the social chandelier. After all, you didn't recognize Cindy when you talked to her outside the hospital. As the story goes, you hit on her. Why is it a stretch to ask how you messed up proposing to her?"

"What's to mess up? I asked her. She seemed excited."

"And then?"

He shifted on the padded chair. "I pointed out all the reasons that it made good sense."

"Be still my heart," she said, fluttering her hand over her chest.

"What? She said, 'thank you, no.' I'm the wronged party here. It's not rocket science."

"You're right," she agreed. "Love is a lot more complicated."

"Love has nothing to do with it."

"That's where you're wrong. Love has everything to do with it."

Nathan refused to confirm that her words eerily echoed what Cindy had said. "In case you forgot, I'm the guy who doesn't believe in love."

"That's a bunch of crap. And you've got it bad." Pity flickered in her eyes. "Otherwise you wouldn't be here on your day off. And the NICU staff wouldn't be wondering what's up with you."

"There's nothing wrong with me."

"Nothing that can't be explained by the fact that you're in love with the mother of your child." When he opened his mouth to protest, she held up her hand. "Save your breath. I've heard it all before. I'll grant you that love is something you can't see or touch. It can't be explained by facts, experiments or data from trial studies. It just *is*. Loving and being loved in return is a miracle and can bring great joy if you're smart enough to hang on."

"Hang on to what? You just said it's not tangible."

"Not in your world." She patted his arm sympathetically. "Your childhood wasn't about emotional growth. It was more like guerrilla warfare. Duck and run."

"A parent's responsibility is to raise their child to function independently."

"And yours accomplished that. But the way they did was more like teaching a baby to swim by dropping them in the deep end of the pool and walking away. It's no thanks to them that you turned out as well as you did."

"That's a compliment, right?"

"Yeah." She picked up a cookie and broke it in half. "The fact that you're a man of science and preaching that there's no rational way to explain love is just your way of being afraid."

"As you so eloquently pointed out, I'm not the brightest

bulb in the social chandelier, but I'd have to guess that's not a compliment."

"I'm your friend. I tell the truth. What you take away from it is up to you. But I'm fairly sure that you're afraid to admit you're in love because when it didn't work out for your parents, you were the one who got hammered. Your reaction to that pain stimuli is avoidance of the offending behavior."

That wasn't news. She'd told him this on numerous occasions, but it always bounced off before. Not this time. Maybe because he was ready to listen and learn. Maybe Cindy had made the difference, laid the groundwork.

"How did you know Ryan was the one?" he asked, wondering about her husband.

"That's easy." Oddly, her eyes filled with tears. "The sex was better than good. The chemistry unquestionable. I knew it—we—were becoming significant, so in the interest of full disclosure before we got to the point of no return, I told him that I couldn't have a baby."

"What did he say?"

"That children were very essential to him and he wanted to be a father. My heart just stopped because I figured it was over. That had happened to me before." She brushed at moisture on her cheek. "Then he said that DNA wasn't the most important part of parenting and there were an awful lot of kids in the world who needed good homes. But there was only one of me and he wasn't willing to let me go. He couldn't imagine his life without me in it."

"And that's when you passed the point of no return?"

"Oh, yeah. I was already in love with him, so that just put the icing on the cake." She turned serious. "I want you to be happy, Nathan. Break the pattern. Take a chance."

He wasn't sure he could do that. She'd zeroed in on his

core belief. It wasn't called *core* for nothing. His deepest truth was that loving someone destroyed everything.

He didn't know if it was possible to break that pattern.

Chapter Fifteen

Nathan got out of the shower, dried off and dressed. He had another day off and nothing to do with himself. Going to the hospital was out of the question. Annie would have him in for a psych eval. Which probably wasn't such a bad idea.

He couldn't stop thinking about Cindy. He wanted to be with her, know how she was feeling, that she was okay. She was sexy and sunny and funny and sweet. There'd been a black hole in his life since she'd refused his proposal.

But love?

Maybe he *was* crazy. He still wanted to marry her—even more than when he'd asked. Not seeing her was driving him nuts. What confused him most was that it wasn't all about the baby. And then he smelled bacon, which convinced him beyond a shadow of a doubt that insanity had set in because no one ever cooked bacon in his house.

He followed his nose to the kitchen, where he found

Shirley standing at the stove, a fork in her hand in front of a pan sizzling with frying bacon.

"What are you doing?"

She glanced over her shoulder and smiled. "What does it look like I'm doing?"

"That's a trick question, right?"

"How can it be a trick?" Shirley's smile didn't falter.

"If I say it looks like you're cooking, you'll say I'm crazy, need my eyes examined, or both." He pointed at her. "Or living in an alternate reality. You're wearing an apron. It has sunflowers on it."

"Well, good morning to you, too. Can't a mother cook breakfast for her son?"

Not in his universe.

"I'm not aware of any laws against it. But this is you we're talking about." He walked around the kitchen island and studied her carefully. "Are you all right?"

"Fine." The smile disappeared but not the cheerfulness.

That was oddly disconcerting. She removed the bacon from the frying pan and placed them on a plate with paper towels, then blotted the crispy strips.

"Would you like hash browns with your breakfast? Or toast? I can do either. Or both."

Frowning, he moved closer and touched the back of his hand to her forehead, checking for fever. "Are you sure you're not delirious?"

"Don't be silly." The Stepford smile was back. "How do you like your eggs? One or two? Or an omelet with vegetables? That would be healthy."

"Stop it," he demanded. "Shirley Steele has never been the domestic type. Who are you and what have you done with her?" Then something else occurred to him. "Or you want something."

"I do. But it's not what you think," she added quickly.

"How do you know what I'm thinking?"

She sighed. "I was sort of hoping this was one of those show-don't-tell moments. But before your head explodes, I guess I better explain."

"I'd appreciate that." He thought about moving a safe distance away but figured holding his own wasn't really a problem.

"I had an epiphany, Nathan."

That's when he did take a step back, then stared at her. "Now I'm really weirded out. And more than a little afraid. Strangely, that wasn't particularly reassuring."

"Maybe you need coffee." The sunshiny expression disappeared, replaced by exasperation that was more Shirley-like.

For some reason he found that comforting. "That would be good."

She poured him some, then looked a little sad. "I don't even know what you take in your coffee. What kind of mother am I?"

"Black is fine." He took the mug she handed him, uneasy now with the way she was acting. "What's going on with you?"

"I need to apologize to you, Nathan."

"Why? Did you burn down the guest house? Paint the walls black?" He smiled at his attempt to cut the tension, but she didn't return it.

"I was a terrible mother. Correction: I still am. I'm self-absorbed and selfish. When your father cheated on me—and make no mistake, it was me he left, not you—I was so completely devastated that I simply couldn't think about anything else. Not even you, I'm ashamed to admit."

"It's okay. I turned out all right."

"No. I mean, yes, you're fantastic, but what I did is not

okay." She met his gaze, her own filled with remorse. "You should have been my primary concern and I'm so sorry that I wasn't there for you. And boarding school." She shook her head. "Ironically that decision was made based on what I thought you needed. I wasn't a positive force in your life under the best circumstances, but when your father left, I just fell apart. I truly believed you'd be better off away from me. What I didn't see until recently was that your world fell apart, too. And you had no one."

For a nanosecond he was that lonely boy again, removed from everything familiar and dropped into an environment so foreign it might as well have been the moon. He didn't know anyone and no one knew him. That was probably the worst. He'd been bewildered and unhappy, but no one had noticed.

Until now. Why?

"That was quite a speech," he said.

"Not a speech. It's from the heart, although I wouldn't blame you for thinking I don't have one." She shrugged. "I'm trying to undo the harm your father and I did to you. He's no longer here, so it's up to me."

His father had died ten years ago. Because the man was a nonpresence in his life, it hadn't left much of an impact. This unexpected change in his mother made him sad for the first time. There was no way to know what a relationship with his father might have been like.

"I'm fine. Don't worry about me."

"I can't help it." She poured herself a mug of coffee and wrapped her hands around it without drinking. "If you were fine, you'd be able to admit that you're in love with Cindy Elliott."

"That subject is off limits." Just hearing her name felt like a punch to the gut.

"Love *is* real, Nathan. If it weren't, your father's rejection wouldn't have hurt me so deeply that I had to hide from life. From you." Her voice caught, but she swallowed hard and continued. "Love exists. It isn't always reciprocated, but it's as real as the heart pumping blood through your body right now."

"Okay."

Nathan didn't know what else to say. She was right. Everything she said rang true and made sense. Especially the part about hiding. He'd been using science and work to dismiss the reality of the emotion and then to hide from it in case he was wrong. Like Annie had said, it was all crap.

"I have a feeling there's more of me in you than your father." Sympathy shadowed her eyes. "When you love, it's deep and forever."

He wasn't going to confirm that he'd just figured out he took after her. "I'm sure my DNA contains characteristics from both of you."

"It's okay to talk to me about your feelings."

"I appreciate that." But he couldn't go there. Not yet.

She tilted her head as she studied him. "Why didn't you tell me the baby is a boy?"

There was only one way she could know that. "You talked to Cindy."

She nodded. "Because you were not acting at all like yourself. I was worried and figured Cindy was the reason. As it happens, I was right. She told me you asked her to marry you. And that she turned you down flat."

There was that fist-to-the-gut feeling again. "She had her reasons."

"She doesn't think you love her," Shirley confirmed. "I think she's wrong, but, along with your fractured childhood, you're still struggling with your guilt that your feelings for Felicia weren't enough."

His gaze jumped to hers and he saw no recrimination there. Only sadness. "Cindy told you?"

"Everything. And for the record, there's no reason to protect me. I'm always on your side. No matter what. What happened to your wife was incredibly tragic. But it's not your fault." She looked down for a moment. "Unlike what you're doing with Cindy."

"What does that mean?"

"All I want is for you to be happy. I'm pretty sure Cindy is the key to that. But you're afraid to take a leap of faith and believe in love."

Taking his breakfast order. Pouring coffee. Wearing the damn apron. It was all to show him that she cared. Food equals love. And then everything clicked. It might be an alternate universe, but he liked it here.

"So that's why you made bacon."

"Now you're cookin'." She grinned. "Your future happiness depends on righting the past. It's my fault your impression of love is screwed up. I'm more sorry about that than you will ever know. Someday I hope you'll be able to forgive me. But now that I've made you aware of the problem, you have to take control. If you mess things up with Cindy now, Nathan, that's on you."

Right again, he thought. The words were invasive therapy to his ailing soul.

He grinned at his mother. "I like my eggs over medium. Hash browns. And wheat toast."

"Coming right up."

She started to turn away, then stopped and met his gaze. "I do love you, son." There was a sheen of moisture in her eyes. "The words sound rusty to me. Probably to you, too. But I promise to practice every chance I get. You'd better get used to hearing them."

"Okay."

"Now, about Cindy—"

He held up a hand to stop her. "I concur with your diagnosis. My resolve is renewed and I will take appropriate steps to get the desired result."

"Then I'm glad we had this little chat and cleared the air."

"Me, too." More than he could possibly tell her.

"For what it's worth, Nathan, I've done your astrological forecast." She shrugged. "Don't look like that. I needed the practice. The thing is, I saw nothing but good things. All the stars and planets are saying love is on the rise. Even the asteroids are—"

"Good to know," he said.

Shirley nodded. "I'm probably the last person you want to hear advice from, but the appropriate steps with Cindy might get a better result if a romantic gesture was included. A really, really big one. That could be just what the doctor ordered."

And it was exactly what Nathan had been thinking.

Cindy pushed her housecleaning cart down the empty hall toward the elevator, really starting to feel the extra baby baggage she was carrying. She planned to work right up until her due date because she couldn't afford to lose the money. In fact, she was worried about how to make ends meet while she was on maternity leave. But then there would be child care expenses when she went back to work.

Marrying Nathan would have solved the problem. Unfortunately it would have created a bigger one. Living without love wasn't really living at all. So, she'd be poor and if not deliriously happy, at least not miserable with a man who buried himself in work to avoid her.

But maybe he would consider a small loan to tide her over. "Cindy. Wait up."

She glanced over her shoulder and saw Harlow. When her friend caught up, she smiled. It was a relief to put her sadness away for a little while. "I heard about the haircut. Very cute."

Harlow automatically touched the sleek, shiny brunette bob. "Yeah? Not too short?"

"No. It's perfect for your heart-shaped face. Sophisticated. Flattering, yet with a hint of sexy."

"You make me sound like a bottle of wine."

"Mysterious, yet bold—"

"Stop." Harlow held up a hand. "Where are you off to?"

"I'm on my way to the NICU." And maybe one day soon she would figure out how to stop hoping to see Nathan there.

"Good. I'm glad I caught you then," her friend said. "Have you heard the rumors?"

"Which one?"

"That you're pregnant."

"Not a rumor. I am pregnant. You know that," she said, putting her hands protectively over her abdomen.

Harlow nodded, green eyes intense. "Well, people are starting to wonder. Is she putting on weight? Or is that a baby bump. Hospital talk about you has gone viral."

In spite of the unease trickling through her, Cindy tried to look unconcerned. "Don't people have better things to do?"

"Well, yeah." Her friend shrugged. "But in between saving lives and getting sick patients well, we love to talk. And you're the current hot topic of conversation."

"Good to know."

"The thing is, Cindy, you need to be ready if

someone confronts you. And they will." Harlow looked very anxious.

"Even though it isn't their concern?"

"Yeah, well, people have a funny way of deciding what is and isn't of concern to them. You can still put them off and keep them guessing, but not for much longer. Then the questions will really start flying."

"Like who the father is," Cindy guessed.

"Bingo." The other woman nodded emphatically, but it didn't shake the worry out of her expression.

"What should I say if they ask me if I'm pregnant?"

"In my opinion as your good friend, the truth would be best. But spilling the father's identity is up to you. I just thought you should know. I really have to run. It's time to start second-round treatments." Harlow gave her tummy a quick, reassuring pat. "Keep the little guy safe. Forewarned is forearmed. Be prepared."

"I appreciate the heads-up."

Her friend started to walk away, then said, "Mary Frances is planning a baby shower. Have you registered yet?"

"No. I'll do it soon."

"Good. How about tonight? We'll have dinner first. My treat."

"In that case, you're on."

"Gotta run."

Cindy watched her friend pick up the pace, then disappear around the corner. She stopped at the elevator and pushed the up button. As she waited, thoughts of her baby's father raced through her mind. She missed him so much. The sudden loss left a hole in her life that could never be filled, not even by the baby. Not completely.

Nathan had so many wonderful qualities. Good-looking, smart and sexy, but so much more. He was kind. And a sense of humor lurked beneath that pretty face. He was noble, dedicated to his work and the tiniest human beings that found their way into his capable hands.

And that's when she knew what she would do if directly confronted about who had fathered her baby.

The elevator arrived and she wheeled her cart through the opening, then pushed the button for the second floor, where it quickly stopped. She got out and headed for the NICU. Stopping in the hall outside, she stepped into the suit and snapped the buttons over her tummy. Her friend's warning had come none too soon. There was very little doubt about her condition.

Bracing herself as best she could, she went into the unit. Automatically looking for Nathan, she was disappointed that he wasn't there. His partner was. Annie was chatting with one of the nurses when she noticed Cindy. She smiled and waved and Cindy returned the greeting before starting her work.

She focused on her job and pushed everything else out of her mind as she picked up discarded packaging from medical supplies. Then she gathered the full bags lining all the generic trash containers, avoiding the ones marked "biohazard" or "contaminated."

She scooped up used linens, then dusted, nearly home free when Barbara Kelly cornered her. To anyone looking on, they were two employees having a casual conversation, but Cindy could feel the vibes. None of them good.

"Hi, Cindy."

"Barbara." Here we go.

"How have you been?"

"Really good. Thanks for asking. You?" Deflect, Cindy thought.

"Not bad." The nurse pointedly lowered her gaze. "What's new?"

And there it was. She was on the spot. To tell the truth

or dodge the issue for a little longer. But maybe this was a good time to get it out there with Nathan not present. He was a doctor, a neonatal specialist who existed on a different plane of existence. If by chance the subject came up some other time in his presence, he could reveal as much or as little as he wanted.

Cindy met the other woman's icy, blue-eyed stare. "I'm pregnant, Barbara."

"Congratulations." There was nothing positive in her tone. "Who's the father? Anyone I know?"

Way to be subtle, Cindy thought. "This may come as a shock to you, but that's none of your business. And it was a rude question."

Barbara shrugged. "Everyone wants to know. But nobody had the nerve to ask."

"How heartening that there are still some people with manners."

Any pretense of civility disappeared and blatant hostility slithered into the other woman's gaze. "Do you really believe you can—"

Just then Nathan walked in. His jeans and white cotton shirt were a clue that he wasn't here for work. He scanned the unit, clearly looking for someone, and Cindy's heart started hammering. The blood rushed to her head, drowning out every other sound.

Finally he glanced in her direction and looked like a predator who just spied his prey. Without hesitation, he walked over and said, "I need to talk to you."

Barbara smiled warmly. "Dr. Steele, what can I do for you?"

"If you'll excuse us, I'd like to speak with Cindy privately."

"Really?" She sounded shocked and disapproving.

Nathan glared at her. "Yes, really."

Cindy was pretty sure Nathan had just put his name at the top of the baby daddy list. Right now she couldn't think about the consequences of that. It was too wonderful just to see him.

"Hello," she said when they were alone.

"Cindy, I know communication isn't one of my strengths. It's unfamiliar to me and I've made mistakes. I'll probably make more. So before I begin, you should be aware that my heart is in the right place."

"I've never doubted that."

"Actually, you have," he pointed out.

"Okay. Maybe at first. Then I got to know you." And love you. She looked at the earnest expression on his face and her heart went all soft and mushy and protective. "Here's the thing. The pregnancy just went public. Pretend you're chewing me out for something then run, do not walk, to the nearest exit. Then no one will know you're the father of my baby."

"I want the whole world to know you're the mother of my child." He stared at her as if she had two heads. "This is the last time I'm going to say this. I *will* be here for you. Always. Publicly. You're the only one who matters to me. If you'll give me another chance, I promise you won't regret it." Then he waited for her to respond. When she didn't, he said, "I wish you'd tell me what you're thinking."

Who could think? "Oh, Nathan—I don't know what to say."

Intensity darkened in his eyes as he said, "Words are highly overrated anyway."

Then he bent and scooped her easily into his arms. She sucked in a breath and threw her arms around his neck as he carried her through the silent NICU while everyone stared open-mouthed. Just before he walked out into the hall, she heard the sound of muffled clapping.

It was a moment.

More than that. It was the most romantic gesture ever.

He took her around the corner to the waiting area, which was empty. Then he set her on her feet and pulled her against him. Seconds later, he kissed her. His mouth was soft, warm, insistent, and her knees literally went weak. Her toes curled and trembles traveled everywhere until she tingled all over. He was so right. When he communicated like this, words were highly overrated.

She had no idea how much time had passed when he finally lifted his head and smiled down at her. She only knew that the emotion so clear in his eyes made her as breathless as his kiss.

"I love you, Cindy."

She'd never expected to hear those words, and they rated really high in her heart. "You do?"

"Yes."

"What changed your mind?"

"I had a talk with Shirley—"

"Your *mom*," she said pointedly.

"Right." He grinned and loosened his hold but didn't let her go. "Long story short, I've been an ass. And I've been wrong. Love *is* real. I see it and touch it every time I look at you and hold you in my arms. I can't see or touch my soul, but I know it's there. As surely as I know it will wither and die without you in my life."

"Oh, Nathan. I love you, too."

"I'm counting on that. Because I'm really hoping that you'll reconsider my marriage proposal what with me not being able to live without you and all."

"Better wed than dead," she whispered, quoting from the movie.

"Pretty much," he agreed.

"Okay, I'll marry you." She smiled up at him. "But only because it's the logical thing to do."

Epilogue

"Is he as beautiful as I think he is?" Cindy stared in awe at the baby in her arms.

"He's the most beautiful baby I've ever seen." Nathan was sitting on the hospital bed beside her, his arm around her and their son, holding them both close. "But we have to find a manlier, more masculine way to say that."

Alexander Elliott Steele.

Cindy hadn't thought she could be any happier than the day she and Nathan were married here in the chapel at Mercy Medical Center, but she'd been wrong. Having their baby made them a family and it was just perfect. She watched him watch the baby, and the love in his eyes was tangible.

He met her gaze and smiled. "I didn't think it was possible to love you more, but seeing what you went through to have our child was just…I don't even have the words."

"I know exactly what you mean." She leaned her head on his shoulder and he pulled her closer, kissing her temple.

She was still sore from giving birth the day before, but the joy of holding her son made the discomfort disappear. The experience was painful and scary but the most awesome thing she'd ever been through. She was strong and would have made it alone, but having Nathan there, encouraging and supporting her was the most beautiful thing. She would never again doubt that he was in it for the long haul. The fact that she knew how much he loved her was a gift beyond price.

She'd thought once that they did everything backward—sex, baby, attraction, love and marriage. But it had all happened in just the right order because they'd actually fallen in love at first sight.

"Hey—" It was a whisper from Shirley who stood in the doorway of the hospital room. "I was hoping Alex would be awake."

"Not now, but it won't be long," Nathan said. "The time will come when we'll treasure these quiet moments."

"I treasure them all now," Cindy said.

"Well, I have a surprise for you and you might want to wake the baby for this."

"Hello, Steele family."

Recognizing the familiar voice, Cindy dragged her gaze away from her son and saw her brother Harry. Her eyes filled with tears because she hadn't known he was coming. "How did you get here?"

"Airplane. Nathan arranged it. Shirley picked me up at McCarran." His dark-blond hair was a little longer than when she'd seen him at her wedding, and he was more muscular than a year ago when he'd gone off to college. He was nearly as tall as Nathan and so handsome. Their parents would be extraordinarily proud.

"Hi, bro." Nathan grinned. "Thanks, Mom."

"Happy to help," she said.

"Hey." Harry walked over to the bed and leaned down to kiss Cindy's cheek. "Hi, sis."

"I'd give you a big hug, but my arms are full."

He grinned down at the baby. "My nephew is a good-lookin' dude."

"He's not a dude," she protested. "But he is beautiful. Would you like to hold him?"

Harry looked horrified. "I think I'll wait until he's a little bigger than a football."

"Coward," she teased. "You've got to man up."

"Don't pick on your brother. Some of us are late bloomers." Nathan had taken naturally to the role of big brother.

Together they'd visited Harry at school in California and he'd come to Las Vegas for long weekends. Her two favorite men had hit it off really well. Now there was a third precious man in her life.

"Well, I'd like to hold him." Shirley moved to the other side of the bed and held out her arms. Her son passed over his son and the new grandmother's eyes went soft and exquisitely tender. "He looks just like you when you were born, Nathan."

"How can you remember back that far, Mom?"

"A mother never forgets."

"I can understand why." Cindy wasn't sure when her husband had dropped the first name and started calling her mom, but that came naturally now, too.

She smiled at her brother. "Harry, wait till you see the mural Nathan's mother painted in the baby's room."

"It's trains and planes and cars right now," Shirley said to the sleeping baby, as she slowly moved from side to side. She tenderly kissed his forehead and said, "But when you get older and we know what you like, I can change it. You can help with the design. We'll talk."

And wasn't that a miracle? The woman who'd run from love had embraced the tender emotion along with her son. Together they'd learned to open up to each other and to her.

After the wedding, Shirley had moved into Cindy's place with their blessing. She and Nathan hoped that the spirit of love permeating the house where she grew up would work as well for his mother as it had for them. And at the astrology store she'd met a handsome, retired Air Force Lieutenant Colonel who was definitely showing interest in Shirley Steele.

But, whatever happened, they were a family now. She and Nathan. Shirley. Harry. And now Alex. This precious baby boy had brought them all together. The sun, moon, planets and stars had aligned on the side of them falling in love.

Cindy and her Dr. Charming had found their fairy tale happy ending.

* * * * *

RICH, RUTHLESS AND SECRETLY ROYAL

ROBYN DONALD

CHAPTER ONE

DRUMS pounded out into the sticky tropical night, their vigorous beat almost drowning out the guitars. Her smile tinged with strain, Hani Court surveyed the laughing, singing crowd from her vantage point at the other end of the ceremonial area.

The village people had thrown themselves into the celebrations with typical Polynesian gusto, the occasion their way of thanking the group of New Zealand engineering students who'd fixed and upgraded their derelict water system.

First there had been feasting, and now they were dancing. A teacher at the local school, Hani wasn't expected to join them.

Instead, watching the whirling, colourful patterns the dancers made, she resisted aching, nostalgic memories of Moraze, her distant homeland. There, beneath a tropical moon every bit as huge and silver as this one, men and women danced the *sanga*, an erotic expression of desire, without ever touching.

Here, half a world away on Tukuulu, the dancing was purely Polynesian but it shared the graceful hand movements and lithe sensuality of the *sanga*.

Six years ago Hani had accepted that she'd never dance the *sanga* again, never laugh with her brother Rafiq, never ride a horse across the wild, grassy plains of Moraze. Never hear her people cheer their ruler and his sister, the girl they'd called their little princess.

Never feel desire again…

Unfortunately acceptance didn't mean resignation. Pierced by longing for everything her stupidity had thrown away, she glanced around. She wasn't on duty, and no one would miss her if she sneaked back to her house in the teachers' compound.

A prickle of unease scudded down her spine. She drew in a breath, her stomach dropping into freefall when her eyes met a steel-blue scrutiny.

Transfixed, she blinked. He was taller than anyone else and the stranger's broad shoulders emphasised his height; hard, honed features provided a strong framework for a starkly handsome face. But what made him stand out in the exuberant crowd was his formidable confidence and the forceful authority that gave him an uncompromising air of command.

Every sense on full alert, Hani froze. Who was he? And why did he watch her so intently?

Quelling an instinctive urge to run, she felt her eyes widen as he walked towards her. Her tentative gaze clashed with a narrowed gleaming gaze, and a half-smile curved his hard, beautifully cut mouth. Colour swept up through her skin when she recognised the source of his interest.

Sexual appraisal.

OK, she could deal with that. But her relief was rapidly followed by shock at her body's tumultuous—and entirely unwelcome—response.

Never—not even the first time she'd met Felipe—had she experienced anything like the surge of molten sensation in every cell as the stranger came nearer, moving through the crowd with a silent, lethal grace. Her skin tightened, the tiny hairs lifting as though she expected an attack.

Warned by that secret clamour, she stiffened bones that showed a disconcerting tendency to soften and commanded her erratic heart to calm down.

Cool it! she told herself. He probably just wants a dance. Followed by a mild flirtation to while away the evening?

That thought produced an even faster pulse rate, pushing it up to fever pitch.

Perhaps he thought she was a local; although she was taller than most of the islanders her black hair and softly golden skin blended in well enough.

He stopped beside her. Bewildered and shocked, Hani felt his smile right down to her toes; it sizzled with a sexual charisma that emphasised the aura of controlled power emanating from him. With a jolt of foreboding she realised he was being eyed covertly or openly by most of the women within eyeshot.

Antagonism flared inside her. Here was a man who took his powerful masculine attraction for granted.

Just like Felipe.

But it was unfair to load him with Felipe's sins...

He said in a voice that made each word clear in spite of the background noise, 'How do you do? I'm Kelt Gillan.'

Struggling to dampen down her wildfire response, Hani smiled distantly, but she couldn't ignore the greeting or the fact that he obviously thought a handshake would be the next step.

Nor could she pretend not to feel the scorching along her cheekbones when she looked up and found his gaze on her mouth. Hot little shivers ran through her at that gaze—darkly intent, too perceptive.

'Hannah Court,' she said, hoping the aloof note in her voice would frighten him off.

Of course, he didn't scare easily. One black brow lifted.

Reluctantly she extended her hand, and his fingers closed around hers.

Hani flinched.

'Did I hurt you?' he demanded, frowning.

'No, no, not at all.' He had, in fact, judged to a nicety exactly how much strength to exert. Fumbling for a reason she could give him at her involuntary reaction, she hurried on, 'Just—I think someone walked over my grave.'

It took every shred of her fragile control not to snatch back her hand. His fingers were warm and strong—the hand of a person who worked hard.

But it wasn't his calluses that sent another bolt of sensation through her, so fiercely intense it numbed her brain and left her with nothing to say.

Rescue came from the band; abruptly, the drums and music fell silent. The dancers stopped and turned to the back of the dance floor.

The stranger looked over her head, his eyes narrowing as Hani found enough voice to warn, 'The elders have arrived. It's polite to be quiet.'

He didn't look like someone who'd care about the rituals of Polynesian society, but after a quick nod he watched the aristocratic council of men and women who ruled Tukuulu file past.

Hani dragged in a deep breath. The leaders would produce their best oratory to thank the group of students, and on Tukuulu it was an insult to leave while they spoke. So although she was stuck beside this man for some time, at least she wouldn't have to talk to him.

She'd have time to subdue the wild confusion attacking her. And then she'd think up some innocuous conversation. Not that she cared if he assumed she was a halfwit, she decided defiantly.

Willing herself to keep her gaze on the elders as they

positioned themselves in front of the crowd, she wondered where he'd come from and what he was doing here. Although his height and those burnished eyes, the cold blue of the sheen on steel, hinted at a northern-European heritage, his olive skin spoke of the Mediterranean.

Perhaps he was Australian, or from New Zealand, although she couldn't recall an accent.

As for what he was doing here—well, right next door was the big nickel mine, Tukuulu's only industry, so possibly he had something to do with that.

If so, Hani thought trenchantly, she'd try to persuade him that the mine company needed to accept some responsibility for the school that educated its workforce.

About half an hour into the speeches, Hani blinked, then closed her eyes against the light from the flaring torches.

Not here, not now, she prayed fervently. *Please!*

Cautiously she lifted her lashes, only to blink again as the flames splintered into jagged shards that stabbed into her brain. Heat gathered across her temples, while a dragging ache weighted her bones.

The fever had returned.

Don't panic—just stay upright. Once they finish you can go.

For almost two months—ever since the last bout—she'd been so sure she'd finally managed to shake off this wretched bug. Fear hollowed her stomach; the last time she'd been ill with it the principal had told her that another bout would mean some months spent recuperating in a more temperate climate.

But she had nowhere to go, and no money…

Acutely aware of the silent woman at his side, Kelt Crysander-Gillan concentrated on the speeches. Although he couldn't follow all the allusions, the Tukuuluan dialect was close enough to Maori for him to appreciate the sentiments and the aptness of the songs that followed each speaker.

Pity the council hadn't waited another ten minutes or so to arrive. Then he'd have had time to introduce himself properly to the woman with the intriguing face and the aloof, reserved air.

Looking down, he realised that she was sneaking a glance at him from beneath her lashes. When their eyes clashed she firmed her luscious mouth and looked away, providing him with an excellent view of her profile.

Kelt switched his gaze back to the orator, but that fine line of brow and nose, the determined little chin and the sleek gloss of exquisite skin stayed firmly lodged in his mind.

An islander? No. Not if her eyes were as green as they seemed to be. And although her silky fall of hair gleamed like jet, a quick glance around the room confirmed that not a single Tukuuluan shared the red highlights that gleamed across the dark sheen. A staff member? Probably. When he'd come in she'd been talking to one of the teachers.

He'd already ascertained she wore no rings.

More than an hour after they'd arrived, the elders finally sat down, giving the signal for the celebrations to continue. Immediately the hall exploded in chatter, swiftly over-whelmed by the renewed staccato thump of the drums.

And the woman beside him turned without speaking and walked away.

An ironic smile pulled at the corners of Kelt's mouth as he watched her. So much for the notorious Gillan pulling power! He couldn't recollect any other woman flinching when he shook hands.

His gaze sharpened when she appeared to stumble. She re-covered herself and stood with bowed head and slumping shoulders.

Without volition, Kelt took two steps towards her, stopping when she straightened up and set off into the hot, dark embrace of the night.

But something was definitely wrong. She wasn't so much walking as lurching down the avenue of coconut palms, and while he watched she staggered again, managed another few steps, and then collapsed heavily against the trunk of the nearest tree.

Kelt set off after her, long legs eating up the distance. Once within earshot he demanded, 'Are you all right?'

Hani tried to straighten up when she heard the deep, cool, aloof voice—very male. Even in her distress she was pretty sure she knew who was speaking.

Weakly she said, 'Yes, thank you,' humiliated to realise she sounded drunk, the words slurred and uneven. She probably looked drunk too, huddled against the palm trunk.

'Can I get you anything?' This time he sounded curt and impatient.

'No.' Just go away, she pleaded silently.

'Drink or drugs?'

She longed for her usual crisp, no-nonsense tone when she responded, 'Neither.'

Instead the word dragged, fading into an indeterminate mutter. Closing her eyes, she tried to ignore him and concentrate on staying more or less upright.

He made a disgusted sound. 'Why don't I believe that?' Without waiting for an answer he picked her up as though she were a child and demanded, 'Where were you going?'

Fighting the debilitating desire to surrender and just let him look after her, she struggled to answer, finally dredging the words from her confused brain. 'Ahead—in house.'

He set off silently and smoothly, but by the time they

reached her door Hani's entire energy was focused on holding herself together long enough to take her medication before the fever crashed her into nightmare territory.

'Where's your key?'

'B-bag.' Her lips felt thick and unwieldy, and she said it again, but this time it was an inarticulate mutter. Dimly Hani heard him say something else, but the words jumbled around in her head.

Chills racked her shaking body as she whispered, 'Cold…so cold…'

Unconsciously she curled into the man who held her, striving to steal some of his warmth. Kelt's unruly body stiffened in automatic recognition and, swearing silently, he took the bag from her limp fingers. His arms tightened around her and he said, 'It's all right, I'll get you inside.'

She didn't appear to hear him. 'B-bedside,' she said, slurring the word.

She was shivering so hard he thought he heard her teeth chattering, yet she was on fire—so hot he could feel it through his clothes.

Kelt set her on her feet, holding her upright when she crumpled. He inserted the key and twisted it, picking her up again as soon as he had the door open. Once inside the small, sparsely furnished living room he found the light switch and flicked it on.

The woman in his arms stiffened, turning her head away from the single bulb. Her mouth came to rest against his heart, and through the fine cotton of his shirt he could feel the pressure of her lips against his skin.

Grimly, he tried to ignore his body's consuming response to the accidental kiss.

Guessing that the open door in the far wall probably led to

a bedroom, he strode towards it. Through the opening, one comprehensive glance took in an ancient institutional bed. A rickety lamp on the chest of drawers beside it seemed to be the only illumination.

He eased her down onto the coverlet, then switched on the lamp. Hannah Court gave a soft, sobbing sigh.

His first instinct was to call a doctor, but she opened her eyes—great eyes, darkly lashed, and yes, they were green.

Even glazed and unseeing, they were alluring.

'Pills.' Her voice was high and thin, and she frowned, her eyes enormous in her hectically flushed face. 'T-top drawer...'

Kelt's expression lightened a fraction when he saw a bottle of tablets; although he didn't recognise the name of the drug, the dose was clearly set out, headed rather quaintly For the Fever.

He said harshly, 'I'll get you some water.'

When he came back her eyes were closed again beneath her pleated brows. She'd turned away from the light, rucking up her skirt around her hips to reveal long, elegant legs. Setting his jaw against a swift stab of desire, Kelt jerked the fabric down to cover her.

'Hannah.' Deliberately he made his tone hard and commanding.

Still lost in that region of pain and fever, she didn't answer, but her lashes flickered. Kelt sat down on the side of the bed, shook out the right number of pills, and repeated her name. This time there was no response at all.

He laid the back of his hand against her forehead. Her skin was burning. Perhaps he should call a doctor instead of trying to get the medication inside her.

Medication first, he decided, then he'd get a doctor. 'Open your mouth, Hannah,' he ordered.

After a few seconds she obeyed. He put the pills onto her

tongue and said in the same peremptory tone, 'Here's the water. Drink up.'

Her body moved reflexively, but she did as she was told, greedily gulping down the water and swallowing the pills without any problems.

She even managed to sigh, 'OK—soon...'

Kelt eased her back onto the pillow and slipped the sandals from her slender, high-arched feet. She wasn't wearing tights, and her dress was loose enough to be comfortable.

To his surprise she made a soft protesting noise. One hand came up and groped for him, then fell onto the sheet, the long, elegant fingers loosening as another bout of shivering shook her slim body with such rigour that Kelt turned away and headed for the door. She needed help, and she needed it right now.

He'd almost got to the outer door when he heard a sound from the room behind him. Turning in mid-stride, Kelt made it back in half the time.

Hannah Court had fallen out of the bed, her slim body twisting as guttural little moans escaped through her clenched teeth.

What sort of fever took hold so quickly?

When he picked her up she immediately turned into him, unconsciously seeking—what? Comfort?

'Hannah, it's all right, I'll get a doctor for you as soon as I can,' he told her, softening and lowering his voice as though she were a child.

'Hani,' she whispered, dragging out the syllables.

Honey? A play on Hannah, a pet name perhaps? She certainly had skin like honey—even feverish it glowed, delicate and satin-smooth.

His arms tightened around her yielding body and he sat on

the side of the bed, surprised when the close embrace seemed to soothe her restlessness. Slowly, almost imperceptibly, the intense, dramatic shivers began to ease.

But when he went to lie her down she clutched weakly at him. 'Stay,' she mumbled so thickly it was difficult to make out the words. 'Stay. Please...Raf...' The word died away into an indeterminate mumble.

Rafe? A lover? Surprised and irritated by a fierce twist of what couldn't possibly be jealousy, Kelt said, 'It's all right, I won't let you go.'

That seemed to soothe her. She lay quiescent, her breathing becoming more regular.

Kelt looked down at her lovely face. His brother Gerd would laugh if he could see him now. This small, stark room couldn't have been a bigger contrast to the pomp of the ceremony he'd just attended in Carathia, when their grandmother had presented Gerd, their next ruler, to the people of the small, mountainous country on the Adriatic.

His brother had always known that one day he'd rule the Carathians, and Kelt had always been devoutly thankful the fishbowl existence of monarchy wasn't his fate. His mouth tightened. His own title of Prince Kelt, Duke of Vamili, had been confirmed too. And that should put an end to the grumblings of discontent amongst some of the less educated country people.

Last year their grandmother, the Grand Duchess of Carathia, had come down with a bout of pneumonia. She'd recovered, but she'd called Gerd back to Carathia, intent on sealing the succession of the exceedingly wealthy little country. The ceremonies had gone off magnificently with the world's royalty and many of its leaders in attendance.

As well as a flock of princesses.

With a cynical movement of his hard mouth, Kelt wondered if their grandmother would have any luck marrying her heir off to one.

He suspected not. Gerd might be constrained by centuries of tradition, but he'd choose his own wife.

And once that was done there would be children to seal the succession again. He frowned, thinking of a Carathian tradition that had complicated the existence of Carathian rulers. It had surfaced again—very inconveniently—just before the ceremonies. Someone had resurrected the ancient tale of the second child, the true chosen one, and in the mountains, where the people clung to past beliefs, a groundswell of rebellion was fomenting.

Fortunately he'd spent very little time in Carathia since his childhood, so his presence was no direct threat to Gerd's rule. But he didn't like what was coming in from his brother's informants and his own.

Instead of a simple case of someone fomenting mischief, the rumours were beginning to seem like the first step to a carefully organised plan to produce disorder in Carathia, and so gain control of over half of the world's most valuable mineral, one used extensively in electronics.

The woman in his arms sighed, and snuggled even closer, turning her face into his neck. Her skin no longer burned and she'd stopped shivering.

He registered that the distant throb of the music had stopped, and glanced at the clock on top of the chest of drawers. He'd been holding her for just over an hour. Whatever the medication was, it worked miraculously fast.

He responded with involuntary appreciation to her faint, drifting scent—erotic, arousing—and the feel of her, lax and quiescent against him as though after lovemaking. Cursing his unruly body and its instant reaction, he moved her so that he could see her face.

Yes, she was certainly on the mend. The flush had faded, and she was breathing normally.

A moment later beads of perspiration broke out through her skin. Astoundingly fast, the fine cotton of her dress was soaked, the fabric clinging like a second skin, highlighting the elegant bowl of her hips, the gentle swell of her breasts, the vulnerable length of her throat and the long, sleek lines of her thighs.

Desire flamed through him, an urgent hunger that disgusted him.

He eased her off his lap and onto the bed. Once more she made a soft noise of protest, reaching out for him before her hand fell laxly onto the cover and she seemed to slip into a deeper sleep.

Frowning, he stood and surveyed her. He couldn't leave her like that—it would do her no good for her to sleep in saturated clothes.

So what the *hell* was he to do next?

The next morning, a little shaky but free from fever, Hani blessed modern medications and wondered who her rescuer— so very judgemental—had been. Kelt Gillan…

An unusual name for an unusual man. She could vaguely remember him picking her up, but after that was a blank, though with an odd little shiver she thought she'd never forget his voice, so cold and unsympathetic as he'd—what?

Ordered her to do something. Oh yes, of course. *Swallow the pills.* She gave a weak smile and lifted herself up on her elbow to check the time.

And realised she was in one of the loose cotton shifts she wore at night.

'How—?' she said aloud, a frown pleating her forehead. She sat up, and stared around the room. The dress she'd worn to the party was draped over the chair beside the wardrobe.

Colour burned her skin and she pressed her hands over her eyes. Her rescuer—whoever he was—must have not only stayed with her until the fever broke, but also changed her wet clothes.

Well, she was grateful, she decided sturdily. He'd done what was necessary, and although she cringed at the thought of him seeing and handling her almost naked body, it was obscurely comforting that he'd cared for her.

But for the rest of that day his angular, handsome face was never far from her mind, and with it came a reckless, potent thrill. Trying to reason it into submission didn't work. Instead of her wondering why she reacted so powerfully to the stranger when any other man's closeness repulsed her, the thought of his touch summoned treacherously tantalising thoughts.

Dim recollections of strong arms and a warmth that almost kept at bay the icy grip of the fever made her flush, a heat that faded when into her head popped another vagrant memory— the contempt in his tone when he'd asked her if she was drunk or drugged.

Although she'd never see him again, so she didn't care a bit what he thought of her…

CHAPTER TWO

THREE weeks later and several thousand kilometres further south, standing on a deck that overlooked a sweep of sand and a cooler Pacific Ocean than she was accustomed to, Hani scanned the faces of the five children in front of her. Though they ranged from a dark-haired, dark-eyed, copper-skinned beauty of about fourteen to a blond little boy slathered with so much sunscreen that his white skin glistened, their features showed they were closely related.

What would it be like to have a family—children of her own?

Her heart twisted and she repressed the thought. Not going to happen, ever.

It was the small blond boy who asked, 'What's your name?'

'Hannah,' she said automatically.

Her accent must have confused them, because the older girl said, 'Honey? That's a nice name.'

And the little boy nodded. 'Your skin's the same colour as honey. Is that why your mum called you that?'

In Tukuulu she'd been Hannah; she liked Honey better. Stifling the hard-won caution that told her it might also confuse anyone too curious, she said cheerfully, 'Actually, it's Hannah, but you can call me Honey if you want to. Now I've told you my name, you'd better tell me yours.'

They all blurted them out together, of course, but six years of teaching infants had instilled a few skills and she soon sorted them out. Hani asked the older girl, 'Kura, where do you live?'

'At Kiwinui,' she said importantly, clearly expecting everyone to know where Kiwinui was. When she realised it meant nothing to Hani, she added, 'It's in the next bay, but we're allowed to walk over the hill and come down here to play if we ask nicely. So we're asking.'

It would take a harder heart than Hani's to withstand the impact of five pairs of expectant eyes. 'I need to know first how good you are at swimming.'

'We're not going to swim because we have to have a grown-up with us when we do that,' Kura told her. 'Mum said so, and The Duke told us off when he caught us only paddling here, and the water only came up to our ankles.'

The *Duke*? Her tone invested the nickname with capitals and indicated that nobody messed with the man, whoever he was.

Curious, Hani asked, 'Who is the duke?'

They looked almost shocked. Kura explained, 'That's like being a prince or something. His nan wears a crown and when she dies his brother will be a duke too and he'll live in a big stone castle on a hill.' She turned and pointed to the headland behind them. 'He lives up there behind the pohutu-kawa trees.'

The Duke's brother, or The Duke? Hani repressed a smile. 'I'm happy for you to play here. Just come and tell me when you're going home again.'

With a whoop they set off, except for the small blond boy, whose name was Jamie. 'Why have you got green eyes?' he asked, staring at her.

'Because my mother had green eyes.' Hani repressed a familiar pang of pain. She and her brother had both inherited those eyes; every time she looked in the mirror she thought of Rafiq.

Surely she should be reconciled to never seeing him again by now!

Jamie nodded. 'They're nice. Why are you staying here?'

'I'm on holiday.' The day after her last attack of fever the principal had told her that if she didn't take up the offer to go to New Zealand—'long enough to get this fever out of your system'—the charity that ran the school couldn't accept responsibility for her welfare. Her air fares would be paid, and the beach house where she'd convalesce was rent-free.

Without exactly stating that they'd terminate her employment if she didn't go, he'd implied it so strongly she'd been persuaded to reluctantly leave the safety of Tukuulu.

Curiosity satisfied, Jamie said nonchalantly, 'See you later,' and scampered off to join the others.

Hani sat back down in the comfortable wicker chair on the deck. Airy and casually luxurious, the beach house was surprisingly big, with glass doors in every room opening out onto a wide wooden deck that overlooked the cove. Her landlord, an elderly man, had met her flight the previous night and driven her here to what he'd called a bach.

Remembering his very English accent, she smiled. No doubt those cut-glass vowels were why the children had decided he must be some sort of aristocrat.

After introducing himself very formally as Arthur Wellington, he'd said, 'The refrigerator and the pantry have been stocked with staples. If you need anything else, do ring the number on the calendar beside the telephone.'

Hani thanked him for that, but realised now that she'd missed telling him how much she appreciated being given the opportunity to stay here.

She'd do that when she paid him for the groceries he'd supplied.

On a long, soft sigh she took her gaze away from the children long enough to examine the cove. Sand like amber suede curved against the kingfisher expanse of water. Squinting against the bright sky, Hani eyed the headland where the landlord lived. Its steep slopes were hidden by more of the dark-leafed trees that lined the beach, their massive limbs swooping down over the sand.

A formal house to match her landlord's formal manner? She hoped not. It would look incongruous in this pristinely beautiful scene.

Loud shrieks from the beach dragged her attention back to the game taking place in front of the bach, one that involved much yelling, more laughter, and some frenzied racing around. For the first time in months she felt a stirring of energy.

Smiling, checking that little Jamie didn't get too close to the water, she failed to notice an intruder until he was almost at the cottage. The soft clink of harness alerting her, she swivelled around and saw a horse—a fine bay, strong enough to take its tall, powerfully built rider without effort.

Her startled gaze took in the rider. He sat easily on his mount—but that wasn't why her pulses revved into overdrive.

For a second—just long enough to terrify and delight her—he reminded her of her brother. Rafiq had the same coiled grace of strength and litheness, the same relaxed control of his mount.

The same air of authority.

Then she recalled when she'd seen this man before, and an odd, baseless panic froze the breath in her throat. In spite of the bout of fever she'd been suffering when she met him on Tukuulu, those hard-hewn features and hooded eyes were sharply etched into her memory.

As was the feel of his arms around her… And the knowledge that he'd stripped her saturated clothes from her and somehow managed to get her into the loose shift she wore at night.

What the *hell* was he doing here?

He swung down, looped the reins over a fencepost and opened the gate to come towards her. Subliminally intimidated by the arrogant angle of his head and the smooth, lethal grace of his stride, Hani forced herself to her feet, stiffening her spine and her knees.

Although tall for a woman, she couldn't match him. Her chin came up; unsmiling, breath locking in her throat, she watched him approach while a feverish awareness lifted the invisible hairs on the back of her neck.

He was—well, *gorgeous* was the only word she could come up with. Except that gorgeous made her think of male models, and this man looked like no male model she'd ever seen. That effortless, inborn air of command hardened his already bold features into an intimidating mask of force and power, emphasised by a cold steel-blue gaze and a thinning of his subtly sensuous mouth.

He was handsome enough to make any woman's heart shake—even one as frozen as hers—but something uncompromising and formidable about him set off alarms in every nerve.

He had to be The Duke. A swift stab of apprehension screwed her nerves even tighter. Felipe, the man she'd once thought she loved, had called himself a French count.

It was stupid of her, but the children's innocent misconception seemed somehow ominous.

Hani knew she should be relieved when he looked at her with a total lack of male interest. Scarily, she wasn't.

OK, so the last thing she wanted was a man to see her as

a sexual being, but… On Tukuulu he'd noticed her as a woman; now he looked at her with complete indifference.

And that stung.

Trying to keep this meeting on a sensible basis, she said warily, 'Hello. I didn't realise that you owned this place. Thank you so much for letting me stay here.'

'I hoped to see you looking a bit better,' he said curtly.

'I am much better.' Yes, her voice was fine—crisp, just as cool and impersonal as his, a far cry from her slurred tone that night at the ceremony. Meeting his merciless survey with an assumption of confidence, she hid her uncertainty with a shrug. 'Another thing I have to thank you for is your rescue of me.'

One black brow lifted. 'It was nothing; I happened to be the closest person around.'

Heat tinged her skin. Trying to sound professional and assured, she said crisply, 'It was very kind of you. I don't remember much—' only the sound of his voice, calm and re-assuring, and the wonderful comfort of his arms when he'd held her until the shivering stopped '—but I know I didn't change myself.'

His eyes narrowed slightly. 'Once the fever had broken I went back to the school dance floor, but everyone had gone by then. It didn't seem a good idea for you to sleep in wet clothes, so I removed your dress.' In a coldly formidable tone, he finished, 'I behaved as a brother might have.'

Colour burned into her skin. Hoping her words mingled the right blend of gratitude and distance, she said, 'Yes—well, I thought as much.' And then, changing the subject without finesse, 'Thanks again for being generous enough to let me stay in this lovely place.'

'You've thanked me enough,' he said a little curtly, adding with a faint smile, 'I went to school with your principal. When he asked if his teachers could use this bach I agreed. It's not used very often, and it seems a waste to have it sit here empty. You're the third teacher to come here, and I expect there will be others.'

So that was the connection. And he was making sure she didn't think she was special.

She said with cool assurance, 'I'm grateful. But to make things very clear, I was neither drunk nor drugged that night in Tukuulu.'

One straight black brow lifted. 'I wondered if you'd remember that. I'm sorry for jumping to conclusions—it didn't take me long to realise you were ill.'

For some reason she wasn't prepared to explore, she didn't want his apology. 'I sent you a letter thanking you for your help.'

'Yes, your principal passed it on.'

He hadn't answered. Well, for heaven's sake, she hadn't expected him to.

Without inflection, he said, 'I'm glad I was there when you needed someone. I'm Kelt Crysander-Gillan—although I don't use the first part of my surname—and I live just up the hill.'

Nothing about being some sort of aristocrat, she noted. Clearly The Duke was just a nickname, perhaps because of the double-barrelled name. They mightn't be common in New Zealand.

And he *looked* like a duke, someone of importance, his very presence a statement of authority. A very sexy duke, sexier than any other duke she'd ever met...

One who'd taken her clothes off and seen her naked...

Firmly she tamped down a sizzle of adrenalin. 'And of course you know that I'm Han-*Hannah* Court.'

Oh, he'd really unnerved her! For the first time in years

she'd almost given him her real name, catching it back only just in time. Startled, she automatically held out her hand.

'Welcome to New Zealand,' he said gravely, and his long, lean fingers closed around hers.

Her heart picked up speed. *Cool it*, she commanded her runaway pulse fiercely while he shook hands.

There was no reason for the swift sizzle of sensation that shocked her every nerve. Acting on pure blind instinct, Hani jerked her hand free.

Kelt Gillan's brows met for a taut second above his blade of a nose, but he turned when the children chose that moment to surge up from the beach, their shouted greetings a melee of sound.

He silenced them with a crisp, 'All right, calm down, you lot.'

She expected them to shuffle their feet, but although they obediently stayed silent their wide smiles told her he was popular with them.

Amazing, she thought, watching as he said something to each of them. And again she remembered Felipe, her first and only lover. He'd had no time for children; there was no profit to be made from them…

Kelt Gillan said, 'Miss Court has been ill and needs a lot of rest, so I want you to play on the homestead beach until she's better.'

Their attention swivelled back to her.

Into the silence Jamie said earnestly, 'I was sick too, Honey. I had mumps and my throat was sore and I couldn't eat anything 'cept ice cream and jelly and scrambled eggs.'

'And soup,' the lovely Kura reminded him officiously.

He pulled a face. 'And some soup.'

'I'm getting much better now,' Hani said, smiling at him. 'And I'm lucky—I can eat anything I like.'

'Honey?' Kelt said on an upward inflection, that taunting brow lifting again as his cool gaze inspected her face. 'I thought your name was Hannah?'

'I'll have to learn to talk like a New Zealander,' she said lightly, irritated by the colour that heated her cheekbones. In the last six years she'd worked hard to banish any vestige of the soft cadences of her birth country.

'Actually, it suits you,' he said, a sardonic note colouring his deep voice. He turned back to the children. 'All right, off you go.'

They turned obediently, all but Jamie. 'Where do you live?' he asked Hani.

Nowhere... 'On a hot little island called Tukuulu a long way over the sea from here.'

An older girl, Jamie's, sister—cousin?—turned. 'Come *on*, Jamie,' she commanded importantly, and the boy gave Hani a swift grin and scampered off.

'What charming children. Are they siblings?' she asked into the suddenly oppressive silence.

'Siblings and cousins. In New Zealand the term *whanau* is used to denote the extended family,' the man beside her said.

'You didn't need to warn them off,' she told him. 'I like children.'

Kelt Gillan said succinctly, 'Honey or Hannah or whoever you are, you're here to convalesce, and it's no part of that healing process to act as unpaid babysitter. Your principal asked me to make sure you didn't overexert yourself.'

His words set off a flicker of memory. The night he'd unhooked her from the coconut palm and carried her home he'd spoken in exactly that controlled, uncompromising tone. As though she were an idiot, she thought angrily.

She didn't care what Kelt thought, but it wasn't fair to

spoil the children's pleasure. 'Both you and he are very thoughtful, but I'm quite capable of making decisions like that for myself. Believe me, it didn't hurt me or tire me or worry me to sit in the sun and watch them. I enjoyed it.'

'Perhaps so,' he said inflexibly, 'but that's not the point. You're here to rest and regain your strength. I'll make sure their parents understand that they stay in Homestead Bay. Don't fret about curtailing their fun—they'll play quite happily there.'

Behind him his horse lifted its head from lipping the grass and took a step sideways, its powerful muscles fluid beneath satiny skin.

In Moraze, her homeland, herds of wild horses roamed the grassy plateau country that surrounded the central volcanic peaks. Descended from Arabian steeds, they'd been brought there by her ancestor, a renegade French aristocrat who'd settled the island with a rag-tag train of soldiers and a beautiful Arabian wife.

Hani's parents had given her one of those horses for her third birthday…

Long dead, her parents and that first gentle mount, and it was years since she'd ridden.

Hani was ambushed by a pang of homesickness, an aching sense of loss so fierce it must have shown in her face.

'Sit down!' Kelt said sharply, unable to stop himself from taking a step towards her.

One hand came up, warning him off. Apart from that abrupt gesture she didn't move, and the flash of something tight and almost desperate in her expression disappeared. Her black hair swirled around her shoulders in a cloud of fiery highlights as she angled her chin at him.

Looking him straight in the eye, she said in a gentle voice with a distinct edge to it, 'Mr Gillan, I'm neither an invalid nor a child. I make my own decisions and I'm perfectly capable of looking after myself.'

He examined her closely, but her lovely face was shut against him, that moment of despair—if that was what it had been—replaced by aloof self-assurance.

Kelt chose to live in New Zealand for his own good reasons, one of them being that Kiwinui had been in his grandfather's family for over a hundred years, and he felt a deep emotional link to the place. But as a scion of the royal family of Carathia he'd been born to command. Backed by their grandmother, the Grand Duchess, he and his brother had turned their backs on tradition and gone into business together as soon as he'd left university. Between them they'd built up a hugely successful enterprise, a leader in its field that had made them both billionaires.

Women had chased him mercilessly since he'd left school. Although none had touched his heart, he treated his mistresses with courtesy, and had somehow acquired a legendary status as a lover.

Women were an open book to him.

Until now. One part of him wanted to tell Hannah Court that while she was on Kiwinui she was under his protection; the other wanted to sweep that elegant body into his arms and kiss her perfect mouth into submission.

Instead, he said crisply, 'And I'll do what I consider to be best for the situation. If you need anything, there's a contact number by the telephone.'

Hani looked at him with cool, unreadable green eyes, the colour of New Zealand's most precious greenstone. 'Thank you; Mr Wellington told me about that.'

Kelt shrugged. 'Arthur works for me.'

Her head inclined almost regally. 'I see.'

'Tell me if another bout of fever hits you.'

'It's not necessary—I have medication to deal with it.' Another hint of soft apricot tinged her exotic cheekbones when she continued, 'As you found out, it works very quickly.'

Clearly, she had no intention of giving an inch. He wondered how old she was—mid-twenties, he guessed, but something in her bearing and the direct glance of those amazing eyes reminded him of his grandmother, the autocratic Grand Duchess who'd kept her small realm safe through wars and threats for over fifty years.

Dismissing such a ridiculous thought, he said, 'Do you drive?'

'Of course.' Again that hint of appraisal in her tone, in her gaze.

'Any idea of New Zealand's road rules?' he asked, making no attempt to hide the ironic note in his voice.

'I'm a quick learner. But how far is it to the nearest village? If it's close enough I can walk there when I need anything.'

'It's about five kilometres—too far for you to walk in the summer heat.'

Warily wondering if he'd given up any idea of looking after her—because he seemed like a man with an over-developed protective streak and a strong will—she pointed out, 'I'm used to heat.'

'If that were true, you wouldn't be convalescing here.' And while she was absorbing that dig, he went on, 'And somehow I doubt very much that you're accustomed to walking five kilometres while carrying groceries.'

Uneasily aware of the unsettling glint in his cold blue eyes, Hani shrugged. 'Don't worry about me, Mr Gillan. I won't be a bother to anyone.'

A single black brow climbed, but all he said was, 'Call me Kelt. Most New Zealanders are very informal.'

She most emphatically didn't want to call him anything! However, she'd already established her independence, so, hiding her reluctance, she returned courteously, 'Then you must call me Hannah.'

He lifted one black brow. 'You know, I think I prefer Honey. Hannah is—very Victorian. And you're not.'

The slight—very slight—pause before he said Victorian made her wonder if he'd been going to say virginal.

If so, he couldn't be more wrong.

Far from virginal, far from Victorian, she thought with an aching regret. 'I'd prefer Hannah, thank you.'

His smile was tinged by irony. 'Hannah it shall be. If you feel up to it, I'd like you to come to dinner tomorrow night.'

Caution warned her to prevaricate, fudge the truth a little and say she wasn't well enough to socialise, but she'd already cut off that avenue of escape when she'd made it clear she didn't need to be looked after by—well, by *anyone*, she thought sturdily.

Especially not this man, whose unyielding maleness affected her so strongly she could feel his impact on every cell. Even politely setting limits as she'd just done had energised her, set her senses tingling, and every time she looked into that hard, handsome face she felt a hot, swift tug of—of lust, she reminded herself bitterly.

And she knew—only too well—what that could lead to.

However, he was her landlord. She owed him for several things; his impersonal care on Tukuulu, the refrigerator full of groceries.

Changing her wet clothes…

Ignoring the deep-seated pulse of awareness, she said, 'That's very kind of you. What time would you like me to be there?'

'I'll pick you up at seven,' he told her with another keen glance. 'Until then, take things slowly.'

His long-legged strides across the lawn presented her with a disturbing view of broad shoulders and narrow hips above lean, heavily muscled thighs. He dressed well too—his trousers had been tailored for him, and she'd almost bet his shirt had too.

Very sexy, she thought frivolously, quelling the liquid heat that consumed her. Some lucky men were born with that *it* factor, a compelling masculinity that attracted every female eye.

And she'd bet the subject of her letting someone know if she had another attack of fever would come up again.

A few paces away he swivelled, catching her intent, fascinated look. A challenge flared in his narrowed eyes; he understood exactly what effect he was having on her.

Hot with shame, she wanted to turn away, but Kelt held her gaze for a second, his own enigmatic and opaque.

However, when he spoke his voice was crisp and aloof. 'If you need anything, let me know.'

It sounded like a classical *double entendre*; if he'd been Felipe it would have been.

It was time she stopped judging men by Felipe's standards. The years in Tukuulu had shown her that most men were not like him, and there was no reason to believe that Kelt Gillan wasn't a perfectly decent farmer with a face like one of the more arrogant gods, an overdeveloped protective instinct and more than his share of formidable male presence.

'Thank you—I will,' she said remotely.

And produced a smile she held until he'd swung up onto his horse and guided it away.

Her face felt frozen when she took refuge in the cottage and stood listening as the sound of hooves dwindled into the warm, sea-scented air. She shivered, crossing her arms and rubbing her hands over her prickling skin.

Again? she thought in mindless panic. The unbidden, unwanted surge of sensual appetite humiliated her. Why on earth was she attracted to dangerous men?

Not that she'd realised Felipe was dangerous when she first met him. And for some unfounded and quite illogical reason she couldn't believe Kelt would turn out to be like Felipe.

As well, the heady clamour Kelt Gillan summoned in her was different—more earthy and primal, nothing like the fascinated excitement she'd felt when Felipe had pursued her. He'd seemed such a glamorous, fascinating man, with his French title and his famous friends. At eighteen she'd been so green she'd run headlong into peril without a second thought.

Six years older, and much better able to look after herself, she sensed a different danger in Kelt Gillan—a more elemental attraction without the calculation that had marked Felipe's seduction.

Desperate to take her mind off her enigmatic landlord and his unnerving effect on her, she went across to the kitchen and put on the electric kettle.

'Displacement activity,' she said aloud, a mirthless smile curling her mouth as she spooned coffee into the plunger.

Wrapping her attraction to Felipe in a romantic haze had got her into deep trouble; this time she'd face her inconvenient response to Kelt Gillan squarely. Coffee mug in hand, she walked out onto the deck and stood looking out over the sea.

No emotions, no fooling herself that this was love, no silly claptrap about soulmates. She'd already been down that track and it had led to humiliation and heartbreak and terror. Felipe had played on her naivety, setting himself out to charm her into submission.

And succeeding utterly, so that she'd gradually been manipulated into an affair without fully realising where she was heading. When she'd realised what sort of man he was she'd tried to break away, only to have him bind her to him with the cruellest, most degrading chains. To free herself she'd had to sacrifice everything—self-respect, love for her brother, her very future.

Closing her eyes against the dazzling shimmer of the sun on the bay, she thought wearily that she hadn't planned for her sacrifice to last the rest of her life.

In fact, she hadn't planned on any further life.

Well, a Mediterranean fisherman with smuggling as a sideline had seen to it that she'd survived. She shivered, and for a foolish few seconds wondered if Kelt Gillan had brought on another attack of fever.

No, her chill was due to memories she wished she could banish.

Only right now she needed them to remind her that no person could ever see into the heart of another, especially when they were blinded by lust.

Ruthlessly she dragged her mind back to the present, and concentrated on the problem at hand—her feelings for Kelt Gillan.

'Just think rationally,' she told herself.

What she felt when she looked at Kelt was a powerful physical attraction for a man both formidable and enormously attractive—a primal arousal with a scientific basis. Humans instinctively recognised the people they'd make superb babies with.

Logic played no part in it, nor did common sense. But both could be used as weapons against it, and if she'd learned anything these past six years it was that any relationship between lovers needed much more than desire to be a success.

And there would be no babies for her, ever.

So she'd have dinner with Kelt and then she'd stay well away from him.

Hani missed the children the next day, and not for the first time wondered what on earth she was going to do for three months. Too many empty weeks stretched before her, leaving her far too much time to think, to remember. Without the steady routine of school she faced more than simple boredom; she'd have to deal with emptiness.

At least the cottage had a set of bookshelves stuffed with books of all ages and quite a few magazines. After a brief walk along the beach that reminded her again how unfit she was, she sank into a chair on the deck with a cup of tea and a volume on New Zealand that looked interesting.

She flicked it open and saw a bookplate. Kelt Crysander-Gillan, it stated.

'Unusual,' she said aloud. There was an inscription too, but she turned the page on that, feeling as though she was prying.

With a name like that, and if Kelt's air of forceful authority had led to a nickname like The Duke, imaginative children could well come up with a crown-wearing grandmother somewhere in Europe.

At precisely seven o'clock he arrived to collect her as the sun was dipping behind the forest-covered mountains that ran down the central spine of Northland's long, narrow peninsula. He drove a large, luxurious four-wheel-drive, which gave Hani a moment of heart-sickness; her brother used to drive the same make...

Hani pushed the thought to the back of her mind. Rafiq thought she was dead, and that was the way she had to stay.

And then Kelt got out, lithe and long-legged, powerfully

magnetic and urbane in a short-sleeved shirt that echoed the steely colour of his eyes, and casually elegant trousers, and the bitter, heart-sick memories vanished, replaced by a reckless excitement.

When he opened the gate she went hastily out into the serene evening. The bach might be his, but she didn't want to sense his dominating presence whenever she walked into the living room.

She knew she looked good. For an hour that afternoon she'd pored over her scanty wardrobe, startled to find herself wistfully remembering her favourites amongst the designer clothes she'd worn in her old life.

In the end she'd chosen a modest dress she'd found in a shop in Tukuulu's small capital city. Although it was a little too loose on her, the clear salmon hue burnished the gold of her skin and the warm highlights in her dark hair.

Tempted to go without make-up, she decided after a critical survey of her reflection that a naked face might make her look conspicuous, and her security depended on blending in. So she compromised on lipstick a slightly deeper shade than her dress, and pinned her badly cut hair off her face with two frangipani clips made from the moonbeam shimmer of pearl shell.

Kelt waited for her beside the gate. Her shoulders held a little stiffly to hide an absurd self-consciousness, she walked towards him, sensing a darker, more elemental level beneath his coolly sophisticated exterior. Trying to ignore the smouldering need in the pit of her stomach, she saw him as a warrior, riding his big bay gelding into battle…

Not, she thought with an inner shiver, a man to cross swords with.

With a carefully neutral smile she met his gaze, and in a

charged moment her wilful memory sabotaged the fragile veneer of her composure by supplying a repeat of how it had felt when he'd carried her—the powerful litheness of his gait, the subtle flexion of his body as he'd lifted her, his controlled strength…

CHAPTER THREE

KELT examined her face with the impersonal keenness of a doctor. 'How are you?' he asked, opening the door of the car.

Hani's smile faded. His persistent view of her as an invalid was—*demeaning*, she decided on a spurt of irritation that didn't quite mask a deeper, more dangerous emotion. After all, in the light of her unexpected attraction, it was far safer if he saw her as an invalid than as a woman.

A desirable woman.

With a hint of frost in her tone she answered, 'Fine, thank you.' And met his scrutiny with head held high and an immobile face that belied the unsteady rhythm of her heart.

'You still have dark circles under your eyes. Lack of sleep?'

Strangely enough, for the first time since she'd come to this side of the world all those years ago she'd slept deeply and dreamlessly, waking with an energy that seemed alien.

'No, not at all,' she told him evenly. Steering the conversation away from her illness, she asked, 'How far away is your house?'

'About a kilometre by road; half that distance if you walk across the paddocks—which I don't want you to do.' He set the car in motion.

'Why?'

He sent her a narrow glance. 'You could spook the cattle.' After a pause, he added, 'Or they might spook you.'

Hani examined some large, square animals, their coats glowing deep red-gold in the rays of the evening sun. 'They don't *look* excitable, but your point is well taken.'

Not that she planned to be going cross-country.

'And you?' he asked levelly, turning across a cattle grid.

She waited until the rattling died away before saying, 'I don't understand.'

'Are you excitable?'

Startled, she looked across at him, saw an enigmatic smile tuck in the corners of his hard mouth, and was shocked again by a fierce tug of arousal, sweet as honey, dangerous as dynamite.

Surely he wasn't *flirting* with her?

She felt winded and fascinated at the same time until a moment's reflection produced sanity. Of course he wasn't coming on to her. Not unless he was the sort of man who indulged in meaningless flirtations with any available woman.

Somehow she didn't want to believe he'd be so indiscriminate. A man with Kelt Gillan's effortless masculinity could have any woman he wanted, and he must know it. And unlike Felipe he had nothing to gain from seducing her.

In her most sedate tone she said, 'Not in the least. Teachers can't afford to be volatile. It's *very* bad for discipline.'

That should tell him she wasn't in the market for a holiday affair. To clinch it, she said, 'Don't worry, I won't walk in your fields or excite your cattle.'

'Paddocks,' he said laconically, explaining, 'New Zealanders call anything with animals in it a paddock. *Fields* are what we play sport on, and as far as we're concerned meadows don't exist.' He nodded at the setting sun. 'And that range of hills to the west is covered in native bush, not forest or woods.'

Intrigued, she said, 'I do know about bush. One of the Australian teachers at the school explained it to me. It's fascinating how countries colonised by the same power could develop such different words to describe things. In South Africa—'

She stopped suddenly, her mind freezing in dismay, then hastily tried to cover the slip by asking the first question that came to mind. 'What are those trees, the ones that grow in groups in nearly all your f—paddocks?'

'They're totara trees.'

'Oh. Do they flower?'

'Not noticeably—they're conifers. As for terminology— well, the world would be a boring place if we were all the same. Settlers in different countries adjusted to different conditions.' He paused a beat before adding casually, 'You're not South African, are you?'

'No,' she said, dry-throated.

'But clearly you've been there.'

Trying to banish any reluctance from her voice, she admitted, 'I spent a holiday there when I was young.'

He accepted that without comment. 'So what made a young Englishwoman decide to spend years teaching in a village school in a place like Tukuulu? The lure of tropical islands I can understand, but once you'd got to Tukuulu and realised it's really nothing but a volcano with a huge mine on it— beaches of dead coral, only one fleapit of a hotel, no night life—what kept you there?'

A little shudder tightened her skin, but she kept her gaze fixed steadily ahead. Let him probe as much as he liked; she had her story down pat.

'I wanted to help. And they were desperate for teachers. It's really hard for them to keep staff. But the principal is your friend so you must know that.'

After a moment's pause he said, 'How long do you plan to live there?'

'For several years yet,' she evaded.

'I imagine it's unusual for anyone to stay for long in a Pacific backwater like Tukuulu.' Let alone a young Englishwoman, his tone implied.

'You're a sophisticated man but you don't seem to mind living on a remote cattle station in a Pacific backwater like New Zealand,' she retorted sweetly.

He gave her swift, ironic smile. 'Don't let any New Zealander hear you call the place a backwater. We're a proud people with plenty to be proud of.'

'The Tukuuluans are proud too, and doing their best to move into the modern world without losing the special things that make their culture so distinctive.'

'I suspect that's an impossible task,' he said cynically.

'I hope not. And I like to think I'm helping them in a small way.'

They crossed another cattle grid and drove through a grove of the big trees she'd noticed before, their great branches almost touching the ground.

'Oh,' she exclaimed in involuntary pleasure, 'the leaves are silver underneath! From a distance the trees look so sombre—yet how pretty they must be when there's any wind.'

'Very, and when they flower in a month or so they'll be great torches of scarlet and crimson and maroon. I'll take you over the top of the hill so you can look over Kiwinui and get some idea of the lie of the land.'

Kelt slowed the vehicle to a stop, switching off the engine so that the silence flowed in around them, bringing with it the sweet scent of damp grass and the ever-present salt of the sea.

Gaze fixed in front of her, Hani said on an indrawn breath, 'This is glorious.'

'Yes.'

That was all, but his controlled voice couldn't hide the pride of ownership as he gazed out at his vast domain.

At the foot of the hill a sweeping bay fronted a large, almost flat, grassed area with what appeared to be a small settlement to one side. More huge trees fringed the beach and a long jetty stitched its way out into the water towards a sleek black yacht and a large motorboat.

'The working part of Kiwinui,' Kelt told her. He leaned slightly towards her so he could point. 'Cattle yards, the woolshed, implement sheds and the workers' cottages.'

Hani's breath stopped in her throat. He was too close, so near she could see the fine grain of his tanned skin, so close her nostrils were teased by a faint, wholly male scent. Hot little shivers snaked down her spine, and some locked, previously untouched part of her splintered into shards.

Desperate to overcome the clamour of her response, she scrambled from the car and took a couple of steps away. When Kelt joined her she didn't dare look at him.

Several measured breaths helped calm her racing heartbeats, and as soon as she could trust her voice she waved a hand at the nearest hill. 'What's that mown strip over there?'

'An airstrip. Kiwinui is too big to fertilise except from the air.' His words held a lick of amusement, as though he had sensed her stormy reaction to him and found it entertaining.

Mortified and bewildered, Hani wondered if the forced intimacy of their first meeting had somehow forged this—this wild physical reaction.

Yes, that had to be it. Relief eased her shame; her response was not some weird aberration or a frightening return to the servitude of her affair with Felipe. Kelt had held her closely, given her comfort while she fought the fever—changed her clothes—so naturally her body and mind responded to his presence.

Well, they could stop it right now. Discipline was what was needed here. She didn't want to feel like this every time she saw him, completely unable to control herself!

Trying to block out his presence, she concentrated on the view. To the north a series of ranges scalloped the coast, the lower-slopes pasture, the gullies and heights covered by forests—no, *native bush*—that reminded her of the jungles of Moraze. Between them she glimpsed a coast of sandy beaches and more green paddocks.

Stretching to the eastern horizon was the restless sea, its kingfisher-coloured expanse broken by a large, high island that formed an offshore barrier.

And, to cap it all, she heard the high, exquisite trill of a bird, joy rendered into song that soared into the golden light of the setting sun. Pierced by sudden delight, Hani dragged in a long breath.

And even as she thrilled to it, she knew that the man beside her somehow intensified her mood, her appreciation, as though his presence had the power to magnify her responses.

Felipe had never done that.

Hani swallowed. 'It's so beautiful,' she managed. 'What's the bird that's singing?'

He gave her a sharp look. 'It's a thrush,' he said. 'They were introduced here by the early settlers. He'll be perched on top of one of the pohutukawa trees.'

Bother, she thought on a surge of irrational panic, oh, bother and double-bother! Too late she remembered a poem

she'd learned at school; if she were as English as her accen
she'd probably recognise a thrush's song…

On the other hand, why should Kelt be suspicious? And
even if he was, he wouldn't be able to find out who she was
Once she'd escaped Felipe she'd covered her tracks so wel
that even he, with all his resources in brutal men and tainted
money, hadn't been able to hunt her down.

Kelt told her, 'The original homestead was down on the
flat, quite close to the workers' cottages you can see, bu
when it burned down early in the twentieth century the new
one was built up here.'

Hani filed away the fact that in New Zealand—at least in the
countryside—substantial houses were called cottages. 'What':
the difference between a cottage and a homestead and a bach?

'A bach is a holiday cottage, always casual, very beachy
They used to be small and primitive, but nowadays that isn'
necessarily so.'

'No indeed,' she said, thinking of the bach she wa
staying in.

He gave her an ironic smile. 'My grandmother made quit
a few renovations to it. She enjoyed the simple life for a shor
time, but had no intention of giving up any comfort.'

His grandmother had clearly been a sophisticate. Wel
Kiwinui was a big farm, and Hani didn't need to know the siz
of his bank balance to accept that Kelt was a wealthy man.

Kelt said, 'As for workers' cottages, the term's a hangove
from the days when they were fairly basic. Nowadays n
worker would be happy with basic housing, and even if he wa
his wife certainly wouldn't be, so they're usually good-size
family homes.'

'And a homestead is where the owner of the farm lives?
she guessed.

'Either the owner or manager's house on a farm or station

Hani nodded. 'Is this estate—Kiwinui—a farm or a station? What's the difference?'

'Basically a station is a larger farm—usually settled early in New Zealand's history. The first Gillan arrived here about a hundred and forty years ago. And yes, Kiwinui is a station.'

Hani looked down at the bay, frowning at the abrupt change of colour in the water. 'It looks as though it gets deep very quickly there,' she observed. 'Surely my cove—' colouring, she hastily corrected herself '—I mean, the one with the bach, would be safer for the children? I truly don't mind them coming, and I'd be happy to supervise their swimming. And young Kura seems very capable.'

'We'll see how things go.' His tone was non-committal. 'When those dark circles disappear then perhaps the children can pay you visits.'

Hani sent him a sharp look. 'The darkness under my eyes will go in its own good time. And I enjoy children's company.'

'You'll enjoy it more when you're stronger.'

His tone left no room for negotiation. Fuming, Hani decided that autocratic wasn't emphatic enough to describe him. Clearly he was accustomed to giving orders and seeing them obeyed.

And yet—she didn't feel suffocated as she had when she'd fancied herself in love with Felipe.

But then, after the first few times she'd never argued with Felipe. Unpleasant things happened to those who crossed him.

Chilled, she turned to get back into the car.

Kelt retraced their path, turning off over a cattle grid when they reached the drive to the homestead. More great trees shaded them, deciduous ones with fresh green foliage. Amongst them she recognised a flame tree, and a pang of homesickness tore through her, so painful she bit her lip and turned her head away. On Moraze the flame trees bloomed like a cloak of fire across the island…

You'll never see Moraze again, she reminded herself starkly

Kelt's fingers tightened on the wheel. The sheen of moisture in her great green eyes struck at something fundamental in him. Just what the hell was going on inside that black head with its gleaming fiery highlights?

Probably nothing more than a lack of control due to her prolonged illness.

Yet behind Hannah Court's cool, serene facade he sensed something stronger, more deeply emotional than a physical weakness, and had to repress an urgent desire to tell her that whatever her problems, he'd probably be able to help.

This fierce urge to protect was something new, and he distrusted it. Because he avoided breaking hearts, he'd always made sure his lovers had been capable of looking after themselves.

Damn it, he didn't want to lust after a woman who was here to recuperate from a severe bout of tropical fever. So it was infuriating that he couldn't prise the image of Hannah, sleek and desirable in the hot, tropical night, from his mind. He felt like some lecherous voyeur.

Abruptly he asked, 'How long have you been driving?'

Her brows lifted, but she answered mildly enough. 'Since I was sixteen.'

For some reason—one he wasn't prepared to examine—her dismissive tone exasperated Kelt. 'And do you have an international licence?'

'Yes.'

He braked as they came up to the portico of his home. 'I'll lend you a vehicle, but you'd better read New Zealand's road rules before you take it out.'

She gave him a startled glance. 'That's very kind of you but—'

'That way you'll be independent,' he said coolly.

Hani chided herself for feeling deflated. Naturally he wouldn't want a total stranger relying on him for transport. Yet her pride baulked at accepting the use of a car.

'Are you sure? I mean—you don't know anything about me. And lending me a car isn't necessary—'

'I've lent the same car to every other teacher who's stayed at the bach, and so far it hasn't had a scratch.' His tone was amused yet definite. 'If I thought you'd break the mould I wouldn't be offering.'

'I—well, thank you very much.' It didn't seem enough, but all she could think of was to repeat lamely, 'It's very kind of you.'

The vehicle stopped. The warm light of the westering sun emphasised the classical framework of his face as he turned to her. In a voice that gave nothing away, he said, 'Welcome to my home,' before opening the door and getting out.

Awkwardly she unclipped herself and scrambled free, wondering why she'd been so affected by the unsmiling look that accompanied his conventional words.

Cool it, she commanded herself; stop seeing things that don't exist. As with the offer of a car, he wasn't being personal. No doubt he said exactly the same words to everyone who came to his house for the first time. She had to stop foolishly seeking hidden meanings in every steel-blue glance, every alteration of tone in the deep voice.

Farming, she decided with a slight shock while she absorbed the full extent of the house, must have been exceedingly profitable during the first quarter of the twentieth century when this was built. The big wooden building had been designed in an Arts and Crafts style that fitted seamlessly into the ageless, almost primeval land and seascape.

Kelt showed no sign of pride when he escorted her to the

door and opened it. Did he take it for granted—as she, in her self-centred youth, had viewed the *castello*, her family home in Moraze?

Trying not to stare around like a tourist, she said, 'This is very beautiful.'

'Thank you,' he responded gravely.

Feeling foolish and gushing, she asked, 'Have you lived here all your life?'

He didn't look at her. 'No.' After a pause so slight she barely noticed he went on, 'My mother wasn't a New Zealander, and I spent quite a lot of time in her country. However, this is my home.'

Another door opened further down, and a middle-aged man came through—her driver from the airport, carrying a large fish in a flax basket. He stopped abruptly.

Absurdly cheered by a familiar face, Hani smiled at him, and said, 'Hello, Mr Wellington. How nice to see you again.'

'Nice to see you again too, Miss Court,' he responded courteously, adding, 'And my name is Arthur.'

Kelt said, 'Hannah thought you owned Kiwinui.'

The older man looked a little taken aback. 'There's only one master here, Miss Court.' His tone indicated she just might have committed sacrilege. He indicated the basket and said, 'I hope you like fish.'

Trying to ease the tension that knotted her nerves, she told him, 'I love it.'

'Good.' He beamed at her. 'This is snapper, freshly caught with my own fair hands today. But when you come next time I'll make sure we have beef—I know it can be difficult to get good beef in some of the smaller islands in the Pacific Ocean.'

'It is, and I'll enjoy it enormously.' Not that she planned to come again...

He nodded and disappeared through another door, presumably into the kitchen.

Kelt indicated a door further down the hall. 'This way.'

The room he took her into opened out onto a terrace; the sun had almost sunk beneath the ranges and the clouds were edged with gold and vivid raspberry and ruby highlights. Hani looked around her, insensibly relaxing in the gracious room, one wall a bank of French windows that opened out onto a terrace. Wide stone steps led down to a lawn surrounded by shrub and flower borders that blended into taller trees.

'Oh, your garden is magnificent.' She gazed across the expanse of stone flagging and took a deep breath, relishing the fresh, summery scent of new-mown grass. Nothing could have been a greater contrast to the school, set in a landscape scarred by its huge mine.

Kelt must have picked up on her thoughts. 'A little different from Tukuulu.'

'A lot different.' This was just an ordinary social occasion, so behave like a normal person, she told herself.

Her appreciative smile faded a little when she met his hooded gaze, but she kept it pinned to her lips. 'Unfortunately the mine is Tukuulu's only source of income.'

'It doesn't look as though its owners care much about their neighbours,' he said austerely.

'I suppose you can't blame them, but—well, most of the mine-workers' children go to the school. You'd think they'd give it some support. That's the problem with big conglomerates owned by people from overseas who have no personal interest in the people they're employing.'

She'd spoken a little heatedly, and he sent her another keen look. Curiosity drove her to ask, 'Was it the first time you'd been to Tukuulu?'

'Yes. Your principal's been suggesting a visit to me for years but it's never been convenient before.'

Hani found it hard to imagine what Kelt had in common with the slightly older man who'd devoted his life to the school he ran on a shoestring.

He went on, 'He needs help, of course, and he'll probably get it. He's an expert at arm-twisting.'

That might be so, but Kelt didn't seem a man who'd yield to persuasion if he didn't want to. 'It's just as well he is,' she said crisply. 'The Tukuuluan government is pushed for money, so the school doesn't get much from them.'

Nodding, Kelt asked, 'Can I get you a drink? Wine? Something a little stronger? Or without alcohol?'

'Wine, thank you, if you have a light white.'

The wine he poured for her had a faint golden tinge, and the flavour was intense—a sensation-burst of freshness that almost persuaded her she was drinking champagne.

In spite of—or perhaps *because* of, she thought mordantly—being so acutely aware of him, she enjoyed Kelt's company. It was stimulating to match his incisive conversation, and a little to her surprise she discovered was he had a sense of humour. The half-hour or so before the meal went quickly.

Yet she had the feeling she was being tested, that for him the innocuous conversation was motivated by something more than social politeness. His hard eyes were always hooded, and she found herself weighing her words before she spoke.

That was worrying; she'd spent the past six years polishing a rather shallow, cheerful teacher persona that seemed to convince everyone she'd met.

Except this man. This man she was fiercely, *mindlessly* attracted to.

So, what was new? She'd felt lust before, and it had taken her into degradation and a never-ending fear that still kept her a prisoner in hiding.

And although there seemed to be a vast difference between her response to Felipe and her host for the evening, it was still lust. Better by far to ignore it—to pretend that she wasn't affected a bit by Kelt, that she didn't notice every tiny thing about him from the boldly arrogant lines of his profile to the easy grace of his movements. Even the sight of his lean, tanned hands on the white tablecloth over dinner sent shuddery little stabs of excitement through her.

Forget that night in Tukuulu. A cold shiver tightened her skin when she thought of what Felipe would do in the same situation. He'd take full advantage of her helplessness and vulnerability.

Kelt hadn't. And she had to respect him for that.

Dinner was served in a conservatory. Intoxicating perfume from the clusters of soft, creamy-pink flowers on a potted frangipani drifted through the room; Hani had always loved the fragrance, but here it seemed imbued with sensuous overtones she'd never noticed before.

But then, everything seemed suddenly more…more *more*, she thought, half-terrified at such foolishness. Colours seemed more luxurious, the food tasted sublime, and light gleamed off the glass and silverware with greater intensity. Just the sound of Kelt's voice produced a blooming of inner heat, a kind of nervous anticipation mixed with an excitement.

'Are you cold?' he asked.

'Not at all.'

Leaning back in his chair, he surveyed her through slightly narrowed eyes. 'You shivered.'

He saw too much. She said stiffly, 'It's nothing. Just someone walking over my grave.'

To her astonishment he leaned forward and covered her hand. His was large and warm and relentless; when shock jerked her backwards his fingers closed around hers, holding her still.

'You *are* cold,' he said, those eyes narrowing further so that he was watching her through a screen of long black lashes.

Apprehension froze her into stillness. But he wasn't like Felipe, and his touch didn't repel her…

She swallowed and said in a constricted voice, 'I'm warm enough, thank you. Let me go.'

Although he released his grip his hard gaze didn't leave her face. 'I'll turn on some heat.'

Her eyes widened. However, one glance at his face told her there was no double meaning to his words.

'I don't need it. I'm perfectly comfortable,' she said curtly, her brows drawing together as she sent him a level glance that should have convinced him.

His brows drew together and he got to his feet. 'I'll be back in a moment.'

Before she could voice an objection he left the room.

Hani swallowed again. He was the most infuriatingly autocratic man—and she didn't want him watching her so closely that he noticed something as inconspicuous as the shiver that had started this. Some men were predators, hunters by nature, and although Kelt didn't show any signs of that, neither had Felipe at first.

Thrusting the vile memories back into the dark cupboard in her brain where she hid them, Hani waited tensely for Kelt to come back.

CHAPTER FOUR

THE wrap Kelt brought into the conservatory matched the intense blue of lapis lazuli, and when he dropped it around Hani's shoulders it settled like a warm, light cloud. 'My cousin left it behind the last time she was here,' he said without moving. 'She won't mind you wearing it—she's the most generous person I know.'

Horrified by something that felt treacherously like a spark of jealousy, Hani said, 'I'll write her a note to thank her for the use of it.' Hairs lifted on the back of her neck, and she had to fight back an instinct to turn around and look up into his face.

'No need,' he said casually, walking away to sit down again. 'I'll tell her you were duly appreciative.'

Hani picked up her knife and fork and applied herself to the food on her plate, exasperated to find that the warmth of the pashmina was very welcome.

'Does Arthur cook all your meals?' she asked into the silence.

'He deals with dinner,' Kelt told her. 'I forage for myself when it comes to lunch and breakfast. As well as supervising the housekeeping and cooking, he likes to garden, and—as you discovered—he's a great fisherman.'

'He's a brilliant cook. This meal is superb.'

'Good. You need feeding up.'

Startled, she said forthrightly, 'That's hardly tactful.'

His answering smile was a masterpiece of irony. 'I'm not noted for my tact. And clearly you've lost weight while you've been ill.'

'I'm feeling much better,' she said defensively.

'You're still looking fragile. When I agreed that you could stay at the bach I was told the chances of you having another attack were pretty remote. However, you still have that delicate look. I'd prefer you to stay here rather than at the bach.'

He spoke as though he had the right to demand her agreement.

Hani's head came up and she stared incredulously at him. Fortunately her days of obeying men were over.

Fighting back a bewildering mixture of emotions—outrage at his high-handedness mingled with an odd warmth because he seemed to care about her welfare—she said evenly, 'That won't be necessary. I carry my medication with me all the time now, so any attack will be stopped before it has time to start.'

Although his expression didn't alter, she sensed a hardening in his attitude. 'Do you intend to stay inside the bach all the time?'

'Of course not, but I won't stray too far from it either.'

He said bluntly, 'No further than a hundred metres? Because that's about how far you were from the party when I found you, and by then you were incapable of moving. If no one had come along you'd have collapsed under the coconut palm you were clinging to.'

Her colour flared, but her eyes stayed steady when they met his. 'The circumstances were unusual.'

'In what way?' Clearly he didn't believe her.

'I knew during the speeches that I was getting an attack, but I stayed because in Tukuulu leaving while someone is making a speech is a huge insult.'

'Your cultural awareness does you credit.' The sardonic inflection in his tone flicked her on the raw. 'You must have realised you were letting yourself in for an attack of fever.'

'It's important to the Tukuuluans,' she retorted.

'Why didn't you get someone to help you to your cottage and make sure you got some medication into you?'

Lamely she admitted, 'I wasn't thinking straight by then. It won't happen again. Normally I just take medication and go to bed. When I wake up I'm fine.'

Heat burned across her cheekbones at the memory of waking and realising he'd changed her clothes. She didn't dare look at him in case he realised what she was thinking—and suspect that occasionally she fantasised guiltily about his hands on her skin, his gaze on her body...

He asked, 'What happens if you delay taking the medication?'

'I collapse, but the fever eventually passes,' she told him reluctantly.

'How long does that take?'

She parried his critical gaze with a level one of her own. Sorely tempted to gloss over the truth, she admitted, 'Quite some time.'

'You're being evasive.'

Her indignant glance made no impression on him. Meeting the burnished sheen of his gaze, she said belligerently, 'The first time I was in bed for almost a week.'

'How soon after the first symptoms do you need to take the drug?'

'The sooner the better.'

'How long, Hannah?'

Hani suspected that he'd continue interrogating her until she told him everything out of sheer exhaustion.

'Oh, about ten, fifteen minutes,' she flashed. 'But you needn't worry. I'm not going to collapse on the beach because—as I told you a few seconds ago—I take my medication with me all the time.'

He frowned. 'It's not good enough. You'd be much better off here where someone can keep an eye on you.'

For years Hani had managed to contain her naturally quick temper, but Kelt's ultimatum set a fuse to it. 'Have you any idea how arrogant you sound?' she demanded before she could bite the words back. 'You have no right—no right at all—to impose conditions on me. I can look after myself.'

'I might believe that if I hadn't *seen* the way you look after yourself,' he countered, startled by a swift stir of sensual appetite.

That serene façade she presented to the world was a sham, a mask to hide a much more animated personality. Her face was made for emotion—for laughter, for anger that came and went like summer lightning…for tenderness.

How would she look in the throes of passion?

His body responded with the now familiar need, hungry and reckless as wildfire. With lethal determination he reined it in, watching with half-closed eyes while she regained enough control to impose a rigid restraint over those mobile features. It was like watching a light being extinguished.

'All right,' she said shortly, 'I actually started to go, but the elders came in before I could. But I do not need cosseting or constant watching or checking. Think about it—*you'd* hate it. Why should I be any different?'

He lifted his brows, but said bluntly, 'I accept that, but I'd be a lot happier if you'd check in each day—say, in the evening.'

Would she recognise the classical negotiation gambit—make an outrageous demand, then offer a compromise? Kelt watched her face, almost sombre as she hesitated. What was she thinking?

Looking up with open challenge in those sultry eyes she said, 'And if I won't?'

He surveyed the lovely face opposite him, her sensuous mouth tightly controlled, and a rounded little chin held at an obstinate angle.

And she called *him* arrogant, he thought with hard amusement. Who exactly was she, and why was her crystalline English accent occasionally gentled by a soft slurring that somehow managed to sound piercingly erotic?

A woman of mystery in many ways—and obviously a fiercely independent one. He'd asked the principal about her background, and been surprised at how little his friend knew. She'd simply appeared one day at the school, offering to help in any way she could.

'Usually people who wash up in Tukuulu are on the run from something,' his friend had told him. 'Alcohol or drugs or the law or the media, or a romantic break-up that's convinced them their life is ruined. They think they can leave it all behind them and make a new start in the tropics, not realising that until they've faced it, everyone carries their past like a burden. People like that are no use to us.'

'But Hannah Court is.'

'Yes, we were lucky. She's great with the children. When we realised she had a talent for teaching she took every extramural course she could, and now she's a fully qualified infant teacher. Better still, she's got a small income from somewhere, so she can manage on the pittance we pay.'

'What nationality is she?'

His friend had looked a little self-conscious. 'I shouldn't be discussing her with you, but I assume she's English.'

'And you know nothing of her past or her circumstances?'

'She never speaks of them.'

'So she's a fugitive too.'

That was greeted by a shrug. 'Possibly. But she's not encumbered by any obvious baggage. And she's kept a low profile—no love affairs, no breakdowns, no binges. What matters to us is that she fits really well into the island culture and she's turned into a good, conscientious teacher.'

Naturally that was all that mattered to the principal of a struggling school in the tropics, Kelt thought dryly now. But it seemed a wicked waste for any woman as young and vibrant as Hannah Court to hide away from the world. No love affairs didn't, of course, mean she wasn't running from one that had gone wrong. But after six years surely she'd have got over such an experience.

That leashed awareness in Kelt stirred into life again.

He frowned, wondering why she intrigued him so much. Partly it was masculine interest—even with the pallor of illness she was lovely, her too slender body alluringly curved, and from the way she'd curled into him he suspected she was no inexperienced virgin. And although he'd learned to control his urges he had a normal man's needs and hunger.

But this wasn't purely sexual.

From the first, even when he'd been sure she was either drunk or stoned, he'd felt intensely protective towards her. What the hell was she hiding from?

She'd blocked his every probe, either changing the subject or simply ignoring his questions, so she was hiding *something*—and that something had to be pretty shattering.

Perhaps he should just let it go, but when he looked at her he sensed a life wasted, a sorrow so deep she couldn't bear to face it.

In Kelt's experience, the best thing to do with pain was meet it head-on, accept it and deal with it, and then move on.

Kelt made up his mind. He'd use kidnapping as a last resort if she refused to compromise. 'If you won't agree to check in, I'll contact your principal.'

Her lovely face set into lines of mutiny. Common sense— and a strong sense of self-preservation—warned him that Hannah Court's past wasn't his business, and that he'd be foolish to tangle himself in her affairs. But he wasn't going to let her retreat to the bach without that promise.

Before she could say anything, he went on, 'And I want your word that you'll let me or Arthur know if you feel another attack coming on.'

Head held high, she met his steady gaze with cold composure. 'If it makes you feel happier I'll let someone know. And I'll ring the homestead every evening.' She added sweetly, 'Anything to please the man who is letting me live in his bach rent-free.'

Hani knew she sounded ungracious, but being backed into a corner made her feel wildly resentful. She'd feared Felipe's brutal domination, but at that age she'd been so sheltered she'd had no way of dealing with it. And then he'd made sure she couldn't escape it.

To be faced now with another dictatorial man angered her more than it frightened her—and that, she conceded reluctantly, was a relief.

'That's not an issue,' Kelt said shortly. 'Certainly not a personal one.'

'You can't actually stop me being grateful,' she snapped, 'but I won't bore you with it.'

'I don't want your damned gratitude!'

She opened her mouth to hurl an injudicious reply, then abruptly closed it before her intemperate words could burst forth. 'How did you do that? I never lose my temper!'

He stared at her, then gave a slow, wicked smile that sizzled through her defences, reducing her to silence.

But his tone was ironic when he said, 'Neither do I. As for how I managed to make you lose yours—according to my brother, a cousin and my grandmother,' he drawled, 'I suffer from a power complex.'

'They know you well.' She didn't try to hide the caustic note in her voice.

Kelt's raised eyebrow signified his understanding of her reluctance, but he appeared to take her surrender at face value, saying coolly, 'Thank you. I'll warn Arthur. He has a first-aid certificate and so do I.'

Irritated again, she blurted, 'I won't *need* first aid—well, not unless I fall off a cliff. I'm perfectly capable of looking after myself.'

There was a moment's silence until he said with silky clarity, 'I hope you don't intend to renege. I really don't like people who lie.'

Then he'd *hate* her—her whole life was built on lies. She said unevenly, 'You're just going to have to trust me.'

He held her gaze, then nodded and stretched out his hand. 'So shake on it.'

She should be getting accustomed to the way his touch burned through her, but it seemed to be getting more and more potent.

Fighting a sensuous weakness as they shook hands, she managed to produce something that resembled a smile. 'I'm sorry, I'm being dull company, but I have to confess to getting tired very early in the evening.'

As she knew he would, he examined her face with that analytical gaze before getting to his feet. 'Far from dull. In fact, the more I know of you the more interesting I find you,' he said ambiguously, 'but I'll take you home.'

His instant agreement should have pleased her. Instead it made her feel as though she'd been rejected. *Idiot*, she scolded herself fiercely and went to put down the pretty shawl.

Kelt said, 'Keep it on. It will be cool outside now, and you'll need it.'

Arthur saw them out, his face crinkling with restrained pleasure when she said, 'That was a superb meal, thank you.'

'My pleasure, miss,' he said with a half-bow.

Kelt was right; the air was much crisper than it had been before sunset, and Hani had to bite her lips to stop them trembling. Snuggling into the shawl in Kelt's big Range Rover, she realised that if she wanted to be comfortable for the next three months she'd have to buy new clothes.

She fought back a twinge of panic. Her trust fund—a secret between them, her godmother had told her with a wink when she revealed its existence on her seventeenth birthday, because every woman needed money she didn't have to account for—provided her with a small income, but it wasn't enough to stretch to clothes she'd never wear again.

Perhaps there was a secondhand shop in a nearby town.

'What's the matter?' Kelt asked as they went over the cattle grid onto the road that led to the bach.

He must be able to read her like a book. Forcing her brows back into their normal place, she said airily, 'I was just thinking I need new clothes. I know it's summer, but I'm used to tropical heat.'

'There are a couple of quite good boutiques in Kaitake, our service centre,' he told her. 'Unless you need the clothes urgently I'll take you there the day after tomorrow. I'm going there on business, and you can have a look around.'

Boutiques she didn't need—too expensive. 'I could walk—'

'No, it's not the local village—that's Waituna, and it's

about five kilometres north, but it's just a small general store and a petrol station. Kaitake is on the coast about twenty minutes' drive away.'

'I see.' After a moment's hesitation she said formally, 'Thank you, that's very kind of you.'

He shrugged. 'You'll find the copy of the road code I promised you in the glove pocket.'

Back at the homestead, Kelt strolled into the kitchen and got himself a glass of water, looking up as Arthur came in through the door that led to his own quarters.

'Tell me, Arthur, what part of the UK does Miss Court come from?'

'She's not English,' Arthur said promptly and decisively.

Kelt lifted an enquiring eyebrow. 'She sounds very English.'

'Not to me. She speaks it superbly, but I'd wager quite a lot of money that English is not her first language.' He frowned and said slowly, 'In fact, I think I detect hints of a Creole heritage.'

'Caribbean?' Interest quickened through Kelt. He set the glass down on the bench.

'Could be,' Arthur said slowly, frowning, 'but I doubt it. I just don't know—but I'm certain she's not English.'

During the night Hani woke from a deep, deep sleep and heard rain quietly falling onto the roof, and in the morning everything outside glittered in the sunlight as though dusted with diamonds.

The water in the bay was a little discoloured, and when she went for a walk after breakfast she discovered one side of the small stream had fallen in, the clay damming the stream so that it backed up and was already oozing up to the farm road.

Back at the bach she rang through to the homestead. And was *not*, she told herself stoutly, disappointed when Arthur answered.

'Right, I'll make sure the farm manager hears about it,' he said. 'Thank you very much for reporting it, Miss Court.'

Later in the day she walked back along the road and came upon someone clearing the stream. One of the huge trees hung over the water there, its leaves sifting the sunlight so that it fell in dapples of golden light across the man in the water.

Kelt, she thought, her heart soaring exultantly.

He'd taken off his shirt, and the sun played across the powerful muscles of his bronze shoulders and back. An urgent heat flamed in the pit of her stomach as her eyes lingered on each powerful thrust of his arms as when he dug through the temporary dam with fluid strength, tossing shovelfuls of clay back up the bank.

Her response shocked her—a wild rush of adrenalin, of heady anticipation, a swift, unspoken recognition in the very deepest levels of her heart and mind.

As if her passionate claiming had somehow sent out subliminal signals, Kelt looked up. His tanned face showed a flash of white as he smiled, but his gaze was coolly assessing.

Without altering the steady, smooth rhythm of his shovelling, he said, 'Good morning.'

'Good morning,' Hani replied sedately, hoping her voice sounded as impersonal as his. Triumphantly she fished in her pocket and held out a container of pill capsules.

His smile reappeared. 'Good girl.'

Reaching up to a low branch, he used it to swing himself up onto the bank. With a smile that turned her sizzling appreciation into a flame, pure and keen and intense, he said, 'And thanks for being a good citizen and reporting the blockage in the creek.'

'It looked as though it might wash out the road.' Hani felt shy and foolish, the urgent instructions of her mind at war with the eager pleading of her body.

'It could have.' He turned and surveyed his handiwork. He'd opened enough of a breach for the discoloured water to start flowing sluggishly out onto the beach. 'Once I took over Kiwinui I started a programme of fencing the gullies and riversides off from stock and planting them up with native plants. This land erodes badly if it's not cared for, and the farm manager who ran it when I was under age cared more for production than for conservation.' He shrugged. 'He was a man of his time.'

Hani nodded. After her father's death Rafiq had introduced a variety of conservation measures to Moraze, somewhat to the astonishment and dismay of many of his subjects. 'How do you stop the bank from eroding?'

He indicated a tray of small plants on the tray of a small truck. 'We run a nursery where we grow seeds from the native plants on the station. Our native flax loves wet feet, and is extremely good at holding up banks. As well, this summer the road to the bach is being moved further up the hill so that it's not running across a natural wetlands area.'

'Are you going to plant those little seedlings?' she asked.

'Once I've finished clearing this away, yes.'

Impetuously Hani said, 'I'll help.'

His brows shot up. 'You'll get dirty.'

She shrugged. 'So? I've been dirty before, and as far as I know it all washed off.'

'You haven't got gumboots.'

'I can go barefoot,' she told him, exasperated by his obvious image of her as a useless creature. She sat down and slid her feet out of her elderly sneakers, aware that Kelt stood and watched her.

When she stood up again he said, 'Do you know how to plant things?'

'I'm not an expert,' she said, sending him a look that held more challenge than was probably wise, 'but if you tell me what you want me to do and where the plants should go, I'm sure I can cope.'

Still with that infuriating air of amusement he did, digging holes for the plants, then going back to clean up the sides of the stream while she planted, patting the earth around each little flax bush with care.

They didn't talk much, although she learned that in this part of New Zealand there were no streams, only creeks. And although she was still acutely, heatedly aware of him, she found the silence and the work oddly companionable, even soothing.

Well, soothing if she kept her eyes on the plants and didn't let them stray to Kelt, she thought mordantly, lowering her lashes after a peek at the smooth sheen of his skin when he threw another shovelful of clay up onto the bank.

'There,' she said when she'd finished.

Two long strides brought him up beside her. 'Well done.' He paused, and into the silence fell a sweet, echoing peal of birdsong. 'A tui,' he told her laconically, pointing out a black bird, sheened with green and bronze and with a bobble of white feathers at the throat. 'They visit the flax flowers to get nectar.'

She eyed the tall, candelabra-like stalks that held wine-coloured flowers. The bird sank its beak into the throat of another one, then climbed to the top of the stalk and, as if in thanks, lifted its head and sang again, its notes pealing out like the chime of small silver bells into the warm, sea-scented air.

Sheer delight prompted Hani to murmur, 'It's just—so beautiful here.'

There was another silence before he said, 'Indeed it is.'

Something in his tone made her glance up.

He was looking at her, not at the tui, and deep inside her desire burned away the warnings of her mind so that they crumbled into ashes. Hani forgot she had muddy hands and feet; she'd wiped sweat off her face and there was probably mud there too.

Under his hooded scrutiny her lips and throat went dry. Tension arced between them like lightning.

Get out of here, she thought frantically, *before you do something stupid, like tilt your head towards him*. She fought back an imperative desire to do just that and find out once and for all what Kelt's kiss would feel like.

As though he sensed her desperate effort to keep calm, she saw him impose control, his eyes darken, and the dangerous moment passed.

Yet he'd wanted her...

Nothing, she thought with a flash of pure rapture, could ever take that away. But far more wondrous was that *she* wanted *him*. After six years of being sure Felipe had killed that part of her, she felt passion and desire again.

Kelt said, 'And it will be even more beautiful when these plants grow. Thank you. Kiwinui will always have some part of you here.'

Unexpectedly touched by the thought, she said, 'I enjoyed doing it.'

'I just hope it doesn't make you feel worse. Remember, any shiver, anything that worries you, ring the homestead.' He glanced at his watch. 'I'm afraid I have to go—I'm expecting a call from overseas.'

Back at the bach she told herself she should be grateful to that unknown person who was calling him long-distance.

Falling in lust with Kelt was one thing, but her headstrong desire to know him far more intimately was a much more dangerous development.

CHAPTER FIVE

WHEN she rang that night, Arthur answered again. He enquired after her health, said Kelt had told him she'd helped plant the flax and hoped her hard work hadn't made her condition worse.

'No, I'm very well, thank you,' she replied politely. After she'd rung off she thought sombrely that Kelt was probably out with some local beauty.

Trying to laugh herself out of that foolish mood didn't work, so she went to bed and dreamed of him, only to wake cross and crumpled in the big bed the next morning.

'Enough,' she told her reflection severely as she applied moisturiser. 'OK, so you think he's gorgeous. No, let's be embarrassingly honest here—you want to go to bed with him. Very, very much.'

And even more since she'd seen him clearing the stream— *creek*, she amended hurriedly—shirtless, his bronzed torso exposed in lethal power and forceful energy.

Her breath caught in her throat. Hurriedly she finished the rest of her morning regime, telling herself sternly, 'But even if he feels the same way, there's absolutely no future for this. In three months' time you're going back to Tukuulu, where you're safe.'

And she'd never be able to forge any sort of future with him—or any man, not so long as Felipe was alive.

But Felipe hadn't found her, she thought, stopping and staring sightlessly into the mirror. And here, in New Zealand, she felt just as safe as she had in Tukuulu.

Perhaps there was a chance...

'Forget it!' she said curtly. 'It's not going to happen, not now, not ever.'

So Kelt had moments when he wanted her. Big deal; for most men that meant very little. If she allowed herself to surrender to the erotic charge between them, he'd probably enjoy an affair, then wave her goodbye at that tiny airport without anything more than mild regret.

Or—even more cringe-making—perhaps he hadn't liked what he'd seen when he'd taken off her wet dress and slipped the shift over her head...

Whatever, an affair was out! So when he arrived in a few minutes she'd be cool and dismissive and completely ignore the chemistry between them.

Dead on time he drove down the track. He was already out of the vehicle when Hani walked out to meet him, her heartbeat racing into an erratic tattoo. Lean and lithe and very big, he surveyed her with an intimidating scrutiny for several seconds before his smile not only melted her bones but also set her wayward pulse off into the stratosphere.

Dizzily she said, 'Good morning,' in her most guarded voice.

Until he'd smiled at her she'd been very aware that this day was considerably cooler than the previous one. Now however, she felt almost feverish.

His gaze hardened. 'You're looking a bit tired.'

'I'm fine,' she said quickly, dismissively.

A glance at the sedan he'd driven made her fight back a

gurgle of laughter. He so did *not* look like that four-cylinder, family-style vehicle! No, he should be driving something wickedly male and dangerous…

So what did it mean that he thought this sedate vehicle suitable for her?

Nothing, she reminded herself staunchly; don't go reading symbolism into everything he does. He was extremely kind to offer what was probably his only spare vehicle; that it happened to be a reliable, boring car was all to the good!

Now, if only she could satisfy him that the past few hours spent devouring the contents of the road code had turned her into a fit driver for New Zealand roads.

'Hop behind the wheel,' Kelt said, making it sound rather too much of an order.

With a touch of asperity Hani said, 'Thank you,' and climbed into the car. Once there, she spent time familiarising herself with the instrument panel.

Kelt got in beside her, immediately sucking all of the air out of the interior.

'Ah, an automatic,' she said, memories of being taught to drive flooding her. 'My brother used to say…'

Appalled, she bit back the rest of the comment, hoping desperately that he hadn't heard her.

Not a chance.

'Your brother used to say—?'

Bending forward, she hid her face by groping for the lever that moved the seat. 'That they're for old ladies of both sexes.'

'I wonder if he'd feel the same once he'd driven on some of Northland's roads,' Kelt said dryly.

'Perhaps not.' Her shaking fingers closed on the lever, but

she was so tense she misjudged the effort needed, and the seat jerked forward. However, the several moments spent adjusting it to her liking gave her precious time to compose herself.

Straightening, she said in her most cheerful tone, 'That's better—I can reach the pedals now. Not everybody has such long legs as you.'

'I wouldn't call yours short.'

An equivocal note beneath the amused words brought colour to her cheeks, but at least she'd diverted the conversation away from Rafiq. 'They certainly aren't in the same league as yours,' she said brightly, and put the car into gear.

On Tukuulu she'd sometimes driven the school's elderly four-wheel-drive, wrestling with gears that stuck, barely functioning brakes and an engine that had to be coaxed, so this well-maintained car was no problem. Nevertheless she drove cautiously, keeping the speed down; the farm road might also be well-maintained, but it wasn't sealed, and the gravel surface was a challenge.

Showing an unexpected understanding, Kelt stayed silent while she found her own way around the instruments and got the feel of the vehicle. By the time she'd taken them past the cluster of workers' cottages and big sheds, she was feeling quite at home behind the wheel, but at the junction with the sealed road she braked, and looked sideways at Kelt.

Eyes half-hidden by thick lashes, he said coolly, 'You're an excellent driver, as I'm sure you know. Your brother taught you well.'

Hoping he didn't notice the sudden whiteness of her knuckles, she loosened her grip on the wheel. 'Do you want to take over now?'

'No. There's not another car in sight. The speed limit's a hundred kilometres an hour.'

'Not on this road, surely,' she muttered, loosening her hold on the wheel to steer out.

'Officially yes, but you're right—most of the time it's safer to stick to eighty. Some of the corners aren't well-cambered.'

Oddly enough, his presence beside her lent Hani confidence. There wasn't much traffic, although she found the frequent huge trucks intimidating.

'It's the main highway north,' he said when she voiced her surprise at the number. 'The railway doesn't come this far, so everything is transported by truck.'

One day, she thought, she'd like to be a passenger and really check out the countryside. She'd seen nothing on that night drive from the airport with Arthur, and her occasional sideways glance revealed a landscape of dramatically bold hills and lush valleys.

'Take the left turn at the next intersection,' Kelt instructed after a few minutes.

It delivered them to a small town situated on an estuary. Shaded by palms and bright with flowers and subtropical vegetation, it looked prosperous and charming. Not even the mangroves that clogged the riverbank could give it a sinister air.

'Kaitake,' Kelt told her. 'Turn right here and then a left into the car park.'

He waited until she'd switched off the engine before saying, 'I'll meet you here at twelve-thirty. That should give you time to have a good look at several of the boutiques before I buy you lunch.'

'You don't have to buy me lunch,' she protested, firmly squelching a forbidden spurt of pleasure and anticipation.

'You drove me here,' he said, not giving an inch. 'One good turn deserves another.'

He stopped any further objection by removing himself

from the car and coming around to open her door. Baulked, Hani grabbed her bag and got out, taking a deep breath.

'That's not so. I'd like to buy you lunch,' she said crisply, looking up into his hard, handsome face.

Bad move; once more her pulses ratcheted up and that odd weakness softened her bones. She had to suck in a rapid breath and steady her voice before she could go on. 'You're lending me the car and, although lunch seems a pretty poor recompense for your kindness, it's the least I can do.'

'The car would be idle if you weren't using it. Are you always so fiercely independent?'

Independence kept her safe. She shrugged, her mouth tightening. 'Yes,' she said in a deliberately offhanded voice.

That disbelieving brow lifted. 'Very well, you can buy me lunch. By now you must know I have a hearty appetite.'

And possibly not just for food... The sexy little thought popped into her head as she forced herself to say airily, 'That's no problem.'

Of course he ate well—he was a big man—but he also exuded a prowling sensuality that probably meant he was an extremely good lover as well.

And no doubt there were plenty of women who responded to that magnetic, masculine charisma. Plenty of women had wanted to go to bed with Felipe—a situation he used with cynical disregard for them. Would Kelt?

She tried to relax her tight muscles. Forget Felipe; it had been sheer bad luck—and her own trusting foolishness—that the first man she'd fallen for had been a career criminal who'd seen her as a means to an end.

'Is something the matter?'

Kelt's voice, forceful and uncompromising, jolted her back to the present.

'I—no, no, of course not,' she said quickly and, hoping to deflect his attention, she went on with a brightness she hoped didn't sound too brittle, 'Nothing could possibly be wrong—I'm about to buy some clothes!'

His unyielding blue gaze held hers a second longer before his mouth curved into a smile that sent a sizzle of excitement through her, one that burned away all her sensible decisions and left her open and exposed to this wildfire hunger, this sensuous craving that was trying to take her over.

He startled her by taking her elbow. At the touch of his hand—strong and purposeful—Hani tensed. Dry-mouthed, she sent him an anxious glance, only relaxing when she saw his calm expression. Swallowing, she concentrated on putting her feet down precisely, every cell in her body taut and alert.

Yet in spite of his closeness and that light grip on her elbow, no panic kicked beneath her ribs; in fact, she thought worriedly, she felt oddly protected and safe.

And that was really, really dangerous.

Talk! she commanded herself.

Aloud she said brightly, 'I didn't expect to see verandas out over the streets in New Zealand. It gives the place a very tropical look.'

'Our sun's not as hot as it is in the tropics, but we live beneath a hole in the ozone layer,' Kelt told her, 'and it can rain just as heavily here as it does there.'

'It's so…fresh.'

'If you're comparing it to Tukuulu, industrial areas aren't noted for their beauty and freshness,' he observed on a dry note.

Several passers-by greeted him, their gazes coming inevitably to rest on her. She felt too conspicuous, their interest setting her nerves on edge. Kelt's compelling combination of raw male charisma and formidable authority would always attract attention, she thought with a hint of panic. So she wouldn't come here again with him.

Uncannily detecting her unease, he glanced down at her. 'What is it?'

Hani said the first thing that came into her mind. 'You promised me boutiques. I can't see any here.'

'There's one about a hundred metres from here, and another just around the corner.' That far too perceptive gaze swept her face. 'You're sure you're all right?'

'I'm fine,' she said, and tried out her best smile, sweetly persuasive.

It failed entirely; if anything, his eyes hardened and his voice turned caustic. 'Stop playing games with me.'

'I will when you stop being so—so mother-hennish,' she retorted, chagrined because he'd seen through her so easily. 'If it helps you to stop fussing, I'll agree that the doctor at Tukuulu was right; I did need a holiday in a cooler place. Since I've been here I've been sleeping like a log, and my appetite's come back. And I feel more energetic. I don't need to be watched and monitored and scrutinised as though I'm going to faint any minute.'

His survey didn't soften, but his mouth quirked. 'Is that what I was doing?'

'That's what it felt like,' she said, startled to realise that, as much as his concern irked her, it satisfied something she'd been unaware of—a debilitating need to be cared for. Her colleagues were kind and helpful and friendly, but they had their own lives, their own affairs to worry about. The friendships she'd formed at the school were genuine, but she'd deliberately kept them superficial.

A voice from behind cooed Kelt's name. Hani's heart clamped when she saw the woman who'd caught them up.

Hardly more than a girl, the newcomer was stunning. Hair an artful shade of auburn, her eyes huge and golden-brown in a beautiful, cleverly made-up face, she looked like sunshine and laughter and innocence, her curvy little body emphasised by clothes that hadn't been bought in any small town.

Her radiance made Hani feel old and tired and depraved, her past cutting her off from such exuberant, joyous youthfulness.

'Kelt, you're the tallest man around. I saw you from the other end of the street,' the newcomer said, beaming at him. She turned to Hani, and her smile widened. 'Hello, you must be the new guest in the bach. How are you liking it?'

'Very much, thank you,' Hani said politely.

In a neutral voice Kelt said, 'Hannah, this is my cousin, Rosemary Matthews.'

'Rosie,' Kelt's cousin said with an admonitory gaze at him. She shook hands with vigour, and added cheerfully, 'No one ever calls me Rosemary. And just between you and me, our relationship is more *whanau* than cousin—so distant it doesn't count.' Her smile turned wicked. 'Consider me one of the aspirants for Kelt's hand.'

Hani's social smile turned into a startled laugh. She glanced up at Kelt, who was studying his cousin with a mixture of austerity and amusement, and asked involuntarily, 'One of the aspirants? How many are there?'

'Dozens,' Rosie told her without any sign of embarrassment, 'if not *hundreds*—they come full of hope, and they go away broken-hearted. I spend quite a lot of time patting shoulders and supplying tissues to weeping women who've realised they don't have a chance.' She heaved a theatrical sigh. 'My heart bleeds for them, but I have to be strong so I can plead my own case.'

'Stop teasing,' Kelt said indulgently. 'Hannah might just take you seriously.'

'She seems far too sensible to do that,' Rosie returned, eyes sparkling with impudence. But when she transferred her gaze back to Hani some of the laughter went from her face. 'Have we met before? I seem to know you—and yet I don't think we've been introduced, have we?'

Of all the people to induce that frantic kick of panic beneath Hani's ribs, this sunshiny girl was the last she'd have imagined. She shook her head and steadied her voice to say, 'This is my first visit to New Zealand.'

Kelt said briefly, 'Hannah lives in Tukuulu—in the islands. She's been ill and needs to recuperate in a cooler climate. What are you doing here? I thought you were going to Auckland with your mother.'

She shrugged. 'I decided not to go—she's off to the opera with the new boyfriend, and you know, tubby little tenors angsting in high Cs at shrieking ladies with huge bosoms are *so* not my thing.' She looked from one to the other. 'Are you going to lunch, because if you are can I come too?'

Amused, Hani glanced at Kelt, who was scanning that vivid little face with a certain grimness.

'No,' he said calmly. 'Hannah needs rest, and you are not restful.'

Hani blinked. He sent her a silent, don't-get-mixed-up-in-this warning.

Mournfully Rosie responded, 'I'll take that as a compliment. Of course, I could just keep quiet and enjoy the ambience.'

'Quiet? You?' Kelt asked, his dry tone not quite hiding his affection. 'Go on—catch up with the friend I can see waiting for you outside the café.'

Rosie gave a wounded sigh, rapidly followed by another of those infectious smiles. 'I try so hard to outwit him,' she confided to Hani, 'but he sees through me every time. It's been nice talking to you—we must get together when you feel up to being stimulated! Although quite frankly, I think Kelt is more than enough excitement for any woman, let alone one who's convalescing!'

With a saucy glance at her cousin, she set off down the street, hips swaying seductively, the sun burnishing her superbly cut hair to copper.

Kelt said dryly, 'She's nowhere near so ingenuous as she seems, but there's no harm in her.'

'She's very forthright,' Hani ventured cautiously, adding because her words seemed like criticism, 'but I imagine she's great fun.'

'She has an interesting sense of humour,' he conceded, checking his watch. 'All right, I'll see you back at the car park. Have fun shopping.'

Hani nodded and walked sedately towards the boutique he'd mentioned, wondering whether his cousin would be lying in wait somewhere. However, there wasn't a sign of her anywhere in the busy street. And one glance at the boutique window told her she couldn't afford anything it sold, but in case Kelt was still able to see her she went inside.

She'd been right. The racks were full of clothes she'd love to buy, but not at those prices. Possibly Rosie had bought some of her outfit here after all.

The quick interplay between the cousins and their obvious affection for each other made her sadly envious. Or enviously sad… Rafiq had been her adored big brother, but he was quite a bit older and their relationship had become less close after their parents had died and he'd had to rule Moraze.

Oh, she'd always known he loved her, but there wasn't the easy camaraderie she'd seen between Kelt and Rosie. And those few minutes in their company had shown her another

side of the man she found so dangerously interesting; they
convinced her that her instinctive trust of him was justified.

After a quick, regretful smile at the saleswoman she left,
resigned to the same experience in the next shop. That wasn't
so upmarket, but still too expensive.

Finally she tracked down a secondhand shop in one of the
back streets, between a pet shop and an internet café.

Ignoring the delectable puppies tumbling around in the
window, she hurried inside the charity shop, and to her relief
found exactly what she wanted—several light tops, a pair of
sleek black trousers in a very fine woollen fabric, a pair of jeans
and two merino-wool jerseys, all good chain-store quality.

'Are you going off on holiday to the northern hemisphere?'
the woman behind the counter asked as Hani examined herself
in the one big mirror in the shop.

Hani said, 'That would be lovely, but no, I've been living
in a warmer climate.'

'They could have been made for you,' the woman said, in-
specting the well-cut trousers and a feather-soft merino jersey
in a soft peach that lent a golden gleam to Hani's skin. 'Look,
if you're cold, why don't you wear them away? They've all
been washed and dry-cleaned. I'll pack your own clothes in
with the other ones you've bought.'

New Zealanders—well, the ones she'd met, Hani thought
wryly as she walked out—were a helpful lot. On the street she
checked her watch, allowing herself another wistful glance at
the puppies before she hurried to the car park.

Kelt was waiting, not impatiently but as though no one had
ever been late for him. He turned as she came towards him,
and once more she saw that gleam in his eyes, a hooded glitter
of appreciation.

Something strange and dramatic happened to her heart;

it seemed to soar within her, and she was filled by breathless anticipation, as though the world was full of wonderful possibilities.

After a swift scrutiny Kelt said, 'You look stunning.'

'I— Thank you.' Too breathless to go on, she groped for the keys she'd dropped into her bag. 'I'll just put my purchases in the car.'

'Do you want to drive again?'

Keys in hand, she looked up at him, his tanned face angular, his expression controlled. 'Aren't we eating here?'

'There's a very good restaurant in a vineyard not far away.'

Too late now to hope it wasn't expensive. She'd thought they'd eat at a café. Abandoning caution, she said, 'I might as well get as much experience as I can while you're here to ride shotgun. I still haven't quite got my bearings.'

'You don't need anyone to oversee your driving.'

'Thank you,' she said, the warmth of his comment lasting until they reached the vineyard in the hills a few kilometres from town.

'It could almost be some part of Tuscany,' she observed when they were seated on the wide terrace beneath a canopy of hot-pink bougainvillea flowers. It overlooked a small valley filled by a body of water too big to be called a pond, too small for a lake.

Kelt asked idly, 'Have you been there?'

She'd spent a holiday with a school friend in a magnificent villa in the heart of Tuscany. 'I've seen a lot of photographs,' she returned, hating the fact that she'd fudged. Still, she might be implying something that wasn't true, but at least she hadn't come out with a direct lie.

Perhaps something in her tone alerted him, because he subjected her to another of those coolly judicial looks. She was prickly with embarrassment when he said, 'A glass of wine?'

'No, thanks.' She gave a rueful little smile. 'I tend to drift off to sleep if I drink in the daytime. Not a good look over the lunch table, or behind the wheel.'

'Not a good look in most places.' A note of reservation in his voice made her wonder whether he was remembering the night she'd collapsed in his arms.

They'd felt so good...

Heat touched her cheeks; she bent her head and applied herself to the menu.

Which, she noted with a sinking heart, had no prices. In her experience that meant the food was astronomically expensive. Well, she'd insisted on paying; no matter how much it cost she'd manage. Thrift was something she'd learned over the past years.

Clearly Kelt was well-known; the woman who'd shown them to their table had greeted him with a warm smile and by his first name. She was too professional to make her curiosity about Hani obvious.

Kelt ordered a beer for himself and freshly squeezed lime juice with soda for her, before saying, 'It looks as though you had a satisfactory morning shopping for clothes.'

'Thank you,' she said politely, adding, 'Is Rosie the cousin who owns that shawl?'

'Yes.' A strand of golden sunlight probed through the leafy canopy over the terrace, summoning a lick of fire from his hair.

A fierce, sweet sensation burst through her, startling her with its intensity. After her treatment by Felipe she'd never thought to experience desire again—in fact, she'd welcomed her total lack of interest in the opposite sex because it kept her safe.

But this was desire as she'd never known it—a cell-deep hunger that pierced her with helpless delight. And with fear. She didn't dare fall in love again.

But she could perhaps exorcise Felipe's malign influence over her life by—

By what? An affair…

Shocked yet fascinated by this outrageous thought, she said in her most sedate tone, 'Then I must write her that note to thank her.'

'Oh, you'll see her again. She's as curious as a cat. In a few days she'll be down at the bach trying to lure you out of your solitude.'

Rosie was a nice, neutral topic. Relieved, Hani seized on it. 'What does she do? Is she at university?'

'Gap year,' he said succinctly. 'Her mother decided she was too immature to be let loose on an unsuspecting world, so she's staying at home.'

Something in his voice made her say, 'You don't approve.'

'I think she should be doing something, not just swanning around having fun,' he said uncompromisingly. 'She's got a damned good brain beneath that red hair, and she needs to exercise it instead of wasting time flitting from party to party.'

'Perhaps she needs a year of enjoying herself. High school is hard work.'

'She's never had to work hard for anything.' He dismissed the subject of his cousin. 'So tell me what you're planning to do while you're here.'

A mischievous impulse persuaded her to say, 'I haven't decided yet. Perhaps I'll do some running around too.'

He cocked that brow at her. 'It shouldn't do you any harm, although you're still looking a bit fine-drawn.'

His tone was impersonal, but a note in it fanned the forbidden, smouldering flame inside her. Ignoring it she said steadily, 'Actually, I'm not the flitting type.'

'Are you going to be able to go back to the tropics?'

Startled, she said, 'Of course. This is the twenty-first century, not the nineteenth.' She lifted her glass of lime juice. 'Here's to the miracles of modern medicine.'

'I'll drink to that,' he said, and did so.

As he set his glass down Hani looked out across the valley and said, 'The vines look like braids across the hillside. They must be stunning in the autumn when the leaves change colour.'

'We don't get intense autumn colours this far north,' Kelt told her. 'For those you need to go to the South Island.'

He'd moved slightly so that his back was presented to a group just being seated, and she wondered if he was ashamed of being seen with her. These women seemed overdressed for a casual vineyard lunch, but their clothes—like Rosie's—bore the discreet indications of skilful design and obvious expense.

Kelt might be a snob—she hadn't seen him with other people enough to know otherwise—but his enviable aura of self-assurance surely meant any embarrassment was unlikely.

He'd certainly shrugged off his *distant* cousin's open claim to him—not to mention her statement that women wept when they realised he wasn't interested in them. And without so much as a tinge of colour along those sweeping, stark cheekbones. Perhaps it was a joke between them?

A comment from Kelt broke into her anxious thoughts. 'That's an interesting expression.'

Hani was saved from answering by the arrival of the first course—iced soup for her, a considerably more substantial dish for him.

As she tackled the soup she thought ironically that she hadn't eaten with a man for over six years, and here she was, for the second time in two days, sharing a meal with the most interesting man she'd ever met.

And one of the best-looking. Apart from Rafiq, she thought loyally, but of course her brother didn't affect her like—

Her thoughts came to a jarring halt.

Well, OK, she *was* affected by Kelt.

But only physically. She was safe from the shattering emotional betrayal she'd suffered at Felipe's hands.

Kelt had shown her he wasn't at all like Felipe—that lick of contempt in his voice when he'd asked if she was drunk or drugged, his affection for his cousin, the children's innocent, open respect and liking…

Any woman who took him for a lover wouldn't end up with splintered self-esteem and a death wish.

And she'd learned a lot in six years, grown up, become a different woman from the child-adult who'd fallen headlong for Felipe's false charm. Even then, it hadn't taken her too long to realise she'd fallen in love with a carefully constructed image, a mirage.

A trap.

And if she wanted to free herself from the lingering after-effects of her experience with Felipe, prove that she was able to handle a mature relationship, then Kelt would be the ideal lover. Miraculously he'd woken the long-dead part of her that was able to respond.

And he wanted her…

Common sense did its best to squelch the secret thrill of excitement, warning Hani not to allow herself the forbidden luxury of impossible dreams. Nothing had really changed; as long as Felipe was alive she'd never be safe, and neither was anyone else she knew.

CHAPTER SIX

KELT'S voice—aloof, rather cool—broke into Hani's tumbled thoughts. 'Don't you like that soup? I can order something else for you if you'd rather.'

'No, it's delicious, thank you.' Startled, she drank some more without tasting it. She was not going to let herself fantasise about an affair with him—it was altogether too dangerous. Reining in her too vivid imagination, she said sedately, 'They have a great chef.'

'She's an American woman with a Brazilian background who met her New Zealand husband in London. When he decided to come back here and grow grapes she set up the restaurant. It's becoming rather famous.'

'I can understand why,' she said, suddenly longing for the potent chilli dishes of her homeland.

A large dog of indeterminate breed wandered around the corner, accompanied by an entourage of ducks. They parted ways, the ducks heading downhill to the pond, the dog stopping to survey the diners. After a few seconds of sniffing, it headed for Hani.

'Shall I send him away?' Kelt said. 'He's well-behaved and very much a part of the restaurant, but if you're wary of dogs he can look intimidating.'

'I like dogs.' Quelling a bitter memory, she held out her hand, back upwards, so that the dog could scent her. It obliged delicately, and with excellent manners refrained from actually landing the automatic lick on her skin.

'Yes, you're a handsome creature,' Hani said softly. 'What's your name?'

Kelt waved away a waiter who'd started towards them. 'Rogue. And he's not allowed to beg.'

'He's not begging, are you, Rogue?'

A woman called from behind a screen, and obediently Rogue bounded off.

'I can see you know how to deal with dogs,' Kelt remarked.

'I grew up with them,' she said simply.

Felipe had bought her a puppy. She'd learned to love it— and then, a month or so later, they'd quarrelled.

She'd gone out, and when she'd got home the puppy was dead. He'd got one of his servants to drown it. To teach her a lesson, he'd said and, when she'd wept, told her negligently that because she'd learned that lesson he'd buy her another one.

That was when Hani had realised that to him she was every bit as expendable as the puppy—something he'd bought, something he could order to be killed just to make a point...

Her throat closed; she swallowed and smiled and said much more brightly, 'I wonder what interesting mix of bloodlines led to Rogue's conformation.'

'German Shepherd, certainly, and perhaps a hint of bull terrier—with border collie? Apart from that, who knows?'

The shutters had come down again, barring him from her thoughts. Kelt's eyes narrowed as he surveyed her calm, emotionless face. Hannah Court's stubborn refusal to give him any information about herself was getting to him.

She was nothing like the women he usually wanted. After

an experience when he was young and callow enough to break a woman's heart he'd been careful to choose lovers as sophisticated as he was. He'd given up expecting to fall in love—and he had no intention of falling in love with Hannah Court either.

But she was an intriguing mystery, one he wanted to solve. He hadn't missed the moment of stiffness when Rosie had suggested she might have seen her before. She wore that disciplined composure like armour, yet flashes of tension broke through it—when he touched her, when she'd inadvertently revealed she had a brother.

He doubted that she'd been involved in anything criminal, but possibly her six years in the mining wasteland of Tukuulu was self-punishment. Was she expiating some sin?

Or was she afraid?

She hadn't pulled away when he'd touched her—she'd actually flinched, as though expecting pain. A violent surge of outrage took him completely by surprise; he had to stop his hand from clenching into a fist beside his plate.

Hani looked up at him, those dark eyes green and unreadable even though she was smiling. 'Probably a couple of other breeds too,' she said. 'I'm glad Rogue's well looked after. People shouldn't have dogs if they aren't prepared to love them.'

Kelt heard the momentary hesitation, the flicker of grief in her voice, and watched with narrowed eyes as she scrambled to her feet and said, 'If you'll just excuse me…'

Without waiting for a response she headed across the terrace and into the restaurant.

What the hell had precipitated that? Bitter memories, or another attack of fever? If she wasn't back in five minutes he'd get the waitress to go in after her. Or go in himself.

He didn't have to wait that long, just long enough to call the waiter over and arrange to pay half of the bill.

'I don't want my guest to know about it,' he said.

The waiter nodded, and left, casting a curious glance at Hannah as she came back.

Leaning back in his chair, Kelt watched her walk towards him, and something tightened in his gut. Unconsciously seductive, the exotic contours of her face were enhanced by the smile that curved her lips. Her hair gleamed in the sunlight like burnished silk, its dense darkness shot with elusive sparks of red. And the graceful sway of her hips had caught the eye of every man on the terrace.

Kelt got to his feet on a fierce rush of adrenalin, an arrogant male need to proclaim to the world that she was with him. Without thinking, he took her hand.

'All right?' he asked abruptly.

She gave him a veiled look. 'I'm fine, thank you,' she said in a tone that had an edge to it.

But her fingers trembled in his, and he could see the pulse beating in the vulnerable hollow of her throat. Fear?

No. Her colour came and went, and her eyes clung to his. A dangerous triumph burning through him, Kelt released her as the waiter came towards them.

Something had happened, Hani realised as they sat down again. Her nerves were jumping in delicious anticipation because she both wanted and feared that *something*.

But she wanted it much more than she feared it. Fortunately she had to deal with the waiter, who was trying to persuade her to order what he described as a sinfully decadent chocolate mousse.

'I'm already full, but you have some,' she urged Kelt, refusing to think of the cost.

He said, 'Not for me, but if you're having coffee I'll have some of that too.'

Still sizzling with a kind of delicious inner buzz, she surrendered to the urge to say yes, to prolong the moment. 'Coffee sounds great.'

After it had been ordered Kelt leaned back in his chair and surveyed her lazily. 'What do you plan to do while you recuperate?'

'I might write a book.'

One black brow hitched upwards. 'Do you write?'

'Not yet,' she admitted, playing with the idea. 'But everyone has to start.'

'Would you make use of your experiences in Tukuulu?'

'No, it would seem like exploiting the school and the pupils.' Another thought struck her. 'Or I could learn to paint. I've always wanted to do that.'

'The local high school has night classes, and I think there's a group that offers lessons as well,' he commented, those dispassionate eyes intent on her face. 'Anything else you can think of?'

'No,' she said quietly, some of her lovely anticipation draining away at the thought of the three long months ahead.

'You could study something that would help you with your career. There's a tertiary institute in Kaitake. Are you a New Zealand citizen?'

Through his lashes he watched her keenly, not surprised when the drawbridge came up again.

'No,' she said crisply. 'And I don't have residency either, which makes study difficult.' And prohibitively expensive.

He frowned. 'So where did you gain your qualifications?'

After a moment's hesitation she said, 'From an Auckland tertiary institute. The principal organised everything.' And the charity had paid the fees.

Uneasily she wondered whether the governing body would want repayment if she couldn't go back to Tukuulu. Brusquely she dismissed the thought; already she felt so much better. The fever had to be on the run.

Kelt said, 'If you want to study, I'd contact the same institute again. But you should make sure you're up to whatever you feel like doing.'

Years of forced independence had made such concern unusual.

And perilously sweet.

Picking up the spoon that came with the coffee, she played with it for a moment before saying with a bite to her tone, 'I certainly don't think I'm likely to collapse in public again. Apart from anything else, it might give people the wrong impression.'

His brows lifted at the allusion. 'I've apologised for my misconception,' he said with formidable detachment.

He had, so why had she reminded him of it again? Because she was reverting back to the terrified woman who'd avoided any sort of emotional connection for the past six years.

She drew in her breath to apologise in her turn, but he forestalled her by holding out his hand.

'Shake on it, and we'll forget it happened,' he said, knowing he wouldn't be able to.

From beneath lowered lids he watched her, noting the subtle signs of unease, the momentary hesitation before she held out her hand.

Why the hell was he trying to help her? If his suspicions were correct she was damaged in some way that needed professional help, possibly several years of therapy. Normally he'd stay well out of it—after making sure she got that help.

So what was different?

Hannah was different, he realised with a shock of anger and

frustration. And so was he. He was already deeper in this than he wanted to be, which meant it was time to bail out.

And even as the words scrolled through his mind, he knew he wasn't going to. This, for example—her initial involuntary flinch at his touch had eased to a certain tension.

He'd like her to welcome the feel of his hands on her skin, not be afraid of it. As she extended her hand he forced himself to be gentle, letting her control the quick handshake.

She gave him a fleeting apologetic smile when she picked up the teaspoon again, glancing away so that she accidentally met the eyes of a woman a few tables away. Skilfully made-up, with superbly cut blonde hair, clothes that made the most of some very sleek physical assets, a very opulent diamond on one elegantly manicured finger—she gave Hani a long, openly speculative stare.

Hani blinked, gave a stiff little nod and turned back to Kelt. He had noticed, of course.

'She's the soon-to-be ex-wife of one of the more notorious property developers. He's just dumped her for a woman ten years younger,' he said dismissively. 'He bought a farm further north—on the coast—and built a large and elaborate holiday house and is trying to deny the locals access to his beaches.'

As though his words had summoned her, the woman at the other table got to her feet and came across.

'Hello, Kelt.' Her smile was as fulsome as her tone, and her eyes flicked from Kelt to Hani, and back again, devouring him with a bold, open appreciation that set Hani's teeth on edge.

'Tess,' he said formally, getting to his feet.

Hani realised they were under intense covert scrutiny from the people at the other table, and wondered what was going on.

Kelt introduced Hani without giving any more information than her supposed name, and their conversation was short and apparently friendly enough, but Hani suspected that not only did Kelt disapprove of the woman, but he also disliked her.

Not that you could tell from his attitude, she thought, wondering whether she was being foolish and presumptuous. After all, she didn't *know* Kelt.

Tension knotted beneath her ribs as Tess Whoever left after one more fawning smile, and walked back to her table.

'She seems pleasant enough,' she said foolishly to fill in the charged silence when Kelt sat down again.

'I suspect I've just been put on a list of possible replacements.' He glanced at her empty coffee cup. 'Are you ready to go?'

'Yes.'

Hani half expected him to insist on paying but he made no attempt to, and to her intense relief the bill was about the amount she'd have expected to pay in a good café.

They had almost reached the turn-off to Kiwinui when she braked and drew into the side of the road.

Kelt asked, 'Something wrong?'

'I just want to look at the view,' she told him.

He nodded and got out with her, standing beside her as they looked out over a wide valley with an immense, slab-sided rocky outcrop almost in the middle.

'That's the remnant of an ancient volcanic plug,' Kelt told her. 'There are burial caves there, and—' He stopped abruptly, turning to frown at a clump of straggly trees on the side of the hill.

'What is it?' Hani asked anxiously.

Over his shoulder he said, 'I heard a noise. Listen!'

Obediently she strained to hear, but heard nothing except the soft sound of the wind in the trees. In a voice pitched barely above a whisper, she asked, 'What sort of noise?'

'A whimper, like something in pain.'

He strode towards the trees, but when Hani caught him up he stopped her with a hand on her arm, and ordered, 'Stay here.'

'Why?' The hair lifted on the back of her neck. Acutely conscious of the latent strength in the fingers curled above her elbow, she looked up into a face set in rigid lines of command.

Blue eyes hard and intent, he said, 'I don't know what it is,' he said. 'I'll go and check it out. I want you to stay here until I call you.'

'Surely you don't think—'

'I don't *know*,' he emphasised. 'And if I yell, run back to the car, lock yourself in and call emergency on the cell-phone you'll find in the glove pocket.'

When she didn't answer he said, 'Perhaps you should do that now.'

'I'll wait by the car,' she said flatly. 'But I think you're overreacting.'

He gave her a thin smile. 'Of course I am. Humour me,' he said, and watched as she walked across to stand by the vehicle.

'Be careful!' she mouthed silently as he walked into the head-high scrub.

Tensely she waited, every nerve on edge, relaxing a few minutes later when he emerged carrying a small black and white animal.

'What is it?' she asked as she ran across to him. 'Oh, it's a puppy!'

Under his breath he said something she was rather glad she couldn't hear, adding distinctly, 'And it's terrified.'

So distressed she had to swallow to control her voice, she said, 'Give it to me!' and held out her hands.

Kelt shook his head and carefully, gently manipulated each fragile limb. The puppy settled down immediately, lifting its sharp little face to him and neither flinching nor whimpering when he ran his lean, competent fingers over it.

'Get into the car and I'll drive us to the vet,' Kelt said austerely. 'It doesn't seem to be in any pain but it needs to be checked in case it's sick, or too young to be separated from its mother. In which case it will have to be put down.'

Hani quelled her instinctive outcry. She knew enough about dogs to realise that he was right.

He looked down at her and the grimness faded. 'I suppose you want to carry it?'

'Of course.'

Kelt put the squirming pup into her eager hands.

'There, there, you're all right,' she murmured, her voice low as she cuddled the little animal to her breast. Immediately it relaxed, staring earnestly up into her face.

Cradling the pup, Hani climbed into the passenger seat. 'She doesn't look sick at all,' she said when Kelt came in beside her.

'She?'

'Yes, she's a female, and she looks really healthy—fat and glossy. Her eyes are clear and bright, and she's alert. She can't have been thrown out of a car. Perhaps whoever did this wanted her to be found.'

Kelt switched on the engine and said harshly, 'If they had they wouldn't have tied her up in a sack and hidden her behind a patch of manuka scrub.'

Wishing he hadn't pointed out that inconvenient fact, she remained silent.

He must have guessed, because he sent her a swift sideways glance. 'It's always better to face the truth,' he said. Once they were on the road he gave a humourless smile. 'Did I sound sententious and smug?'

'Yes, you did,' she told him spiritedly, stroking the puppy's downy little head. 'Unfortunately that doesn't make what you said any less true.'

'In my experience almost as much havoc is wrought by people who stubbornly make excuses for inexcusable behaviour as by the people who indulge in that behaviour.'

'Oh, dear, as well as sententious and smug you sound very old and jaded,' she teased.

To her surprise his mouth twitched at the corners, but he didn't answer, and her gaze drifted to his hands on the wheel—sure, competent, controlled...

He'd handled the pup so carefully, his long fingers gentle as he'd manipulated the tiny limbs. Into her head there sneaked an image of those hands on her skin, their lean, tanned strength a potent contrast to her pale gold.

That secret warmth blazed into life, sending a wave of hot excitement through her. Stunned, she banished the seductive fantasy and sat upright, concentrating on the animal now asleep in her lap.

But before long she stole a glance at the man beside her, unconsciously measuring the arrogant profile—all angles and straight lines except for the sexy curve of his lips.

'OK?' he asked without looking at her.

How did he know she'd been watching him? Confused by her reaction, she swallowed and said, 'Yes, she's asleep, poor little scrap. How *could* anyone be so cruel as to abandon her like that to a lingering and painful death? It's—just horrible.'

'They probably couldn't bring themselves to kill her, so they stuffed her into the sack like rubbish and dumped her—out of sight, out of mind.' Kelt's tone was coldly disgusted.

Chilled, because Felipe always had someone else do his dirty work for him, she said thinly, 'That's appalling—horrifying.'

'Indeed.'

The vet, a middle-aged woman with an expression that told them she'd seen worse things than this, said, 'She's in excellent condition. I'd say she was the only pup in the litter and that she's just been taken from her mother. She's about two months old—part border collie with something like a corgi.' She looked at Kelt, her eyes amused. 'She'll probably make a good cattle dog, Kelt.'

He smiled at that, looking at the puppy protectively cradled in Hani's arms.

'What do you want done with her?' the vet asked.

Hani said, 'I'll look after her.'

She felt the impact of Kelt's frown without seeing it, but his tone was neutral and dispassionate when he said, 'Are you sure? Puppies are a bit like babies—they need fairly constant attention and that often means getting up at night to take them outside.'

'I know.'

'You'll be sorry when you have to leave her behind.'

'Surely someone—perhaps on the station—will adopt her once I've got her housetrained and taught her some simple commands?'

'Every child on Kiwinui will want her,' Kelt said dryly, then shrugged. 'Your decision,' he said, and turned to the vet. 'Thanks for looking at her. We'd better buy some necessities before we go.'

The vet said, 'Well, let me sponsor her for that, anyway. Quite frankly, I'm glad you're not leaving me with the problem of what to do with her.'

Kelt said ironically, 'I'll stand godfather and buy her first lot of food.'

'It's all right—' When he lifted that quizzical brow Hani

stopped, realising she couldn't accept the vet's professional services then refuse Kelt's offer.

Lamely she said, 'Thank you very much, both of you.'

Halfway home Kelt asked, 'What will you call her?'

'I don't know.' She laughed. 'My brother always said dogs choose their own names if you just give them a bit of time.'

And stopped, her heart banging uncomfortably in her chest. For years she'd never spoken of Rafiq—tried not to even think of him because it hurt so much—yet somehow this man had got through her guard enough for her to mention her brother twice in as many days. She'd have to be much more careful.

He said casually, 'Your brother is probably right. You could call her Annie.'

For a horrified second she thought he'd said Hani. The puppy squirmed in her lap as though sensing the panic that kicked beneath her ribs. Then she realised what he'd actually said. Relief cracked her voice when she replied, 'Annie?'

'Little Orphan Annie, alone and friendless in the world.'

The allusion clicked into place. She kept her eyes fixed on the pup, asleep again. 'Well, she's probably not an orphan, and she's certainly not alone or friendless now—thanks to you.'

She sensed rather than saw his broad shoulders lift. 'You're the one who made the decision. I just hope you're not too shattered when you have to leave her behind.'

Hani bit her lip, then was struck by a thought. '*If* I have to leave her behind. I might be able to take her with me. I can't see why not.'

For the first time since she'd fled Felipe she was ready to risk loving again. An emotion unfurled inside her, softly and without limit, a sense of freedom and relief.

She'd believed Felipe had killed an essential part of her—

that part willing to give trust and love—when he'd ordered the death of her puppy.

But he hadn't.

It had just gone into hiding.

So she'd allow herself to love this helpless, abandoned little thing, and she'd fight to take her back to Tukuulu. After all, she'd saved the pup's life, and saving something meant it was up to you to look after it to the best of your ability.

Feeling slightly winded, as though she'd taken a huge step into the unknown, she stroked the puppy again.

'The vet said she'll grow into a working dog,' Kel reminded her.

'So?'

'That means she'll need constant stimulation—work to occupy her mind—or she'll become frustrated and neurotic.'

Hani digested that silently before saying, 'I'll see how things go.' She sent him a quick, defiant look. 'But whatever happens, I'll always be glad we stopped to look over the valley.'

He nodded. 'Me too.'

CHAPTER SEVEN

THE PUPPY SETTLED DOWN well in her new basket, but in the middle of the night Hani woke with a headache and the telltale signs of a bout of fever. Glumly she gulped down her medication, then remembered her promise to Kelt; aching and reluctant, she forced herself out to the telephone, squinted at the number she'd been given, and fumbled to press the buttons.

When she finally got the combination right Kelt answered. 'I'll be right down,' he said tersely. 'Get back to bed.'

By the time he arrived she was shivering under the covers, and the low hum of his approaching vehicle was probably the most wonderful sound she'd ever heard.

Learning to rely on Kelt would be almost more dangerous than falling in love with him, but at that moment she was utterly grateful he had an overdeveloped sense of responsibility.

Although she strained to hear, she didn't realise he was in the house until he opened the bedroom door and the puppy, secure in her basket in the corner of the room, woke, made a funny squeak and scrabbled at the side of her basket.

'Go back to sleep,' he said, and of course the little thing settled down again.

He came silently across to the bed and scrutinised Hani, and in spite of her heart's warning she relaxed and closed her eyes, allowing herself to yield to the effortless authority emanating from him.

'You've taken your medication?'

He frowned, because her smile was a pale imitation of the real thing. 'Yes, sir.' The words were slurred and unsteady, and she spoke with difficulty, but she added, 'I'm glad you're here.'

Kelt took her hand, surprised at the way her fingers curled around his. 'Try to relax. I'll get you a drink. Hot or cold?'

The narrow brows pleated as though she didn't understand, and a minuscule nod was followed by another shiver that racked her slender body.

'Hot,' she whispered.

He made tea and brought it in, scooping her against his chest and holding the cup to her lips as she took tiny sips of the warm liquid. He didn't know if adding sugar would help, but on the chance it might he'd sweetened it. Although her brows drew together again, she drank most of it.

To his critical eye this attack was nowhere as severe as the first one he'd witnessed, but it was bad enough. She was on fire and in pain, and there was nothing he could do but hold her and wait for the fever to subside.

He looked down at the even features, the flushed, honey-coloured skin like silk satin. She might pretend to be English, but with her superb eyes closed a heritage of more exotic bloodlines was obvious. Those eyes were set on a slight upwards tilt, their long lashes flickering and her sensuous mouth tightening as the fever burned mercilessly through her.

The thought of her enduring this alone and uncared for roused a fierce, powerful compassion in Kelt, fuelling his helpless anger at knowing the only thing he could give her was the comfort of his arms.

Eventually the fever broke dramatically, and once again she

was drenched. Relieved, he glanced at his watch. This bout was over in half the time of the previous one.

Meanwhile, what to do about her soaked clothes? She'd hate it, but she was just going to have to deal with the fact that once again he'd got her out of the wet garments and into something dry.

At the thought his body quickened, protectiveness replaced by a rush of forbidden desire. He gritted his teeth and set her back onto the bed.

Her lashes flickered again, then lifted, forced up by sheer will.

Hani stared at the dark, stony face above her, familiar yet strangely alien. Slowly her sluggish brain processed enough information for her to recall what had happened. Although exhaustion softened her bones and loosened her muscles, she shuddered at the feel of her wet hair against her throat and the clammy embrace of her clothes.

After a couple of tries she managed to say, 'Th-thank you.'

The steely blue gaze that held her prisoner didn't change. 'Do you think you can shower by yourself?'

Shying away from the only alternative, she muttered, 'Yes.'

When she tried to pull herself up he said curtly, 'Stay where you are. I'll turn the shower on and carry you in.'

But when he came back she was sitting on the side of the bed, brows knotted and panting slightly.

'I said I'd carry you in,' he said, but his tone was resigned rather than irritated.

'I can manage,' she said, defiance plain in her tone.

To her surprise he didn't object. 'OK, give it a try.'

Hani eased her feet onto the floor and grabbed the headboard, exerting the very last of her strength to stand up. Her legs shook so much that she might as well be shivering, she thought miserably.

Kelt didn't say anything; he just picked her up as effortlessly as though she were a child and carried her across the room. As the door closed behind them she saw the puppy's eyes on them.

'I'm glad you can smile,' he said, easing her onto the chair he'd put in the shower.

'The puppy thinks we're crazy,' she managed to say, her voice wobbling.

Eyes revealing grim amusement, he examined her through a haze of steam. 'She's almost certainly right,' he told her. 'If you think you can cope, I'll leave you to it. If you can't, I'm afraid you're just going to have to grit your teeth and bear my ministrations.'

Again—only this time she was conscious. Colour prickled up from her breasts. 'I can do it,' she said quickly.

He gave her another hard stare and nodded. 'Yell if you need help,' he said succinctly, and left her.

Gathering strength, she sat for some moments just relishing the clean warmth of the water on her sweat-soaked body, but when she tried to get out of her clothes that same water made her clothes clinging and uncooperative. Gritting her teeth, she was able to wriggle free of her briefs, but the top resisted her every attempt.

She was shaking with useless frustration when there was a knock on the door. 'J-just a moment,' she called desperately, tugging at the recalcitrant shift as it refused to come over her arms.

Humiliatingly exposed, she looked around for her towel, then grabbed the one he'd put outside and wrapped it around herself. Where, of course, it immediately got wet. Hot, furious tears welled up in her eyes and ached in her throat so she couldn't produce a word.

He said, 'Hannah?'

Her silence brought him straight inside; he took in the situation immediately and said, 'It's all right.'

She flinched away as he opened the door into the shower. Face rigid, he paused for a second to strip off his shirt, then reached in and turned off the shower.

Hani could have died with embarrassment, but to her amazed bewilderment she wasn't afraid. Efficiently and without changing expression he removed her top and, while she blushed from her waist to the top of her head, he got his shirt and cocooned her in it, hiding everything down to her thighs.

'Let that wet towel drop now,' he said.

Her hands were shaking so much she couldn't even untie the one she'd knotted around her waist. Embarrassing tears filled her eyes. In a goaded voice she said, 'I f-feel so useless...'

'Nobody is at their best after a bout of tropical fever,' he said in a cool, level voice, and undid the towel for her, letting it drop.

His hands against her were—wildly exciting. They set her skin on fire.

No, they set her whole body alight. Dumbly, she stared at him, and started to shake again—delicious, fiercely erotic tremors of sensation that filled her with a tempting strength. Hani forced herself to lift her eyes from his torso—a powerful incitement in itself, strong and lean and bronze, the muscles flexing slightly as though he stayed still only with a great effort.

She met his eyes, recklessly responding to the glitter of hunger in their blue depths.

For—how long? Measured by heartbeats, an eternity. His fingers tightened around her waist, almost easing her closer, and she held her breath, everything in her focused on the warmth of his hands on her skin, the faint, primal body scent that was his alone, emphasised by the shirt she wore.

Somehow the fever had sensitised her whole body so that it longed for his touch. More than anything in the whole world she wanted him to take that final step, wanted to let her head rest on his broad shoulder, let him...

His eyes went cold, and he set her away from him, his hands closing on her shoulders to propel her out of the shower and into the bathroom.

'You need to sleep,' he said, his voice totally lacking inflection. 'Have you got a hairdryer?'

'Yes.' Every bit of passion drained away, leaving her cold and so utterly humiliated it took all her energy to produce the word.

She wanted to insist he let her walk into the bedroom, but he gave her no choice; he simply picked her up and carried her through, depositing her on the side of the bed. In spite of her bitter embarrassment Hani thought she'd never felt so safe in all her life...

'The puppy wants to go outside,' he said, and left the room.

As she shed the bath towel and struggled into a gaily-patterned wrap he'd found, she heard him talking to the puppy. The outside door rasped open, closing again a few moments later.

From the bedroom door he asked, 'Are you OK?'

'Yes.'

He came in with a dry towel, which he used to dry off her hair. He was so gentle, she thought dreamily, by now so tired she couldn't produce a coherent thought. Tomorrow she'd wake and remember what he looked like—strong and lithe, the light burnishing his tanned, powerful shoulders.

Then he turned on the hairdryer, saying grimly, 'I should have called Rosie for this part.'

Hani gave a prodigious yawn. 'You're—it's fine,' she murmured. Her half-closed gaze lingered on the scroll of dark hair across his chest.

His detachment should have reassured her. Shamefully, she was undermined by another, more searing emotion—a fierce resentment that he could be so unaffected when she felt like melting like a puddle at his feet.

Eventually he said, 'It's dry now.'

She fell onto the sheets, eyes closing as she felt the covers being pulled over her. Dimly she realised that he'd changed the bedlinen, and then exhaustion devoured her.

Kelt looked down at her. Hannah—Honey suited her much better, he thought sardonically—lay on her side, a cheek cupped in one hand, her breath coming evenly between her lips and her colour normal.

He glanced at his watch again. If she followed the previous pattern she'd sleep like that until morning, and wake up in remarkably good shape.

So he could go home to his very comfortable bed in his own room.

He picked up his shirt and pulled it on again, stopping as the faintest fragrance whispered up to him from the cloth. Jaw set, he went into the living room and opened a door onto the deck. Little waves flirted onto the sand. The tide was going out, he noticed automatically, and looked along the beach.

Mind made up, he came back in and lowered himself onto the sofa.

Hani woke to a plaintive little snuffle from the puppy, and cautiously stretched. She felt—*good*, she decided, and eased herself out of the bed.

'Yes, all right,' she said softly. 'Just give me time to find my feet…'

The medication had worked its magic; she was still a bit

wobbly, but that would go once she got some food and a cup of good coffee inside her.

Heat swept up from her throat at all-too-vivid memories of Kelt's impersonal, almost indifferent ministering to her—until the moment when his hands had released the towel around her waist.

And then, in spite of his cool self-possession, for taut, charged moments he hadn't been able to hide his desire.

For her…

Hani's breath came swiftly through her lips as she relived her own emotions—a hungry passion backed by intense confidence, as though this mutual desire was *right*, the one thing that could bring some peace and harmony to her.

OK, so he'd controlled his own reaction immediately. She wished he hadn't.

More colour flooded her skin when she remembered her dreams—tangled, happy, erotic fantasies without the shame and fear that usually dogged her night visions. Last night they'd been a fairy tale of love and passion and peace, and she'd woken with a smile.

As she scooped up the puppy and carried its wriggling body across to the door, she reminded herself that dreams were all she dared to savour as long as Felipe Gastano was alive.

She pushed the door open and stopped abruptly, eyes fixed on the man asleep on the sofa.

He'd stayed? Warmth suffused her, and a kind of wonder that he should feel so responsible for someone he didn't really know. He looked raffish, the arrogance of those strong features neither blurred nor gentled by the dark stubble of his beard.

The puppy wriggled, and she looked down at the little creature, realising that she had on only the thin cotton wrap. Torn, she half turned to get her dressing gown, but it appeared that things were getting desperate for the puppy, so she tiptoed across the room, holding her breath as she eased the door onto the lawn open.

Once placed on the grass the puppy obliged, and Hani smiled, remembering other occasions like this. Although the *castello* had been run efficiently by a team of servants, her parents had always insisted she look after her own pets.

Now, damp grass prickling the soles of her feet, she shielded her eyes against the sheen the rising sun cast on the sea, and the edge of shimmering gold outlining the big island that sheltered this coastline. Her lungs expanded, taking in great breaths of salt-scented air. She had never been in a place so beautiful, so free.

She could live here very happily, she thought wistfully. Perhaps she was attuned to living on an island in the middle of a vast sea...

Moraze was smaller than New Zealand, Tukuulu even smaller, a mere dot in the ocean, but all were thousands of miles from the nearest country, and perhaps such places bred a different kind of people.

Whatever, she could learn to love New Zealand. This part of it anyway.

The puppy sniffed its way back to her and licked her bare toes. 'Hello, little thing,' she said softly, and stooped to pick it up. 'I hope you find your name soon, because I can't go on calling you puppy, or little thing. It's demeaning. What do you think, hmm?'

The puppy swiped her chin with a pink tongue, then yawned, showing sharp white teeth in excellent condition.

On a quiet laugh Hani turned and walked back to the bach, hoping fervently that Kelt was still asleep. It seemed stupid and missish that after last night she should be so embarrassed—

the wrap covered her from neck to ankle—but she couldn't help it.

Any more than she could help that *frisson* of excitement that ran down her spine whenever she met his eyes, or the suspicious heat that smouldered into life at his lightest, least erotic touch.

Again she held her breath, keeping a wary eye on the sprawled figure dwarfing the sofa. Her breath came noiselessly between her lips as she passed the sofa, only to have that relief vanish when his rough, early-morning voice stopped her in her tracks.

'How are you feeling?'

'Good,' she blurted, turning to face him with the puppy clutched to her breast like a squirming shield. Guiltily she loosened her hold and added brightly, 'It was very kind of you to come down.'

He lifted his brows, and ran a hand across the stubble. 'There's no need to thank me.' His tone changed from the gravelly drawl to a clipped note that barely concealed anger. 'Have you had to suffer all your other attacks by yourself?'

'I managed,' she said defensively.

'Why wasn't someone with you? Once you start to shiver you have no idea what you're doing.'

Heat burned along her cheekbones. What *had* she done? Only shown him that she wanted him.

Defensively she said, 'I'm getting much better.'

'And you'd rather suffer in silence than ask for help,' he said curtly. 'But your colleagues must have known you needed help, even if you refused to ask for it.'

'I asked for it last night,' she pointed out, chin lifting.

He showed his teeth. 'You didn't, you simply told me you were coming down with another bout, and you only did that because I extracted a very reluctant promise from you.'

Her silence must have told him that he was dead on the mark. The puppy wriggled in Hani's hands again and his frown disappeared. 'Put her down. She probably wants to explore the place.'

Sure enough the little thing started to sniff the sofa leg. Hani said, 'She should know it well enough by now—she spent most of yesterday afternoon either sleeping or smelling around.'

'It will take her more than a few turns around the room to get used to being here.'

A single lithe movement brought him to his feet. Automatically Hani took a step backwards. He was so tall he loomed over her, and he had a rare ability to reduce her to a state of shaming breathlessness.

His eyes hardened. 'Why are you afraid of me?' he asked in a level voice that was more intimidating than a shout would have been.

Not that she could imagine him shouting. He'd lose his temper coldly, she thought with an inward shiver, in an icy rage that would freeze anyone to immobility.

'I'm not.' It sounded like something a schoolchild might blurt.

His brows climbed. 'If you're not afraid of me, why did you jump backwards just then, as though you think I might pounce on you?' His steel-blue eyes surveyed her mercilessly.

Very quietly, she said, 'You take up a lot of room.'

He frowned. 'What does that mean? Yes, I'm a big man, but that doesn't make me violent.'

'I know that.' She was making a total hash of this, and she owed it to him to explain that he was reaping the heritage of another man who hadn't been violent either—not in action. Felipe had never hit her. His speciality had been mental torture, a feline, dangerous malice that had irreparably scarred her.

But the words wouldn't come. After a deep breath, she continued, 'I suppose the… I feel embarrassed by being such a weakling.'

'You're not weak,' he said impatiently, 'you're ill. There's a difference.'

Rattled, she floundered for a few seconds. 'I mean, I'm grateful—'

He cut in, 'I've done no more for you or with you than your brother or father would have done. There's no need for gratitude, and certainly no need for the kind of fear you seem to feel.'

'I know,' she said quickly. 'You've been amazingly kind to me, and you don't…I don't…' She took another jagged breath. 'Look, can we just leave it?'

He said abruptly, 'Sit down.'

And when she continued to hover, he continued, 'It seems to me that you're either a virgin—'

Her abrupt headshake stopped him. The thought of Hani helpless and brutalised fanned a deadly anger inside him that demanded action. Unfortunately he had no way of finding out what had happened without forcing her to relive the experience.

Keeping his voice level and uninflected, he went on, 'Or you've had a bad experience.'

At her involuntary flinch, he said in a silky voice that sent shudders down her spine, 'So that's it.'

Hani bit her lip. 'No, actually, it's not what you're thinking.'

'Care to talk about it?'

The thought made her stomach lurch sickeningly. 'No.'

After several charged moments he said in a level, objective tone, 'You need help—therapy, probably.'

'I'm fine,' she returned, automatically defensive.

'That's your attitude to everything—just leave me alone, I'm fine,' he observed with a sardonic inflection. 'Unfortunately it doesn't seem to be working.'

Pride lifted her head. 'Sorry, I don't feel like being pyschoanalysed.' His narrowing eyes made her add tautly, 'Neither your kindness nor my gratitude gives you any right to interfere with my life.'

'The fact that you're staying in my house on my property means I've accepted some responsibility for your well-being.'

'I'm a grown woman. I'm responsible for myself—and apart from these bouts of fever I'm perfectly capable of looking after myself.'

He looked at her with an irony that was reflected in his words. 'Really? You could have fooled me.'

'That is ridiculous,' she retorted hotly. 'In fact, this whole conversation is ridiculous!'

'It's a conversation that should have taken place years ago between you and a therapist,' he said evenly. 'Before you decided that the only way to expiate the sin of being brutalised was to devote your life to doing good works.'

She went white. 'You don't know what you're talking about.'

'You flinch whenever a man comes near you. Nothing and no one has the right to do that to you.'

'I do not!'

Eyes half-concealed by those dark lashes, he covered the two paces that separated them and took her by the upper arms, holding her with a gentleness that didn't fool her—if she struggled those hands would pin her effortlessly.

Fierce heat beat up through Hani, an arousal that softened her bones and rocketed her heartbeat into panicky, eager anticipation that undermined her anger and outrage.

'You're not shaking—yet,' he said calmly. 'But if I kissed

you you'd faint. You're clenching your teeth now to stop them chattering.'

'You're an arrogant lout,' she flung at him. Desperate to banish from her treacherous mind the image of his mouth on hers, she surged on, 'Why are you doing this?'

'By *this*, do you mean holding you close?' His eyes gleamed with the burnished steel of a sword blade, but his voice was level and uninflected. 'See, you can't relax, even though you must know I won't force myself on an unwilling—or unconscious—woman.'

Neither had Felipe. He'd been able to make her want him—until she'd understood the true depths of his character, and fear and loathing had overwhelmed that first innocent, ardent attraction. And by then it was too late to run...

Still in that same neutral tone Kelt said, 'If you're afraid, Hannah, all you have to do is pull away.' He loosened his already relaxed grip.

Something—a wild spark of defiance—kept her still. A basic female instinct, honed by her past experiences, told her she had nothing to fear from Kelt—he didn't possess Felipe's cruelty, nor the lust for power that had ruled him.

And Kelt's taunt about devoting her life to good works stung. Running away had eased her visceral, primal terror for her own safety, but she'd chosen to teach because she'd wanted to help.

Staring up into the hard, handsome face of the man who held her, she realised that Kelt had somehow changed her—forcing her to face that what she was really hiding from was her own shame, her knowledge that she had let her brother down so badly.

It was as though a switch clicked on in her brain, bringing light into something she'd never dared examine. Before she could change her mind she said quietly, 'I'm not afraid of you.'

Kelt's expression altered fractionally; the glittering steel-blue of his gaze raked her face.

Hani held her breath when his mouth curved in a tight, humourless smile. 'Good.'

And she closed her eyes as he bent his head.

CHAPTER EIGHT

HANI had no idea what to expect; eyes clamped shut, she waited, her heart thudding so noisily she couldn't hear anything else.

'Open your eyes,' Kelt ordered softly, his voice deep and sure and almost amused.

'Why?' she muttered.

His laughter was warm against her skin, erotically charging her already overwhelmed senses, but a thread of iron in his next words made her stiffen.

'So you know exactly who you're kissing,' he said.

'I do know,' she whispered. 'The man who looked after me last night.'

Impatiently, every nerve strained and eager, she waited for the touch of his lips. When nothing happened she opened her eyes a fraction and peered at him through her lashes.

In spite of the smile that curved his mouth his face was oddly stern. 'The man who wants you,' he corrected.

Colour burned her cheeks. When she realised he was waiting for an answer she mumbled, 'It's mutual.'

He gave her another intent look, one that heated until her knees wobbled. And then he bent his head the last few inches and at last she felt his mouth on hers, gentle and without passion as though he was testing her.

Into that fleeting, almost butterfly kiss she said fiercely, 'I'm *not* scared of you.'

'You can't imagine how very glad I am to hear that,' he said, his voice deep and very sure, and he gathered her closer to his lean, hardening body and kissed her again.

Hani felt something she'd never experienced before—a sensation of being overtaken by destiny, of finding her heart's one true fate.

The warnings buzzing through her brain disappeared in a flood of arousal. Kelt tasted of sinful pleasure, of erotic excitement, of smouldering sexuality focused completely on her and the kiss they were exchanging, a kiss she'd never forget.

She was surrounded by his strength and she wasn't afraid, didn't feel like a stupid child who'd fallen into a situation she didn't understand and couldn't control...

It shocked her when he lifted his head a fraction and said something. 'Hannah?'

No, my name's Hani! But of course she couldn't say that. Hani de Courteville no longer existed; she'd drowned six years ago. This kiss was for Hannah Court, not the pampered darling of an island nation who'd failed everyone so badly.

Opening dazed eyes, she tried to regain command of her thoughts. 'Yes?' she asked in a die-away voice.

'All right?'

From somewhere inside her she found the courage to say with a smoky little smile, 'Right now I don't think I've ever felt better. Kiss me again.'

He laughed, and she raised a hand and traced his mouth, the beautifully outlined upper lip, the sensuous lower one that supported it. Something hot and feverish coiled through her. Felipe had never wanted her caresses—forget about Felipe, she commanded wildly. He'd never made her feel like this, either—so deliciously wanton, confident in her own sexuality.

Kelt's lips closed around her finger and he bit the tip delicately, sending more erotic shivers through her.

His breath was warm against her skin when he said, 'I will, once you stop playing with my mouth.'

Greatly daring, she cupped his jaw with her two hands, relishing the opportunity as her fingertips tingled. He let her explore, and when at last she dropped her hands he caught them and pressed the palm of each to his mouth before pulling her back into his arms and kissing her again.

No butterfly touch this time, but one that frankly sought a response from her, a response she gave eagerly, losing herself in the restrained carnality of their kiss.

Until Kelt lifted his head to say on a note of laughter, 'I think your small protégé needs another run outside.'

'Oh!' She pulled away, hiding her disappointment by bending to pick up the puppy, which was making plaintive noises at her feet.

'I'll take her,' he said crisply.

She handed the puppy over and while he took it through the door into the sunlight she dashed into the bathroom and combed her tumbled hair into some sort of order.

More of those sexy little chills ran through her as she remembered him holding her head still while he'd kissed her, doing with his mouth what her fingers had done to the jut of his chin and the clean, unyielding line of his jaw.

She'd been completely lost in passion, so far gone that nothing but Kelt's kiss had been real to her. She hadn't even heard the puppy.

But Kelt had.

'Oh, dear God,' she whispered, pressing a cold cloth to her hot cheeks and tender mouth.

Was she doomed to be attracted to inherently cold men totally in control of their emotions, their passions?

After she'd realised that Felipe's interest in her had been only because she was Rafiq de Courteville's sister, she'd vowed never to lose her head over a man again.

But Kelt had been so kind, some pathetic part of her pleaded. Felipe had teased and amused her, flattered and caressed her, but she could never remember him being kind…

OK, so Kelt wasn't like Felipe, but he was still dominant, accustomed to being in charge.

So was Rafiq.

Tormented, she stared at her reflection—big dark eyes still slumberous in her flushed face, her trembling mouth full and well-kissed. She simply didn't know Kelt well enough to even guess what sort of man he really was.

Quite probably he'd kissed her on a whim—or because he'd rather liked what he'd seen when he'd helped her out of the shower.

He certainly couldn't feel anything more for her than a physical desire.

But that's what you want, she reminded herself. This is just sexual passion, nothing more. You're not in love with him. You don't want him to love you.

Yes, I do.

With a horrified inward groan, she turned away and grabbed a towel, hiding her face in it for a second before turning to face her reflection.

All right, she silently told the wanton woman in the mirror, falling in love with Kelt Gillan is simply not an option. So you'll call a halt right now. Yes, it's going to make you feel like an idiot, but you've been behaving like one, so it serves you right.

She dried her face, applied a light film of gloss to her mouth, then turned away, squaring her shoulders, and walked out into the sitting room just as Kelt, this time with the puppy gambolling at his heel, walked through the French door into the room.

Her gaze skipped from broad shoulders to the width of his chest and the narrow, masculine hips. One of those sensuous little shivers scudded down her backbone.

Abruptly, before she could change her mind, she blurted, 'I hope you don't think that this…ah, those…what we did…'

'Those kisses?' he supplied smoothly.

His cool, confident tone gave her the strength to say stolidly, 'Yes. I hope you don't think they meant anything.'

'Beyond that you want me?' This time his voice was cynically amused.

'Exactly,' she said, almost cringing at the undercurrent of embarrassment in the word. However, having handed him the opportunity to mock her, she just had to wear it with as much grace as she could.

Quailing inside, she called on every scrap of courage she possessed to meet his coolly measuring survey with a pretence of confidence.

'I assume you're trying to tell me that, just because you kissed me with enthusiasm and a charming lack of pretence it doesn't mean you're going to sleep with me,' he said blandly

Shaken by his bluntness, Hani bought a moment by stopping to pick up the puppy, who licked her chin lavishly and promptly dozed off.

'That's exactly what I mean.' She prayed she could bring this awkward and humiliating conversation to an end withou' seeming any more foolish than she already did.

He said with cutting emphasis, 'A few kisses, however hungry and sweet, don't constitute an invitation to sex, so you can relax. Don't ever judge me again by whatever bastard made you so afraid of men. When I feel the urge to take you to bed, I'll make sure you know well ahead of time, and I'll let you make the decision.'

Hani said in a goaded voice, 'I'm sorry—'

'Like your gratitude, an apology isn't necessary,' he cut in without emphasis. He looked down at the sleeping puppy. 'Has she decided on a name for herself yet?'

Hani forced herself to respond. 'I don't think Sniffer would be a nice name for a puppy,' she said, hoping he didn't notice her brittle tone. 'I'll wait a few days, and if she doesn't come up with something more suitable I'll have to choose a name myself.'

Kelt nodded. 'In spite of what your brother said. Where is he, by the way?'

Hating the lie, Hani said shortly, 'He's dead,' and turned away. 'I'll just put her in her basket.'

He stopped her with one hand. 'I'll go back to the homestead,' he said, blue eyes hooded and unreadable as he scanned her face. 'But just for your information—although I find you very attractive, you're quite safe with me. And if you're thinking that naturally I'd say that—'

Wishing she could deal with this with a light hand and not make blunder after blunder, she broke in, 'Look, it's not important. Truly. I suppose I overreacted—just like you did when you heard her whimpering.' Colour high, she met his opaque gaze with desperate candour. 'Of c-course I find you attractive too, but I'm not—I don't want to embark on an affair that will have to stop when I go back to Tukuulu.'

Kelt's arrogant black brows drew together. 'You must

realise by now that this latest bout of fever reduces your chances of going back to Tukuulu.'

She stared at him. 'What do you mean?'

His frown deepened. 'If you go back to the tropics the fever could well recur.'

'That's not much of a problem; the medication works every time. You've seen how well I respond to it.'

He said harshly, 'Constant use produces a raft of quite nasty side-effects.'

Her eyes widened, then went blank. 'The attacks are getting further and further apart.'

'Because you're in New Zealand,' he told her with brutal honesty. 'People can become permanent invalids from this, Hannah. Some still die. If you go back to Tukuulu that's a possibility the school has to take into account.'

Grabbing for composure, she babbled, 'No, that won't happen. The medication works really well.'

'How well are *you* going to work if you keep having attacks? How much use will you be to the school?' He switched subjects. 'As for the side-effects—do you have a computer?'

She shook her head.

'Then come up to the homestead and I'll show you the information I found in a search that took me five minutes.'

Torn, she hesitated, but this was important. 'I have to get dressed—'

Ten minutes later, clad in trousers and one of her new jerseys, she found herself inside his Range Rover, the puppy in her lap. While Kelt drove silently towards his house she stared out through the window, worrying away at his statement.

Stop it, she told herself sturdily. He might be wrong.

But he wasn't a man who made mistakes.

Though hadn't she read somewhere that only the naïve trusted everything they'd read on the internet?

It wasn't until she sat in front of his sophisticated computer set-up in his scarily modern office that panic closed in on her, producing something terrifyingly close to nausea.

'How do I know this is accurate?' she asked thinly, staring at the words that danced on the screen. She blinked several times and they settled down, spelling out a frightening message.

'Because it comes from a respected medical journal.' He waited, noticing the absolute rigidity of her spine, as though if she relaxed something might shatter. Frowning, he said, 'Finish it.'

Dark head bowed, she read silently and swiftly. Once she finished she didn't turn to look at him, but dropped her gaze to the keyboard.

And when at last she spoke her voice was flat and completely without emotion. 'I wish they'd told me.'

'Your doctor should have,' he said, coldly angry because nobody seemed to care much about her.

'He's old, and…' She couldn't go on.

'It's not the end of the world,' he said calmly. 'A couple of years in a temperate climate will almost certainly make sure you recover.' Without giving her time to digest that he went on, 'Do you want me to get in touch with the expert in tropical medicine they quote?'

She couldn't afford some expensive expert. And if she couldn't get back to Tukuulu… Panic kicked Hani beneath the ribs, temporarily robbing her of rationality.

She had nowhere else to go, nothing else she could do. Her homeland was forever banned to her. Rafiq would never forgive her for putting him through the agony of losing a sister who'd not only figured in a sleazy scandal, but had also tried to take the easy way out by committing suicide.

Besides, he was married now, and a father. She'd picked up an elderly magazine in the hospital in Tukuulu, and seen a photograph of the ruling family of Moraze—a wife who'd looked like someone Hani could love, and two handsome sons. Rafiq had other people to love, closer to him than a sister could ever be.

She'd felt she was doing something worthwhile in her job on Tukuulu, but if she couldn't go back...

Her godmother's inheritance wouldn't support her, and she suspected that her qualifications wouldn't help her find a job in New Zealand unless she actually emigrated. And she didn't want to do that; it would mean too much enquiry into her past.

Kelt said crisply, 'I'll make an appointment with the specialist.'

'No,' she said thinly. She turned and met his eyes, shivering a little at the burnished sheen that made them unreadable.

'Why not? If you're worried about money—'

'No,' she repeated more briskly this time, and got to her feet, taking in a deep breath as he put out a hand to help her.

Hani ignored it, but in spite of the scared thoughts churning in her brain, his closeness triggered a swift, uncontrollable excitement. His kisses had sensitised her to him, linking them in some intangible way so that her body ached with forbidden longing.

What was he thinking?

She tried to smile. 'If that's true, then it looks as though my time on this side of the world could soon be over,' she said, struggling to project a voice that sounded light and casual.

So much for thinking she could learn to love this place!

'You'll go back to the UK?' Kelt asked neutrally.

'Where else?' she said, trying to avoid a direct lie. She hated the falsehoods her foolish decisions forced on her; they made her feel cheap and dirty, a woman tarnished by her many mistakes.

Kelt's scrutiny hardened, and this time the shiver down her spine had little to do with the erotic physical excitement he conjured in her. Apprehension was a much colder, more threatening sensation.

'If you don't want to go back to England you could always stay here.' His tone and expression gave nothing away.

In spite of that, her foolish heart leapt in her breast. Hastily she said, 'Emigrate? I doubt very much that I have any skills New Zealand requires.'

'We always need good teachers. You'd probably have to do some more teacher training, but I'm sure you could manage that.'

She didn't dare. If anyone ever suspected that Hannah Court was the supposedly dead sister of Rafiq de Courteville, ruler of the island of Moraze, the news would be splashed across the world media, just as her death had been! In Tukuulu she'd arrived as a tourist, her passport barely glanced at. Once she'd been asked to stay on at the school she'd been accepted with no further enquiries.

Coming into New Zealand on leave had been simple enough, but emigration was a whole different affair. She struggled to control her fear, reminding herself that her passport was perfectly legitimate. Her mother had been the daughter of the ruler of a small Middle Eastern state, and her children held dual citizenship.

But emigration officials might probe deeper than that. She didn't dare take the chance.

Shrugging, she said lightly, 'Well, I'll wait until I know for certain whether I can go back to Tukuulu.' She gave the computer a quick glance. 'But thanks for finding that information for me. Just in case, I'll do some serious thinking about the future while I'm here.'

'Get better first,' he advised, still in that coolly objective tone. He indicated the puppy, snoozing on a rug. 'And find a name for that dog.'

Pretending an amusement she didn't feel, she said wryly, 'Right now, I think Sleepy would be perfect.'

A knock turned his head. 'Yes?'

Arthur peered around the door. After a quick smile at Hani he said succinctly, 'Your cousin's here.'

'Thanks,' Kelt said, his voice giving nothing away.

'I'll walk back,' Hani said immediately. Right then she didn't feel like dealing with the ebullient and rather too frank Rosie Matthews.

'Nonsense,' Kelt said, black brows meeting for a second as he looked down at her.

Rosie appeared in the doorway, looking theatrically stunned. 'Good heavens—you've let her into the inner sanctum!' she exclaimed. 'What an honour! He must be in love with you, Hannah! Nobody ever gets into Kelt's office—it's *verboten*!' She stared around as though she'd never seen it before.

Although Kelt's mouth curved, he said evenly, 'Knock it off, Rosie. All those exclamations will frighten the puppy.'

'*Puppy?*' Her mobile features softened when her gaze fell on the small animal curled up on the mat. 'Oh, what a charmer,' she crooned, and glided gracefully into the room. 'But not your style, Kelt—it looks a definite bitser. You like brilliantly pedigreed Labs.'

Briefly he explained the circumstances of the puppy's arrival.

Rosie looked at Hani with interest. 'What are you going to call her?'

'I suggested Annie,' Kelt told her.

'As in Little Orphan?' When he nodded, she said indignantly. 'No, that's horrible. Besides, she isn't an orphan any longer.'

Hani said, 'She'll find her own name soon enough.'

Rosie looked up at her cousin and fluttered her lashes. She had, Hani noticed with a hint of chagrin, very long, very curly lashes.

'Actually, Kelt,' she said in a syrupy voice that made Hani's mouth curve, 'I came to ask a favour.'

One black brow lifted. 'Ask away.'

She sighed. 'I don't know how just lifting one eyebrow is so intimidating, but it works every time,' she complained.

'Stop stalling.'

Hani said, 'Perhaps Rosie would prefer to talk to you alone.'

'She would not,' Rosie said immediately. She took a swift breath and said, 'I thought you might like to give a party.'

Kelt asked, 'Why can't your mother do it?'

'Because she's in Borneo.'

This time both brows rose. 'Your mother?' Kelt asked with an edge to his voice. 'In Borneo? I thought she was going to Auckland to the opera.'

Rosie shrugged elaborately. 'Well, this new man in her life has a thing about orang-utans, and there's this place where they introduce baby ones back into the wild. She thought she'd rather do that than see *Carmen* again, especially as she doesn't like the tenor—'

'Spare me,' Kelt cut in dryly. 'So why can't you ask your father to give you this party?'

Rosie sent him a look. 'You know very well he's writing another book.' Her tone indicated that this was answer enough.

'I'll remind him he has a daughter,' Kelt said grimly.

Kelt's open protectiveness for his cousin reminded Hani of

her brother; he too had been protective—possibly too much so. If she'd had half of Rosie's sophistication she might not have fallen for Felipe.

'No, don't do that,' Rosie said swiftly.

Kelt frowned, but didn't press the issue. 'Who do you want to invite?'

'Oh, just the usual crowd.' Rosie looked vague.

Relentlessly Kelt asked, 'Who in particular?'

Flushing, his cousin admitted, 'There's this man—he's staying with the O'Hallorans at their bach. I thought it would be a neighbourly thing to have a party for them.'

'What's his name?'

With an exasperated glower Rosie said, 'Alonso de Porto, but he's got a stack of other names to go with that. He's from Spain. He's been doing a grand tour of New Zealand.'

Hani froze, her skin leached of all colour, and beads of sweat burst out at her temples. Desperately she stooped and picked up the puppy, hoping the abrupt movement would hide her shock.

CHAPTER NINE

YAWNING sleepily, the pup snuggled into the cup of Hani's hands. She kept her eyes on it for as long as she could, forcing her mind into action.

The Alonso de Porto she'd known was a handsome boy who'd hung about on the fringes of Felipe's circle for a few weeks until his parents whisked him out of harm's way.

It couldn't be the same man. New Zealand was as far from the jet-setting sophistication of Europe as he could get.

Or be sent.

After all, if his parents had sensibly removed him from Felipe's influence once, possibly they'd had to do it again. But to New Zealand?

Entirely too much of a coincidence, she thought frantically, all her illusions of safety shattered.

Could Felipe have found her and sent Alonso…?

She took a deep breath. Why would Felipe use a Spanish grandee to track her down when he had professionals to do that sort of thing?

But if it *was* the Alonso she remembered, would he remember her?

She tried to calm her racing heart and dispel the coldness spreading beneath her ribs. When they'd met she'd been at university, struggling to fulfil her study obligations in spite of Felipe's obstruction, so she hadn't seen a lot of young de Porto.

And then relief washed through her as she realised she'd been so busy panicking she hadn't thought of the most obvious way of avoiding discovery. All she had to do was stay safely hidden at the bach!

Forcing herself to relax, she let her lashes drift cautiously up. Her stomach clamped when she met Kelt's cool, hard scrutiny. *He knows,* she thought for a taut second, feeling the familiar chill of shame.

But of course he couldn't.

Easing her grip on the squirming puppy, she parried Kelt's gaze with all the composure she could produce, forcing her brows upwards in a questioning look.

'I think I've met him,' Kelt said neutrally. 'A nice enough kid, and surprisingly unspoiled for the scion of a Spanish family with a pedigree that goes back a thousand years or so, and a fortune to match.'

Oh, God, that sounded like the Alonso she knew…

She steadied her breath, willing her heartbeat to settle down and her legs to stop shaking.

Rosie glared at Kelt, then laughed. 'Of course, you know everyone who's anyone, don't you? Although it's a bit daunting to hear the best-looking man I've ever seen described as *"a nice enough kid"*. Kid? He can only be four or five years younger than you!'

Kelt eyed her with amusement. 'All right, you can have this party, but you'll organise it yourself. Arthur will have enough to do with the cooking.'

'Super.' Rosie hurled herself into his arms, kissed his cheek with fervour, then tore free.

Hani felt a pang of—jealousy? Surely not, she thought, horrified.

That horror was intensified by Rosie's next enthusiastic words. 'I thought a nice *casual* party, a beach-and-barbecue sort of thing, starting around seven because it's such a super time in summer. One for Hannah—to introduce her to everyone.'

'So it could,' Kelt said, his keen gaze on Hani's face.

Stricken, she said as lightly as she could, 'Oh, no, you mustn't. A summer party doesn't need a reason beyond the season, surely?'

'But this would be perfect!' Rosie swept on. 'After all, if you're going to be here for three months you might as well meet all the usual suspects. And their visitors,' she added with a brilliant smile.

'Just remember Hannah's here to convalesce,' Kelt said. He gave his cousin a direct, intimidating look. 'I don't want her roped into helping you.'

'Cross my heart,' Rosie said after a speculative glance at Hani.

'I'm getting better, not dying,' Hani said briskly, earning herself another thoughtful look from the younger woman.

'Cool. We must get together some time and have lunch,' Rosie said, then blew an airy kiss to Kelt and whirled out of the room, leaving Hani breathless.

So much for hiding…

Still, she had the perfect excuse—her illness.

To the sound of his cousin's teasing voice in the hall and Arthur's indulgent replies, Kelt said ironically, 'Don't let her bulldoze you into doing anything you don't want to.'

'That's very thoughtful of you,' Hani said, 'but I wish you hadn't given her the impression that you had any right to monitor my behaviour.'

'I doubt if she's at all surprised. She frequently tells me I'm arrogant and overbearing, not to mention inflexible and old-fashioned.'

'She knows you well,' Hani said on a false, sweet note.

Kelt's answering smile sent excitement curling through her. His kisses were thrilling, but his smile had the power to reduce her to abject surrender. Not that it softened the hard lines of his face, but there was genuine humour behind it, and an appreciation of her tart irritation with him.

'I'm the big brother she never had,' he said. 'Or possibly the father. Her own is so wrapped up in his work he can only see her as an interruption.'

Hani's face must have shown what she thought of this, because he said, 'Oh, he loves her, but more when she's at a distance. That's why she lives with her mother.'

'Poor Rosie,' she said involuntarily. 'What sort of books does her father write?'

'He's a historian.' He gave her a sardonic look as though expecting her to be bored. 'At the moment he's writing a tome on Chinese exploration in the Indian Ocean; he's planning to head off to Moraze, an island a thousand miles or so off the coast of Africa, to research some ruins there. He's convinced they're Chinese.'

Hani froze. She knew those ruins.

It seemed everything—from Alonso de Porto to Rosie's father's sphere of interest—was leading back to her old life.

Oppressed by a feeling of bleak inevitability, she said brightly, 'How interesting. And don't worry about me—I won't overdo things.' Grateful for the excuse he'd given her, she said, 'I doubt if I'll get to Rosie's party so I'll make sure she doesn't use me as the reason for it.'

'Leave Rosie to me,' he said briefly. 'You look as though you could do with a cup of tea. Or coffee, perhaps.'

Right then she just wanted to get away and hide. The unexpected links between her old life and her new had shattered her precarious composure. She produced a smile, hoping he'd put its perfunctory nature down to tiredness. 'Thank you, but actually I'd rather go back to the bach.'

And met his keen survey with as limpid and innocent a look as she could manage.

His brows drew together but he said evenly, 'Of course. Rosie tends to have that effect on people. If we could harness her energy we'd probably earn megabucks from selling it to the national grid.'

Hani's gurgle of laughter brought an answering smile to his mouth, but the hard eyes were still uncomfortably intent.

So she said brightly, 'I can walk back. I could do with some fresh air.'

'I'll take you back.'

And that was that. He left her at the bach with an injunction to rest, and a feeling of being safe and protected by his concern.

You don't need care and concern, some tough inner part of her warned.

After all, she'd been independent for six years, forging her own way. And in the process she'd discovered things about herself: that she was good with children, that she could teach, that she liked the satisfaction of working hard and making a difference. Life at Tukuulu had shown her that she could cope without the protective influence of her older brother.

Her mind skittered away from the memory of Kelt's kisses. One lesson she'd learned thoroughly before she washed up on Tukuulu was that men didn't necessarily feel anything for the women they made love to. Felipe had seen her as a tool he could use, deliberately wooing and seducing her with no more emotion than lust and a desire for power.

Oh, he'd enjoyed their lovemaking; with a shudder she thought he'd found some vile satisfaction in debauching innocence.

Driven by restlessness, she got to her feet. 'How about a walk on the beach, little one?' she said to the puppy.

Once breathing in the clean, salt-scented air, the sun warm on her head and the sand firm and cool beneath her bare feet, with the puppy snuffling happily around a piece of dried seaweed, she thought that at least there had been no undercurrent of exploitation in Kelt's kisses; he'd treated her as an adult fully aware of what she was doing. And she'd been gripped by a far more primal, intense chemistry than when she'd been so sure she was in love with Felipe.

A sweet, potent warmth washed through her. She didn't dare let things go any further, but she'd always treasure the memory of Kelt's kisses.

And not just his kisses. Somehow, just by being his masterful, enigmatic, uncompromising self, by looking after her, even because of the way he dealt with Rosie, he'd restored her faith in men.

But was it wise to trust her instincts?

'Probably not,' she said to the puppy, who startled them both with a high-pitched yap.

The little animal sat back on its haunches and stared at Hani as though suspecting that the noise had come from her.

'Hey, you can talk!' She bent to stroke her, and received a lick on the wrist and another little yap.

'OK, that clinches it,' Hani said, chuckling. 'You've found your name. How do you do, Gabby?'

Gabby cocked her head, then yapped again and scratched

herself with vigour, sending a spray of sand a few centimetres into the air.

Hani felt tears burn her eyes. It had been so long since she'd dared to love; the puppy had broken through her protective armour, opening her to emotions she'd shunned for six dark years.

Actually, no—meeting Kelt had cracked that shell she'd constructed around herself with such determination.

She stooped to pick up a bleached piece of driftwood and drew a pattern in the sand. Just because she'd met a man who made her feel like a woman with heated passions and deep-seated needs didn't mean she could allow Kelt to become important to her in any way. Caution warned her that this new-found capacity to feel could hurt her all over again.

The puppy came up to investigate this new activity, pounced on the stick and promptly fell over.

'Oh, poor baby!' Hani said, then watched, intrigued, as Gabby got up and sank her tiny needle-teeth into the wood, growling fiercely.

'You've probably got it right, Gabby,' she said aloud. 'Fall over, pick yourself up and start over again. And again if necessary. Perhaps that's what I should have done instead of running away.'

Except that she'd had bigger issues to deal with than a dose of heartbreak—staying alive and out of Felipe's clutches being the most important.

Resolutely pushing the grim memories to the back of her mind, she walked up to the bach, stopping halfway to rescue the exhausted Gabby, who drank lavishly once they got back then sprawled out in the sunlight on the floor and went to sleep.

Smiling, Hani made herself a snack and sat down to eat it,

but pushed it away as the memories intruded. Could Alonso still be part of Felipe's circle?

If he was, and he recognised her and mentioned it to Felipe, she'd be in danger. Before she'd 'died' she'd told Felipe she was leaving him.

He'd been quite calm about his response, wielding his power with consummate artistry. 'Of course you may go if you no longer want to stay with me. But if you do, you will be signing your brother's death warrant as well as your own.' He'd watched the colour drain from her skin and smiled. 'And neither his death nor yours will be quick,' he'd said calmly.

Desperately she got to her feet and walked the length of the terrace, her haunted eyes ignoring the beauty before her.

That was what had pushed her into informing Rafiq that Moraze was threatened, and her despairing decision to kill herself. Although she hadn't managed to achieve that, she'd managed to convince the world she was dead, buying six years in a peaceful limbo.

If those years had taught her anything, it was that losing your head only made things worse.

First of all, she needed to know if this Alonso de Porto was the same one she'd known back then, and if he still made up part of Felipe's circle.

If only she had a computer she could go onto the internet and search for Felipe's name. He'd be easy enough to track down—presumably he still figured in the social pages of various glossy magazines.

If Alonso was still part of his circle she'd have to leave Kiwinui.

Running again, around and around like a rat in a cage…

Although she'd occasionally used the one school computer

she'd never dared look for Felipe, or even for Rafiq and Moraze. Tracking software enabled the teachers to check on the sites the students visited.

Into her mind there sprang the image of the superb set-up in Kelt's office. No doubt he needed to keep up-to-date with farming matters, but a smile hovered on her lips because it seemed the impregnable farmer was a techno-freak.

He had no children to guard, so there'd be no need for him to have tracking software.

She could ask…something…and if he offered her the use of his computer…

Appalled, she pushed the idea away.

But during the rest of the afternoon it came back to her again and again, and that night it vied with other, more tender images of Kelt's kisses, until in the end she woke sobbing from a nightmare in which Kelt had morphed into Felipe.

Shaking, she made herself a cup of tea and sat out on the deck watching the sea wash gently in and out on the beach, the moon catching the white tips of the waves as they broke into lacy patterns on the sand.

She'd been passive for too long. Now she needed to take charge of her life. And she could only do that if she had information.

And then she remembered seeing an internet café close to the pet shop.

'Oh, for heaven's sake!' she whispered.

So much for taking charge of her life! Why on earth hadn't she thought of that hours ago? No need to ask Kelt—no need to do anything more frightening than pay for half an hour of internet access. 'Tomorrow,' she promised herself, half-terrified, half-eager.

The next morning Kelt rang. 'I'm going into town

shortly,' he said, 'and I wondered if you need anything or if you'd like to come.'

Hani's first instinct was to say no, and drive into town later when he was safely home again. But she thought of passing his house, or just possibly seeing him on the farm...

So she said, 'Well, yes, as it happens I do.'

'I'll pick you up in half an hour.' He rang off.

The day was warm, so she chose a pair of loose-fitting cotton trousers the same green as her eyes, and topped them with a neat cap-sleeved T-shirt that matched her skin colour. All she needed to complete the theme, she thought with wry humour as she applied lip gloss, were black shoes that gleamed red in the sun like her hair. Failing those, she made do with a pair of tan sandals.

'I won't be too long,' she promised Gabby, who blinked at her and went straight back to sleep.

Her heart jumped when the car came down the hill, and jumped again when Kelt got out. What he did to her nerve cells, she thought with an involuntary shiver, was positively sinful...

He subjected her to a long, considering look, then smiled. 'You've obviously been sleeping very well.'

'I have,' she replied, hoping her sedate tone didn't tell him that it was his presence that gave her cheeks colour and lightened her step.

Kelt closed the door behind her and slid behind the wheel. 'And how is the puppy?'

'Her name is Gabby.' Hani grinned at his cocked eyebrow. 'She's just discovered that she can yap, and she's been practising often. But she only woke me once last night.'

All morning she'd been fighting a faint nausea at the prospect of seeing even a photograph of Felipe again, but Kelt's arrival had put paid to that. In his company everything seemed at once infinitely more complex, yet straightforward; colours were brighter, scents more seductive. His presence sharpened her appreciation of the blue of the sky and the brilliant green of the fields—*paddocks*, she corrected herself with a half-smile—and the stark loveliness of the countryside.

It wasn't exactly comfort—let alone comfortable—but she was buoyed by a sense of exhilaration, a feeling that life could be filled with richness and delight if she allowed herself to deserve it.

That newly awakened confidence faded fast once she walked into the internet café. Heart pounding and the nausea returning in full force, she sat down and keyed in the search engine, then glanced around. There were only two other people there—tourists—and they couldn't have been less interested in her.

Twenty minutes later she paid her money and sat down limply at one of the tables, waiting for the strong black coffee she'd ordered.

Felipe was dead. The words echoed in her head. He'd died on Moraze four years ago in a shoot-out with the military. The news items had been brief and carried very little information. Clearly Rafiq had clamped a lid on Press speculation.

Hani waited for relief, for joy, for anything but this vast emptiness. Nothing came.

She could go back home.

No, she could never go back. Rafiq wouldn't welcome her— how could he, when she'd caused him so much grief and pain?

She had chosen to die, and it would be far better for those she'd left behind if she stayed as dead as they thought her. She glanced around the shop, the customers drinking tea and coffee, the people walking the streets outside, the sights and smells of normality…

Here she could build a new life. The thought lingered. No one knew her here. She could start afresh...

Her mind returned to those moments she'd spent in Kelt's arms, his mouth on hers producing such ecstatic excitement that she could feel it now in every cell of her body, like a delicious electric current that revived joy and brought a kind of feverish hope.

'Hannah?'

Kelt's hard voice broke in on her scattered thoughts, making her jump. Thank God, she thought in a spill of relief, she'd finished at the computer before he came in.

The concern in his tone warmed her. 'Oh—hi. I'm waiting for my coffee.' Surprisingly, her voice was level. She indicated the chair opposite her. 'Why don't you join me?'

The coffee arrived then, and he ordered for himself, then settled back in his chair and said, 'You looked—a bit disconnected.'

She shrugged. 'Just daydreaming.'

'About what?'

'Nothing,' she said instantly, flushing under his sardonic gaze.

His beautiful mouth tightened. 'It didn't seem a pleasant daydream.'

'Daydreams are pleasant by definition, surely?' She drank some of her coffee. The excitement he roused in her returned, bringing with it the feeling that everything could work out, that the world was a better place when she was in Kelt's company. She set the cup down on its saucer and finished, 'Anything else would be a daymare, and I don't think there is such a thing.'

CHAPTER TEN

HANI said lightly, 'The thing about daydreams is that we control them, so they're always wish-fulfilment. Therefore they're always pleasant.'

Kelt eased his big body back into the chair. 'So tell me, what's your favourite daydream?'

She stared at him, saw his mouth curve, and said demurely, 'When I was five it was to be a bareback rider in a circus. I wanted to wear a short, frilly skirt with sequins all over it, and have long, golden hair that floated behind me while I rode a huge white stallion around the ring. What was yours?'

'When I was five?'

He accepted the coffee from the waitress, a woman who'd given Hani only a perfunctory smile. Her interest in Kelt was obvious, her smile broader and tinged with awareness, her eyes lingering on his hard, handsome face.

Hani squelched the same unwelcome prickle of jealousy she'd felt when Rosie had kissed him. Darn it, she thought in frustration, she was behaving like an idiot, so caught up in his male physical magic that she'd lost all sense of proportion.

OK, so he'd kissed her, and she'd kissed him back, lost in some rapturous wonderland she'd never experienced before. But honing a natural talent to his present expertise probably meant he'd kissed a lot of women. It was just plain stupid to feel that his care for her when she'd been feverish had somehow impressed her body so much it craved his touch.

'When you were five,' she reminded him once the waitress had reluctantly taken herself off.

Broad shoulders lifted in a slight shrug. 'A very boring ambition, nothing as romantic as yours; I wanted to be an astronaut, the first man to stand on Mars. Then I decided that an explorer—Indiana Jones-style—would be even more interesting. We had an old bullocky—a bullock driver—living on Kiwinui then, and he showed me how to use a whip. The first time I got it to crack I thought I'd reached the pinnacle of life's achievements.'

When she laughed delightedly, he smiled. 'That was just before my pirate period, when I roared around the Caribbean on my ship with a loyal crew of desperadoes and gathered vast amounts of treasure.'

Hani had a sudden glimpse of him as he must have been— always a leader, even as a child, his innate authority bred in him.

She opened her mouth to tell him that Moraze had an interesting history of fighting against and sometimes in alliance with the corsairs who'd once infested the Indian Ocean. Just in time, she called back the words, but he'd noticed.

He always noticed, she thought, confused by mixed emotions.

'You were going to say?' he prompted.

She summoned a smile. 'Just that we've both proved my point—it's impossible to have unpleasant daydreams because we always star in them.'

'You have an interesting habit of appearing to be about to speak, only to check yourself and come out with a platitude.'

His voice was conversational, but when she glanced up at him his eyes were uncomfortably keen.

She parried, 'Learnt from experience; teachers who blurt out comments or statements without thinking first can get themselves into trouble.'

Although he gave her abraded nerves a chance to settle down by steering the conversation into neutral channels, she suspected that every slip of her tongue was filed away in his mind.

But on the way home he asked, 'What are your plans if you aren't able to return to Tukuulu?'

Tension tightened her skin. 'I'll leave making plans for when I'm sure I can't go back—*if* that happens.'

'So you're determined to return if you can?' At her nod he said with cool detachment, 'You're a very dedicated teacher.'

'It's what I do.'

Again she endured that penetrating survey. 'No daydreams of children of your own, a husband, of falling in love?'

Her chin came up. 'I could ask you the same question,' she evaded. 'After all, you're quite a bit older than I am.'

'I'm thirty.'

'Well, why—at six years older than I am—are you still single?'

He looked amused. 'I haven't met anyone I'd like to marry.'

'Same with me.' And that, she thought with a quiver of pain, was yet another lie to add to her list.

He undercut her momentary triumph by saying, 'So we're both unattached.'

His tone hadn't altered but something—an edge to his words that hadn't been there before—set her senses onto full alert. 'I am,' she said, holding on to her reserve with determination.

'I am also. Completely.'

Hani had no idea how to reply to this, or what to do. Was

this how he wooed a possible lover, or was he warning her off? Excitement roiled through her in a series of sparks, setting fire to her imagination and her body.

Why not? Why not follow this wildfire attraction and see where it led?

Kelt wasn't like Felipe. She knew that in her innermost heart.

No, it was impossible. She realised they were passing the stream where she'd seen him digging out the blockage. Felipe would have considered such work degrading.

Just *stop* this, she told herself. Stop comparing Kelt to Felipe.

She said, 'So none of the women Rosie has comforted meant anything to you?'

His expression was amused. 'Rosie is a born exaggerator,' he said dryly, 'and you realised that five minutes after meeting her, so don't use her to back up your decision.'

A decision? As the car approached the bach, she gathered the courage to say carefully, 'I'm not sure what's going on here.'

He didn't reply until he'd stopped the car and switched off the engine. His silence was too intimidating, she thought, and scrambled out, turning to face him with her chin held high as he came around the car to stand in front of her.

His expression unreadable, he asked, 'How old were you when you went to Tukuulu?'

After a moment's hesitation she answered, 'Eighteen.'

'Barely more than a child,' he said, frowning. 'What the hell were your family thinking?'

'I have no family,' she said, hating the lie.

'And since then you've had no relationships?'

'That's none of your business,' she said coldly, aware that heat was emphasising her cheekbones.

'In other words you haven't.'

Reduced to frustrated silence by his blunt statement, she gave him a haughty glare and started off down the path towards the bach.

From behind he said deliberately, 'I'm trying to tell you that I find you very interesting—and very desirable. Did you enjoy being kissed?'

Keeping her head down, she groped in her bag for the key and said the first thing that came into her head. 'If I hadn't I'd have slapped your face.'

Oh, how banal! Hastily, her skin by now scorching, she found the key and unlocked the door. Without turning her head, she said, 'But I'm not in the market for a casual affair.'

'It wouldn't be casual,' he said mildly enough, and when she lifted her astonished face towards him she saw something like amusement glitter in his eyes.

Only it wasn't; her heart quivered in her breast as he smiled down at her with a narrowed intensity.

Why not? she thought again, unbearably tempted by a passionate longing that urged her to fling away common sense and accept what he was offering.

Even feverish and barely able to see him, she'd been aware of his potent masculine impact, her body responding instinctively and instantly.

The breath stopped in her throat when she realised that this was already more than simple sexual hunger. Oh, she'd be physically safe, but if she surrendered to this overwhelming need, she'd face a far greater risk—that of losing her heart irretrievably and forever.

The sudden flash of understanding gave her the strength to pull back. Quietly, steadily, she said, 'I don't—I don't think I'm ready for any sort of relationship right now, Kelt.'

It was the first time she'd said his name except in her mind.

He looked at her for too long, his gaze so piercing she had to stop herself from closing her eyes against it, and then he nodded. 'Perhaps it's for the best,' he said with a cool smile. 'And don't let Rosie talk you into any of her mad schemes.'

Aching as though she'd been beaten, Hani went inside while he walked down the path. Later that afternoon, Arthur Wellington drove the car down.

'Before he left, Kelt said to tell you it's fully insured and that you're to use it as much as you like,' he said.

'That's very kind of him.' She didn't have any right to ask where Kelt had gone.

He gave her a thoughtful look. 'He can certainly be kind,' he agreed.

Although the sun shone from a brilliant sky she felt cold and bereft, as though she'd thrown away something of great value.

But she'd have ended up paying a bitter, lifelong price for passion, she thought, trying to fortify her resolve. Because Kelt had offered her nothing beyond that.

Even if he had, she'd have been forced to refuse; it was bitterly ironic that Felipe's death resolved nothing except the fear that had been an ever-present shadow. She couldn't, with honour, return to Moraze or resume her old life.

The thought of media attention filled her with horror. Far better to stay dead.

The next afternoon she drove into town to buy groceries and check Alonso on the internet; although he and his family were easy to find, in all the references and photographs there was nothing that could connect him to Felipe's circle.

But even so, she didn't dare run the risk of him recognising her and remembering her supposed death.

As Gabby played with leaves and spindrift, and made her first forays into the sea, her mistress tried to map out a future.

Without success; her thoughts kept finding their way to Kelt. Unconsciously she'd grown to rely on seeing him, and it was painful to discover just how empty and barren life without him could be.

Her heart felt like a stone in her breast, and her dreams became forlorn affairs of pain and loss and frantic searching, as though some essential part of her was missing.

So when Rosie arrived just after lunch one day she greeted her with real pleasure until she started to discuss her plans for the beach party—plans that involved Hani as guest of honour.

'No,' Hani said firmly.

After her attempts at persuasion had failed, Rosie pulled a face. 'You're just as stubborn as Kelt! He said I wasn't to bother you, and threatened to call the whole thing off if I asked you to do *anything*. All I said was that this beach would be wonderful for the party—it's so pretty and sheltered, and it's great for swimming—but he vetoed that too. And now Alonso's gone back home!'

'Kelt's got this thing about my illness,' Hani offered, so relieved by this that she felt giddy for a moment. At least she wouldn't have to skulk around the bach for three months!

'How are you?' Rosie examined her. 'You look fine— much better than you did the first time I met you, actually.'

'I feel great.' Hani smiled. 'Gabby's seeing to it that I get a fair amount of exercise, and it's so beautiful here. I expected the water to be too cold for me, but I love its briskness.'

'Oh—hasn't Kelt forbidden you to swim alone?' Rosie sounded surprised.

'No.' Paddling was as far as she'd got; she hadn't swum for six years. 'And I doubt if I'd take much notice of him if he did. Why would he do that?'

'His mother drowned while she was swimming on her own off Homestead Bay. He found her body.'

'Oh, how awful,' Hani said involuntarily, repressing memories she tried to keep in the darkest recess of her mind. 'Poor Kelt.'

'Yes. She was a darling.'

The next day, shopping for groceries, Hani realised that the school holidays must have started. The car parks were full and there were children everywhere, fizzing with a palpable air of enjoyment beside their harried parents.

Summer holidays, she thought reminiscently, eyeing a small tot in a frilly sundress with an old-fashioned sun bonnet protecting her freckled face—apparently the latest fashion for under-twos here.

Kelt's words came to her: '—a husband, children...'

By cutting herself off she'd given up any hope of such a future. In fact, she thought now, she'd simply given up hope. Her attempt to kill herself had failed, but in a way she'd committed emotional suicide.

For the first time she appreciated the full impact of the decision she'd made at eighteen. As she was convinced that not only had she failed to live up to her brother's standards, but also that she was a definite threat to him and to the islanders her family had ruled for hundreds of years, the decision had been understandable.

Now she realised that her shamed self-absorption had prolonged Felipe Gastano's power over her. And in a way, her refusal to accept Kelt's delicately worded proposition had been a continuation of that mortification.

But Felipe was dead. Did she dare emerge from her exile and take what she could from life?

Even if it couldn't lead to anything permanent?

Back at the bach she unpacked her purchases and put them away, then took Gabby for a short run, before curling up on a lounger in the sun, the puppy a sleepy little bundle against her bare legs.

'No, no playing,' she said, stroking the soft little ears. 'I have to sort out my thoughts.'

Her gaze drifted to the top of the tree-clad ridge between her little cove and Homestead Bay. Only a few weeks ago her actions had seemed perfectly logical and sensible—until Kelt woke something inside her, a yearning that had turned her life upside down.

'So instead of just reacting,' she told Gabby, 'I need to think this through carefully.'

Except that it was so easy to let her mind drift off into wonderful daydreams. Ruthlessly banishing them, she began to make mental lists.

Surely it would be safe to settle in New Zealand? After all, her qualifications were New Zealand ones; that would help her case. And the charity that ran the school on Tukuulu was based here—maybe they'd organise her a job.

She might even be able to marry...

No, that was just another daydream, a fantasy like her dreams of being a circus rider. Marriage would involve trusting someone with her secrets.

'Stop right there!' she said out loud, astonished by her wayward thoughts.

Gabby woke with a start, and after a lavish yawn that revealed every one of her needle-teeth indicated that she wanted to get down. Once on the ground, she staggered across to drink heartily from her water bowl, then arranged herself in the sun for another nap.

Not marriage—not that. Not ever. Marriage would mean

living a lie, because she couldn't tell Kelt—any prospective husband—about that sordid episode in her past, and her cowardice.

But an affair was a different matter. Excitement beat through Hani—sweet, intense, potent. Softly, her eyes on the little dog, she said aloud, 'I want to know what desire—what passion—is like when there's no hidden agenda, when the emotions are open and honest and not confused with love.'

No marriage, no commitment—just a straightforward, uncomplicated relationship between two people who wanted each other and had no reason not to act on that erotic attraction.

'A thoroughly modern affair,' she said into the heavy air, scented by sun and sea and greenery.

Her breath came faster between her lips, but her voice trailed away. So how did a woman go about indicating to a man—whom she'd already rebuffed—that she wasn't averse to changing her mind?

She had no idea.

But nothing ventured, nothing won.

A large motorboat swung around the headland and roared into the bay, its huge wake creaming the water before crashing into the rocks at the base of each headland.

Gabby woke with a start and let off a couple of startled yaps. 'It's all right,' Hani soothed her, picking her up and holding her in her lap. 'They'll go as soon as they've had a look around.'

But they didn't. A few metres off the beach the engine cut and the anchor rattled down. The silence was broken by loud yells as the people on board—all men, she noted—dived over the side.

With a shock she realised they were naked and the hair on the back of her neck lifted in a primitive intimation of danger.

She bit her lip. No, she was being foolish. Clearly they thought they were alone in the bay, and on such a glorious day, why not swim naked?

She took Gabby inside and tried to read, but while the sun eased down the sky her apprehension grew stronger as she listened to the new arrivals' increasingly raucous yells and laughter.

She'd made up her mind to ring Arthur when she saw a car heading down the drive. With a sigh of relief she went out to the gate.

Her relief turned to joy when she realised that the driver was Kelt. One hand clutching the gatepost, she watched him get out of the big farm vehicle, and her heart expanded within her and soared.

Yes, she thought, giddy with elation, yes, this is what I want. This is right for me now.

The future could look after itself. She might grieve when this was over, but she'd never regret it.

After one searching scrutiny he demanded, 'Have they come ashore?'

'No. No, I'm fine, but I was getting a bit worried.'

He said austerely, 'I've only just got home. Otherwise I'd have been down sooner.'

'They're not actually doing anything I could object to, just making a noise,' she said, adding, 'But I was about to ring. How did you know they were here?'

'I checked the bay when I drove in. I know the owner of the boat; his son and some of his friends—all at university— have been on a cruise around the Bay of Islands, and this is their last night. They're good enough kids, but clearly they've been drinking.' As if it was an afterthought, he went on, 'A lot of deaths at sea are linked to alcohol.'

Of course, his mother had drowned. Quietly Hani asked, 'What can you do?'

'Hail them from the beach, then take them back to the marina.'

Unthinkingly she said, 'How will you get home? Arthur?'

He gave her another keen glance, something kindling in the depths of his eyes that set her pulse dancing. 'Arthur's planning to go out tonight. Why don't you drive to Kaitake and pick me up from there?'

Hani realised that she'd been offered her chance to countermand her rejection. A wild, sweet excitement charged her body with delight. 'Yes, of course.' Before she could say anything else a particularly noisy yell made her glance anxiously over her shoulder. 'But will you be safe? They sound violent.'

'They're just horsing around,' he said with such rock-solid confidence that she almost stopped worrying. 'To be fair, they probably don't know there's someone in residence here.'

Apprehension warred with acceptance. One of the reasons she'd learned to trust Kelt was that sense of responsibility; he wouldn't have been Kelt if he hadn't decided to take them back.

But when he turned to go she grabbed his sleeve. 'Kelt—wait. I don't think—'

He looked down at her. 'Don't worry,' he said calmly. 'I'm not stupid. If I didn't know them I'd get back-up, but they're not bad. Just a bit wild and, at the moment, more than a bit drunk.'

Hani stared at him, then reached up and kissed his mouth. He went rigid, and she was just about to pull back in sick humiliation when he snatched her into his arms and returned the kiss with an uncompromising passion that sent hunger rocketing through her.

Eyes gleaming, he put her away from him and surveyed her with narrowed, glittering eyes. 'You shouldn't do that sort of thing if you don't want to arouse false hopes.'

'I do,' she said, flushing hotly.

'Do what?'

That fierce kiss had unsealed something inside her, let loose a need that ached through her like a sweet fever.

'Do want to arouse,' she repeated, holding his gaze as more colour scorched across her face. 'And the hopes wouldn't be false.'

CHAPTER ELEVEN

EYES narrowed and intent, Kelt looked down at her. Hani gave him a tremulous, shy smile. He made as if to step towards her, then stopped. His hands clenched at his sides, and he said between his teeth, 'I'll hold you to that.'

Hani's heart pounded, almost blocking out the sound of the waves on the sand. *What had she done?* But it was right; some primal womanly instinct told Hani that if she didn't surrender to this moment, this man, she'd regret it for the rest of her life.

Trying to look cool and sophisticated, she said, 'I'll see you at the marina.'

'It will take the cruiser about half an hour to get there.' He paused another charged moment, then turned and strode off towards the beach without looking back.

Tensely, anxiously, Hani watched him come to a stop just above the tidemark. He didn't have to hail the boat; the men on the cruiser saw him, and after a short shouted exchange of words a small rubber dinghy came hurtling recklessly towards the shore, grounding on the sand with a jerk that almost hurled the driver overboard.

Kelt said something that set the driver laughing as he collected himself. With one strong, sure movement Kelt heaved the dinghy into deeper water, then swung lithely into the craft and took the controls.

Hani relaxed, thinking with a trace of irony that her anxiety had been entirely wasted. But she stayed there, fingers knotted together, her straining gaze fixed on his tall, athletic figure until he climbed into the cruiser. The other men crowded around him, clearly welcoming his arrival. Ten minutes later the anchor rattled up, and the big boat swung smoothly around, a faint wake feathering the water as it made its way out between the tree-clad headlands.

Almost half an hour later to the minute, Hani watched the big cruiser ease into a mooring at the marina. The disembarked sailors were less noisy by now, and became noticeably more subdued when they were met by a man—presumably the owner of the boat. Kelt spoke to him, and the two men shook hands before Kelt started towards her.

Her heart picked up speed again, and her eyes turned hungry. He looked…wonderful. Tall and lithe and—hers. For tonight, anyway.

Oh, she hoped so.

'Everything's OK,' he said briefly as he got into the passenger seat.

Feeling oddly pleased that he trusted her to drive him home, she put the car in gear and concentrated on backing out. 'Obviously you didn't have any trouble with them.'

He looked a trifle surprised. 'Not after I pointed out that by letting me take them back they might—*just*—be trusted to take the cruiser out again, whereas they wouldn't have a show if I had to ring the owner and ask him to come and deal with the situation.'

Her laugh took him by surprise. Low and huskily seductive, it rippled through the car like music. 'You should do that more often,' he said without thinking.

'What? Reverse?'

'Laugh. I don't think I've heard it before.'

What the hell had happened to her? Something so traumatic that it had killed her laughter.

Her sideways glance reminded him of a hunted animal, but her voice was level and cool. 'I'm sure you must have—or am I that glum?'

'I wouldn't describe you as glum.' Look at the road, he told himself. If he kept his eyes off her perhaps he could restrain his reckless hunger, so heady it threatened to unleash the control he'd always kept over himself.

He'd never had any worry about restraint before, but tonight, with Hannah, he'd need to temper his carnal craving. She'd had at least one bad experience; he didn't want to terrify her, or hurt her.

He wanted to make it perfect for her.

She startled him by saying, 'If I haven't laughed in the time you've known me I must be lousy company.'

'Fishing?' he asked laconically, because talking nonsense might help. 'You must realise that I find your company extremely—stimulating. Your laughter was worth the wait.'

More than anything—even more than satisfying the carnal hunger that prowled through him—he wanted to hear her laugh again.

Fiercely Hani concentrated on driving. His words twisted her heart, adding something vital to the purely physical charge between them.

If she kept on this way, she thought in a sudden panic, she might end up loving him, a willing prisoner of desire.

She didn't dare.

She just didn't have the courage to open her heart again, to accept the possibility—no, she admitted starkly, the *inevitability*—of pain.

About to tell him she couldn't go through with it, she clamped her lips together. Don't dress this up as love, she advised herself trenchantly. You did that once before, and look where it got you...

Think of making love to Kelt as medicine you have to take to get well again.

Nice medicine...

And could have laughed at the banality of her thoughts. Making love to Kelt would be a sensuous, mind-blowing delight, nothing like medicine.

And she was going to do it because she'd let Felipe's brutality crush her instincts for far too long. But more—oh, so much more, some hidden part of her jeered—because she *wanted* Kelt. Wanted him so much she could actually taste the longing on her tongue; she ached with it, afire with the hunger that now seemed so normal, so natural. Anticipation ran hotly through her, melting her racing, tumbled thoughts, her inhibitions in a flood of hungry desire.

She said, 'I'll see to it that I laugh more, then.'

'I'll look forward to it,' he told her with a narrow smile that made her concentrate on keeping her breath steady.

The rest of the trip home was conducted in almost complete silence.

Home? she thought in bewilderment, shocked at the mental slip. Moraze had always been her one true home, but somehow this beautiful, peaceful place had become precious.

Slowing down as they approached the turn-off to his house, she said, 'Oh, I forgot. Your car is at the bach.' She flashed him a glance. 'Would you like to stay to dinner?'

She didn't dare look at him again during the short silence before he said, 'Thank you, yes. I need a shower, so drop me off here and I'll walk down.'

Obediently she did that, saying just as he got out, 'I've already made chilli, but I like it hot. If you don't I can make something else, although it won't be meat.'

'Don't worry, I like it hot too,' he said, his cool tone very much at variance with the dark gleam in his eyes.

Hani drove off, wondering what on earth had pushed her into that invitation. A weak effort to give their lovemaking some context, a feeble pretence that it meant more than a soulless connection of bodies?

Probably, she thought, but at least this time she knew what she was doing.

Gabby greeted her with joy from amidst a newspaper in shreds over the sitting-room floor. Laughing, Hani cleared it up, took the pup for a short walk outside, then hurried through the shower and into a sunfrock with a pretty little bolero to cover her upper arms as the sun went down.

As she took the chilli from the fridge she wondered whether she should try to reduce its bite. Well, she had a large pot of New Zealand's superb yoghurt and some coriander. If Kelt burnt his mouth he could ease it with that.

With it she'd serve rice and a large green salad, followed by strawberries and the yoghurt. A bubble of anticipation expanded in her stomach.

But she had no wine. After a moment she shrugged. It wasn't necessary, and besides, wine and chilli didn't always go well together. Anyway, she didn't need alcohol; she was half-intoxicated already, as though the very best French champagne were circulating through her veins.

When Kelt came in through the door the feeling of delirious lightness morphed into something darker, more potent. Deep inside her a smouldering erotic hunger blazed into desperate life at the hard-honed angles of his handsome face, the air of power and command that controlled his compelling masculinity.

In a raw voice he said, 'I brought some champagne, but I don't need it. Just looking at you is enough to make me drunk.'

Hani had no idea what to say. Unevenly she finally managed, 'Put it in the fridge.'

She'd imagined them sitting outside as the sun sank over the hills, talking a little, but suddenly she felt she couldn't wait. Trying to hide the heady clamour of desire, she stirred the chilli, but when the silence stretched too far she had to glance up.

He was still watching her, his eyes narrowed and intent, his mouth a hard, straight line.

Hunger tore at her. Smiling tremulously, she put the spoon down.

He took a step towards her before stopping to say in a thick, driven voice, 'I'm not going to touch you. Not yet.'

Something splintered into shards of sensation inside her. In a tone she didn't recognise she said, 'In that case, do you mind if I touch you?'

'Hannah,' he said, and then with a tight, humourless laugh, 'No, you should be Honey. It suits you much better. Warm and golden and sweet—you've been tormenting me ever since I saw you. Once you touch me I doubt very much if I'll be responsible for anything that happens.'

Dazzled by the thought of affecting him so strongly, she came slowly towards him, eyes darkening as she took in the control he was exerting, the clenched hands, his waiting, predatory stillness.

She should be afraid, she thought exultantly, but she wasn't scared of Kelt.

Hands behind her back, she stood on tiptoe and kissed the tanned hollow of his throat. He made a muffled sound and his arms came around her, pulling her against him so hard she could feel every rigid muscle, the powerful male strength he was keeping in check, the rapid uneven pounding of his heart—and the hunger that met and matched hers.

And then he lifted her, and she remembered how amazingly safe she'd always felt in his arms. Hers tightened around his neck as he shouldered through the door into the bedroom and across to the big bed, sitting her down on the side with a gentleness that reassured every drifting, hardly recognised fear.

He dropped a swift, famished kiss on her throat, then straightened, looking down at her with a glitter in his eyes that set her pulses racing so fast she thought she might faint with anticipation.

'I don't even dare undress you,' he said with a taut smile. 'I might tear this pretty thing, and that would be a shame.'

He was talking, she realised, to ease the tension that gripped them both. A swift relief swept over her at his understanding. In a soft, low voice she said, 'Then perhaps we should undress ourselves.'

'An excellent idea.' He stepped back and his hands went to the opening of his shirt.

Fascinated, she watched his lean fingers flick open the buttons to reveal the broad chest beneath, his powerful muscles emphasised by a scroll of hair across the sleek, tanned skin. Excitement clamoured through Hani, a fierce demand she'd never known before.

When he'd shrugged out of his shirt she said on a sharp, indrawn breath, 'You are—magnificent.'

'Thank you.' One black brow rose when she continued drinking him in.

Flushing, she pulled off her tiny bolero, revealing her bare shoulders. Heat kindled in the cold blue flames of his eyes, but he made no move towards her as she eased the sundress over her head.

Too shy to let it drop to the floor, she let it hang loosely in front of her. Dry-throated, she said, 'I think it must be your turn.'

He removed his shoes and socks, then let his trousers drop to the floor.

Hani dragged a startled breath into empty lungs. Long legs, strongly muscled from riding, narrow hips, and he was—big, she thought, her eyes darting from the sole part of his anatomy that was still clothed.

'May I?'

Closing her eyes for a second, she nodded, opening them only when he'd taken her dress from her nerveless fingers and put it on the chair beside the bed.

Clad only in one small scrap of cotton, she had never felt so naked.

Harshly he said, 'You are utterly beautiful.'

And for him she felt beautiful. With a trembling smile she held out her arms, and he came down beside her with a rush, tumbling her backwards so that her breasts were exposed and open to his eager mouth.

But first he kissed her lips—tender, quick kisses that stoked the fires between her loins unbearably. Then he possessed himself of her mouth, plunging deep in an imitation of the most intimate embrace of all. Almost immediately she shuddered with hunger, her straining body afire against the hard, potent length of his, her breath coming in short, hoarse pants, her eyes wild as she stared up into his face.

Hani expected him to take her there and then, but instead he kissed her breasts, made himself master of her body, caressing with his hands and his tongue so that her every cell recognised and responded to his touch.

And he gave her the freedom to do the same to him until she learned intimately the swell of muscle and line of sinew, the fine matte texture of his skin, the contrast with the scrolls of hair across his chest, the way his body tensed beneath her seeking hands…

Frantic, driven by a voluptuous desire, a longing so desperate all her fears disappeared, she pulled at him, her hands tightening across the sleek skin of his back, her voice urgent and importunate.

Until at last he moved over her and with one smooth, easy thrust took her.

Every muscle in Hani's body contracted, welcoming him, clinging to him, beginning an involuntary, automatic rhythm that soared higher and higher into a place she'd never known, so when at last the climax overwhelmed her in delight and ecstasy she cried out and surrendered completely.

Only to be hurled further into that unknown rapture when he joined her there, his big body tense and bowed, his head flung back. Locked in erotic union, they reached that place together, and eventually came down together, slick bodies relaxing, their hearts slowing into a normal rhythm until Kelt turned to catch her in his arms again and pull her against him.

He kissed her wordless murmur into silence, and said against her lips, 'Tired?'

'Mmm,' she said, and he laughed, and held her while she slid into sleep unlike anything she'd ever known before.

It was dark when she woke, and she knew instantly that he was awake. She was sprawled across him, her head pillowed on one shoulder, her hair streaming across his chest.

He must have sensed her wakening, because he said, 'It's almost midnight.'

'Oh, lord,' she said, suffused with guilt, 'and I haven't fed you! How long have you been awake?'

'Long enough.' He dropped a kiss on the top of her head.

'Long enough for what?'

The silence was so short she thought it hadn't happened until he drawled wickedly, 'To work up an appetite.'

She spluttered into laughter, and hurtled off the bed. 'Then we'd better eat that dinner—if it's still edible,' she said, climbing into her dressing gown.

Smiling, he got up, and together they ate, took Gabby out, and drank a little champagne, only to leave it unfinished when desire overpowered them once more.

Hani slept again, but woke to tears aching behind her eyes, tears that spilled across Kelt's chest. Grateful that he stayed asleep, she surrendered to bitter-sweet joy. In his arms she'd found true fulfilment, and now she knew that when this interlude was over she'd spend the rest of her life longing for him.

But she had never been so happy. Making love with Kelt had been—amazing and wonderful and glorious and sensuous and…just plain *magnificent*.

Just as amazing was that she hadn't thought of Felipe once. For the first time she felt well and truly loved in every respect.

Except the emotional, she realised as days and nights passed in a voluptuous feast for all her senses—a dazzling, mind-blowing parade of sensuousness in which Kelt taught her just how wonderful making love could be.

Each day she fell deeper and deeper into love—and knew with a hopeless hunger that Kelt didn't love her. Although he showed her he could be tender and generous as well as passionate and demanding, she sensed an unbridged distance between them.

She didn't ask for anything more; she even tried to convince herself that she was well content. But as the summer lazed on, she found herself wondering if perhaps—just perhaps—they might some time cross the invisible, unspoken boundaries they'd set on their affair.

Daydreaming again…

One evening, coming back into the bay after a picnic on a tiny offshore island, he asked, 'It's over six weeks since you had that bout of fever.'

Hani trailed her hand in the water and frowned as she counted the days. 'So it is.' She watched him rowing the old wooden dinghy, letting her eyes drift meaningfully over his shoulders, the muscles bunching with each smooth flick of the oars. 'I've been occupied with other things,' she said sweetly, and flicked some water his way.

He grinned. 'Mind over matter?'

'Or the placebo effect.'

He laughed, his eyes gleaming. 'Perhaps there's something to it. We could get all scientific about this; I have to go away in three days' time, so we could see whether you keep count of the time while I'm away.'

Lost in the wonder of being his lover, Hani had to bite her tongue to stop herself from asking him where he was going.

'I'll be away about ten days,' he said calmly. 'I'd ask you to come with me—'

Before he could come up with whatever excuse, she shook her head and interrupted. 'No.' Her heart twisted. Not ever.

She hurried on, 'As for the fever, I think it's gone. I feel—strong, somehow. Good.'

The dinghy grounded on the sand and things went on exactly the same—at least, that was what Hani told herself. But for the three days she found herself tensing whenever he came, almost as though she had to extract every ounce of pleasure, commit to memory every tiny alteration in his deep voice, the way his smile melted her bones—even the exact shade of his eyes, so close to the border between blue and steel-grey that it was impossible to state categorically what colour they were...

And that, she thought robustly, was stupid. He'd only be away for a week and a half.

The days dragged. Oh, she had the delicious memories of the night before he'd left when he'd made love to her as though—as though he wasn't coming back, she thought, trying to laugh at herself.

But memories weren't enough. She wanted Kelt. No, worse than that—she *needed* him.

The night before he was due back restlessness and an oppressive cloud of foreboding drove her to seek refuge from her own thoughts and longings, and she sat with Gabby in her lap—a bigger and more sturdy puppy now, showing every sign of developing a strong character. The soft, warm weight comforted her a little, but she longed to see Kelt again, to tell him...what?

I love you? 'Not likely,' she said forlornly, and got up and turned off the television.

Later, she heard the low sound of a car come down the hill. She began to shake, then got to her feet and walked carefully to the door, opening it as Kelt raised his hand to knock.

His face was drawn, but he was smiling. Every cell in her body recognised him with joyous outcry. Holding out her hands, she drew him in with her and lifted her face in mute invitation.

He kissed her with a famished intensity that banished every last inhibition. When at last he lifted his head, she said, 'You were away nine days, eleven hours and forty-three minutes.'

'I know.' His eyes gleamed with sensuous amusement. 'And every one of them dragged.'

'I know.' She laughed softly, huskily, and kissed his throat. 'Food first?'

Or do you want to go straight to bed?

Her unspoken question astonished her. How had she summoned the courage to be so—so brazen?

A darting look up from beneath her lashes revealed the strong framework of his face, as though the tanned skin had tightened over it.

And his voice was raw when he said, 'If you keep that up we won't make it to the bed.'

Boldly she lifted her head and kissed his chiselled mouth, then outlined it with the tip of her tongue. His heart thudded against her, strong and fast. Heat bloomed her skin, and she could have breathed in the faint, elusive male scent of him, tangy and arousing, for the rest of her life.

'That would probably shock Gabby,' she murmured. And added, because she had to, 'You guessed I'd had a bad experience. It's—finished with, Kelt. I'm not afraid any more.'

He looked down at her, eyes narrowed into blazing slits, so piercing she could hardly meet his gaze. 'You're sure?'

'Completely sure.' And to seal it she initiated another kiss, one that was frankly voracious, showing him just how much she wanted him.

This time he returned it—with interest—before sweeping her up in his arms and carrying her once more into the bedroom.

This time—oh, this time there was none of the practised gentleness she'd come to expect. Kelt made love to her as though he'd spent just as many lonely night hours longing for her as she had for him, as though they were lovers separated by years that had only whetted their desire, once more together.

Glorying in his ardour, she allowed her needs and desires free rein, responding to each kindling caress, each sensuously tormenting kiss, with everything she was, everything she felt.

And although their lovemaking was fast and fierce, when that moment of release came again it threw her even higher as wave after wave of pleasure surged through her, sending her to that rapturous place where desire and satisfaction melded into mutual bliss.

Much later, safe in his arms, she accepted that she loved him. And that it didn't matter. The sheer grandeur of her feelings for him outweighed the knowledge of pain to come, when she left him.

She murmured, 'You were away too long.'

'I won't need to go back to Carathia for a while,' he said calmly.

'Carathia?' She yawned. 'Isn't that a little country on the edge of the Adriatic? What were you doing there?'

'I was there on business, but in the end I helped my brother put down a rebellion,' he said dryly.

Love-dazed, her tired mind barely registered the words, but when they sank in she sat up and stared down at him, her heart shaking inside her at the sight of him, long and lean and tanned against the white sheets.

He was smiling, without humour, and his eyes were sombre.

'What? *What* did you say?' she spluttered.

'My brother is the ruler of Carathia.' His expression hardened. 'I went there because there was a spot of bother, and he needed me.' He smiled and pulled her down again, kissing the swell of her breast. 'Mmm,' he murmured against her skin, 'you smell delicious. I sometimes think it's what I miss most about you.'

Little tremors of sensation raced through her, urgently and pleading. Ignoring them, she whispered, 'What do you mean— the ruler?'

The children on the beach had called Kelt the Duke, and talked of a grandmother who wore a crown. Oh, God, why hadn't she listened? Why hadn't she asked?

Kelt turned her face up so that he could see it, and a frown drew his black brows together. 'My brother, Gerd, is the new Grand Duke of Carathia.'

Dreams Hani hadn't even recognised crashed around her. Unbeknown to herself she must have been fantasising— *hoping?*—that somehow, she might be able to forge some sort of connection with Kelt. That with him she'd be able to make a life here in this enchanted place.

That perhaps there might be a future for them if she could trust him enough to be able to tell him about herself and her past.

'I didn't know,' she said in a stunned voice. 'No one told me.' No one but the children…

'Most people around here are aware of it; my grandparents used to come and stay here on occasion, and my brother and I spent all our holidays here.' He finished coolly, 'It's no big deal.'

Hani turned to hide her head in his chest. His casual words had killed every inchoate, wordless hope. She didn't dare have any sort of relationship with a man whose wealth and good looks and ancient heritage made him food for gossip mills. Even as his mistress she'd shame him—she cringed thinking of the way the tabloids would treat her reappearance.

Kelt asked, 'What is it? Tell me.'

'I didn't know,' she said faintly. And because she couldn't tell him what that knowledge had done to her, she asked, 'But why do you live here—in New Zealand?'

He shrugged, and his arms tightened around her. She lay with her face against his heart, listening to the slowing beat, inhaling his beloved scent, and felt her world crumble around her again, her splintered hopes painfully stabbing her.

'It's no big deal,' he said again casually. 'Our grandparents met while my grandmother was fighting a nasty little rebellion amongst the mountain people, one fomented by her sister. Our grandfather was a New Zealander, and he saved her life in an ambush. Kiwinui was his heritage, just as it's been mine. They were married, and had one son. Our mother was a Greek princess. We spent quite a lot of time here as children. My brother has always known he'd be Grand Duke one day. I've always preferred New Zealand.'

Hani sensed that he wasn't telling her everything, but she didn't dare speak. Instead she nodded, letting loose a swathe of black hair across his skin. Their hips met, moved together with sensuous languor, and she felt him stir against her.

Tomorrow, she thought weakly. She would steal one more night of paradise in his arms, and tomorrow she'd tell him that it was over.

CHAPTER TWELVE

HANI woke, to find Kelt, fully clothed, bending over her. She smiled and he bent and kissed her.

Against his lips she murmured, 'What…?'

'I am expecting a call from Gerd,' he told her. Then he smiled, and said in a warmer voice, 'Go back to sleep.'

But by then she'd remembered, and her eyes were agonised when he turned and walked out of the door into the half-light of dawn.

When the sound of his vehicle had died away she got up and put Gabby outside. A sliver of golden light against the horizon heralded another summer day, but in her heart it would always be winter.

Dragging her footsteps like an old woman, she walked into the bedroom, Gabby gambolling at her heels. She had to get out of here, before he came back. She'd take the car into Kaitake and catch a bus to—to anywhere. No, to Auckland because it was big enough to get lost in. She'd leave Gabby with plenty of water and food and ring tonight to make sure they knew she was there. She wasn't worried about getting Kelt; Arthur answered the phone at the homestead.

She'd leave Kelt a note. Feverishly she started composing it in her mind: *It's been great, but I have to go—than you so much for all you've done for me. Please look after Gabby for me...*

He'd never know just how much he had done for her. Making love with him had wiped the tainted memories of the past, leaving her whole again and stronger than she'd ever been.

'No,' she said out loud, startling herself. 'No, he deserves better than a stupid note.'

Last time she'd run without telling anyone it had been for her life. This time it would be sheer cowardice. She wouldn't leave Kelt without an explanation of why she had to go. Although it would be savagely painful and embarrassing to tell him that she suspected she was falling in love with him, he could at least salvage some sort of honour.

By lunchtime her suitcase was packed and she'd rung for the bus timetable, and was taking the coach that came through later in the afternoon.

A knock on the door froze her into place. She didn't need Gabby's happy little greeting to tell her who it was. I'm not ready, she thought, panic-stricken, knowing she'd never be ready.

Dragging a deep breath into her compressed lungs, she came out of the bedroom and closed the door behind her.

Gabby was prancing around the door, her tail wagging. White-faced, Hani opened the door to Kelt, who took one look at her and demanded, 'What the hell is the matter?'

Before she had time to think, she blurted, 'I have something to tell you.'

His eyes hardened, but he came in and closed the door behind him. 'Are you sure? It's early days yet, but don't worry. We'll get married.'

Hani's heart gave a great leap, then settled like a lead weight in her chest. Retreating a few paces, she said, 'I'm not pregnant.' Pain stabbed her, sharp and brutal.

His brows drew together and she saw the warrior, angular and relentless. 'All right, what is it?'

'I'll be leaving soon,' she said quietly. 'I just wanted you to know that you've made me very happy and I'll always remember you.'

His eyes narrowed. In a silky voice he said, 'If that's so why are you going? And before you say anything, I know you love me, so it has to be something else.'

Hani stared at him. 'How arrogant you are,' she said, but the spark had gone from her voice and she had to force herself to meet that merciless gaze. 'We made love, that's all. There's a difference.'

A cold kick of fear silenced her as she watched his hands clench into fists by his sides. 'Is that all it was?' he asked in a voice like molten metal. He smiled, and came towards her and for the first time ever she felt truly afraid of him.

Yet she didn't flinch when he raised his hands and his fingers settled gently around the golden column of her throat. He was so close she could see the pulse beating in his jaw, smell the hot, primal scent that was his alone; if she lifted the hand that itched to move of its own accord, she'd feel the heat of his fine-grained skin against her fingertips.

And she'd melt in abject surrender.

He said softly, 'How could it be so unimportant when it made you cry? That first night—you thought I was asleep, but I heard you, felt the hot tears soak into my skin, and I knew then that whatever you felt for me wasn't something you'd ever forget.'

Do it now. Make it clear. Head held high, she met his narrowed gaze and said coolly, 'I had issues from the past. You showed me how unimportant they were. I'll always be grateful to you for that.'

'I don't believe you,' he said between his teeth. 'Tell me the truth, Hannah.'

If she did he'd despise her. Dumbly she stared up into icy eyes.

His fingers smoothed over the rapidly beating pulse at the base of her throat, then he dropped his hands and stepped back, smiling without humour. 'So you've had your *past issues*—' he said the words with caustic emphasis '—resolved by extremely good sex, and now you're leaving, no bones broken, no hearts cracked.'

Instantly Hani felt cold, abandoned. She owed him the truth. In a low, shamed voice, she said, 'Why didn't you tell me you weren't what I thought you were, an ordinary New Zealand farmer—?'

'I *am* a New Zealand farmer—'

'You're much more than that. Your grandmother is a grand duchess, and you are not only rich, you're also hugely powerful. You must have known I didn't know.'

'Oddly enough,' he said in a caustic voice, 'I found your attitude interesting, and very refreshing. But what difference does any of that make?'

She braced herself. 'A lot. You really don't know anything about me. I'm afraid I've lied to you again and again.' It took all of her courage to go on, but she had to make him understand. 'Starting with my name. It's neither Hannah nor Honey. Until six years ago I was Hani de Courteville, and my brother was Rafiq de Courteville, the ruler of Moraze.'

'Moraze?' She watched as his keen mind processed the information and slotted it into place. His lashes drooped. 'Go on.'

Everything about him—tone, stance, the formidable intensity of his gaze—was intimidating, but he didn't seem shocked. In fact, she thought wonderingly, her revelation seemed to have confirmed something he'd already suspected.

A small warmth of hope gave her the impetus to continue.

'I spent my childhood there, and went to boarding-school in England, and then to a French university. I was eighteen, and too young—too stupid—to be let loose.' She took another agonising breath. 'My brother organised a chaperone-cum-companion for me, who introduced me to a man called Felipe Gastano. He said he was a French count; later I found out that it was his half-brother who had been born to the title. Unfortunately the brother died conveniently from a drug overdose not long before I met Gastano.'

'Keep going,' Kelt ordered, his gaze never wavering.

She looked down at her hands. The knuckles were white and she was holding herself so stiffly her spine ached. 'He was enormous fun and possessed great charm. I won't bore you with details of our affair; it began with me convinced I had found the man I wanted to marry, and ended when I tried to commit suicide, and only failed by good luck. Or bad luck, as I thought it at the time.'

He said something in a lethal voice, then in a totally different tone, 'My poor girl.' And then his voice changed. 'So why do you plan to leave?'

She could have held out against his anger; that flash of tenderness struck home like an arrow.

In a thin thread of a voice Hani said, 'Felipe introduced me to drugs. I know now that he did it quite deliberately. By the time I decided to commit suicide I was an addict and in desperate trouble.' She didn't dare look at him. 'Felipe intended to take over Moraze and use it as a depot to ship drugs to Europe.'

'How?' Kelt demanded forcefully. 'Your brother would never have allowed that.'

'I was the lever, the hold Felipe would have had over Rafiq. And he—Rafiq—was the lever Felipe used on me.'

A flash of fury in the steel-blue eyes was swiftly extinguished, but she felt it emanating from him, fiercely controlled but violent. Before he could speak she hurried on, 'I told him I was leaving him, but he threatened to have Rafiq killed if I did.'

'Go on,' Kelt said evenly.

She could read nothing—neither condemnation nor sympathy in his expression. Chilled, she forced herself to continue, 'I knew then that the only thing I could do was die. But not before I'd written to Rafiq, telling him what Felipe planned to do. Then I went to a small Mediterranean island where Rafiq and I had holidayed once. I just walked into the water, and it was such a relief when I finally gave up swimming and surrendered to the sea.'

She could see the rigid control he was exerting, and some part of her was warmed by it.

'So how did you survive?'

'I don't know,' she said simply. 'I lost consciousness, but before I could drown a fisherman found me.'

Kelt said through his teeth, 'You should have told your brother what had happened to you—he wouldn't have blamed you.'

She gave a bleak, cynical smile. 'Perhaps I should have, but I was an addict. They don't make sensible decisions.' And he'd been so bitterly ashamed. She still was.

'So why did the fisherman not turn you over to the authorities?'

'He was a smuggler, but he was a kind man. He dragged me into his boat and took me to his family. I pleaded with them not to tell anyone where I was.'

'So you could have another go at killing yourself?' he demanded harshly.

'At first,' she admitted, pale and cold under his implacable gaze. 'His wife and mother nursed me through the aftermath of drug addiction, and they all kept quiet about the fact that I'd survived. I owe my life and my sanity to them, and although I was sure I'd never, ever be happy again, they made me promise not to try to kill myself. They said I owed them that, as they'd saved me.' She gave a pale smile. 'The grandmother told me I had to live so that I could make amends for what I'd done.'

In a voice she'd never heard him use before Kelt said, 'I'd like to meet that family. But I would like even more to meet this Gastano.'

'You can't—he's dead; I searched for him on the internet that day in Kaitake. It's horrible—wicked—to be glad a man is dead, but I am.' At least Kelt and Rafiq were safe now. 'Felipe didn't kill people himself—he ordered others to do it, and it would have been done.' She shivered. 'Even a puppy he bought for me—once he asked me to do something—' She stopped, unable to go on.

'What exactly did he want from you?' Kelt's voice lifted every tiny hair on her body in a reflex old as time.

She'd started this; she had to finish it. 'I'd agreed to go out to lunch with a friend from school. Felipe didn't want me to go, but I made a feeble attempt at asserting my independence and went anyway. He got his chauffeur to kill the puppy while I was away.'

'What happened to him?' Kelt's voice was corrosive.

'Felipe must have tried to use Moraze anyway, because he was killed there in a shoot-out with the military. I suppose he thought that even without me to use as a hostage he could force Rafiq to obey him.' She said in a shaking voice, 'He didn't know Rafiq, of course.'

'When you found out this Gastano was dead, why didn't you let your brother know you were alive?'

'I am ashamed,' she said in a low, shaking voice. 'There are people who know what I was reduced to—who know about me. Young Alonso de Porto, for one.'

'You were targeted and preyed upon,' he said between his teeth. 'Who cares about them?'

'If only you were an ordinary New Zealand farmer it wouldn't really matter,' she said passionately, dark eyes begging him to understand, her voice completely flat, without hope. 'But you're not—you are rich, you have royal links and if we…if we continue our affair, it would soon turn up in the tabloids and then—I'd be found again!'

'Why is that a problem?' he asked relentlessly.

Hani was wringing her hands. Forcing them into stillness, she took several deep breaths and looked him straight in the eye. 'You deserve better than to be embroiled in such a scandal.'

It was impossible to read his face when he demanded, 'Do you love me?'

Don't do this, her heart whispered. She hesitated, huge, imploring eyes fixed on his face. 'I—' She swallowed, unable to say the words. Why wasn't he satisfied with what she'd already told him? Did he want her heart on a plate?

Ruthlessly he said, 'I didn't think you were a coward. Do you love me, Hani?'

Hani flinched. The sound of her real name was inexpressibly sweet on his tongue. 'Think of the uproar if it ever got out that I am alive and was your mistress! Like Rafiq and his family—his wife and two little boys—you'd be shamed in the eyes of the world.'

Willing him to understand, she gazed at him pleadingly, but his expression was controlled, all violence leashed. 'Answer my question.'

Something in his tone alerted Gabby, who stretched elaborately and climbed out of her basket, fussily pacing across to sit on Hani's feet, where she indulged in a good scratch.

Hani hesitated again, her breath knotting in her throat.

'One simple word,' Kelt said inflexibly. 'Either yes or no.'

'I'm afraid,' she whispered.

'I know. But you have to say it.'

She licked her lips. 'I—oh, you know the answer!'

'Tell me.'

Tears magnified her eyes. He didn't come near her, but she could feel him willing her to answer. And from somewhere she found the courage. Unable to bear looking at him, she said in a muffled voice, 'Yes. Yes, of course I love you. I would die for you. But I couldn't bear it if you were humiliated or hurt or made a laughing stock because I was stupidly naïve and—'

'Very young,' he said, and at last came across and took her into his strong embrace.

'But once people know who I am, the whole sordid story will be in every tabloid, and people will sneer at you.' She stared up into his dark, beloved face, then grabbed his arms in desperation and tried to shake some sense into him. It was like trying to move a rock. 'Have you thought of that?'

He asked, 'Have you ever been tempted to use drugs again?'

'Oh, no.' Near to breaking, she shuddered. 'No, not ever again. That was why I came down with such a bad case of fever—I don't like taking anything in case I become addicted.'

'Then you can chalk the whole hideous experience up to youthful folly.'

Unevenly she said, 'Kelt, it's not so simple. What will your brother think?'

He gave her a little shake and said, 'Look at me.'

Slowly, not daring to hope, she lifted her eyes.

Speaking firmly, he said, 'I don't care what Gerd or anyone

else thinks. I'm not going to let you spend the rest of your life expiating sins you didn't commit. You were young, and you were deliberately targeted by an evil man.'

She had to make him see sense. 'Rafiq,' she said urgently. 'My brother—'

Frowning, he interrupted, 'If it had been your brother this had happened to, would you turn away from him?'

More tears ached behind her eyes. 'Of course not,' she said quickly, 'but—'

'I understand why you had to escape, but that reason no longer applies,' Kelt said, his calm tone somehow reinforcing his words. He paused and let her go, taking a step backwards and leaving her alone and cold and aching with love.

When she said nothing, he went on, 'It comes down to one thing only; either you join me in my life and trust me to look after you and our children—stop shaking your head, of course we'll have children!—or I will simply have to kidnap you and keep you here, chained to my side.'

Colour came and went in her skin, and a wild, romantic hope warred with fear. She stared at him, saw uncompromising resolve in his expression, in the straight line of his beautiful mouth, and although her heart quailed joy fountained up through her.

'You're a hard man,' she said, her voice shaking. 'And I love you. But I can't, Kelt. I don't—I just don't have the courage.'

'You had the courage to tell your brother what was going on, to try to sacrifice yourself for him and your country, to hide to keep them safe. You have the courage to do this.'

Her breath caught in her throat. 'You make me out to be more than I am.'

'You are much more than that, my valiant warrior, and I look forward to a long life together so I can convince you of that. I don't blame you for not wanting your story blazed across the media, but it can be managed. I can protect you, and together we'll stare the world down.' Then he smiled, and her heart melted. 'So, can you take that last step and tell me where you'd like to live?'

Hani drew in a sobbing breath and surrendered. He hadn't said anything yet about loving her, but she didn't care. As long as he wanted her she would treasure each day she spent with him.

'I'll live wherever you are,' she told him quietly, her gaze never leaving his beloved face. 'Because if I don't, I won't really be living at all—just existing, as I have been for years. But—could it be here? I love this place.'

This time the loving was different. She expected—longed for—a wild triumph from him, but he was all tenderness, a gentle lovemaking that was strangely more erotic than anything they'd shared before, spun out so long that she lost her composure completely and gave him everything he wanted, demanded everything from him.

And when it was over he cradled her into his lean body and said against her forehead, 'I love you. I want you to marry me as soon as you can organise a wedding.'

Astounded, Hani stared up at him. 'All right,' she whispered, then wept into his shoulder.

'I didn't know,' she finally muttered when he'd mopped her up.

'That I love you?' His voice was harsh, raw with an emotion she had to accept. 'Of course I love you. I've loved you ever since I saw you. Never doubt me.' He paused, his face hardening, and said, 'But before we marry, you need to get in touch with your brother.'

'I—' She froze. 'Oh, God,' she whispered, her throat closing.

'You know you must,' he said quietly. 'I intend to show the world that, whatever happened in the past, I'm not ashamed of loving you. I want to flaunt this precious gift I've been given, and I can't do that if you insist on hiding away like a criminal. You can do it. You're no longer the terrified girl who tried to kill herself and then had to run, and I'll be with you.'

She dragged in a shivering breath. Like this, skin to skin, the sound of his heart in her ears, his body lithe and powerful against her, here in his arms, she could be brave.

And his words had made her think; she would never have turned away from her brother.

'How can Rafiq forgive me for everything I did?' she asked in a muffled voice. 'Most of all for my cowardly silence, allowing him to think I was dead, after the suicide attempt.'

'You'd forgive him.'

'Rafiq would never be so weak—so stupid. He is strong.'

'So are you,' Kelt said, his voice very tender. 'And you're no longer the green girl he once knew—you've grown and matured and gained self-command.'

She looked up into his beloved face. 'And if I don't do this I'll be letting Felipe win.'

He nodded, holding her eyes with his. If Rafiq rejected her she'd be devastated, but she wouldn't be alone. Not any more.

Capitulating, she dragged in another shuddering breath. 'Then I'll go to Moraze.'

'I'll come with you.'

Thirty-six hours later she was walking down the steps of the private jet Kelt had chartered, her knees shaking so badly she didn't dare look around the international airport at Moraze. Kelt slung an arm around her shoulders.

'Relax,' he said calmly. 'Everything will be all right.'

'I know.'

An hour previously she'd rung Rafiq's personal number, and the memory of that conversation was seared in her brain. He had organised for them to land in the military area and a helicopter was standing by to take them to the *castello*.

Sitting tensely in the chopper as it approached the grey castle that once kept watch over the approach to Moraze's harbour, she clutched Kelt's hand.

'It will be all right,' he repeated calmly, sliding his arm around her.

'I c-can't—he *cried*, Kelt. He *cried* when I convinced him that I am alive.'

He kissed her into quietness. 'Of course,' he said. 'If I had a dearly loved sister returned to me from the dead I'd weep too.'

Fortified by her love and Kelt's unfailing support, she no longer automatically assumed every man was like Felipe Gastano, but this startled her into silence.

'I should have met you six years ago,' she said forlornly, then added, 'No, I was too young. Tukuulu taught me things I'll never forget—that I can survive on my own, that I can do work that is worthwhile, that there are people infinitely worse off than I could ever be, and that people are basically the same the world over. I grew up there.'

She wore sunglasses, keeping them on even when the servant—someone she didn't know—ushered them through the *castello*. Kelt's steady hand at her elbow gave her comfort and resolve.

The servant opened the door into Rafiq's study. Her brother was standing by the window, but he turned to look across the room as she took off her sunglasses and produced a wobbly smile for him.

'I'm so sorry,' she said uncertainly. 'So sorry I let you down, and so very sorry I let you believe I was dead.'

He still said nothing, and she went on in a muted voice, 'You see, I thought then it—it was best.'

He came towards her then, his handsome face set in lines that showed her how much control he was exerting. In their shared language he said quietly, 'I have always blamed myself for letting you go without a proper person to look after you.' He held out his arms.

With a choked little cry she ran into them, and for long moments he held her, gently rocking her as she wept on his shoulder.

At last, when she was more composed, he held her away from him and said in English, 'You were always beautiful, but you are radiant now.' His green eyes flicked from her face to that of the man watching them. 'So, having had you restored to me, I understand I am to lose you again? Introduce your man to me.'

Much later, when she and Kelt were alone on the terrace in the shade of the starflower tree, with the moon shining kindly down onto a silver lagoon, he asked, 'All demons slain now?'

'Yes, thank God,' she said soberly, so happy that it hurt. 'When Rafiq told me that everyone in Felipe's organisation was either dead or in prison, I felt a weight roll off my back.'

'I can't help but wish I'd had some hand in Gastano's death,' Kelt said evenly.

She shivered. 'He was an evil man, and nobody will be sorry he's dead.'

'Those who live by death and treachery, die that way,' Kelt said, his tone ruthless.

She was silent for a few moments, then turned and looked up into his face. Kelt could be hard and she suspected that he could be even more dangerous than Felipe had ever been, yet he'd shown her tenderness unsurpassed, and understanding and love.

Stumbling, her words low and intense, she tried to tell him what he meant to her. 'You have stripped his memory of power. You have shown me that there is nothing more potent than love. I'll never be able to thank you enough—'

'Thanks aren't necessary or wanted,' he broke in, his voice rough. 'Will you be happy with the life we'll lead? It will be mainly in New Zealand, because I can't live in Carathia.'

Something in his tone alerted her. 'Why not?' she asked anxiously.

'In the country districts there is a legend that the country will only ever be at peace when the second child in the royal family rules. The rebellion my grandmother fought off was an attempt by her younger sister to take the throne from her. I am the second child.'

She stared at him. 'And this is a problem for your brother?'

'At the moment, yes. The legend has resurfaced, and with it stirrings of rebellion, only my security men have discovered that it's being fomented by a cartel that want to take over the mines.'

'Like Felipe with Moraze,' she said in a low, horrified voice.

'Indeed.' His tone was layered with irony.

Slowly, wondering at the coincidence, she said, 'So you understand.'

'I do indeed. Except that for me there has never been any sense of exile. I have no desire to rule Carathia, and since I was young I've always considered myself more of a New Zealander than a Carathian. I can run our enterprise as easily from New Zealand as Carathia, although there will always be occasions when I have to travel.'

'I'll come with you,' she said quickly. 'But is everything all right for your brother now?'

'Yes, the rebellion has been well and truly squashed.'

'How? Were you—was there fighting?'

'No,' he said calmly. 'I toured the area and told the people that I would never rule Carathia, that I was planning to marry and live for the rest of my life in New Zealand. It seems to have done the trick; once they realised I was in earnest, the agents who were stirring the trouble were greeted with curses.'

She said fiercely, 'It must have been dangerous. Don't you ever dare to do anything like that again.'

He drew her to him, his expression softening. 'You and our children will always come first with me.'

The kiss that followed was intensely sweet. When at last he lifted his head she clung, so filled with joy she couldn't even stammer a word.

He said, 'And once we've said goodbye to Rafiq and Lexie you have my family to meet. You'll like my brother—and he'll like you. Hell, you'll probably even like Rosie's mother, who's as flaky as they come!'

'I can deal with flake,' she told him exuberantly, eyes mischievous in the glamorous witchery of moonlight. 'I'm so happy I can deal with anything. I can't wait to marry you and live with you in your house on the hill overlooking our bay.'

He laughed, drew her into the warm circle of his arms, and kissed her again. Home at last, Hani knew that from now on she would always be safe in Kelt's love.

ACCIDENTAL CINDERELLA

NANCY ROBARDS THOMPSON

For Michael for all the wonderful meals
over the years.

Chapter One

"**Y**ou almost make a girl believe in fairy tales." In this rare intimate moment amidst the festive chaos, Lindsay Bingham reached out and tucked a stray strand of hair into her friend Sophie Baldwin's bridal veil.

Sophie looked every bit the princess she was. Literally. *A real princess.*

The wedding was magical and the reception was the social ticket of the year, Lindsay marveled. It was still hard to believe that salt-of-the-earth Sophie Baldwin from Trevard, North Carolina, was full-fledged royalty.

Last year, she'd discovered her birthright—or maybe it was more apropos to say her birthright finally found her—and she'd been swept away to the island of St. Michel in imperial fashion. As if that weren't enough good fortune, she'd just married her prince in a gorgeous December wedding.

Right on cue, tall, handsome Luc Lejardin whirled by on the dance floor with another woman in his arms. But as he caught and held his bride's gaze, it was perfectly clear he only had eyes for one woman.

Lindsay sighed. She would've gladly relinquished rights to an entire kingdom to have a man look at her that way.

"If I keep humming, 'Wish Upon A Star,' will I get my turn as Cinderella?"

Sophie smiled. "Maybe, but since that song belongs to Pinocchio, you might end up with a fibbing bad boy rather than a handsome prince."

Fibbing bad boys. The story of her life.

"That's right," she conceded. "Cinderella's fight song was 'A Dream Is a Wish Your Heart Makes....'"

Sophie winked at her. "A little dream-wishing never hurt anyone."

"Yeah, but for the foreseeable future, I'm going to do my best to do more than dream. I'm getting my life together. I'm calling it the 'New Me' plan."

Yeah, rather than the old "Plan of Self-Destruction." A strategy that involved seeing how many years she could accrue at her dead-end job as a receptionist at Trevard Social Services and how many Mr. Wrongs she could pack into one lifetime.

She sighed against the beat of protest that thrummed inside her. Frankly, her "New Me" plan was a lot easier in theory than in practice. Her receptionist job was comfortable. It was so simple she could do it on autopilot. Even though her boss was a colossal pain in the butt, it was definitely one of those *devil-you-know* situations. Or so she told herself.

But the job was getting her nowhere.

As were the men she sometimes dated.

From her perspective, the journey toward true love sometimes seemed akin to walking a tightrope strung across a dark, scary abyss. She'd walked that rope before, holding the hand of a man she loved and trusted, a man who, once upon a time, said he wanted to spend the rest of his life with her. Ultimately, he'd not just let go of her hand; he'd shoved her into the darkness below.

She'd nearly drowned in the misery.

Even now, almost seven years later, when she thought about the man who'd broken her heart, the pain resurfaced like it was covered by fading Novocain.

To numb herself, she dated. She'd even had relationships—if you could call them that. The men all had one thing in common beyond the tall, broad-shouldered, feral masculinity: none were husband material.

She preferred it that way. By dating the perennial bad boy, it was a given that those relationships wouldn't last. She kept a firm grip on her heart. That way it couldn't be broken.

Sophie squeezed Lindsay's hand. "I think focusing on *you* is a wonderful idea, and to help you with that, I have a surprise for you." Sophie's face lit with a certain look Lindsay had seen before. A look that meant Lindsay should probably run the other way—as fast as she could.

Her friend always meant well, and she could also be extraordinarily generous, as evidenced by the way she'd packed the past month full of fabulous surprises—from daylong, head-to-toe spa days, to designer clothes, shoes and handbags, to the custom-made Cartier diamond necklace and earrings she'd presented her attendants to wear with their bridesmaids dresses.

"What are you up to now?" Lindsay narrowed her eyes, playing along with the tone Sophie had set for this one.

"I'll tell you in a minute. First, I have to say hello to someone."

She followed Sophie's gaze to a short, slight man who was making his way toward them.

"Your highness, such a lovely wedding." The man had a thick Italian accent. He bowed and dusted Sophie's hand with a kiss. "It is a great honor to bear witness to such a momentous occasion."

Okay, this could take a while. But Lindsay had monopolized Sophie long enough. It was time to relinquish her friend and give others a turn. It was a good time to get a drink. The guests didn't want to talk to her, and that was okay. Really, it was. She didn't want to stand there, awkward as a sixth finger while this man did what every guest at this wedding endeavored to do: endear himself to the future queen of St. Michel.

She turned to Sophie. "Will you excuse me for a moment?"

Sophie smiled. "Is everything okay?"

Lindsay nodded. "Absolutely, I need something to drink. Would either of you care for something?"

"Nothing for me," said the Italian. "But please allow me to be at your service."

"No, no, thank you. You stay here and talk. I'll be back."

"You don't have to leave," Sophie whispered.

She'd been so good to make sure Lindsay didn't feel out of place during her stay at the palace. The poor woman must be exhausted.

"I'm fine," Lindsay assured her. "I'll find you later."

"Okay, don't forget. Your surprise."

Sophie had been so generous already. Lindsay couldn't imagine what else she could pull out of her crown. Especially tonight. Sophie's big night. It felt wrong for her friend to take time away from her wedding to give her something else. If anyone should be fussed over tonight, it was the bride.

Across the room, Lindsay spied a tux-clad server with a tray of champagne flutes. She walked over and helped herself, then turned to survey the crowd. The guest list was studded with several A-listers who melded so well with the others that sometimes Lindsay had to do a double take before she could identify them. But she was careful to not be too obvious. No one here gawked or gushed.

That's why it was important that she honored the agreement she'd made with herself and remained cool—and not go stark raving fan girl, even though *Johnny Depp* was sitting directly in her line of vision at a table for two, with his arm draped around a petite woman.

Lindsay bit her bottom lip instead.

Johnny. Depp.

She watched as the actor lifted a cigarette to his lips, taking a long drag. It was just as well she didn't try to engage him in conversation, because with all this pent-up nervous energy, she'd probably end up saying the wrong thing or bleating like a startled goat rather than forming words that made any sense.

Her toes curled in her custom-made Jimmy Choos (one of the bridesmaid gifts from Sophie), and she exhaled a full-body sigh, reluctantly tearing her gaze from him.

As she skimmed the crowd, she stopped suddenly, backtracking to a familiar face. A sulking hulk of hand-someness and broad shoulders sat alone at a table toward the back of the ballroom.

It was that famous chef. Oh, what was his name…?

As she studied his ruggedly attractive face, the olive skin and perpetual five o'clock shadow, Lindsay's mind flipped through names one by one, but she couldn't quite pin it down.

A couple of years ago, he'd been the poster boy of the trashy tabloids. Oh, what was his name…? He used to have a show on Food TV…but something had happened. She couldn't remember what. In fact, she couldn't remember the last time she'd seen him on television. Not that she'd ever been a big fan—but boy, he was even better-looking in person than on TV, and the tabloid photos didn't do him justice.

Montigo.

Carlos Montigo.

Yes! That was it.

She snapped her fingers. As if he'd heard her, which was impossible over the clamor of conversation and music, his dark gaze slid to hers and locked into place.

Her stomach performed a curious lurching summersault. Good grief, the guy was handsome. But based on the headlines, he was no Prince Charming. Not by any stretch of the imagination.

Still, she couldn't make herself look away.

Ping. There it was. That steel-to-bad boy magnetic draw of attraction—pulling her in a direction her better judgment warned she shouldn't go.

He kept watching her and she kept watching him back, over the top of her champagne flute.

She'd known guys with bad reputations like him. He was exactly the type of guy she was drawn to.

If there was one thing her résumé of postengagement relationships had taught her it was you can't re-habilitate a bad boy.

That was the short-term draw.

A slow, lopsided smile that barely turned up the corner of Montigo's lips promised trouble. Those were definitely bad-boy eyes gazing at her. Dark, sexy, bad-boy eyes that were meandering brazenly down the length of her body.

It wasn't the way Luc looked at Sophie. No, this was something altogether different. Her mind skittered through all sorts of possibilities involving bare broad shoulders, rumpled bed sheets and a lot more skin than he was showing now....

It kind of took her breath away.

It *was* her last night in St. Michel....

Even if he wasn't part of her "New Me" plan, she'd never see him again.

But then the strangest thing happened. Her better judgment kicked in.

What was the point of a one-night stand—besides a night of great sex?

Back home, her friend Ida May Higgins, the woman who'd known Lindsay since she was born, who'd cared for her after her mother died and had in many ways been a surrogate mother to her, insisted that the only way Lindsay could fix what her former fiancé, Derrick, had broken was by simply taking the time to be alone so that she could get to know herself.

Alone.

As in no one-night stands.

Besides, Sophie had yet to cut the cake and toss the bouquet. As the maid of honor, Lindsay needed to be available for Sophie, not formulating a plan to hook up with Mr. Hottie.

Willing herself not to look back at him, Lindsay swallowed the rest of her champagne, set the empty glass on a busing tray and made her way toward the terrace for a breath of fresh air.

Something—anything—to clear her head.

If she were at home right now, she'd pull out her mother's recipe book—a small red notebook filled with pages of handwritten recipes, mostly desserts—and bake. The kitchen was her sanctuary; baking helped her keep her sanity.

Even though she'd been so young when her mother had died she didn't have memories of her, she had her recipes. And bringing them to life somehow made Lindsay feel connected to this woman she never really knew.

She'd brought the red notebook to St. Michel with her but she hadn't been near a kitchen in the month she'd been there. So, since baking wasn't an option, she made her way toward the ballroom's open doors.

The terrace was dotted with a smattering of people. Mostly couples who'd stepped out into the moonlight for a little romance, it seemed, from the way people were paired up, some with arms entwined, others stealing little kisses—one couple, off in the far corner, getting a little too frisky for public decency.

Lindsay hated intruding on the romance, but she couldn't go back inside. Not just yet. To give them some privacy, she walked to the other end of the terrace, leaned against the ornate wrought-iron railing and tilted her face into the briny breeze that blew in off the ocean.

It was a gorgeous night. In North Carolina, she'd need a parka and gloves to be outside on a December evening. Here, the temperature was a little chilly, but it was brisk and fresh—just what she needed. She was already starting to feel revived.

After being in St. Michel a month, Trevard, North Carolina, seemed like a vague smudge on a distant horizon. It was hard to believe she'd be going home tomorrow. She blinked away the thought. No way would she waste her last night dwelling on the mundane. She'd have her fill of that soon enough.

She looked around, taking in the huge moon hanging over the water like a brilliant blood orange, spilling diamond seeds across the inky sky and into the restless sea below. Such a beautiful moon on Sophie and Luc's wedding night, as if the heavens were bestowing a special blessing upon their union.

It was all so romantic.

A shooting star burst across the sky like a Roman candle. Remembering her earlier conversation with Sophie, a chill skittered over her. She crossed her arms to rub away the goose bumps, then closed her eyes and wished…

When she was done, she looked around, blinking a couple of times at the couples paired up on the terrace.

Well, Cinderella, you're certainly not going to find your prince at Lover's Lane. Better get back inside.

As she turned to leave the happy couples to their romantic seclusion, she nearly bumped into someone. Backlit by the warm glow of the ballroom, he was silhouetted and she could barely make out his features. But she didn't need better light to recognize Carlos Montigo.

"It's a beautiful night," he said with a melodic Spanish accent, warming her from the inside out.

"It is beautiful. I was just—"

"If you're cold, I'd be happy to offer you my jacket."

"I appreciate the offer, but I'm fine."

He nodded and stepped up to the railing next to her. Looking at him from this angle made her draw in a quick breath. He might've been born of the bad-boy mold that attracted her, but something in his voice and in the way he carried himself suggested he was different. But exactly how, she couldn't discern.

"You made a beautiful bridesmaid for the princess."

"Thank you. Are you a friend of the bride or the groom?"

She cringed at the inane question. This was not North Carolina. Sophie hadn't met three-quarters of the guests, and she'd bet good money that Sophie and Luc didn't know most of them personally. That was what famous people did—hang out with other famous people. Go to their weddings. Whether they knew each other or not.

"I am acquainted with the Henri Lejardin, St. Michel's minister of art and culture, the brother of the groom. I have catered events for him in the past. I am in town for another occasion—the St. Michel Food and Wine Festival—and he invited me tonight.

"I am Carlos Montigo." He offered a hand and she took it.

"Lindsay Bingham," she returned.

He lifted her hand to his lips. She liked this gallant European custom.

His gaze slid to hers and locked into place.

An electric jolt coursed through her, and she couldn't look away. Even though she knew she should.

Oh, boy, she was in trouble.

But then, with the same air of rogue regality he'd shown when he so blatantly perused her from across the room, he released her hand and did a sweeping search of her face, his gaze finally lingering on her lips, which were suddenly so dry she had to moisten them before she could speak.

"Where are you from?" she asked.

"Florida."

"Really? I had you pegged for a European all the way."

"All the way?" he said, mimicking her slight southern accent. His mouth quirked up at the corner, forming a sexy half smile that Lindsay would've bet money had driven more than one woman wild.

"You're definitely American, and judging from the accent, from somewhere below the Mason-Dixon line. Am I right?"

"No, you're not. I don't have an accent."

He stood about a foot taller than Lindsay, yet now that her vision had adjusted to the moonlit terrace, she could see that his eyes were actually a deep shade of green rather than brown as she first thought.

"Yes, love, you do."

Oh, boy, indeed. Tall. Broad shoulders. Green eyes.

A lethal trinity, and if she didn't watch herself, she could find herself in a lot of trouble. A cool breeze blew in across the water. She tipped her face up to it and closed her eyes, hoping it would help her regain her senses.

"Mmm, that's nice. Isn't it?"

"Paradise," Carlos murmured. "I think I may have just found paradise, Lindsay Bingham."

What?

"Really?" She leveled him with a bemused gaze. "And I think I've just heard the cheesiest pickup line ever."

They laughed, and his eyes did that face-searching thing again that made her feel completely and deliciously devoured.

"May I buy you a drink?" he asked. "Seeing that it's open bar."

"Only if it's the best champagne."

He smiled. "Wait right here. I'll be back. With a bottle."

She was definitely in trouble. Especially since in the five seconds that he'd been gone, she'd already begun to tell herself that Florida and North Carolina weren't that far apart. At least there wasn't an ocean between them.

Even so, it didn't mean she had to sleep with him just because the guy was coming on to her….

A little dose of harmless flirtation might be good for her. So why not?

Because.

That soothing breeze blew in again, caressing her. Not in a seductive way, but in a way that reminded her of her "New Me" plan.

In answer, she tipped her face into the breeze and breathed in deep.

Even though Carlos Montigo was tempting, she was tired. And if she was completely honest with herself, she didn't have the energy to play games. Because her gut was warning that if she laid one hand on the Montigo burner she would surely get burned.

"Lindsay? There you are."

It was Sophie. In that split second before Lindsay realized it, she'd checked her posture and smiled. Reflexive moves, thanks to the ever-present paparazzi that had been milling about the past month. Not because of how Carlos Montigo's gaze had just shamelessly undressed her, and in response she'd thanked him with her best *what happens on my last night in St. Michel stays in St. Michel* smolder….

Her cheeks burned, and she strengthened her resolve to resist temptation.

"I thought you were coming back?" Sophie said. "We've been looking for you." With her head, she gestured to Carson Chandler, who waited in the doorway. "Carson wants to talk to you."

Talk to me?

Sophie had introduced Lindsay to Chandler earlier that week. Tonight, as she and Sophie walked toward him, he'd acknowledged her with a polite, "Good evening, Ms. Bingham. Lovely to see you."

Why did he want to talk to her?

The billionaire media mogul had turned a travel guide business into an empire. Everyone knew his name. Sort of like how people *knew of* the Rockefellers or William Randolph Hearst.

Sophie gave Lindsay a look and mouthed, *surprise!*

"What?" Lindsay mouthed back.

But Sophie ignored her, turning instead to Chandler. "Carson, would you do me a favor?"

He smiled. "Certainly, your highness, your wish is my command."

"Will you dance with Lindsay? My *handlers* are beckoning." Sophie rolled her eyes and gave her head a quick shake. "Don't think I'll ever get used to having *handlers*. Or, for that matter, the fact that I need to be *handled*."

She turned on a flourish of tulle and silk, leaving Lindsay and the older man alone. There was an awkward pause during which Lindsay's mind spun. Carlos would be back any minute with the champagne. She couldn't just leave without excusing herself. What kind of surprise could Carson Chandler have for her? He was handsome in an aloof, moneyed way, but then again didn't all men look gorgeous in white tie? Still, he was old enough to be her grandfather. She resisted the urge to fidget, or worse yet, glance around for Carlos.

Finally, Chandler tilted his head to one side in a regal gesture and offered his arm. "Shall we?"

Feeling suddenly shy and exhausted, Lindsay tried to let him off the hook. "Please don't feel obligated to entertain me."

She was the kind of wrung-out tired that made even the thought of dancing feel like an effort. Since she was leaving tomorrow, what she really wanted to do was go upstairs and enjoy one last long, hot soak in that huge, marble tub in her suite.

"Dancing with you, Miss Bingham, would be my honor," said Carson. "Besides, I have something I need to talk to you about."

"Oh. Well, then." How could she deny a man his *honor?* One quick dance wouldn't hurt. In fact, she might even be back before Carlos returned with the champagne. "But please call me Lindsay."

She took his arm and walked back into the ballroom with him. When he smiled, he vaguely reminded her of Ricardo Montalbán sans accent. Of course he would. Because wasn't St. Michel *Fantasy Island?* How could she have missed that? A place where her best friend got to be a princess and Lindsay had been able to play Cinderella. For an entire month.

Here she was at the ball. Even though tomorrow her coach would turn back into a pumpkin and she'd board a plane homeward bound for Trevard, she'd had the time of her life.

Of course, she wished her Cinderella fantasy came with Prince Charming and happily-ever-after. But as

Carson Chandler whirled her around the gilded and mirrored ballroom, she glanced up at the crystal chandeliers, admiring the way the light played through the facets, illuminating the cut crystal like brilliant diamonds.

How many women got to attend a royal wedding in their lifetime? She should be grateful for the experience, even if the handsome prince didn't come chasing her across the Atlantic to see if the slipper fit.

Her gaze wandered back to the doors to the terrace. She wondered if Carlos was back yet. She hoped he didn't think she'd run out on him. Surely he'd wait. Wouldn't he? A ridiculous tangled sense of conflict flooded through her.

Oh, well. They'd just met and tomorrow she'd go home. Her "New Me" plan didn't call for leaving one Jimmy Choo behind on the palace step with the slim hope a man—even Carlos Montigo—would find it and bring it to her on the other side of the ocean.

"The princess tells me you've worked in television, Miss Bingham."

Carson's voice startled her back to the present.

"Excuse me?"

The orchestra was loud. She must not have heard him correctly. He leaned in closer. A little too close for Lindsay's comfort.

"You're such a beautiful woman. Actually, I haven't been able to stop thinking about you since we were introduced earlier this week. Princess Sophie tells me you have broadcast journalism experience?"

Her cheeks warmed and graceless dread unfurled in her belly, working its way up until it blocked the words to explain her short-lived journalistic career. The question unlocked a door in the recesses of her mind behind which she'd stashed a very bad memory. The memory of an incident that cost Lindsay her dream.

"I was curious about the type of television work you'd done?"

Sophie was one of the few people who knew of this thwarted dream. Why would she tell Chandler?

"I don't know what Sophie told you." *Or more important, why.* "But in college, I majored in broadcast journalism, and I reported for a network affiliate for a short time."

"Why for only a short while? I have a feeling the camera would love your face."

Lindsay stiffened, suddenly aware of his hand on the small of her back. Nothing improper, but now the door that had been closed tight for years had opened and a flood of bad memories…of a powerful man taking advantage…poured out.

"Relax, Miss Bingham, I didn't mean that the way it sounded. I'm a happily married man."

Okay.

She felt a little silly for jumping to conclusions. With her penchant for bad boys, obviously, she was no prude, but those relationships had always been mutual and consensual. Even if the men in her past had ended up being bad choices, she'd never sold herself for a job. And she never would. That's why she'd left the television industry in the first place.

"You didn't answer my question, Miss Bingham. Why are you no longer working in television?"

She wished she'd simply told him she had no experience rather than opening this can of worms. Oh, Sophie, what did you do?

"It just wasn't the career for me."

Again, his hand pressed into the small of her back as he gently led into a turn on the dance floor.

"Do you work now?" he asked.

She laughed. She couldn't help it.

"Well, yes. Of course I do. Not everyone here is royalty or independently wealthy."

Ugh, that sounded rude. She hadn't meant it to.

"I work for Trevard County Social Services in North Carolina. That's how I know Sophie."

"The same line of work as the princess's former job?"

"No. Not exactly."

"Well, what exactly do you do?"

She bristled. Why the game of fifty questions? She wasn't embarrassed by where she came from or that she'd chosen not to be a television talking head. She had an honest job. That was more than some could say— those who had no qualms about sleeping with a married man on their quest to the anchor desk.

"I'm the office manager."

"And do you enjoy your work, Miss Bingham?"

No.

"It's Lindsay." She glanced up at him, frowning. "Do you always ask so many questions, Mr. Chandler?"

"Only when I'm trying to decide if I'll invite someone to interview for a job."

A job?

The music stopped. Carson Chandler escorted Lindsay off the dance floor.

Wait! What job?

As they reached the edge of the parquet, he said. "Thank you for the dance. Miss Bingham, er, Lindsay, Chandler Guides produces a three-minute segment that airs on Food TV between full-length shows. It's called *The Diva Dishes.* The spots highlight travel, food and festivities of various destinations. Have you seen the spots?"

Lindsay nodded. She was addicted to Food TV.

"The *mini-sodes,* if you will, have the potential to boost the sales of our travel guides. But in the first year, increases didn't live up to our expectations. Because of that we let the host go. She didn't have that *diva* spark I was looking for. That *je ne sais quoi* that captivates."

He paused and put a hand to Lindsay's chin, looking her over appraisingly. "You really do have the most exquisite eyes, my dear. I'm sure everyone tells you so."

Lindsay's guard went up again like steel trapdoors. She was just about to pull away, a split second before Chandler dropped his hand.

"I digress," he continued. "Monday, right here in St. Michel, we will conclude auditions for the new host. The person we choose will start right away because we're taping this weekend at the St. Michel Food and Wine Festival. I'm inviting you to audition."

Every nerve in Lindsay's body went on hyperalert. The St. Michel Food and Wine Festival? Wasn't that the event Carlos mentioned?

But...but she couldn't audition. She was flying out tomorrow. Mary was expecting her back at work bright and early Monday morning. Plus, Chandler made her uncomfortable. Brought back too many bad memories.

He must have read the hesitancy in her expression, or perhaps she didn't return a properly enthusiastic response.

"Hundreds have auditioned, Lindsay. To be quite honest, you will be the only one we see Monday. I'm sure I needn't remind you that you have a fabulous friend in the princess. She was quite generous with her praise of you, and quite convincing that you are the diva for whom I've been searching."

An awkward pause followed this unexpected compliment. Boy, Sophie wasn't kidding when she said she had a *surprise.*

As Lindsay searched for how to respond to Chandler, the clock in the castle tower tolled midnight. Out of the corner of her eye, Lindsay glimpsed Carlos walk through the doorway that led in from the terrace, but then she lost sight of him as he was swallowed up by the crowd.

Chandler reached inside his breast pocket and produced a business card. In the style of a magician weaving a coin through his fingers, he presented it to her with a flourish.

"Call my assistant for the location of the audition. It will be a very nice, lucrative opportunity."

She took a deep breath, glancing around, trying to locate Carlos as she gathered the words she needed to nip Chandler's wild idea in the bud.

"Thank you for the offer, Mr. Chandler. I'm flattered, really I am. But it's been several years since I was in front of a camera. As tempting as the opportunity sounds, I'm afraid I'm not the person you're looking for."

"Oh, but I believe you are. Don't misunderstand, I'm not offering you the job on the spot." He smiled. "We'll have to see how you look on camera, but as I said earlier, I have a hunch the camera will love your face. And, Miss Bingham, my hunches are always right."

Chapter Two

"You left?" The vein in Max Standridge's forehead pulsed like it might explode. Normally, Carlos Montigo would rib him about it, but better judgment warned, *not today*.

Instead he settled into the hotel suite's couch, shrugged and pierced Max with his best *what of it?* stare.

Max pounded his fist once on the desktop. "You know the hoops I jumped through to wrangle you an invite to that wedding, Montigo. It was an opportunity, man. Why'd you leave? You could've at least made contact with the minister of art and education. We talked about how important that was."

"Why did I leave?" Montigo stood and grabbed the *La St. Michel* social page off the coffee table, took a few steps and flung it onto the desk. It careened across the glossy surface until Max stopped it with a slap of his palm.

"That's why I left."

He gestured to a front-page photo of Lindsay Bingham in her sexy red dress, wearing that drive-a-man-to-madness smile.

In the photo her arms were outstretched, the bridal bouquet was in midair, poised to fall gracefully into her elegant hands.

Max sneered. "You have something against brides tossing flowers?"

"Yeah, I'm a conscientious objector to weddings in general." Carlos rolled his eyes. "Especially when they toss the damn flowers eight times to get the right photo to con the world into buying the fairy tale wedding bull. What a crock of sh—"

"What does that have to do with anything?"

Max looked perplexed.

Carlos stared at the photo, into the eyes that had captivated him last night…at the face that had danced through his restless dreams making sleep fitful and his mood edgy because he was so damn tired today.

Max was his best friend, but there was no way Carlos could tell him that he'd narrowly escaped letting the woman get under his skin. But she'd ditched him while he went to get drinks, for a media mogul who could've bought and sold most of Europe.

Why should he be surprised that yet another woman followed the scent of money? Didn't they all?

If he told Max that, the guy would have license to mock him for a year, ribbing him about his bruised ego and poor choice of woman. So instead of fessing up, he improvised.

"It's fake," Carlos said. "The first toss hit her in the head. Nearly put her eye out. Since that wasn't the perfect *fairy tale* outcome, they did it again. And again. Eight. Times. It wasn't a wedding. It was a three-ring circus full of barracudas, phonies and opportunists."

Max pressed his hands to his eyes, then raked his fingers through his hair, pulling so tight that for a moment his eyes were drawn into slits. Carlos couldn't bear to look at him. So he turned around and reclaimed his spot on the sofa. The wedding had been closed to the paparazzi. The royal image makers were, no doubt, doling out the photos and video clips they wanted the world to see. How long would it take for the press to dig up the *real deal?* A rogue video or an embarrassing picture taken with a camera smuggled in by some opportunistic schmuck hungry to sell secrets?

"I'm your manager, Montigo, not a miracle worker. I can't help you if you won't help yourself."

Help me? He leaned back and laced his fingers behind his head.

"I'm not a charity case, Max."

"I didn't say you were, but you have to lose that chip on your shoulder if we're going to make this work."

For the love of God, the guy nagged more than Montigo's ex-wife, Donna.

The ornate hotel room with its frilly pink cabbage rose wallpaper was closing in on him. Just like the ballroom had last night. The only reason he didn't walk out right now was because Max, unlike Donna, hadn't walked out on him when the chips were down.

They needed one more good run.

Get in. Make money. Get out.

This cookbook needed to sell. Then Carlos could repay Max and use the rest for a project none of the beautiful people cared to touch.

Damn hypocrites.

And that was fine by him.

All he wanted was a restaurant where he could cook what he wanted to cook and play by his own rules. A place where he could open his doors to kids who'd screwed up and give them a fighting chance in this world.

Because didn't everyone deserve a second chance?

He'd had it all once—right in the palm of his hand. Until his fall from grace, when he'd lost everything.

The past two years had changed him. Rearranged his priorities. Proven that there were more important things than money and parties.

But it also showed him how much he valued his independence.

Now that the dust had settled and he'd begun to pick up the pieces, he knew he didn't need the pretty people to succeed. The ones who once called him friend, but now pretended to not remember his name. But that was fine—life in the fast lane came with too many strings and always, always too high a price.

He would make his own way as he'd started to before Donna and all her glitzy ambitions. He would be beholden to no one.

"So I guess this means I need to cold-call Lejardin's office and try to get us in sometime in the next week," Max muttered, pensive, as if contemplating an impossible task.

"No need," Carlos said.

Max sighed, a weary, exasperated sound.

"Lejardin's stopping by the booth on Wednesday. Though you might want to call his assistant and confirm, things were pretty crazy at the wedding. They only had to do the garter toss six times. But still. Since he was in the wedding party, he was a little distracted. But I had to get out while I could. Before I hurt someone."

Carlos smiled at his own joke. Dazed, Max opened his mouth to say something, but nothing came out. He snapped his jaw shut.

Carlos reached inside his shirt pocket and pulled out a business card. "Here's his direct line. Should get you right through."

The trip to the airport where the St. Michel state jet awaited to fly Lindsay home to Trevard was a scenic fifteen minutes by limousine from the *Palais de St. Michel.* Lindsay settled into the soft leather seat, savoring her final glimpse of the St. Michel coast and the last vestiges of *the good life.*

Who knew when she'd return? She wanted to commit this parting scene to memory, to drink it all in. Even though she wanted to think she'd visit Sophie regularly, she didn't expect her friend to send a jet to fetch her every time they wanted a girls' weekend. And God knew she'd have to miser away every spare cent and every minute of vacation time before she could afford to take another trip abroad.

She sighed as they passed the yacht club, boats bobbing in the azure water, crisp, white sails billowing in the wind. Most of the vessels were larger than the modest apartment Lindsay called home.

Pointedly, she ignored the nagging question that kept forcing its way to the front of her mind—just how did one go back to Trevard after living like this?

Experts claimed it took twenty-one days to make a habit. She'd been here exactly thirty-two days. Not that it had taken anywhere close to twenty-one days to get used to the St. Michel life.

But the habit rule also worked in reverse, she reminded herself. She had a good job back in Trevard. A life there—no matter how much she'd love to stay in St. Michel, no matter how tempting Carson Chandler's offer to audition for *The Diva Dishes,* Lindsay had been away long enough.

The longer she put off going home, the harder it would be to go back. Besides, judging by the hoops she'd jumped through to get the time off—even though she had the vacation days—she didn't dare ask her boss for a single day more.

As the limo passed through a seven-story carved stone archway that resembled the *Arc de Triomphe,* a blue funk threatened to envelope Lindsay. She fought off the mood by reminding herself to look at the good. How many people had flown by private jet, been chauffeured by limousine and lodged in a five-hundred-year-old castle?

It was good while it lasted, and she needed to make the most out of these last moments rather than waste them brooding.

She grabbed her handbag, a cavernous Marc Jacobs—another bridesmaid gift from Sophie—and foraged for a compact and tube of lipstick to touch up her face before they arrived at the airport.

Instead of the makeup, her fingers found their way to Carson Chandler's business card and plucked it from the inner pocket where she'd stashed it. She ran her finger over the black letters embossed on the ivory-colored linen, then flipped it over and studied the bold script he'd used to write the contact number for his assistant, Sheila.

It would be a very nice opportunity for the right

person. And I believe you might be the right person, Miss Bingham.

Sophie had promised Chandler was a gentleman, "…happily married for nearly fifty years."

Interesting, since the man had a reputation in the business world for changing his mind as often as the wind changed directions. Even the spot he'd invited her to audition for seemed tentative.

"I'm not supposed to tell you this," Sophie had confided. "So you can't breathe a word, but you know he just purchased the Epicurean Traveler Network. Well, he wants to eventually turn the three-minute *Diva* spot into an hour-long show. You have to do this, Linds, because this little spot could turn into something really big."

Yeah, right. And it could be a dead end if he hired her and later decided to go with someone else—as he'd fired the previous Diva *host.*

Lindsay closed her eyes, trying to get Sophie's voice out of her head. "Cinderella certainly didn't get to the ball by locking herself away in the tower. She saw the opportunity and she took it."

Lindsay couldn't help but smile at the Cinderella metaphor. Wouldn't it be nice if life were simply one big fairy tale?

Then she wouldn't have to worry about cads who lied and cheated to get what they wanted.

Lies that cost Lindsay her fiancé, her job as a television reporter and her dignity.

"Chandler knows if he does you wrong he'll suffer the wrath of the future queen of St. Michel."

Lindsay sounded a humorless chuckle. God, Sophie almost sounded serious.

"Should I call you Ann Boleyn?" Lindsay had asked.

"*Nah.* Your royal highness will suffice." Then it was Sophie's turn to laugh. But her laugh was genuine. "You know I'm right, Linds. You've been hiding behind the reception desk. You're wasting your talent answering phones."

Really, when it came down to it, it wasn't the bad taste her foray into journalism left in her mouth as much as it was the uncertainty of the job in question.

Even if *The Diva Dishes* did have the potential to morph into a full-fledged television show, Chandler seemed too likely to change his mind midstream. His vision seemed too fickle. Sure, she had the future queen of St. Michel on her side—she still couldn't wrap her mind around the reality of Sophie's new life—but Chandler was a businessman and he'd make decisions based on what he deemed good for business, as evidenced by the way he fired the former host when she didn't live up to his expectations.

What if Lindsay couldn't pull it off? Her job at Trevard Social Services wasn't ideal, but she'd been there so long. It was comfortable—well, as comfortable as Mary Matthews allowed you to become. Lindsay's salary, though not huge, was enough to make ends meet, and you couldn't beat the government benefits.

Plus, she wouldn't be able to give two weeks' notice. Mary was certain to get her panties in a wad over that. She'd fussed over Lindsay taking time off for the wedding—even though Lindsay had more than enough accrued vacation.

No. Quitting on a whim just wasn't practical.

Sheila's number was one Lindsay wouldn't need, except for possibly making a courtesy *thanks-but-no-thanks* call.

An awkward uncertainty bubbled to the surface. Carson Chandler hadn't invited her to a party. So it wasn't as if she needed to RSVP, but he'd offered her a good opportunity. And she was the only one they were seeing at the St. Michel audition. Surely they'd have to arrange a camera ahead of time. It was rude to not call and tell them she wouldn't be there Monday.

The pang of missed opportunity pierced her, as she decided to call. If she'd learned one thing this month in St. Michel it was *when in doubt, err on the polite side.*

Lindsay pulled her cell phone out of the bag and switched it on. It had been off the entire week of the wedding when the battery had died, and she'd been too busy to worry about recharging it. She wasn't expecting any calls.

This morning, she'd remembered it needed charging and plugged it in, an afterthought as she prepared to leave. But she'd only bothered to turn it on now. And what she saw made her flinch: thirteen missed calls had gone to voice mail. All from her boss Mary Matthews over the past two days, Lindsay discovered, as she flipped through the call log.

Undistilled dread coursed through her as if someone had uncorked a bottle of something bitter and upended it into her system. *What did Mary want?* What was so darned urgent it couldn't wait until Lindsay was back in the office?

A multitude of possibilities sprang to mind, ranging from Mary wondering where she could find fresh file folders to her asking, "what's the phone number of that little sandwich shop that delivers?"

To Mary Matthews, a paper clip could be urgent if she couldn't put her fingers on one when she needed it.

Lindsay tapped a French manicured nail on the phone, debating whether to pick up the messages now or wait until tomorrow morning. When she was back on the clock.

After all, what could she do from this side of the Atlantic?

Tap. Tap. Tap. Tap.

But what if it *truly was* an emergency?

She struck the key that connected her to the voice mailbox.

The first message contained no greeting. No *I'm-sorry-to-bother-you-on-your-vacation-but* niceties.

It simply consisted of two words: "Call me."

After not hearing Mary's voice for so long, it was both familiar and strange, grating and startling in Lindsay's ear. It reminded her of how long she'd been away, and worse yet how she hadn't even missed home. Not once.

The second call was a bit more forceful: "Lindsay, did you receive my message? I need you to call me."

Followed by: "Lindsay, this is the third time I've called. I don't understand why you're not returning my calls."

Which was followed by: "Lindsay, I am furious. We agreed you could take a month off as long as you remained available to me. You're not upholding your end of the bargain. Call me ASAP or—"

Lindsay clicked off the phone.

Call me ASAP or—or what?

How like Mary to call before Lindsay's vacation was over, assuming it would be no bother, no imposition to drop what she was doing and serve her.

Mary's voice had been adamant and crackling in that last call, like a live wire one wouldn't dare cross. But it was that call, that self-righteous tone of voice that suddenly shocked some sense into Lindsay.

Like a bolt out of the blue…

Shining a bright, hot spotlight on her cold, pathetic life.

This was what Lindsay was going back to. No family, a handful of lukewarm friendships, Mary Matthews and an unfulfilling office manager job that she'd fooled herself into believing was important. Rather than the dime-a-dozen job it was.

And if that realization wasn't enough, then…

She didn't waste time thinking about the consequences of ignoring this epiphany. As the limo driver turned left onto the runway access road that led away from the public portion of the airport back to the private hangars that housed the royal jet, Lindsay dialed the number Carson Chandler had written on the card.

Chapter Three

Never before had Lindsay landed a job *that* fast. After placing the call on Sunday, she went in the following day for a test taping. Now, here she was on Tuesday morning, standing amidst a maze of white tents that an army of workers were busily erecting on the St. Michel *Parc Fête* green.

She'd called Ida May, who had graciously agreed to continue looking after the house. And with that squared away, she was the new host of *Chandler Guide's Diva Dishes*. Rather than sitting behind the Trevard Social Services reception desk taking orders from Bloody Mary, she was on assignment at the St. Michel Food and Wine Festival.

Oh. My. God.

She shuddered as a giddy sense of possibility seemed as if it might lift her off the ground.

In the distance a symphony of hammers and power tools rang out a determined song. Drawing in a deep breath, she inhaled the scent of lumber, freshly mowed grass and the odor of the hard work that was happening all around her.

Tomorrow the place would be filled with epicures and delectable aromas from the various booths and cooking shows and demonstrations, but today the place more closely resembled a construction site.

Lindsay watched in wonder, trying to imagine how they would pull it off and have everything ready in time. Or, more aptly, tried to imagine how she would be ready for her first show by tomorrow.

She'd seen several of the previous *Diva* spots that had aired last year with the former host whom, Chandler proclaimed, came across like a cold fish. He was depending on Lindsay to breathe new life into the show, to deliver an edgier, more provocative performance that would boost recognition and sales of Chandler Guides. They were going for a younger, hipper image. And, he added, almost as an afterthought, he wanted her to be the sand in the oyster that produced a pearl. How was she supposed to accomplish that? By simply being herself, Chandler said.

Herself?

Edgy? Provocative? Gritty?

Oh, boy.

Quite frankly, the thought made her head spin. It felt as if she were on a wild ride, hanging on for dear life. She didn't dare loosen her grip or risk being flung out into the stratosphere. Only, for once in her life, she felt as if she just might be on a ride that would actually take her somewhere.

"There you are. Okay, here's what I've got." Paula English, *Diva Dishes* segment producer, rushed into the press tent, talking as she scribbled notes on a clipboard. The woman elevated multitasking to a new level. "We can talk with a French vintner or a local cheese maker...."

As her words trailed off, Paula frowned and gnawed her bottom lip, continuing to write notes to herself.

"Those are two of the most boring ideas I can think of," said cameraman Sam Gunn, who had trailed in behind Paula. Sam rounded out the three-member *Diva Dishes* team. It was a lean operation, and Paula pulled no punches upon their introduction when unsmiling, she sighed and said, "Oh goody. I get to train *another* new host." Then she promptly informed Lindsay that each person, *especially* Lindsay, was expected to pull his or her weight.

"There's no room for slacking and no time for learning curves," she'd said. "You'll have to hit the ground running if we're going to make our deadline."

Lindsay couldn't tell if Paula's brusqueness was simply business, or if it was passive-aggressive resentment toward the new girl.

Whatever. The vacation was over, and the pressure was on Lindsay to not only show Chandler he'd made the right choice in hiring her, but to prove to herself she hadn't made a fatal error by quitting her job back in Trevard.

"So that's all you've got?" Sam shook his head. "I hope to hell Lindsay is good at improvising because it's going to take a genius to make something brilliant out of that."

Improvised brilliance? A solid lump formed in Lindsay's throat, then it dropped like a lead ball into the pit of her stomach. Improvising had never been her strong suit. She'd learned late in the game that it was one of the things she hated about news reporting. Improvising meant saying the wrong thing. Embarrassing herself. She thought she'd outgrow the fear with a little experience under her belt. Her career had never made it to that point.

Paula lifted her gaze from the page and glowered at Sam. "Do you have a better idea?"

She didn't call him a moron, but her tone implied it. The tension between them was nearly palpable.

Sam arched a brow. "Last time I checked, I was the cameraman and you were the producer."

Sam gave Lindsay a conspiratorial wink that implied he was choosing sides. While it was good to have an ally in Sam, she didn't want the team to be divided. They had to work together or they'd go nowhere fast.

Paula tucked her pen behind her ear. "Quit heckling me and make yourselves useful."

She nodded at Lindsay. "Come on, let's go have a look around and see if we can come up with something better. Sam, you go scout locations."

Unsmiling, Sam stared at Paula long enough to raise the possibility of a showdown. But then he broke the standoff.

"This is your show," he said to Lindsay. "Don't let her push you around."

Paula frowned and looked as if she might spit nails. She hissed, "Meet back here at 5:30 p.m., Sam. We have a dinner meeting with Chandler."

Then Paula muttered under her breath as he walked away. Something that sounded suspiciously like, "That's why you don't sleep with your coworkers."

Lindsay's jaw dropped. "You and Sam?" The words fell out before she could stop them.

Paula turned her wary gaze on Lindsay and seemed to sum her up for a moment. Then, to Lindsay's surprise, Paula nodded. "Yeah. It was sort of messy. We were the inspiration behind Chandler Guide's Gunn-English policy."

"What?" Why was Paula telling her this?

"The Gunn-English policy." There was no warmth in her expression. "A *no fraternizing* policy."

Was this Paula's not-so-subtle way of saying hands off? Because it sure didn't feel like girl talk.

"*Ah,* thanks for the heads up," she said cautiously. She wasn't the least bit interested in Sam.

No way. No how.

She'd been through that before—she and her ex-fiancé, Joe, had worked at the television station—he'd been an up-and-coming anchor. She'd been a general assignment reporter. Their problems started when she confided in him about the uncomfortable advances their boss, Gerard Webb, was making when they were alone. After all, if you can't trust your fiancé, who can you trust?

But Joe shocked her by getting mad at *her,* saying "Don't blow it out of proportion, Lindsay, and most important, don't do anything stupid that will jeopardize our jobs."

How could she not say anything? How could he not stand up for her? But when it all hit the fan, Joe proved whose side he was on. When she filed the complaint against Webb, Joe broke off their engagement, claiming she must have been leading Webb on, doing something to give him the wrong impression. In other words, she "must have asked for it."

"There's no sense in the two of us staying here," Paula said. "I'm going to go talk to the festival coordinator. You stay here." She gestured to a table full of literature on the far side of the tent. "See if you can find something better for the show in the press kits."

Then without so much as a goodbye, Paula turned and walked away, leaving Lindsay on her own.

It was make-it-or-fall-flat-on-her-face time. Since the latter wasn't an option, she had to get her rear in gear. The best place to start was to find a knockout idea for the first show, proving that she could pull her weight.

Dodging a team of men hauling a stack of boxes, she made her way to the publicity table. She scanned the various brochures, press kits and photos stacked neatly on the cloth-covered rectangular table. A familiar face snagged her gaze. Smiling up at her from a photo pasted on the cover of a blue folder was none other than Carlos Montigo.

Lindsay's stomach performed an erratic somersault that drew a defensive hand to her belly.

With her free hand, she reached for the folder.

The press kit was printed on glossy paper. No expenses spared. Impressive. It had all the makings of a staged comeback.

Lindsay opened the folder and pulled out a bio, which gave the general who—Carlos Montigo; what—self-taught chef; when—he'd been cooking all his life; where—born in Madrid, raised in Paris, and subsequently made his mark after he moved to Miami; and why—because food was his passion, *yada yada yada*. But no mention of his hiatus.

Of course not.

Behind the bio was one of his signature recipes for

beef bourguignonne and several eight-by-ten glossy black-and-whites: Montigo working in a restaurant kitchen; Montigo on the set of a cooking show; Montigo smiling warmly and toasting the camera with a glass of wine. Good photos of a gorgeous man— longish, glossy dark hair. Great bones that the camera loved. The trademark dark stubble on his jaw that made him look ruggedly handsome, but there was something about his crooked nose and the look in his eyes that promised danger. Good lord, the man made her squirm, and if there was one thing she couldn't resist it was a man who made…a good subject for the third *Diva Dishes* segment.

Lindsay had been out of the television business for several years, but despite advances in technology, one truth remained: a good reporter did her research before an interview.

She had a lot to learn about Carlos Montigo, and what she learned this afternoon—without letting his sexy smile and rugged good looks cloud her judgment— would tell her whether she'd pitch the story to Carson, Paula and Sam.

Sure, *The Diva Dishes* wasn't *60 Minutes,* but her gut told her there was a story here, and she was bound and determined to have a meaty idea to present to them at five-thirty.

So, she went back to the hotel and booted up the MacBook Chandler had given her when she accepted the job.

Leaning back against a stack of pillows, she performed a Google search of Montigo's name. One hundred fifty thousand matches came up.

The first listing was a *Wikipedia* entry. She clicked on it and the page opened, revealing a color photograph of Carlos that made her bite her bottom lip. Underneath the photo it said:

Carlos Montigo is a restaurateur and celebrity chef. The former owner of South Miami Beach's Prima Bella Donna starred in one season of Food TV's You Want A Piece of Me?

He was born in 1972 in Madrid, Spain and raised in Paris, France. He moved to Miami, Florida after meeting Donna Lewis and together, the two opened Prima Bella Donna. The couple divorced in 2006 citing irreconcilable differences. Lewis is now sole owner of the restaurant and has employed three different chefs in the two years since Montigo has been gone.

Montigo was the center of controversy when a reporter for the Miami Herald *initially set out to write a story about Montigo's refusal of a Michelin star and in the process discovered that the chef had lied about his credentials.*

Following the exposé, Food TV terminated Montigo's contract on the show You Want A Piece of Me.

Lindsay blinked. He lied? Why on earth would a man who was seemingly sitting on top of the world fake his credentials?

She scrolled down to a list of resources the author used for the story. She found a link to the *Miami Herald* story and clicked on it.

Miami Herald *February 10, 2006*
Celebrity Chef Spices Up Resume

Carlos Montigo, the celebrity chef/owner of Prima Bella Donna in South Beach, who rose to fame on the wings of the Food TV show You Want a Piece of Me *has caught his pants-on-fire. It seems Montigo, 35, falsely positioned himself as a culinary hotshot with hoity-toity credentials. In response, Food TV executives have relieved him of the remainder of his contract. They will show reruns of the episodes that have already been taped.*

According to Montigo's biography on FoodTV.com the chef claimed to hold a diploma from the prestigious Le Cordon Bleu culinary arts school in Paris. Au contraire, say school officials. "Our records cannot substantiate a connection between Monsieur Montigo and the school. He did not earn a Grand Diplome from our institution and should cease and desist connecting himself to Le Cordon Bleu."

Also, he maintained he was formerly a chef at the Élysée Palace in Paris, the official residence of the French president. That assertion also was proven to be a lie.

Montigo and his representatives did not return phone calls before the publication of this article.

It was like reading about a train wreck. What would possess him to do that? How did he think he could get away with falsifying his background? When you're in the public eye, you're begging people to ask questions and snoop around. Well, that's exactly what she'd ask him tomorrow when they met.

Her conscience protested.

It would be awkward digging up the past, rehashing things he probably wanted to put behind him—asking the tough questions was another aspect she'd found difficult about journalism.

She stared at the black-and-white photo of Carlos on the screen, a shot of Carlos in a leather jacket and a tough look on his handsome face, a publicity shot for *You Want A Piece of Me.*

But surely if he was promoting himself at the festival he had to know that media would ask questions.

She'd have to. It was her job—especially since Chandler wanted edgy.

Well, as edgy as you could get in a three-minute spot.

She searched some more and viewed Carlos's Web site, which was all about pitching his new cookbook—published by Lone Wolf Press.

Hmm…never heard of that house.

It also had recipes and a bio that didn't reveal anything new. It only mentioned his brief relationship with Food TV and his old stomping ground, Prima Bella Donna, in passing.

Nothing about the controversy.

The Food TV site was even less revealing. There was no mention of Carlos Montigo. It was as if he'd never existed in their realm.

She searched hundreds of articles that appeared in her Google search, but they were simply rehashings of the *Herald* article and didn't offer anything new.

Until she clicked on one that showed Carlos and a attractive brunette toasting each other on a Mediterranean-styled terrace with a gorgeous water view behind them.

The title of the article, which was presumably written before all hell broke loose, was *The Chef and His Prima Donna*.

Lindsay skimmed it, wanting to know more about this woman who, according to the article, was no wallflower, and what caused their irreconcilable differences.

They looked so happy in the photo.

According to the article, equal parts of Carlos's cooking and her charm were responsible for growing their Prima Bella Donna into the toast of the South Beach restaurant scene.

So this was his ex.

Lindsay studied her pretty face and the way Carlos was smiling at her. It reminded her of the way that Luc looked at Sophie.

But no! That was completely different.

Sophie and Luc were happy.

Carlos and Donna were…divorced.

Does love ever last?

How do you go from looking at each other as though the sun rose and set in your love's eyes to being…irreconcilable?

She blinked away the thought. She had just opened a word processing program on her computer and began to write notes and interview questions when her cell phone rang.

"Hello?"

"Lindsay? It's Sophie. How are you?"

Thrilled at the sound of her friend's voice, Lindsay sat up. She set the laptop aside and swung her feet over the side of the bed.

"Sophie, hi! It's so good to hear your voice, but why on earth are you calling me? You're on your honeymoon."

Sophie laughed. "Are you kidding? Do you think I could wait another two weeks to see how your meeting with Carson went? Besides, Luc went down to consult with the concierge about a trip we want to take tomorrow. So I have a few minutes. Tell me how it went."

For a split second, Lindsay considered playing a joke on Sophie—like they used to kid each other when they worked together—she thought about saying she'd gone home without talking to Chandler…or better yet, that Chandler said, "Thanks, but no, thanks." But she didn't have the heart. Not when her friend had been so good to give her this opportunity, and she didn't want to waste the precious little time they had to talk playing a prank.

"He offered me the job."

Sophie squealed. "And?"

"And we start shooting tomorrow at the St. Michel Food and Wine festival. In fact, I was working on my interview questions. Oh, Sophie, I don't know how I will ever repay you for this."

"You can repay me by knocking the socks off Chandler…and your admiring public."

"No pressure, huh? Couldn't I just take you to lunch the next time I see you?"

They both laughed.

"Lunch would be good. Could we set a date for a return visit now?"

Lindsay sighed. "I wish we could, but with work, I don't know when I'll be able to make it back to St. Michel."

"Oh, Linds, I'm so happy for you. Not to bring up a sore subject, but how did Mary take it? I'll bet she had a fit."

Lindsay sighed. "That's putting it mildly. I thought she was going to reach through the phone and strangle me. I've never quit a job without giving at least two weeks' notice."

Lindsay cringed at the thought.

"Right, but she should understand you're not just ditching her. This is the opportunity of a lifetime."

"I hope so because if not, I've just blown years of my life because Mary informed me she won't give me a good reference—no way, no how."

"Well, you won't need one. Despite my prodding, Carson wouldn't have chosen you if he didn't see something special in you, Linds."

"Here's my idea." Lindsay took a deep breath and placed Carlos Montigo's press kit on the restaurant table in front of Carson Chandler. She, Paula and Sam were having dinner with Carson to firm up their game plan for the first show.

They still hadn't ironed out the focus of the show. When they met back at the press tent, Lindsay, giddy with possibility, had spouted her idea. Even though she'd anticipated Paula being a hard sell, Lindsay had no idea that woman would be so disagreeable and dead set on her wine and goat cheese man.

It was clear that Paula was turning the show content into a competition when she grabbed the first opportunity to present her idea to Chandler—before they'd even been seated at the restaurant.

Chandler had nodded politely, and asked as they walked to the table, "But where's the edginess in wine and goat cheese, Paula? Remember, we're making the jump from run-of-the-mill to edgy and provocative."

When Paula didn't reply, Lindsay decided it was time for her pitch. She took a deep breath and twisted her hands into the napkin on her lap.

"Do you remember that Food TV chef, Carlos Montigo?" Lindsay asked. "The one who got the boot because he lied about his credentials? Well, he's here at the festival and it looks like he's staging a comeback."

Paula grimaced as she opened the menu. "Why would you want to give him free press?"

"It's not free press," Lindsay said. "It's a chance to

give Carson the type of story he wants. Something with an edge."

Lindsay glanced at Chandler to gauge his response, but he was staring at the menu. She wasn't sure if he'd heard her. If he had, he didn't look enthused.

Over the menu, Paula regarded Lindsay with arched brows and a smug smirk that gave her pessimistic mouth an ironic upturn. No backing there—no surprise. So, Lindsay looked to Sam for support, but he was busy buttering a dinner roll. For a moment, an awkward silence enveloped them.

Okay.

She took a deep breath, inhaling the delicious aroma of herbed bread baking in a wood-burning oven. The enticing scent of rosemary and thyme filled the restaurant and fueled her courage. Giving the napkin one last twist, Lindsay decided it was time for the new girl to prove her mettle.

"In all my research, I couldn't find anything telling his side of the story," Lindsay said. "This is a chance to ask him *why* he lied and to hear about his future plans."

Paula closed her menu and shook her head, as if Lindsay had proposed a feature on *The Wiggles* or something else laughably inappropriate and ridiculous.

"Who cares?" Paula choked on an incredulous laugh, then pursed her lips as if stifling the urge to guffaw. She looked at Chandler as if she expected him to have the same reaction.

"Who cares?" Lindsay countered. "A lot of people would find the story interesting."

"Maybe we can catch up with him for another episode," Paula dismissed. "Since we're in St. Michel, we'll go with the wine and goat cheese theme."

Chandler held up his hand. "Not so fast, Paula. You haven't made a case for your goat man."

Paula laughed again, as if she expected Chandler to join in on the joke. But his serious expression warned otherwise.

"I think Lindsay is onto something with the Montigo story," he said. "Let's move forward with it."

Chapter Four

Carlos's role in the food and wine fest was three-fold and simple: He'd host a one-hour, audience-interactive cooking demonstration; join five chefs in presenting a charity fundraiser "celebrity chef" dinner; and sign books at a launch party celebrating the release of his new cookbook, *Carlos in the Kitchen.*

The launch party, sponsored by the publisher, Lone Wolf Press, was his last event in the lineup. And, by all accounts, the most important to him.

There was a lot riding on this book.

As the taxi stopped in front of the Hotel St. Michel, Carlos tucked a copy of the new cookbook under his arm.

No one need know that Carlos and Max were the driving force behind Lone Wolf. It wasn't ideal to self-publish and throw a party for himself. But his former publisher had dropped him and these days corporate sponsors were hard to come by.

The way he and Max had sheltered the publishing house, no one need be the wiser. Right now, that was the last thing on his mind. Things were off to a great start. Max, who deserved a huge bonus once they got on their feet, had secured an interview with the new host of *The Diva Dishes*. That interview was the reason he'd rushed back to the hotel.

Now, as he stood in front of the door to the hotel suite he shared with Max, he raked a hand through his hair and took a moment to get his head in the game before he entered the room.

He'd thought a lot about what Max had said about losing the chip on his shoulder and he supposed his friend was right. Sometimes Carlos could be his own worst enemy. He'd lived a desolate, flatlined life since his fall from grace.

That's what caused his career to self-destruct. Now that he'd quit feeling sorry for himself and was trying to rebuild his life, he could either go with the flow or make it an uphill, and quite possibly losing battle. He might be proud, but he wasn't stupid.

This was an opportunity, a means to an end. He would go in there and charm the media into an endorsement.

He practiced a smile, which felt tight and insincere at first, but gradually eased into something that felt like a pleasant expression. One more deep breath, then he opened the door.

Okay. Showtime.

"Carlos, my man." Max stood and spread his arms wide. Yep. Nothing said *showtime* like Max in amped-up PR mode. "Come in. Come in. We've been waiting for you."

He hadn't even closed the door behind him when his gaze locked on the blonde sitting on the couch.

Lindsay Bingham?

What the—

Only, today she wasn't swathed in the low-cut, curve-hugging gown that had mesmerized him Saturday night. She'd traded it in for a sleek black, knee-length skirt and white button-down blouse that should've spelled sensible, but on her it looked even sexier than that gown that had been cut to places that might've been illegal in some cultures. Her long, straight, blond hair was loose today, framing her face. He tried not to stare at the way her skirt was hitched up over her knees—rather pretty knees at that, and long, slender legs that were enough to drive a man to distraction.

What was she doing here?

There were few things that Carlos hated more than being caught off guard. Unpredictability was one of the things he hated most about being in the limelight. He wanted to follow the script—like an old reliable recipe—but invariably surprises sprang up.

He hated surprises.

So why was it that underneath the *surprise* of finding this unpredictable woman in his hotel room, he was happy to see her?

Carlos walked over to the party of five gathered in the living area and placed the cookbook on the coffee table, front and center.

"I'd like to introduce you to the crew of Chandler Guides's *Diva Dishes*," said Max. "This is Carson

Chandler, CEO of Chandler Guides and the show's executive producer."

"Carlos Montigo," he said, shaking Chandler's hand. For the first time since he'd seen Lindsay with Chandler at the wedding, he felt a surge of possibility. Pieces were starting to click into place. He hadn't considered the possibility that Lindsay's relationship with Chandler might be strictly business. Experience—Donna, his mother—had proven more often than not most women followed the money.

"This is *Diva* cameraman, Sam Gunn," Max continued, "Segment Producer Paula English, and Lindsay Bingham, the show's new host."

Lindsay held out her hand and dazzled him with a smile. Even wearing muted tones, she looked impossibly brilliant against the room's prim floral motif. As if her energy claimed physical space.

"I believe we've met," he said, taking her hand.

"Yes, we have," she said. "You disappeared the other night. I didn't get to say good-night."

Her skin was as soft as he remembered, and her handshake firm, yet every bit as feminine as he thought it would be. Since Saturday, visions of this woman had lingered in his mind. Without warning, that face—with those haunting brown eyes, those full, tempting lips—had randomly popped into his thoughts, leaving him vaguely wanting and unsettled.

And here she was standing in front of him. Again.

Did she have her manicured fingers in every news-making pie in St. Michel? Maid of honor to the princess. Headline-grabbing bouquet catcher. Chandler Guides's brand-new Diva.

Whatever the case, he was glad to see her. Because,

of course, he wanted to be sure the diva worked her magic promoting *Carlos in the Kitchen.*

"Here's a copy of Carlos's itinerary for the duration of the Festival." Max handed each of them each a crisp white sheet of paper.

"How did you want to do the interview?" he asked. "Do you want to start here or on location?"

The *Diva* crew glanced at the papers.

"The segment will only be three minutes," Paula said in a slightly irritated deadpan. "We want to shoot during his audience-interactive cooking demonstration. His show's scheduled for two o'clock. We'll meet you backstage at one o'clock."

"No preliminary interview?" Carlos asked.

"No time," Paula answered.

"But we'll get to see the script first, right?" Max asked.

Though Carlos didn't think it was possible, Paula's face hardened even more. "We don't use a script. We wing it."

There was something about that woman he didn't trust. Something about her that didn't sit right. He took people at face value now. Because of Donna, he didn't make excuses for anyone anymore. He heeded his gut's warning. With his ex-wife, he'd brushed off *this,* made allowances for *that.* In the end, Donna had made a fool of him. He'd seen it coming, yet he'd sat back and let her have her way until she'd systematically ruined his life.

He had no one to blame but himself. But one thing was for damn sure: it would never happen again.

"I'm not comfortable with winging it," Carlos said. "So, thanks for your interest, but I can't help you with your show."

Max shot him a *what-the-hell-are-you-doing?* look as Carlos turned to walk out of the room.

"What Paula means," Lindsay interjected, "is that we take an *organic* approach when we film. Tomorrow, we'll play off the audience, talk about what you're cooking and go with the general mood of the show. No worries. I promise."

Carlos stopped, his back to the *Diva* crew and considered her words for a moment. Why should he trust her any more than the woman she worked with?

"I have an idea," Chandler offered. "Why don't we have dinner tonight? We can get to know each other. You know, break the ice before tomorrow."

Carlos turned. "No. I don't want a group get-together, but I will reconsider if Lindsay will agree to have dinner with me. If we have too many cooks in the kitchen, it'll be counterproductive. Since she'll be interviewing me, we're the ones who should meet."

The Rivera Ivoire on the Boulevard St. Michel was an intimate jewel of a restaurant. It wasn't a three-star establishment, but it had a solid reputation for stellar food. It was one of his favorites. So it was the only possible choice for dinner with Lindsay. Not to mention, here he didn't know the chef and that was fine with him.

Despite his reputation as the outcast who'd lied about his credentials, two years out of the game, few industry professionals acted like they recognized him. Of course, that meant no chef-to-chef professional courtesies. But he wasn't looking for special treatment. In fact, he preferred to remain anonymous.

Carlos stood when Lindsay walked into the dining

room, lighting up the place like sunshine through gray clouds. More than one head turned as she walked by.

She looked bohemian in her flowing cobalt-blue skirt, gauzy white peasant top and brocade shawl. Still graceful and beautiful, but staggeringly different from the elegant socialite in red who'd caught the princess's bridal bouquet—and his eye. And different yet again from the businesswoman who'd appeared in his suite earlier today.

The woman was a jumble of contradictions, and the sight of her as she walked toward him made him smile despite himself.

The way she carried herself with her long hair swinging loose about her shoulders made her look like a gypsy. *Maybe she'd bring him good fortune?*

Yeah, right. How could he even contemplate such crap? She was here to get a story, and he needed to make damn sure he steered the direction that story would go.

She smiled as she walked toward him, and he could've sworn sparks ignited the instant their eyes met.

"Sorry I'm late." She offered him her hand. He held on to it and gazed at her, happier to see her than good sense warranted.

"I got tied up going over the camera shots with Sam." She pulled her hand from his. "Time got away from me, but it's going to be a great spot."

"No problem." He pulled out a chair for her, and she sat. "I haven't been waiting long."

Her bracelets chimed as she pushed her long hair over her shoulder, no doubt sizing him up as he took his seat across the table from her; reconciling the man before her with the cad the news stories had concocted.

Hell, everyone he met looked at him that way these days, since his life hit the fan and the intimate details of who he was or, more important, who he *wasn't,* flew out into the open for all to judge.

Still, even though the media had burned him, to get what he wanted, he needed some good press to turn his ship around. That was the only reason he was going through with this interview on *The Diva Dishes.*

He picked up the open bottle of wine and poured some for her.

"This is a Chateau Troplong Mondot Saint Emilion 2000. I hope you like red."

"I do," she said. "Thank you."

He handed her the goblet and touched his to hers.

"Here's to a good show."

"Cheers," she said, and lifted it to her full lips, sipped, then considered her glass. "I thought you said you hadn't been waiting long?"

He shook his head as he savored the classic, rich berry, cherry and spice of the full-bodied wine. "It needed time to breathe before we enjoyed it."

She grinned. "You haven't been waiting long, yet you had ample time to order and aerate a bottle of Saint Emilion—and quite a nice one, I see."

With his forearms resting on the edge of the table, he toyed with the knife at his place setting. "So maybe I was early. You caught me."

She clucked her tongue and tsk-tsked. "Punctuality is such a bad habit. You really should do something about it."

She smiled warmly, a glint of mischief sparkling in her brown eyes. He was suddenly very glad they were dining together.

After officially meeting Carlos Montigo in his hotel suite earlier that day, Lindsay's first impression was that he was an egomaniac—wanting to dictate the direction of the show, and threatening to pull out when things didn't go his way.

But as they ordered and Carlos gradually let down his guard, he seemed…charming. Before talking to him, she would've expected a Muzak orchestra to break into a chorus of "You're So Vain" when he walked into a room.

Now she was willing to give him the benefit of the doubt. Maybe she'd misjudged. Either the tabloids were wrong or the man was a veritable Jekyll and Hyde. Even though there was usually a grain of truth in tabloid headlines, she'd certainly never placed much stock in them. Never had a reason to until now. They were just something to look at in passing. Something to read and secretly roll her eyes at as she waited in the checkout line at the supermarket.

But now that she'd met Carlos, the truth suddenly mattered. That was what she intended to get to the bottom of tonight.

The conversation flowed naturally and fluidly. Mellowed by the wine and lulled by his silken, slightly-European accent—Spanish tempered by his years in France and the States—she was swept up in the ebb and flow of his voice as he candidly talked about his early years in Spain and France; how he learned to cook in his grandmother's kitchen—nothing she didn't already know from her research, but it was interesting hearing it from him.

It was strange knowing so much about someone she'd just met. It almost felt a tad stalkerish, but it was all in a day's work. It was her job to do be well-informed and armed with pertinent questions.

"What happened with Food TV, Carlos?" she asked.

She could almost see the wall going up around him. It was a physical shuttering of the sexy, funny man who'd beguiled her with candid tales of his early years.

"I'm sure you know the story. You've done your homework."

"Yes, I have." She toyed with her bracelet before looking up at him. "Over and over again, I read the same account of how you falsified your credentials. But nowhere did I read your side of the story. How come, Carlos?"

His expression was impassive. Yep, the wall was firmly in place. And it was steely and cold.

"For the interview, I'd prefer to look forward, not back."

"But you've never told your side of the story. Why?"

He smiled without warmth and shook his head, then looked down into his wineglass and gave it a swirl. "What good would that do? The media has already told the story it wants to tell. If I offered a rebuttal two years after the fact, it would do nothing but open old wounds. After all this time, it's old news. There's no sense in rehashing that can of worms. However, I would like to focus on what the future holds."

Ugh. Okay. Fine. He wins.

She'd always been bad at asking the hard questions. That was one of the excuses that Gerard Webb had used for firing her.

She certainly wasn't going to sit here and fight with him. Because even then she wasn't sure he'd trust her with the information. Extracting the truth out of an interviewee just wasn't her strong suit. That's why she wasn't a good journalist.

She sighed inwardly.

"So what does the future hold for Carlos Montigo?"

"I'm getting back to my roots. I haven't been to St.

Michel in ten years, and now here I am touring Europe—at least for now—promoting my cookbook. Life is good, Lindsay. It'll be even better when I can return to my house in Cedar Inlet. But for now, I'll enjoy St. Michel and the company of a gorgeous woman."

He raised his glass to her, and the way he looked at her left her strangely breathless, but if she stuck to her mental list of interview questions, she'd get over it.

"What about South Beach?" Lindsay asked. "Do you miss it?"

A smile tugged at the corners of his mouth, but it didn't reach his eyes. He took a slow sip of wine as he pondered the question.

Finally, he said, "I don't miss it a bit. Not a single thing about it."

"Why did you pass on the Michelin star?" She held her breath, aware that he'd never gone on record answering that question.

For an awkward moment Carlos didn't answer, and she feared that he wouldn't.

"Again, I'd rather not dwell on the past, but if you promise me this is off the record…give me your word that tomorrow these questions won't be part of the interview, I'll tell you."

Her heart pounded against her rib cage. "Of course."

He regarded her warily. "I would've sacrificed a lot of my freedom in exchange for those stars. Since I was away from the restaurant more than I was there, it seemed to be better for the restaurant for me to pass on the honor."

"In other words it would've been too much pressure to keep up?" she asked.

Carlos shrugged, pulling that impassive look again.

"Interesting. Your trying to keep your freedom was exactly what led to the media investigation that robbed you of all you'd worked so hard to build?"

Another awkward moment flared. Only this time, it soon became clear, as Carlos crossed his arms over his chest, he had no intention of answering the question.

Whatever had passed between them earlier had evaporated. "Earlier, you mentioned Cedar Inlet, Florida. I'm not familiar with it. How is it different from South Beach?"

Carlos chuckled and she was relieved he seemed to have loosened up again. "They're like black and white," he said. "Day and night. One is all about glitz and money, seeing and being seen. The other is natural and laid-back—it works with your rhythms, whereas you have to get in tune with South Beach rather than it synching with you. You see, I have this dream that—"

He stopped and shook his head as if he'd caught himself in the nick of time.

"A dream?" she asked. "Go on."

"It's not important."

"Dreams are always important. Sometimes they're the only thing that keep us sane."

"I understand that, what I meant is that it's not important that I share that information with you."

His words crashed down like a wave pulling her under for a moment, then spitting her out, disoriented, on the shore. He must have read the bewilderment on her face, because he said, "That was rude. I apologize. What I meant is it's not relevant to our interview and I'd rather focus on the cookbook."

She shrugged. "Maybe the next time I interview you, it will be about that dream."

* * *

He wasn't trying to be rude, not on purpose, though he could be when it served him. He hadn't expected the flash of hurt on her face when he steered the conversation back around to the purpose of this dinner. Maybe Lindsay Bingham was more human than media automaton after all.

A curious thrill shot through him. He couldn't quite figure her out, but one thing was certain, she was one hundred percent woman—a smart, funny, richly complex woman. Someone he definitely wanted to know better.

The waiter brought the bill, and Carlos reached for his wallet.

"Mr. Chandler has already taken care of the tab." Lindsay smiled triumphantly. "This is just a receipt."

He sat back in his chair.

"Thank you, but it wasn't necessary," Carlos said. "When I invite a woman to dinner, I pay. Business or not."

His words, *business or not,* seemed to reverberate in the ensuing silence. They begged the question—*was this business...or not?* Because somehow suddenly the mood had shifted, the air between them seemed charged and for a reckless moment, he wanted to trust her, wanted to open up and share.

"Come on, let's get out of here," he said. "I want to show you something. Do you feel like taking a walk?"

"Sure," she said tentatively. "Where to?"

He gave her his warmest smile, taking in the alluring contrast of her dark eyes and her pale blond hair. "It's a surprise."

They stood. She grabbed her handbag, and he helped her with her wrap.

Soon they found themselves out in the chilly night air walking past the casino through streams of well-dressed people, toward the beachfront park.

"So what's it like being Chandler's new Diva?" he asked as they walked.

A Diva? Me?

She decided to not take the question literally.

"Actually, this is my first show. I've had the job for all of three days."

"Really? What did you do before?"

And as they made their way along the ancient cobblestone street that led through the heart of downtown St. Michel, Lindsay regaled him with the story of how, with a little nudge from her good friend the princess of St. Michel, she'd landed the position as the show's host.

Amusement lit his eyes. "You must lead a charmed life to stumble upon a job like this."

She shrugged. "Hardly, but I am fortunate to have such a good friend as Sophie. I wouldn't be here right now if not for her. Now, if you want to talk about someone leading a charmed life, she's the one."

A strange sense of irony tugged at her insides. Yes, indeed, if not for Sophie, Lindsay *wouldn't* be here right now in St. Michel, walking with this gorgeous man, feeling as if anything were possible.

Maybe some of Sophie's charm had rubbed off, Lindsay thought as she stole a quick glance at Carlos. His profile wasn't perfect, which was reassuring. His nose was slightly too big and there was a bump on the bridge that made it a little crooked—but that simply added to his charm.

They walked in comfortable silence for a few minutes, listening to the *whoosh* of cars whizzing by, intermittently muting the conversations of giddy passersby en route to the casino and various clubs and restaurants that lit up the Boulevard St. Michel.

It was so intimate walking with him, the two of them together, making their way through the throngs of people. They walked so close, yet didn't touch. That made her all the more aware of him. It was as though she could feel the heat radiating off him, beckoning her closer.

"So, a man who cooks," Lindsay said, feeling suddenly brave. "Why hasn't some lucky lady snapped you up? Unless someone already has?"

She hadn't thought of that until now. Nothing had been written about him since the initial media nightmare about losing the show and his divorce. Maybe he'd found someone. But that would be part of the story, and it was her job to ask questions like that—for the story.

"There's been no one recently I've wanted to be involved with."

His answer made Lindsay bite her lip. "Oh, I'm sorry." *Sort of.*

"We've talked about me all night," he said. "Tell me about you."

She tucked a strand of hair behind her ear.

"Talking about *you* was the purpose of the dinner," she said.

He pinned her with a devastatingly persuasive look, and something in the way his eyes crinkled at the corners when he smiled made her happy he wanted to know about her.

"Well, let's see…I was born and raised in Trevard, North Carolina. This trip to St. Michel is my first trip out of the United States."

"Really? You seem so worldly."

"Worldly? Somehow that doesn't sound like a compliment."

"Oh, but it is." He winked at her. "At the wedding, I had you pegged as a jet-setter. You know, one of the beautiful people."

She smiled and ducked her head a little, embarrassed.

"So you must like Trevard to have stayed there so long?"

She shrugged. "Life sort of dictated my staying put."

"Really?"

She nodded. "My mother died when I was young. It was just my father and me for so long. I guess felt a little responsible for him. Especially since I never really knew my mother." She glanced up at him to gauge his reaction, unsure if she'd said too much. But the warmth in his eyes spurred her on. "All I have of her is her old recipe book. It's this little red notebook. All the recipes are handwritten. I've always had this crazy notion that if I could master all those recipes, I might know her somehow...."

She gave her head a slight shake, wishing she hadn't said it.

"I'm sure that sounds ridiculous. Just—" She waved her hand, as if she could erase the comment. He wasn't interested. He was just being polite.

He shook his head. "Why would that sound ridiculous? I think you can tell a lot about a person through the things they cook. If she's anything like you, I'll bet she was a wonderful woman."

Heat crept over her like a shadow.

"So what's in her book?" he asked. "If you don't mind telling me?"

His genuine interest surprised her.

"Sweets, mostly," she said. "Apparently, she was quite a baker."

"*Ah,* pastries." A wicked grin spread over his face. "That means she was sweet."

Lindsay blew out a breath. "That's not a cliché at all, is it?"

Carlos chuckled. "What's wrong with that? People who bake tend to be kind and homey by nature—think grandmas. I, on the other hand, am a savory man. Not a sweet bone in my body."

"Well, you've got a point there. But I'm sure some big, burly pastry chef would just love to hear himself described as *sweet.*"

They laughed together.

"So you and I have losing our mothers in common."

Lindsay pursed her lips against the pang that inevitably pierced her heart when the subject of death came up. Even though she'd lost both of her parents, it didn't make it any easier to console others. Plus, was this off the record or part of the interview? It would be heartless to ask.

As if reading her discomfort, Carlos shrugged. "Not much love lost there. First, she abandoned me to my *abuela*'s care, then she went out and drank herself to death."

He said the words matter-of-factly. She grimaced. "I'm sorry."

He waved her off. "Nah. No need. What my mother lacked in affection, *Abuela* made up for tenfold."

"This is the grandmother who taught you to cook?"

He nodded, and a warm glow enveloped her at the thought of a little Carlos with his *abuela.*

"Were you an only child?" she asked.

"Yes."

"Me, too. Were you a lonely kid?" she asked, sensing that they just might have that in common, too.

He turned to her, looking very serious. But he didn't answer her. Their gaze linked, and the night suddenly seemed very quiet except for the faint roar of the sea. Only then did she realize how far they'd walked—all the way down the path that stretched from the city center down to the cliffs that bordered the beach—far enough to escape the hustle and jostle of the city to the natural roar of the water.

Funny, it didn't seem as though they'd walked that far. But they had, lost in each other's company, discovering that they had more in common than they might've imagined.

She crossed her arms, surrendering to a shiver that wasn't completely caused by the drop in temperature.

"Are you cold?" he asked. "Here, take my jacket." Before she could protest, he'd already draped it around her. It held the warmth of his body and smelled faintly of soap, leather and spice…and something indefinable that made her want to bury her nose in the collar and breathe in deeply.

He walked over to the waist-high retaining wall that bordered the sheer, rocky drop down to the water below.

"This is what I wanted to show you." He gestured for her to join him.

"The beach?"

Curious, she made her way over to stand beside him.

"Do you hear that?" he asked.

They stood silent for a moment, Lindsay straining to hear something, but just what, she wasn't sure. All she could discern was the sound of the wind and the waves slapping the rocks below.

"Earlier, you asked about the difference between South Beach and Cedar Inlet. It's similar to the contrast between downtown St. Michel and this." He made a sweeping gesture toward the sea. "Though South Beach might be a little rowdier and this beach a bit more extreme than Cedar Inlet. But at heart, the contrast is the same. I guess I've always connected better with nature than with people—well, most people. Let's just say there are certain types I prefer more than others."

They leaned on the wall, their shoulders a breath apart, not quite touching, but the vibrations radiating off each other were nearly palpable.

"If you're not a people person, then how the heck did you end up in the restaurant business?"

He shrugged. "Funny the path life sends us down, huh?"

The lilt of his accent set loose a swarm of butterflies swooping in Lindsay's stomach. Or maybe it was the nearness of him and the realization that they were alone—and the sudden rush of desire that trailed in the butterflies' wake.

"I *was* a lonely kid," he said. "The kind of lonely that can only be understood by someone who's felt it, too. You know, not belonging. I can't imagine that you were that kind of kid."

"Ah, but I was," she said. "Sometimes I still am."

"I don't believe it." His voice was a sexy whisper. "You can talk to anyone. You fit in anywhere. How is it that the lonely child in you overcame her affliction?"

She shrugged, aware of how he was looking at her. "It was difficult growing up under my father's roof. He was good to me—always made sure I had what I needed. But no matter what I did, it felt like I never quite measured up to his expectations. I suppose I was always trying to prove to him that I wasn't a failure. The only time I came close to making him proud was when I was reporting for WKMO. He took such pride in telling everyone that his daughter was on television every night. But then when I…"

She stopped, backpedaling away from the bad memory. She didn't want to get into it. Why ruin an otherwise good evening by drudging up parts of the past that couldn't be changed? *Her past.* They were supposed to be talking about him, for God's sake.

"You were saying?" he prodded.

"Let's just say one of the biggest disappointments of my father's life was when I lost that job."

He reached out and touched her arm.

"*Lost* the job?"

She held up her hand. "I don't want to talk about it."

"Fair enough," he said. "But look at you. You've come a long way since then. I think he'd be proud of who you are now."

Would he?

He smiled. In the clear moonlit night, she could see that the smile reached his eyes. Mmm, those incredible green eyes that looked darker than ever tonight.

"Funny thing is, sometimes I don't quite know who I am." The words escaped before she realized what she was saying. She should leave. Because her head was swimming and she was saying way too much. She was supposed to interview this man tomorrow. Supposed to be professional. She needed to have the upper hand, be the one in control. But he was looking at her mouth and she was leaning into him. When he took her chin in his big hand and drew her closer, she felt his warm, wine-scented breath so near that every feeling—every dream and desire she'd had since the first moment she'd set eyes on him that night at the castle—shimmered to the surface. Since then, all she'd thought about was the way his arms would feel around her, the way his lips would taste….

Then he kissed her. Despite the longing, the kiss surprised her. The tentative touch and softness of his lips were a sexy contrast to his masculinity. The warmth lingered, burning away the chill in the air. His mouth was so inviting and even though a voice of reason sounded in a distant fog in the back of her mind—she really shouldn't be doing this—she had to have one more taste.

He pulled her closer, enveloping her in that scent that threatened to drive her insane. Again, he dusted her lips with a featherlight kiss, then a playful nip. When his mouth finally covered hers, he kissed her with such an astonishing passion, it felt like it came from the soul.

The deep, demanding kiss had her reeling, as yearning pulsed through her body. And the way he touched her…one hand in her hair, holding her possessively in place, while the other slid down, caressing her back, edging its way underneath the hem of her blouse until the skin-on-skin contact made it exceedingly hard for her to catch her breath.

A low groan of desire broke through the sound of the elements, and she realized it had come from her. If she knew what was good for her she'd stop now….

Or…in a minute…. She just needed…one…more…taste—

Without warning, Carlos pulled away. Muttering something about it being late, needing to get back. The contrast was jarring, and she stood blinking, trying to regain her equilibrium. He'd gone from heated passion to cool business in the time it took to extinguish a flaming burner on a gas stove.

"What's wrong?" she asked.

"I just realized how late it is," Carlos said.

The excuse sounded ridiculous, even to himself. But how could he explain that he'd stopped kissing her because he never should've started in the first place? That he had no idea the taste of a woman could potentially drive him over the edge, making him want things he had no business wanting? Not right now.

He led her away from the wall, back on the path toward town. They walked in awkward silence.

Tonight, he'd been way out of line, asking her too many personal questions when he should've kept the focus on business. On tomorrow's interview.

Even more important, he should've never lost sight of his plan. A plan that didn't include a woman in his life. Even so, something at the most base level urged that not only did Lindsay have the potential to be part of the plan, but she could be the center of his world.

Donna had taught him a hard, expensive lesson about the cost of building his life around someone else. And because of that he'd promised himself it would never happen again. Of course, that didn't mean he'd become a monk. There'd been women since Donna. Several, in fact. And each one had been a beautiful distraction, but nothing more. Not a single one had cut to the core of him like Lindsay had, making him want things he hadn't thought about in a very long time.

Even if he went back on the promise he'd made to himself, with everything he'd planned for the next year, the timing was bad. It was the wrong time to start something. And even worse to start something he couldn't finish.

Hell, maybe it was even wrong to agree to the interview because it was crystal clear that when it came to Lindsay Bingham, he had very little control.

Somehow she'd managed to break through the barriers he'd erected. And tomorrow, they'd both go their separate ways. He was off to the Vienna Food Show, and she'd go wherever the *Diva* path led her next.

The chance of their paths crossing again was slim to none. Unless one of them compromised.

Compromise was too great a sacrifice to ask of either of them.

Chapter Five

It was just a kiss, Lindsay reminded herself as she walked the six blocks from the hotel to the festival grounds.

The thought made her head hurt almost as much as the bright St. Michel sun glaring on the white tents dotting the *Parc Fête* green. The morning was much warmer than the previous night. St. Michel weather was schizophrenic. Its warm days almost made a person forget it was early December.

Very much in the same way that Carlos Montigo made her forget herself last night.

She blinked away the thought as she neared the festival entrance. Despite yesterday's disarray, the workers had miraculously managed to pull everything together in time for the show. Too bad she hadn't been able to pull herself together rather than necking with Carlos Montigo like a hormone-ridden teenager.

"Bon jour," she said as she flashed her press credentials at the security guard posted at the entrance. He smiled appreciatively, muttered something in French, and motioned her through the gate.

"Merci. Au revoir," she said.

Even though hours had passed, she could still feel Carlos's kiss on her lips. She touched her mouth, but the sensation didn't go away.

In the bright light of day, she didn't know which hurt more—the wine-induced headache or her pride for his having kissed her and run.

Actually, it was her conscience that was giving her the most trouble.

She was such an idiot.

What was she thinking, jeopardizing her job by kissing the subject of her first interview?

Self-destructive idiot—as evidenced by the way her body reacted as she remembered Carlos Montigo's kiss.

She pressed her fingers to her lips, leaving a smudge of red lipstick on the tips.

After more than seven years away from the camera, not only did she have the pressure of filming her first segment in front of the boss, but now she'd compounded the difficulty by adding a headache and a dash of sexual tension.

She'd never been much of a drinker and she should've known better than to indulge in more than one glass of wine with dinner. But she and Carlos had talked so easily. And he kept pouring. All too soon she'd lost track of where one serving started and the next began.

Honestly, it was hard to tell which had been more intoxicating, the wine or the man.

Ha. Both were the cause of a massive headache.

Last night, he'd been so interested in her. Asking her questions. Absorbed in her answers. Drawing common parallels before he led her to that secluded, moonlit spot where he'd kissed her senseless.

Even thinking about it made butterflies flutter in her stomach.

Thank goodness, after today she wouldn't have to worry about being sucked in by Carlos Montigo's tractor beam. After today, she'd never have to see him again. It was a good thing, but for some ridiculous reason the thought left her feeling more empty than relieved.

Again, she held up her identification to security. This time she entered the press tent, happy to take shelter from the bright morning.

Since Sam had some preliminary camera work to take care of early this morning, Paula, Chandler and Lindsay had agreed to meet at the tent an hour before taping the show. Leaving her sunglasses on, she set her purse on a table and fished for more lipstick, some antacid and aspirin, swallowing the latter down with bottled water.

She was starting to feel better. Thank goodness the dry toast and weak tea, which she'd gotten from hotel room service, combined with fresh air and pharmaceuticals were already starting to make her feel human again—except for the uncomfortable memory of last night and the awkward mix of dread and anticipation of seeing Carlos again.

A mélange of food aromas filling the air didn't exactly help things. Ordinarily, Lindsay would've found the smells irresistible, but her stomach had churned itself into a nervous knot as she watched Chandler and Paula walk toward her.

"Lindsay, my love," Chandler greeted her with a kiss on each cheek. "You look beautiful this morning, darling. Are you excited?"

Okay. Well, so far so good. At least she didn't look like death warmed over.

"Paula wrote a wonderful script for you." He nudged her. "Give Lindsay a copy so she can study her lines."

Script? What script?

Paula set a pile of white poster boards on the table behind her and offered Lindsay a stack of smaller stapled white pages, but she didn't make eye contact as the paper changed hands.

"Since when do we use a script? Yesterday, you pointedly told Montigo we didn't work that way, that we wing it."

Paula acted like she didn't hear her.

"Well, today we do," Chandler said. "Things change all the time. While you were out wining and dining, Paula stayed up all night putting this together, and I must admit, I'm over the moon for it. It's brilliant. Exactly what I want. Smart. Edgy. Provocative. Just the direction I want to take the show."

Provocative? Edgy? Oh, God.

Lindsay flipped past a cover sheet to the first page and what she saw nearly made her choke: a total rehashing of the scandal.

It was a complete bait and switch from what they'd discussed with Carlos yesterday in his suite.

"I can't say this." She glanced up at Chandler, horrified. "I promised him we'd look forward, not back."

Paula, who was uncharacteristically quiet, looked impassive as she gazed at a spot somewhere over Lindsay's shoulder, still refusing to meet Lindsay's gaze.

Chandler frowned.

"You can't promise things like that, Lindsay. Especially when the mission of our show is to dig into *uncomfortable* territory."

He paused and the silence was deafening.

Oh, God. He was right.

She just hadn't expected her first assignment to be *this* uncomfortable. Under other circumstances, it wouldn't have been. Stupid mistake to let fleeting attraction cloud business.

"Why don't you give it a read through?" Chandler suggested. "Take it from the top."

Lindsay hesitated, and he rotated his hand in an impatient gesture that suggested she should get on with it because he was losing his patience.

Lindsay swallowed against the lump in her throat.

"*Er*...okay...*um*...I'm here with celebrity chef, Carlos Montigo." Lindsay knew her delivery was flat, but what did they expect on a cold read? She cleared her throat.

"He's staging a comeback with a new cookbook. But I'm getting ahead of myself. You remember the big debacle a couple of years ago, don't you? The refusal of the much-coveted Michelin star, which prompted the *Miami Herald* to dig into his background? The falsified résumé eventually cost him his job. Carlos, give us a little background. What possessed you to lie? How did you think you could get away with it? And most burning, who are you to turn up your nose at such an honor?"

There was a note written in the script, which Lindsay read aloud:

"At the end she should make a crack about it taking

a person with a huge ego to refuse a Michelin star…? Possibly tease that he should change his name to Carlos Mondo Ego."

What the—?

Now it was *her* turn to frown at Chandler and Paula.

Paula spoke for the first time. "I figured the crack would come more naturally if you worked it out on your own. But consider the Mondo Ego bit. It's funny."

"No, it's not."

Oh. My God. There was no way.… It was one thing to craft a report herself—in her own words—but it would be too difficult to regurgitate someone else's barbs.

Especially when she'd given her word to Carlos that she wouldn't delve into that territory.

And *Mondo Ego?*

All Lindsay could do was shake her head.

Chandler frowned so hard his brows nearly formed a single line across his forehead.

"Why are you shaking your head?" he asked.

"Seriously," Paula muttered. She rolled her eyes. Then, for the first time, her gaze locked with Lindsay's and the tiniest gleam of passive-aggressive self-satisfaction betrayed her motives.

She knew exactly what she was doing. She'd embarrassed herself by offering up the idea of the wine and goat man. When Chandler had reinforced how off the new track her segment idea was, Paula knew she had to redeem herself—and all the better to take a stab at Lindsay in the process.

Two birds. One stone.

Lindsay glanced at her watch. "We tape in less than an hour. I don't see how you can change plans the morning of the show and expect me to—" Lindsay fanned through the pages and shrugged. "I won't have this memorized before we tape."

Paula smirked. "I figured as much. That's why I made cue cards."

She turned and lifted the stack of poster board off the table. Sure enough, written in bold, black letters, each piece of poster board contained part of the script—verbatim.

"We need to practice before we start taping," Paula said. "Why don't we take it from the top again, and this time do a complete run-through."

We?

There was no "we" in this whatsoever.

"No," Lindsay said. "I need to work on this alone."

Paula sighed. It was the sound of someone at her wit's end.

"There's no time." Paula snapped her fingers. "Come on. Start at the beginning. Let's go."

Lindsay fought the anger spinning inside her.

She had to hold her breath for a moment until an eerie calm settled around her. But in the span of a few seconds her head cleared and she felt more in control.

"I am going to go over there." She pointed at an empty table on the other side of the tent. "I'm going to sit there *alone* and go over my lines. I don't need a coach. I don't want any feedback. I need to do this by myself."

Her voice was so low and steady that she almost didn't recognize it.

Paula opened her mouth to say something, but Chandler cut her off with a wave of his hand. "Leave her alone, Paula. She knows what she needs to do to prepare. Let her do it."

Lindsay mustered her best professional smile for

Chandler, nodded and walked away, knowing exactly what she had to do.

The only problem was, she had no idea how the heck she was going to do it.

The outdoor kitchen stage where Carlos would do the cooking demonstration was abuzz with last-minute preparation—food handlers were chopping and dicing; prop masters were moving and arranging; light and sound techs were testing and adjusting. People were rushing around, as busy as ants in a colony.

As the audience began to fill with early arrivals, Carlos waited backstage, out of the fray, sipping a triple espresso, trying to read the *New York Times*, trying not only to wake up, but to shore up his concentration. It was difficult with all the commotion—and everything that had transpired over the past twelve hours.

Maybe he should've stayed at the hotel until just before showtime. But he'd been antsy and needed to get out and clear his head so he could think. A lot of good it was doing him since all he could think about was seeing Lindsay before they came face-to-face with a television camera pointed at them.

Even the thought of the cameras made him a little anxious. *Maybe this wasn't such a good idea after all.* But just about the time he'd reached the edge of his mental ledge, he'd think of Lindsay and he'd back away from the edge.

If he'd known how he'd lose himself in the taste of her gorgeous mouth, would he have gone to dinner with her? *Probably.*

He gazed up at the cloudless sky. It was so clear this

morning, that perfect robin's egg–blue that Mother Nature reserved solely for December. He wished he could borrow a bit of that clarity and put everything into perspective.

He'd awakened with the taste of Lindsay on his lips. Wrapped in a gauzy fog of half sleep, he'd craved more. He'd even reached for her, but all he'd found was the cool, unused pillow on the empty side of the king-size bed.

The bite of disappointment had jolted him fully awake, and he knew it was a good thing he hadn't found her in his bed. Not with the day they had ahead of them. Not only were they taping the segment, they'd be doing so in front of a live audience coming to see a cooking demonstration—the first live show he'd done since his life was turned upside down.

Even that didn't stop his body from responding to the thought of waking up with her naked and in his bed.

As he'd showered, shaved and prepared for the day, his mind kept drifting to the way she'd looked in the moonlight, to the moment his lips met hers. He couldn't stop thinking about the way she tasted, the way she felt in his arms.

Now here he was on the set, pondering at least one hundred reasons why kissing Lindsay Bingham had been a bad move. Reasons such as how he needed to focus; how he needed to reclaim some of the career ground he'd lost over the past two years; how getting involved with a woman right now was absolutely impossible—especially one like Lindsay Bingham who'd hit him like a drug.

He stretched his legs out in front of him and tilted his face into the sun, soaking in the warmth. His mind drifted to the way she'd looked last night with the moon shining on her blond hair; her eyes looked as dark as the sky.

A man carrying a table of props stumbled over Carlos's legs, nearly falling. But he caught himself in time.

"Sorry, man." The guy was American. "Didn't see you there."

"No problem. Are you okay?"

"Yeah, no harm done," the guy said.

Carlos scooted his chair back farther into the corner, between the backside of the stage and a stack of crates that jutted out, forming a half wall. Out of the line of traffic, he refolded his paper and tried to concentrate on the latest news in the United States.

Until he saw her.

Maybe he'd glimpsed her out of the corner of his eye. Maybe it was a sixth sense that alerted him to her presence. But there she was, with Chandler, Paula and Sam huddled around her.

Sam looked casual and Paula looking uptight and awkward as she shifted a bulky pile of what looked like white poster boards in her arms.

When she unloaded the stack on the table, Carlos saw that there was writing—bold, black letters that he couldn't quite make out.

Cue cards? Maybe if he could have a look at them he could get an idea of the questions Lindsay was going to ask him. Normally, he would've just been straight-forward and asked. What was the harm?

But they were so adamant yesterday about not script-ing the show. Well, it didn't take a rocket scientist to know that you had to have a script to have cue cards.

There must be a reason for the secrecy, and he

would've bet money that the crew would refuse to enlighten him before they started taping.

Well, even if he got a look at only the first couple of questions he'd have an idea of the tone of the interview.

He'd just have to wait until the right moment.

Just then, right on cue, Max rounded the corner and slapped Chandler on the back. Working it, just like a good PR flack should.

He laughed and talked with the *Diva* crew for a moment. Then he gestured toward the steps that led to the stage. They all followed him and disappeared through the curtain at the top, leaving the cue cards on the chair where Paula had deposited them.

He made his move quickly, picking up the cards and reading through each one.

"What the hell?"

It was an entire rehashing of the scandal. Exactly what Lindsay had promised him they wouldn't do.

His blood boiled.

The only mention of the new cookbook was a passing reference at the very end. But there'd be no time to talk about it. Not when her three-minute spot was spent raking the muck.

He was stupid for trusting her. Because all reporters were obviously cut from the same mold.

For a split second he considered simply refusing to do the interview. He didn't have to do it. He could do his cooking demonstration without *The Diva Dishes*. It was no skin off his nose.

But even though it would put Lindsay behind schedule taping her show, his refusal didn't seem like it would set her back much. After all, she had the entire Food and Wine Festival to draw from.

Well, as far as he was concerned, they'd sealed their deal with a kiss last night. While he was never one to kiss and tell, he intended to collect the endorsement he was due.

Chapter Six

"Cut!" Paula yelled, tapping the cue cards. "Why aren't you following the script?"

"Script?" Carlos frowned. "What script?"

"While we were out last night, Paula wrote a script," Lindsay whispered.

Carlos looked warily back and forth between Paula and Lindsay. "May I see it?"

"No!" Lindsay and Paula yelled at the same time.

At least they agreed on something.

Carlos shot her a knowing look, as if he sensed a conspiracy and wasn't a bit happy about it.

"What's going on here?" he whispered, exasperation weighing down his words.

"Nothing, just follow my lead," she whispered back.

Suspicion darkened his eyes. He even looked a little

disgusted, like he didn't trust her. With how this must look, she didn't blame him.

"Lindsay, would you please join us over here?" Chandler waved her over. Paula and Sam were already huddled around him.

"We're looking unprofessional," Chandler said as he frowned. "We need to get our act together. Pronto."

"If *she'd* just follow the script," Paula demanded, "we wouldn't have a problem."

Okay, this was war. Enough was enough. Lindsay had had her fill of Paula's attitude and she was tired of making excuses for the woman. Especially since Paula was making her look bad in front of Chandler on the day when she most needed to prove that he hadn't made a mistake by hiring her.

"You see, the thing is, the script stinks." Lindsay looked Paula square in the eyes and held her gaze for a beat before she turned to Chandler. "I won't do it. It's not…"

As she searched for the words she needed, she glanced at Carlos, who was staring a hole through them. It was obvious he could hear what they were saying. Why had they even bothered stepping away from him?

"It's not natural," Lindsay finally said. "I would never say the things Paula's written, and I don't see how you can justify springing a script on me one hour before we tape—even if you do have cue cards. You can't expect me to change course when I already had something in mind. You know, after last night—" She glanced at Carlos who smiled at her—kind of sarcastically. She looked away and lowered her voice. "After having dinner with Carlos. Talking to him. Interviewing him."

Kissing him.

Her cheeks flamed. Resisting the urge to press her

hands to her face, she hoped to God the blush wasn't obvious to the others.

Chandler scowled. Arms crossed over his chest, one hand stroked his chin in a contemplative manner. Lindsay couldn't tell if the gesture was positive or negative.

"Come on," Paula prodded. "The audience is getting restless out there."

"Yeah," the stage manager chimed in. "He needs to be on stage. Now."

"All right," said Chandler. "We can't hold them up. We need to get with the program or we'll miss our shot. At this stage in the game, Lindsay needs to do the interview the way that's most comfortable for her. You two need to get on the same page."

The look that flashed in Paula's eyes could've sparked a fire of global proportions, even though the evil eye was only directed at Lindsay. Not the boss, of course. Even though she was cloaked safely for now in Chandler's special dispensation—Lindsay knew there'd be hell to pay after this segment was complete.

Carlos watched as Chandler's huddle broke. Something didn't smell right.

"Sorry about that," Lindsay said. "Why don't we take it from the top?"

"Would you care to let me in on the secret?"

"Secret? There's no secret," she said. "Just a little confusion, but we're good now."

"Are we?"

She nodded, all business. There was no trace of the soft, vulnerable woman he'd held last night.

"I guess I'm a little confused over this phantom script, since you told me you didn't work with one."

"There is no script."

He quirked a brow. There was no way he'd let it go that easily.

"You told me Paula wrote a script."

"She did, but we're not following it."

"Why not?"

"It wasn't the direction I told you we'd go with this interview. And, I…I keep my promises."

If she hadn't thrown him a curveball before, she had now. "So, you and your producer are at odds? That doesn't exactly instill a sense of comfort."

"I guess you just have to trust me."

Yeah, right. There it was. That word.

"Why should I trust you? First you say there's no script, then we get to the set and—"

"Because I'd say at this point you don't have much of a choice, do you?"

"I don't have to do this interview."

Of course, he didn't mean it. But he wanted her to sweat for a moment. He was well aware that Chandler and his crew were listening. Where was Max? He could use a little backup right about now.

"Look, that's your prerogative. But backing out right now won't do either of us any good."

The woman didn't give up easily, and he found that devastatingly appealing. Even so, this was no time to let down his guard any more than he already had. He simply needed to get through the next few hours, and then he never had to see Lindsay Bingham again.

He ignored the strange way his insides constricted at the thought. That was the only way to get through this. The way it had to be. But in the meantime, it didn't mean he couldn't have a little fun reminding her of the deal they'd sealed with that moonlit kiss.

"I'm backstage at the St. Michel Food and Wine Festival with Carlos Montigo," Lindsay said to the camera.

She knew she'd be nervous, but she had no idea just how rusty she'd be. She felt clunky, as if the muscles in her face weighed tons. The camera light was impossibly bright. It was all she could do to keep from drawing a complete and total blank as she spoke, making herself look like a deer caught in headlights.

Maybe in the future a script would be a good idea— as long as she wrote it and didn't leave Paula to her own devices.

So Sam could get the shot in the tight confines of the backstage area, she and Carlos had to stand so close their arms pressed against each other. Hers were slightly in front of his and she couldn't tell if the heat she felt was nervous energy or if it came from him.

In a very strange way, this heat was her touchstone, the thing that kept her going.

"So, Carlos, you've done it again, you've written another cookbook, which you're releasing here at the festival. Can you tell us a little bit about it before you go out and cook for your fans?"

There was a flash of something in his eyes—something that resembled surprise, but she couldn't quite define it. It was there one instant and gone in a flash.

"Sure Lindsay, thanks for hanging out with me today." He moved his arm ever so slightly, leaning into her as he talked. "This cookbook means a lot to me, because it lets me get back to my roots."

Something brushed her back. It was so whisper soft,

that at first, she wondered if she might simply be imagining it. But then the pressure was unmistakable—it was Carlos's fingers stroking her bare back beneath the hem of her blouse, dipping just slightly below the waistband of her skirt.

Lindsay flinched. "What are you doing?"

His hand fell and he flashed a killer smile that could've charmed a nun out of her habit.

"I'm glad you asked." His hand was on her arm now. Yes, it was definitely the heat of him she'd felt before. "I'm heading out on stage, because they're telling me it's time for the cooking demonstration I'm doing here at the festival."

His gaze snared and held hers for a couple of beats more than was strictly professional, then, for a split second his eyes dropped to her lips. "I do hope you'll join me because I have lots of things to show you, Lindsay."

Then he winked.

And that was all it took to render her speechless. What the—?

"Carlos, what are doing?" she whispered.

"Come with me and I'll show you."

With that, he mounted the short flight of wooden steps that led to the stage, pausing at the top to turn and crook his index finger, beckoning her to follow.

He was messing with her. That's what he was doing.

Had he lost his mind? Touching her like that on camera—even though no one could see? But they could certainly see him leering at her like he was ravenous and she was prime rib.

If this was about the script—she glanced at Paula, who was standing with her hands on her hips, sporting a bemused expression that said loud and clear she was fully enjoying watching Lindsay flounder.

Out of the corner of her eye, Lindsay saw Chandler making a hand motion, indicating he wanted her to follow Carlos onto the stage.

Ugh…

For lack of a better idea—or a plausible reason to avoid walking into Carlos's fire—she did just that. With Sam in front of her, she ascended the steps that led to the stage.

It was make it or break it time. This was becoming her mantra. Holding on to the rickety metal handrail, she shored up her courage and decided, if Chef Boy Mondo Ego could dish it out, he'd darn well better be able to take it.

As soon Carlos saw her peering through the curtain that cordoned off the backstage entrance, he said to the audience, "There she is, ladies and gentlemen, *The Diva Dishes'* Lindsay Bingham."

The crowd broke into spontaneous applause.

"Didn't I tell you she was beautiful? Come out here, darling."

Darling?

As the audience applauded, she cringed inwardly, but resisted the urge to fidget, determined not to act as awkward as she felt.

She met Carlos center stage at the kitchen island and resolved that it was time to take control of the situation.

Her mind raced, discarding options such as secretly goosing him in the manner that he'd surreptitiously slipped his hand beneath the back of her blouse and trailed his fingers along her bare skin, or reverting back to Paula's script, calling him Carlos Mondo Ego. But she knew better than straying from the high road.

One had to be quick on her feet to play dirty pool in front of a live audience and not come off looking like a jerk. Since Lindsay was more the type to think of the perfect comeback fifteen minutes after the fact, sparring and digs weren't a luxury she could indulge in with the camera in her face.

"Well, this is quite an audience, Carlos," she said, instead. "Thanks for letting *The Diva Dishes* join you today."

"My pleasure," he said. "I've cooked up all kinds of surprises for you."

Surprises? There was that word again. His grin was a side dish of pure mischief.

"I'll bet you have." She smiled as she held his gaze. "You seem like the kind of guy who'd just be full of *surprises*. I'm going to keep my eye on you."

The audience unleashed a collective *ooh* that only seemed to egg him on.

"That would probably be a good idea, love."

More *oohs*.

"Oh, come on now," she said. "Don't encourage him." They laughed.

Okay. That was good. A friendly crowd.

She felt her body loosen up.

"So, Carlos, your new cookbook, *Carlos in the Kitchen* is published by a house called Lone Wolf Press. *Hmm*, Lone Wolf? That's fitting, isn't it? Given your history as a guy who seems to enjoy being the only cook in the kitchen?"

"Lone Wolf is a small press, and I was honored to have them publish my book. Today, I'm preparing a recipe from *Carlos in the Kitchen*. Would you like to help me?"

"I'm not a chef, but I'd be happy to assist you."

"That's the point of this book," he said. "Actually, that's my philosophy as a chef. You don't have to be classically trained to prepare delicious meals."

"And you are self-taught, correct?"

He narrowed his eyes at her, as if he wasn't sure where she was going with this. He was probably bracing for her to dredge up the dirt that got him fired in the first place.

Good. It was nice to turn the tables on him—even if would only be for a moment.

He started it. What did he expect?

He picked up a knife and cut the end off an onion, then quirked a brow at her.

A challenge.

"We're roasting a chicken and vegetables today. A perfectly roasted chicken is easy and elegant, but at the same time, it's also the world's best comfort food. But before we begin, does everyone know how to chop an onion easily and safely?"

He was talking to the audience again, and they murmured their curiosity.

"Okay, let me show you," he said. "Lindsay, my love, would you please help me?"

He was baiting her, calling her *love* and *darling*. If she ignored it, maybe he'd stop.

"I don't know, Carlos. Onions have the same effect as tear gas on me. Will your method keep me from crying when I chop?"

"Only if you work fast, which this method will allow you to do. But until you master the technique, I suggest that you light a candle when you're chopping—the flame will burn away the sulfuric fumes, and that's what makes you cry."

"Really?"

"Well, that and cutting your fingers. So come over here and help me demonstrate the best way to hold my...*utensil*..."

Oh my God. He did not—

The audience *oohed* suggestively. Lindsay want to drop down and crawl into a cabinet. Instead, she kicked Carlos as hard as she could and still remain inconspicuous.

"People, people, people," Carlos tsked. "I don't know what your dirty minds are thinking, but Lindsay is a lady. Let's keep it clean. I want to show her how to hold a knife so that she keeps all her digits."

He took her hand and raised it to his lips the same way he had that night at the wedding. Only this time he nipped at her knuckle. She flinched. What the heck was he doing?

He handed her a large knife and moved a small cutting board with an onion on it in front of her.

"First, you need to hold the knife right." He slid her hand down and repositioned her grip so she held the handle where it met the blade. "This gives you more control."

Control was good. She'd certainly felt out of control since meeting Carlos Montigo.

"Curl the fingers of your left hand—the one holding the onion—under, and angle the top of the blade toward your left hand, so that the sharp edge goes away from your fingers that are holding the onion."

She squinted up at him, unsure of what he meant. That was the problem with letting her mind wander.

"Let me show you," he said.

He came up behind her and slid his arms around her, his right hand on her hand that was holding the knife, his left on top of her hand that was holding the onion.

As the audience whistled, egging him on, every nerve in Lindsay's body sang.

His arms around her made her feel strangely breathless, but if she stuck to her mental list of interview questions, she'd get through it.

Wouldn't she?

"Like this." He applied enough pressure to gently curl the fingers of her left hand back. He turned the knife in her right hand so that the blade angled away from the fingers holding the onion, so that the top of the blade grazed her fingers, but the sharp edge posed no danger.

"This technique has saved countless fingers." He said the words in her ear, even though he was talking to the audience. His breath whispered across her temple, sending shivers skittering up her arms.

"You see," he continued while holding her hand, guiding her as she chopped the onion. "With your fingers curled under and the blade angled away, you won't get yourself into trouble. Although, something tells me you like finding trouble."

More applause and whistles.

She found herself extremely conscious of him—his scent, clean, with a hint of spice; and his body, how it was pressed against hers, engulfing her as he invaded her space. She hated herself for it, but her body responded to the sheer virility of him.

Her head spun and she drew in a deep breath, inhaling a strong whiff of raw onion.

The ensuing burn was all it took to set the tears flowing.

Pulling out of his grasp, she swiped at her eyes. The onion-induced tears were starting to cloud her vision.

"See, I told you," she said.

He looked her over seductively and her heart turned over in response.

"Don't cry," he joked. "Here, let me help you with that. Was it something I said?"

He reached out and with the pad of his thumb, wiped a tear that had just spilled over her bottom lashes.

More *whoops* and cheers from the audience.

"It's just the onion." She swatted his hand away. "Umm…thanks, I've got this."

Carlos smiled, then picked up the cutting board with the remnants of the onion and set it on a counter behind them, out of camera range. In short order, a stagehand removed it.

He handed her a white dish towel.

"I'll bet you make all the girls cry," she said as she dabbed at the remaining tears.

"When I make a girl cry I always kiss the hurt and make it better," he said with a sly grin.

Again, the audience cheered. "Kiss her and make it better," someone called.

A rush of heat started at her neckline and spread upward. She racked her brain for a segue back to the cooking demonstration, but before she could open her mouth, Carlos had swept her into his arms as if she were weightless. She gasped as he dipped her back in a fashion that would've made a tango master proud.

She was putty in his arms. He bent over her, his lips a breath away from hers, and the audience went wild. She could feel his uneven breathing and her heart hammered foolishly.

The audience cheered and chanted, "Kiss her! Kiss her! Kiss her!"

But he didn't.

Thank God, because if he had, she probably would've melted into a puddle right there in the middle of the stage—she wasn't sure if it would've been from embarrassment or desire or because the world seemed to whirl around her in this upside-down predicament. She caught a glimpse of Chandler frowning from the side of the stage.

Oh, God. She'd blown it.

Utterly.

Completely.

Then, just as fast as Carlos had swept her into his arms, he righted her and started saying something about putting the onion in the chicken cavity after he slipped some herbed butter under the bird's skin.

Lindsay stood there blinking, wondering why the heck she hadn't stuck to the script.

Chapter Seven

"Why didn't you stick to the script?" Paula demanded once they were in the car headed back to the hotel. Lindsay had considered walking back alone rather than getting into a confined space with Paula and Sam, but somehow walking back to the hotel alone would've seemed like a walk of shame.

No, it was better to leave as a team and hold her head high.

"I thought the spot was *hot*," Sam said.

Both women looked at him—Paula glared, Lindsay tried to figure out whether he was being facetious.

The spot was a disaster. She was sure Paula was secretly celebrating, reveling in the chance to skewer Lindsay with a chorus of passive-aggressive I-told-you-so's.

"Well, it *was* hot," Sam persisted. "The audience thought so, too."

Good old Sam. After working with him for less than a week, Lindsay liked him. He was the team's optimist— at least they had one. Casual and laid-back, Sam seemed to find the good in everyone and go wherever the wind blew him—or wherever *Bossy* led him.

Paula might be able to get away with leading Sam around by the nose, but she had another think coming if she thought she could push Lindsay around. A heart-to-heart was long overdue, and Lindsay knew it needed to happen sooner rather than later. Maybe tonight after the production meeting Chandler had scheduled to discuss the future production schedule.

Lindsay stared out the window and watched picturesque St. Michel roll by. Of course, that was *if* there'd still be a meeting later—since Chandler had left before they'd finished taping.

Her insides constricted at the thought. But before she could fall down the slippery spiral of self-doubt, Lindsay steeled herself, determined not to read anything into his leaving—because it wouldn't do any good. It would only drive her crazy.

She needed to borrow some of Sam's optimism.

Even if Lindsay had felt awkward, the audience *had* responded well. And Chandler hadn't stopped the taping. He certainly would've been within his rights to do so, if he'd thought the content was totally unsalvageable.

Unless he was just being courteous to Carlos, not interrupting the flow of his live show.

Oh, God.

Her head spun and she wiped her clammy palms on her skirt.

Stop it!

She could go back and forth all day, but he'd certainly tell her his thoughts in no uncertain terms at the meeting. Right now, it would only drive her crazy to ponder the what-ifs.

She just wanted to get past this debacle and move on. That's why she'd bolted before Carlos had finished his show. They'd finished taping, but he still had an autograph session to attend. It was Lindsay's perfect escape. She took it.

She didn't have to face him after the way he'd made a fool out of her in front of all those people. What hurt the most was how he'd made a mockery—albeit a private joke—out of what had happened between them the night before.

The jerk. If he'd been upset by the script, couldn't he tell she wasn't following it? After all, he was the one leading the show.

Next time she'd be the one in control.

"A complete and utter disaster," Paula muttered, and it was all Lindsay could do to hold her temper.

"I'm sure there's at least three minutes of footage we can—*use* for the spot." She'd almost said *salvage* but she'd caught herself just in time. She wasn't going to give Paula the satisfaction of knowing she was sick about the segment. "And just so we're clear, Paula. In the future, I'll write my own scripts."

She'd intended to keep the issues between her and Paula. To hash it out in private, not in front of Sam—or the driver. But suddenly this seemed as good a time as any. Especially since Paula couldn't seem to leave it alone.

"If there is a next time." Paula smiled. She looked absolutely evil.

Lindsay whipped her head around to look the woman dead in the eyes. "Excuse me?"

Paula smirked. "You just don't get it, do you?"

The car pulled up in front of the hotel.

"I certainly don't understand *you*. You've had a problem with me since day one, and I think it's time you and I got to the bottom of it. Let's go somewhere and talk about this."

But before Paula could respond, Lindsay's cell rang. Chandler's name flashed on the LCD screen.

"Hello?" She hoped to God her voice didn't shake.

"Lindsay, it's Carson. Please come up to my suite. We need to talk."

Carlos walked into the living area of the suite he and Max shared. Max was sitting on the couch, leafing through some papers.

He looked up and saw Carlos. "How'd the signing go? Sorry I had to bolt, but I had some business to take care of."

Carlos shrugged. "I sold about fifty books. Which, on paper, sounds impressive, but since there were upwards of two hundred people in the audience, I don't know if it's anything to get excited about."

"That means a quarter of the audience went home with a book. I have a feeling the other hundred and fifty will soon be clamoring for a signed copy."

Carlos shot him a questioning look.

"I just made some coffee," Max said. "You might want to pour yourself a good strong cup and sit down. We have something important to talk about."

At first, Carlos thought Max might give him hell about crossing the line with Lindsay, a don't-mess-with-the-one-who-gives-you-free-publicity speech.

He served himself a cup of Italian roast, and he began

formulating his defense. The show was over and done with. He'd just have to take his hand-slapping like a big boy and move on.

"Look, after today I'll never see her again," he said, taking a seat across from Max. "We left things on good terms and I think the segment was terrific."

Liar.

Lindsay left without as much as a farewell. He had come on a little strong today, but he'd trusted her. And she'd broken her promise.

She'd obviously done what she needed to do to get the story she wanted. In turn, he did what he needed to do.

All's fair...

"My philosophy is," Carlos said, "sweet talk them so they say sweet things about me."

Max looked confused. "What are you talking about?"

Carlos shrugged and sipped his coffee. He didn't have to explain himself. Besides, it was a moot point. It was over. He'd never look back except to ride the momentum the *Diva* spot would give him.

Max shook his head. He seemed to do that a lot these days, but that was part of the reason they got along so well. Max knew when to shut up and give Carlos room. Knew when not to push. Knew when to change the subject.

"So, I was talking to Carson Chandler. He, uh, has a business proposition for us. *Er*—for *you.*"

Carlos wrapped both hands around the coffee cup, enjoying the soothing warmth.

"What kind of business proposition?"

The guy was into all kinds of industry. Maybe he published cookbooks? If he wanted to pick up *Carlos in the Kitchen,* they could talk. Hell, if the offer was good enough just about anything was possible.

"He just bought the Epicurean Traveler Network and wants to expand this three-minute *Diva Dishes* infomercial for Chandler Guides into a full-fledged, hour-long show."

Max paused and fixed Carlos with a knowing look. Carlos wasn't quite sure what this had to do with him—except that maybe the spot would be an hour rather than three minutes. Did they have enough footage? Because if they needed more they'd have to follow him to Madrid for his next scheduled appearance.

In an instant, images of rediscovering his hometown with Lindsay on his arm and in his bed flashed through his mind. There would be no script. Just instinct and spontaneity.

Weren't they at their best together when things were spontaneous?

Nice daydream. But it would never happen.

"I'm sure you're aware Epicurean Traveler is a direct competitor of Food TV," Max said.

The mention of the Food TV bastards zapped the rush Carlos had been feeling and landed him in a bad mood.

"Right, and he needed your approval for this latest scheme? He's not trying to hire you away from me, is he?"

"Possibly, but it would be a package deal since he wants a male host to join Lindsay Bingham on the new show."

Another knowing look. This time with a broad smile.

"Montigo, he's considering *you* for the spot. He loved the chemistry between you and Lindsay. Said that was exactly the type of fire he wants for the show. This could be the answer to our prayers."

Carlos's mouth went dry as Max's words sank in. An unsettling bittersweet feeling loomed, setting off a war of conflicting emotions. On one hand this would be an opportunity to see Lindsay every day. On the other hand…he would see Lindsay every day.

Not to mention getting caught up in the grind of a network series again. He frowned at the thought of being owned by a television network—something he'd sworn he'd never endure again.

"I don't know, man," Carlos said. "It was such a mess last time."

"Chandler's astute. He's coming into this knowing damn well who you are, and more important, who you *aren't*. He doesn't care what happened before. If anything he'll parlay that into good PR for the show."

"No. No way." Carlos held up his hand as if he could repel the repugnant idea.

"But don't get ahead of yourself," Max soothed. "We have some negotiating to do."

Max held up the file. "This is the contract. We need to go over it. Chandler wants to meet face-to-face this afternoon."

For a long moment neither of them said a word. The silence was heavy. But finally, as if he couldn't contain himself any longer, a broad smile overtook Max's face.

"You're back, my man."

Max let out a whoop.

"Now look who's getting ahead of himself." Carlos took a long draw of his coffee, wishing the hot liquid could either infuse him with the same certainty and enthusiasm that had gripped Max—or at least wash away the longing to see Lindsay that was building inside him.

"It's my job to be optimistic about you. It's also my job to advise you. We're going to ask for better money— twice what he's offering."

"Twice? Wait a minute."

"If we ask for twice, we'll get a better deal."

Carlos set his mug on the glass-topped coffee table and then rested his elbows on his knees, pressing his hands to his eyes.

"I don't know, Max."

"What do you mean, you don't know? Most people would kill for a second chance like this."

Carlos was all about second chances. That was exactly the principle behind the restaurant he wanted to open. Giving kids who'd screwed up a second chance at life—a chance to learn a trade so that they could do an honest day's work and sleep at night with pride that they were making it on their own.

"I know that, but you know television isn't exactly the direction I wanted to go. I don't know if I have it in me to run that rat race again."

Max sobered. "It's either the rat race for the short run or you'll be on the road for God knows how long hawking your self-published cookbook out of the trunk of your car."

Though Max hadn't come right out and said it, there was an undertone that suggested if Carlos refused this offer, he'd be working out of the trunk by himself. Who could blame Max? He'd stuck with Carlos through the worst and here was their opportunity to dig themselves out.

The reality hit him like a strong punch to the gut.

Carlos leaned his head back on the sofa cushion and closed his eyes, trying to erase the image of Lindsay that kept running through his mind.

If this was going to work—if they were going to work together—they had to come at this platonically. The last time he'd let business become personal it nearly destroyed him and his career. But now he was stronger than that.

"Let's roll up our sleeves and hammer this out," Carlos said.

Chapter Eight

Lindsay stopped by her room to touch up her face before going up to Chandler's suite. On the phone, his voice had held his own particular brand of Carson Chandler urgency that suggested she get there sooner rather than later, but if he was going to chew her out—or worse—she wanted to go in with the confidence of knowing she wasn't a shiny mess.

Now, standing outside his door, she knocked straight-away rather than pausing to collect herself, because if she had, she might not have knocked at all.

"Come in," he called. "It's open."

When she reached for the door, she realized her hand was shaking. She took a deep breath, checked her posture and mustered her most confident smile before walking in.

"Hello." At least her voice sounded steady.

Chandler held up a hand, and she saw that he was sitting in a chair by the window, talking on the phone.

Oh. Oops.

"Can you be here by two-thirty?" he said.

She glanced at the grandfather clock. It was just after two o'clock now. Who was he talking to, she wondered idly as she looked around the suite, taking it all in—the antique furniture, the realistic Impressionist replicas, the marble-topped bar with its fine crystal stemware and Cognac decanter, the fresh flowers in the porcelain vase on the mirrored buffet.

In all her years she'd never been around such finery. Her father had always provided for her and done the best he could, but luxuries like this weren't part of their world. If he could see her now, he'd be happy that she was finally "doing something" with her life.

How many times had they fought about that?

A stinging lump formed in her throat.

If she thought about her father too hard, she'd get emotional. Right now she needed to stay positive and strong.

If Chandler was unhappy with her performance, she'd convince him she'd do better next time.

She *couldn't* lose this job.

"I know it's earlier than what we'd discussed." There was an edge to Chandler's voice. "I would really appreciate it if you could move it up in your schedule."

Suddenly, for the first time in a long time, a sense of purpose rooted inside her. She knew this job was something to fight for. She couldn't just stand by and let it slip through her fingers.

She'd approached this job tentatively, almost expecting it to end. Because didn't everything good eventually play out? Like Cinderella finally making it to the ball only to have everything she'd worked so hard for evaporate at midnight?

Maybe it was time she wrote Cinderella a new happy ending. For a nanosecond her thoughts skittered to Carlos and his kiss, his arms around her today.

This chapter of her Cinderella story wouldn't necessarily include a prince—at least not Carlos. Because right now, the story was about her.

If this job turned into a pumpkin, she'd have nothing. Not even her old Social Services job.

"Sorry about that, Lindsay." Chandler's voice startled her. She hadn't heard him hang up. "I had to take that call. Come over here and sit down. Tell me, how do you think today went?"

She studied his expression as she made her way toward him, but it was unreadable, which rattled her nerves again.

"Today was...interesting. It was a little...*unpredictable,* but I suppose that stands to reason since it was my first shoot in seven years. The important question is what *you* thought."

Her stomach churned.

Chandler frowned.

When he didn't say anything, fear knotted inside her. *Ooh. Oh, no.*

She braced herself, waiting for the fallout.

Then a wide smile overtook Chandler's face. "I thought today was remarkable. *Perfect.*"

She had to purse her lips to keep the elation from escaping.

Then, slowly, she relaxed. For the first time since she'd awakened this morning, she was able to draw in a full breath.

"Thank you," she uttered.

"I must admit," he said. "After getting off to such a rough start, I was a bit skeptical at first. But as soon as the two of you got going, the chemistry between you and Carlos Montigo was mind-blowing. I came back and looked at the raw footage and I loved it."

Chemistry?

Mind-blowing?

Was it that obvious?

She bit her bottom lip at the memory of Carlos's kiss. She willed herself not to blush. Miraculously, somehow she was able to maintain her composure.

Everything was going to be okay. No, it would be more than okay. She still had a job, and from that moment she vowed to do everything in her power to make sure each show going forward was the best she could deliver. She would write her own scripts. She'd remain perfectly professional and not cross the line with the subjects of her interviews. She'd—

"Which brings me to something else I wanted to discuss with you." Elbows on the arms of the chair, Chandler steepled his fingers. "Do you remember me expressing my wish to expand *The Diva Dishes* into a full-length show?"

The bottom of Lindsay's stomach fell, causing her to inhale sharply.

"Yes."

Was this going where she thought it was? Ooh. She shouldn't get her hopes up. She nodded, trying to act casual. Not like she was about to jump out of her skin.

"Since purchasing the Epicurean Traveler Network, I've been in a position to expand the show. The only thing holding me back was finding the right hosts."

Hosts? As in plural?

"Today, that search came to an end."

The pause was almost as tantalizing as the prelude to a first kiss. The silence lingered, hovered, like lips destined to meet. Almost…but not quite…yet. The vision of Carlos with his fingers laced in her hair, his mouth a whisper's distance from hers…the chemistry…the—

"I believe I have found that dynamic duo in you and Carlos Montigo."

She bit her bottom lip. Those were the words she'd anticipated. The offer she'd hoped for finally presented itself.

And with *Carlos?*

A warm glow flowed through her.

"Of course, the potential change was written into your contract," he said, "but there is an escape clause if need be. So tell me, is this something you'd be interested in?"

Her heart sang with delight.

"Absolutely."

Chandler nodded his approval. "Very good."

"Is Carlos already on board?" If it was the pair of them he wanted—a package deal—it certainly sounded like it.

"I made the offer to his agent earlier today. In fact, that was him on the phone when you arrived. We have some minor details to iron out, but I can safely say, yes. He is on board."

Her stomach performed an odd little somersault.

"When I first saw you," he said, "I had a hunch you'd be perfect. I simply wasn't one hundred percent sure if you were the woman for the full-length episode, because much of that hinged on finding the right cohost. You and Montigo absolutely cemented that today. Of course there will be a pay increase commensurate to the expanded camera time. My dear, I'll say this as a friend—you really should have an agent. So…?"

Her head spun. Chandler must have sensed as much because he spread the new contract out on the coffee table and pointed out the pay increase and the terms: four episodes to be filmed over the span of a month, one episode per week. Contract terms would either be renewed or terminated upon completion of the fourth episode.

Her body vibrated with new life.

She really did need an agent—or a lawyer. Someone to guide her through this. But reality was overshadowed by another feeling that kept bubbling up—the impossible joy of getting to see Carlos.

Every day.

She hadn't realized what an effect he'd had on her until now.

Of course, they'd have to set some things straight. Keep things platonic. There was no other way this would work. She'd nearly lost her head today. She hated being out of control like that.

There was a lot at stake, but she could handle it. The secret was to start thinking of Carlos Montigo strictly as a business associate.

From this moment on, that would be the extent of their relationship.

As the old grandfather clock struck two-thirty, there was a knock on the door.

"Ah, right on time. Come in," Chandler called.

Carlos and Max walked in, followed by a room service attendant pushing a cart heaped with a bottle of champagne in a sterling wine bucket, four crystal flutes and a mountain of strawberries surrounding a bowl of luscious-looking chocolate sauce.

* * *

She looked like a ray of sunshine, Carlos thought, as he gazed at her from across the room.

Their eyes locked and he sensed her stiffening. Her brown eyes grew a shade darker even though she smiled. For all outward appearances, she appeared happy to see him. He was probably the only one who sensed the whisper of a strain in her expression as she looked away, turning her attention to Chandler, who had leaned in to say something in her ear.

It wasn't exactly jealously, but there was definitely a proprietary tug as he spied Chandler's arm around her waist. It was a ridiculous reaction. He had no claim on her, especially if they were to work together for the next month.

Then in a flash, Chandler was walking toward them, welcoming Max and him, with handshakes and jovial slaps on the back.

"How wonderful to have my new cast together for the first time," Chandler said. "This calls for a toast."

The room service attendant popped the cork and poured the Dom Perignon into the glasses, handing each one to Chandler, who, in turn, passed them out.

"To the newest show on the Epicurean Traveler Network, *The Diva Drives.*"

They raised their glasses. As they sipped the bubbly, he snared Lindsay's gaze again, causing a tingling in the pit of his stomach. This time she looked away, with an odd twinge of disappointment.

"Diva Drives," Chandler repeated. "That will be the name of the show. Please have a seat and I'll tell you about the premise."

"Well, here we are," Carlos said as he settled next to her on the sofa.

"How about that," she answered, sounding almost glib.

The way the morning had turned out, he couldn't blame her. He supposed he'd have to explain his actions at some point. To clear the air so that they could work together.

Platonically.

But how ironic that if he hadn't set out to push her buttons, if she'd just come in and done the traditional interview about a new cookbook, perhaps they wouldn't be here now.

Not that it was all his doing. It was their—how did Chandler put it?—*chemistry* that sealed the deal.

The question was how were they supposed to maintain that chemistry and keep things platonic?

It would be like holding a lit match to a gas tanker—explosive.

Chandler sniffed his champagne, held it up to the light and regarded it for a moment before he sipped it.

"I had this vision of the two of you in a car driving through Europe," he said. "Hence the name, *The Diva Drives.*

"Of course, you'll get out and visit notable locals, interview interesting people, dine at fabulous restaurants. But the premise revolves around the chemistry of the two of you in the car. It will be as much about the journey as the destination."

Wasn't that the truth.

Chandler leveled Lindsay and Carlos with a knowing look. "Judging from the chemistry, if I didn't know better, I'd swear that the two of you were involved. But we all know how mixing business and pleasure can get tricky."

"No!" Lindsay said. "We're not."

Chandler flashed a patronizing smile. "I see the way

he looks at you." He turned to Carlos. "And I see you looking back."

"It was part of the show," Lindsay said.

"No, I'm talking about when the camera's not even on you."

So it began. You signed a contract and they took it for granted that they own you. Carlos waited for Chandler to throw down the gauntlet and prohibit personal involvement. There'd been nothing in the contract, so there was no way he could control their personal lives.

He slanted a glance at Lindsay, who stared straight ahead, her body language betraying nothing, despite the defiant set of her jaw and the slight upward tilt of her chin.

He couldn't blame her. It was insulting.

Then again, it was only for a month. For the money Max had managed to negotiate for him—enough to give his Cedar Inlet restaurant a healthy start—he could play by Chandler's rules in the short-term. Then he could take the money and run—whether they offered a new contract or not. And if this was anything like his experience on *Piece of Me,* he wouldn't want to sign on for an endless tenure of being owned.

He tried to ignore the voice inside that asked *what about Lindsay?*

"I'd like to take the footage we shot today, add to it and expand it into our first hour-long show. This works so well. We hadn't yet invested anything in a new intro for the new *Diva Dishes*—that was on the schedule for tomorrow. So we can fold in today's footage and we haven't lost anything."

"When did you want to start?" Carlos asked.

"Tonight," Chandler said as if it were a given.

Tonight. The guy didn't waste time.

Thinking of the appearances he had lined up for the next month, Carlos looked at Max, who seemed to read his mind.

"We have a slight problem," Max said. "Carlos is booked at various festivals around Europe. It could get costly if we back out at the last minute."

Chandler waved away the concern as if it were merely a pesky gnat. "E-mail my assistant a list and she'll take care of it. We'll pay any cancellation penalties incurred. I want to get this show on the road right away. Literally."

Chandler chuckled at his own joke and chased the humor with another sip of champagne.

So this was really going to happen, Carlos thought, as he glanced at Lindsay, who'd been unusually quiet. Probably for the best that they jump right in, because if he had a chance to think about it too hard, he might remember exactly what he was getting himself into—again—and run in the other direction.

"What about the production?" Max asked. "This is a much larger scale than *The Diva Dishes*."

Chandler nodded. "Very good question. We will increase the crew, of course. Something of this scale requires at least four cameras and upwards of a ten-person production team. The good folks at Epicurean Traveler are gathering the crew, probably as we speak. The larger scale of this show is one aspect that makes it so exciting."

"Will you keep Paula and Sam?" Lindsay asked.

Chandler tilted his head to the side and considered her question. "I hadn't really given it much thought. But now that you mention it…hmm. One thing will be paramount is that we all work well together as a team. We will be pulling exceptionally long days. There won't be time for artistic clashes if we're going to shoot an episode a week. Lindsay, I realize there's been a personality clash between you and Paula. If you'd rather not work with her, I have no problem letting her go."

Chapter Nine

Lindsay wasn't avoiding talking to Carlos about what had happened between them earlier that day. Really, she wasn't.

The only reason she left the meeting so fast was because she had to talk to Paula.

She and Carlos would talk. Eventually. There was no avoiding it.

First, she had to talk to Paula.

It felt weird holding the fate of someone's livelihood in the palm of her hand.

That was essentially the way Chandler had left it. He'd gotten a call and had ended the meeting as quickly as he'd called it. He'd asked Lindsay to decide within the hour whether Paula and Sam stayed or went.

They had no idea how tenuous their jobs were. Chandler hadn't yet broken the news about the new show to them because he wanted to wait until Lindsay and Carlos were locked into place to avoid potential media leaks.

Apparently, Sam and Paula had been afterthoughts. It bothered her that Chandler could consider them so expendable. Maybe it was because she was in a there-but-for-the-grace-of-God-go-I state of mind, because hadn't she been fearing for her job when she walked into Chandler's suite?

As fate would have it, she happened to be on Chandler's sunny side at the moment. But she'd been in the fragile position of being superfluous before and the memory still haunted her. She wouldn't wish it on anyone.

Sam was a given. Of course he'd stay. He was talented and easy to work with. Plus, he'd been her ally from day one. Loyalty was important, especially in this business.

Still, despite all the friction with Paula, Lindsay couldn't in good conscious save Sam's job and kick Paula to the curb.

Maybe she was an idiot for giving Paula the benefit of the doubt. But since the woman had been with *The Diva Dishes* from day one, Lindsay wanted to give Paula a chance to save herself. She wasn't going to make the woman grovel, just simply explain why she had such a problem with Lindsay.

Maybe she was naive, but Lindsay clung to the belief that people were inherently good. If someone acted like a jackass, there was usually a reason. Not that it excused bad behavior, but in a gesture of goodwill Lindsay wanted to give Paula the chance to explain herself and to clear the air.

What Paula chose to do with that opportunity was up to her. It was a good sign that the woman had agreed to meet Lindsay for a cup of coffee. She hadn't pulled a sorry-I'm-busy, we'll-schedule-it-when-it's-convenient-for-me excuse. She'd agreed straight off, which made Lindsay believe that Paula really did want to work things out. To be fair, Lindsay had decided to be up-front with her right out of the starting gate.

The mood was tense as they placed their orders, but as soon as the server stepped away from their table, Lindsay said, "Thank you for agreeing to talk to me. I really want to get to the bottom of the friction between us."

Paula crossed her arms. A defensive gesture.

"I have to admit, part of me was curious to see if you still had a job," Paula said.

Okay. That wasn't exactly the tone she was hoping for.

The woman definitely knew how to push Lindsay's buttons.

"Look, I'm going to be frank with you. I still have a job. It's yours that's in question."

The look of utter astonishment on Paula's face was equal parts heartbreaking and vindicating.

"Mr. Chandler called the earlier meeting to tell me about some changes to the show. Some very exciting changes, I might add. My place is secure, but since the new format will require a solid team, he left it up to me as to whether you'd stay on with us. He told me to consider whether I could work with you, Paula. I have to be honest, at this point it's looking doubtful."

Paula opened her mouth to say something, but all that came out was a tiny sound, something like a cough.

"I'm not trying to be mean or rub your nose in it. I just want to know why you have such a problem with me."

Paula grunted and screwed up her face.

Strike two. *Come on, Paula. You're about to strike out.*

"Why? So you can torture me? Why don't you just make this quick and painless—"

Lindsay slapped her hand down on the table.

"Can't you see I'm trying my hardest to find a reason to keep you on? Just be straight with me. If it's one of those cases where you just don't like my face, then fine. Tell me it'll never work and we can make it as painless as that."

Her incredulity morphed into astonishment. "Why? Why would you do this for me?"

Then she did the last thing Lindsay expected. The woman buried her face in her hands and cried.

She sobbed for a full five minutes, during which the server brought their order. He shot Lindsay a questioning look, and she shook her head and mouthed, *it's okay.*

Finally, Paula composed herself and with mascara-streaked cheeks, at which she dabbed with a napkin, she explained that somehow Chandler never seemed to notice her. That she'd wanted the job as host, and after training three failures for the position, she'd misjudged Lindsay as another in a long line of self-absorbed divas. None of them had ever treated her with respect, certainly never given a second thought as to whether she should keep her job.

"I'm sorry," Paula said. "And I'm not just saying that so you'll put in a good word for me with the boss. I misjudged you. I was rude and nasty. And I truly am sorry for that. You'd have every right to send me packing and if that's what you choose, I'll live with it."

Lindsay regarded her for a long moment. "Did you ever tell Chandler that you wanted a shot at hosting the show?"

Paula had pulled a compact out of her purse and was

working with a tissue and the water from her glass to clean up her face.

She shook her head. "I...no. I didn't."

Lindsay smiled. "Well, rule number one in this business is that you have to make sure that the powers that be know what you want. And then when you want something that bad, you have to go for it."

Lindsay's mind skittered back to Carlos and the thought of him gave her a little jolt. She blinked away the longing that fought to be recognized. Because just as it was important to make what you want known, it was equally important to recognize the pitfalls that could block your path to getting there.

She knew instinctively she and Paula would be fine. Given Chandler's noninvolvement mandate, she wished she could be that confident about her relationship with Carlos Montigo.

Carlos had thought about calling Lindsay and asking her to have a drink with him, but wine—and this undeniable chemistry—was what had gotten them into trouble in the first place.

So he hadn't called. He'd simply thought about her and the noninvolvement mandate that Chandler had placed between them.

The following morning—the first day of taping—as they sat in the red Ferrari F430 that Chandler had procured for the show, Carlos took a deep breath and asked Lindsay, "Are we okay?"

"We?" she repeated. This was the most she'd said all morning. Just like yesterday, she'd been quiet this morning as they sat in the parking lot of the St. Michel royal palace, waiting for Paula to get the all-clear from palace officials so that they could film the two of them driving up to the gates.

"Are *you* okay?" he said.

Someone had to break the ice since they were going to be working in such close confines.

She nodded.

He ran his hand over the dashboard. It was a lean machine and when Carlos first got a look at it, he was nearly dizzy at the thought that he'd be driving it for the next month. Only now that he was actually sitting in the driver's seat with Lindsay beside him, he felt a little subdued.

Whatever had initially passed between them had vanished. This cool, remote woman beside him wasn't the woman who'd inspired him to lose control. Because that's what had happened yesterday during the cooking demonstration. Even if he'd started out with the intention of teaching her a lesson about baiting and switching, somewhere between the feel of his hands on the bare skin of her back and dipping her into the almost-kiss, he'd lost control. He'd wanted to kiss her. Now, he desperately wanted to tell her so.

But all he could do was ask whether she was okay.

That was such a farce.

He wasn't okay and obviously she wasn't, either. So he resorted to generalities.

"Look," she said in a small voice. "I guess at this point it's best to just be straightforward."

He looked at her, trying unsuccessfully to see her eyes through the dark lenses of her sunglasses.

"I don't want to play games," she continued. "I don't understand what you were trying to prove yesterday. Acting like that...on the set."

He started to explain, or at least offer a reason, but she held up her hand and stopped him.

"I don't need explanations. I want your word that it won't happen again. We're on the same team now. We have to work together for this show to fly. So, truce?"

He reached out and pushed her glasses on top of her head.

"I need to see your eyes," he said.

She raised her chin defiantly, but her eyes belied her hard stance, suggesting that this was just as hard for her as it was for him.

"Truce," he agreed, gripping the steering wheel rather than giving in to the urge to run his finger down her jawline. "I think I mentioned at dinner the other night that I didn't enjoy working in television during my last show."

She angled her body toward him. "Actually, you didn't mention it. You were pretty tight-lipped about the past that night. Why do you bring it up now?"

She met his gaze.

Why *was* he telling her this now?

"Because as you said, we're on the same team now. Yesterday, you were the media trying to report the story you needed to report."

She started to protest, but he held up a finger.

"When I was in television before, I was burned very badly by the media and others I trusted. My actions toward you—right or wrong—were reflexive. I think we've both learned a lesson about not trusting. So as you said, truce."

She nodded in agreement.

"Just so you know, I didn't go back on my word to you. The story they wanted me to report wasn't my story. They had no idea I'd promised you we wouldn't look back—"

"I didn't know that then, but I do now. So let's leave that in the past."

They sat in silence for a moment, watching a tall, dark-haired man greet Paula and three production assistants. Comprised of sixteen members, the new crew was decidedly larger than the former *Diva* operation. It included four camera operators—of which Sam was the team leader—two audio technicians, and a ten-person production team. Chandler had kept Paula on, but he hadn't put her in charge of production. Strangely enough, the woman didn't seem to mind. In fact, she'd mellowed out, was actually trying to work as a team player.

"Is that Henri Lejardin?" Lindsay asked.

Her voice had lost its edge. She sounded more like herself.

Carlos shaded his eyes from the early-morning sun. Sure enough, it was St. Michel's minister of Art and Culture. As he'd promised at the wedding, Lejardin had dropped by the signing. Then after the new deal was signed and sealed with Chandler, Max had called him and arranged for the show to shoot some footage in and around the palace. Lejardin and Paula were walking toward the car.

As Lindsay and Carlos got out of the car to greet Henri Lejardin, Lindsay was once again overwhelmed with awe that this grand palace was now her good friend Sophie's home, and the country's handsome Minister of Arts and Culture was Sophie's brother-in-law.

Still, even that wasn't nearly as baffling as realizing that the man she'd been sitting next to in the car was turning out to be more real than she'd ever imagined. He'd actually cared enough to clear the air—to drag the issue out into the open and leave it there until they were both satisfied with the resolution.

Usually she was the one doing the repair work.

This was a refreshing change.

She found his openness devastatingly sexy, much to her dismay. If she knew what was good for her she'd check all sexy thoughts at the door. The pain of the sexual harassment complaint she lodged against her former boss still plagued her. Because of it, she'd lost her fiancé and her job. Even though that was in the past, the bottom line was Chandler had made it perfectly clear that he didn't approve of romantic fraternizing. Her head knew that was plenty enough reason to shelve any romantic notions of Carlos Montigo.

Now, if she could only convince her heart as much.

"Mademoiselle, so nice to see you again," Henri Lejardin said as he planted a kiss on each of Lindsay's cheeks. "Much has changed for you since the wedding. I must congratulate you on your success."

Henri was a tall, striking man. His perfect English was embroidered with enough of a French accent to add to his charm. His dark good looks hinted at a slight resemblance to his brother, Luc, Sophie's new husband, but Henri was not quite as intense as his older sibling. He was less reserved, and there was a hint of flirtation in his smiling eyes. Or perhaps it was just that certain brand of magnetic charm that was organic in wealthy, good-looking men in lofty positions. Where Luc could be compared to a French James Bond, Henri was more like Hugh Jackman with a French twist—a sexy turn that had nothing to do with the hairstyle, of course.

"Thank you, Henri," she said. "Have you met my co-host, Carlos Montigo?"

"Yes, we met at the wedding and then again at his cookbook release party at the festival."

The two men shook hands.

"Very nice to see you again," Carlos said. "I can't tell you how much we appreciate your allowing us to shoot at the palace on such short notice."

Henri's eyes twinkled as he flashed a blinding grin at Lindsay. "How could we refuse someone with such excellent references? Besides, her beauty makes us look good."

The compliment made Lindsay smile. "I'll bet he says that to all the girls." She turned to look at Carlos and—

Oh—

The way he was looking at her…

She was accustomed to men's appreciation—to looks of lust even—but Carlos's eyes held something altogether different. It was almost heartbreaking because they couldn't explore it as long as they worked together.

Chapter Ten

Working with the footage they'd already shot during Carlos's cooking demonstration, it only took three days to shoot the rest of the first episode in and around St. Michel. After that, they spent a week in Cannes shooting the second spot. Now they were in Toulouse, France, for the third *Diva* installment.

This morning, Carlos waited alone in the French Provincial dining room of the Leblanc Inn, the quaint bed-and-breakfast that had become the temporary Toulouse headquarters for the cast and crew. He popped the last bite of fresh-baked baguette—which he'd slathered with butter and homemade apricot preserves—into his mouth, and washed it down with a swallow of good, strong black coffee.

Men had waged wars for less, he thought as he heaved a silent sigh of satisfaction. The least they could do in this episode was pay homage to the delicious breads baked by Babette Leblanc, the proprietor of the Leblanc Inn.

He'd suggest it as soon everyone gathered for the daily production meeting. Right now, the dining room was empty. The dozen small tables, topped with lace cloths, waited unmussed for the *Diva Drives* barrage, which, according to his calculations, should hit any moment. Collectively, the group ran like a well-oiled machine adhering to plans and schedules.

It was amazing how seamlessly everything had fallen into place for the new show format. Here they were, already taping the third installment—three-quarters of the way through the contracted commitment. What a change from his experience on *Piece of Me,* which felt like an uphill battle from the get-go.

There was only one area that felt a bit shaky...his off-camera relationship with Lindsay. Since that first day in the car, she'd remained distant when they were alone.

Cordial.

Professional.

Platonic.

Actually, now that he thought about it, they never really had that much time alone. Whenever it was just the two of them, she'd find one reason or another to excuse herself.

When they were in a group, she was herself—smart, funny and open. What he liked about her was that somehow she always managed to cut through the crap and get right to the heart of the matter. But when they were alone, she'd close up tight as a clam. Her distance was her protection. He understood that because the two of them weren't so dissimilar in that department. They both could put on a good front when it mattered, but the armor was always at least part of the way up.

As if on cue, Lindsay entered the dining room. Chandler and Max were with her. All three offered Carlos hearty greetings.

Carrying herself with self-assured grace, Lindsay looked gorgeous. Her pale pink sweater brought out the rose in her cheeks and hugged her curves in a way that a man couldn't help himself but to do a double take. Paired with trim black slacks, the sweater looked so soft it begged to be touched. At the thought, blood surged from his fingertips to his toes.

Carlos fisted his hands into his napkin and cleared his throat. "Good morning."

"I'm glad you're here, Montigo," Chandler said over his shoulder. "We're on a tight shooting schedule today. All week for that matter. In fact, they're bringing Bella around in fifteen minutes."

Bella was what the cast and crew had affectionately named the red Ferrari.

As Chandler, Max and Lindsay helped themselves to coffee from the silver server on the buffet, Babette Leblanc entered the room with a tray of steaming brioche. She offered Lindsay first choice, and Lindsay plucked one out of the basket and held the warm bread up to her nose, savoring the aroma.

"Ah, *merci*." She sighed. "This is heaven. Right here in my hands. And if I keep eating this way, Carson, I won't be able to fit into the car and you'll have to fire me."

"But what a way to go," Max said as he placed his saucer of coffee on Carlos's table and helped himself to two brioches.

"Carson," Lindsay said, "we need to work a segment

on Babette." Lindsay gestured to the woman, then to the room. "This place and her fabulous bread."

Great minds.

Chandler considered the suggestion. "That might make a nice starting point for the segment. We could open here and close at the winery in Bergerac. Talk to Paula about it."

Lindsay nodded and started to set her breakfast down at the small table next to Carlos, but hesitated when Chandler pulled out a chair next to Max.

As Carlos motioned her over, their gazes locked. It was the first time she'd looked at him in the past ten days. Since they'd been working together, she'd looked past him. Through him. At everything but him. But now she was finally looking at him. In that split second, in which time seemed to grind to a screeching halt, her eyes spoke volumes. And what they said hinted at plenty of unfinished business.

"Lindsay, join us over here," Chandler said.

As she tore her gaze away, Carlos wondered if the tension was as obvious to Chandler, because to Carlos, it felt as palpable as the thick home-churned butter on the table.

Lindsay set her plate down and Carlos stood and pulled out a chair for her. The gesture seemed to startle her, but she recovered fast.

"Thank you." Her voice was light—almost unnaturally so. But what did he expect with the boss sitting between them?

Then the rest of the crew began to stream into the dining room, and Chandler asked them to serve themselves coffee and whatever they wanted to eat. "But be quick about it because I have a full agenda to discuss and you must be on the road to our first location within the half-hour. No time to waste or we won't get everything done."

In short order, everyone gathered around.

Chandler brushed the crumbs from his navy blue fisherman's sweater and called the meeting to order.

"I appreciate how hard everyone's working during this holiday season. That's why I feel a little guilty leaving you all today to go back to New York, but I'm thrilled with the St. Michel and Cannes episodes we've shot and in my absence, I have all the confidence that you will continue the good work you've been doing. I must have one more meeting with the executives at the television station to tie up some loose scheduling ends. Then I will head home to spend Christmas with my family. If I don't, my wife will never let me hear the end of it."

A round of obligatory laughter rippled through the room as several people nodded their understanding of his predicament.

He went over the schedule.

"Christmas is five days from today," he continued. "That's one reason I'm rushing to get this shoot wrapped up, so that you all can spend Christmas with your families."

Carlos blinked at the realization. Despite the near freezing temperatures and homey holiday decorations strung up around the inn, Christmas had snuck up on him.

Further south, St. Michel and Cannes had offered balmy days and pleasant evenings. Besides, they'd been so busy it hadn't dawned on Carlos that it was Christmas week.

Since his divorce he hadn't enjoyed the holidays. Not that Max wasn't good company. But it would be nice, for a change, to kiss someone under the mistletoe and hold her tight at the stroke of midnight as they ushered in a new year.

Reflexively he glanced at Lindsay, who sipped her coffee and listened as Chandler detailed the schedule and what they needed to accomplish so they could have the week off. They'd be trekking through a cheese cellar in Roquefort, France, and then tomorrow, they'd pack up camp and head three hours northwest to Bergerac, home of some of the most incredible French vineyards and wineries.

After that, they were free until after the new year, when they'd reconvene in Paris.

Paula cracked a good-natured joke about how she was *finally* getting her wine and cheese segment, which encouraged more laughter. The woman had done a serious attitude about-face.

He might as well work through Christmas, Carlos thought as he listened to everyone making merry after learning of Chandler's gift of a week off.

How was he going to spend the holidays?

The thought of ringing in the new year alone rang hollow.

It was the smell of him that undid her, Lindsay thought as the two of them sat in Bella. It was all she could do to resist the urge to lean in and bury her nose in that place where his neck met his shoulder, the way she had that night at the beach, and breathe in that intoxicating mix of soap and leather that was so distinctly Carlos.

It had taken an extraordinary amount of willpower to resist.

Iron willpower.

But she'd managed.

That's why she'd insisted on driving the majority of the time. In the driver's seat, she could keep her eyes on the road and her hands on the steering wheel.

So, on the occasion when they were confined to the close quarters of Bella, the seat belt, steering wheel and ribbon of highway before her were her safety net.

Or chastity belt, of sorts.

Maybe that was a little extreme, but they hadn't slept together. Thank God. And this arrangement was meant to keep it that way.

Remarkably, Carlos had been amenable to her being in the driver's seat. Most men, she mused, would've demanded at least equal time putting a car like Bella through her paces.

That's why it caught Lindsay off guard when Chandler had insisted that they mix it up a bit today, that Carlos should drive in this episode. Of course, Lindsay was smart enough to know that a person who valued her job wouldn't argue with the likes of Carson Chandler. Nope, she'd hand over the keys and strap herself in for a long, bumpy ride.

Figuratively speaking, of course.

They were taping the journey from the inn to the cheese cellar today. On the way to meet the *affineur,* it felt a little awkward not being able to drive. Of course, they wore mics and had cameras in their faces, which left little time for personal small talk.

They still weren't working from a formal script, but one of Paula's jobs was to come up with specific talking points she constructed from the lightning-fast research she did on each area they featured on the show. The talking points were designed to keep the conversation natural and flowing. Relevant.

Even armed with those talking points, she felt as awkward as a teenager on a first date—unsure where to look or what to do with her hands.

So she kept her hands in her lap and looked straight ahead out the window. She never looked directly at the camera, except for an intimate aside in response to one of Carlos's particularly flirty or suggestive remarks.

Never directly at Carlos, if she could help it.

But she couldn't always help it.

As they drove to the cheese cellar, Carlos followed close behind a flatbed truck with a camera mounted to it for the tracking shots.

Toulouse was a beautiful city with a spicy blend of cosmopolitan and history. Lindsay had read that some of the city's old mansions dated back to the Renaissance. Filled with gardens and squares, it was an exciting commingling of past and present, preservation with accents of modernity.

Carlos and Lindsay wore small earpieces that fit inside the ear with wires that wardrobe had tucked away down collars and underneath scarves, so that the apparatus was invisible to the camera, but Carlos and Lindsay could still hear cues from the director, David Crawford.

"Okay, everyone, listen up," David said. "We're about ready to approach the area where I want to film the drive-by. Start with the first talking point, Carlos, in three…two…one…go—"

"So, Lindsay, you're finally giving me a turn behind the wheel. You're not one of those women who always has to *drive,* are you?"

Slanting a glance at her, he chuckled, playing it up for the camera.

She feigned offense.

"What, are you suggesting I'm controlling, Carlos?"

He shot the camera a do-I-even-have-to-answer-that look.

"But Carlos, sweetheart, I'd never dream of trying to control you, oh, unmanageable one."

He tore his gaze from the road to give her a smoldering reaction. That made it suddenly very hard to breathe. But it was all for the camera, she reminded herself.

In turn, she shot the camera a look of her own, which inspired Sam to give them a thumbs-up.

"Cut!" David called. "That was great. Perfect. You smoked it."

"We smoked it." Carlos held up a fist for Lindsay to bump. She did. He kept his eyes on the road and it gave her a chance to look at him.

On the way to the cheese cellar, they skirted Carcassonne, a walled medieval city that rose like a mighty dragon in the distance. Since they were on such a tight schedule, Lindsay and Carlos didn't stop to tour it—a small crew would film what they needed and the editor would splice together audio and video of they city with footage of Carlos and Lindsay in the car.

On cue, Lindsay said, "Oh, look at that. It's as if we've time-traveled to a medieval storybook city."

"Carcassonne dates all the way back to the twelfth century," Carlos answered. "It's one of Europe's best-preserved walled cities, complete with turreted towers—fifty-two, to be exact—and Gothic architecture. It's perched high on a prominent headland that overlooks the vineyards of the Languedoc region. Even from down here, the view is extraordinary."

"It really does look like a picture from a book of fairy tales. I wish we could go inside."

He smiled. "Princess, I should've known you'd fall in love with Carcassonne. But sorry, if we stop, we'll miss our appointments with the cheese maker and the vintner. Maybe next time?"

Lindsay sighed. It wasn't all affect for the camera. Even though she'd spent a month in the St. Michel palace, Carcassonne called to her.

Maybe next time.

"That was perfect, you two," David said into their ear pieces. "Let's do the short intro to the cheese caves and then you two can hang out until we get to the cheese man. Sound good?"

They agreed and without much ceremony went right to their talking points.

"So, Lindsay, did you know that the Languedoc area, where we are now, isn't one of France's best know gastronomical regions?"

"Really?"

"Yeah, it's sort of had a tumultuous history—at one period, the southern region of France spoke an entirely different language from the rest of the country, called Occitan."

"Is it still spoken today?"

Carlos shook his head. "Not by many people, but this area still remains sort of an anomaly because of its geographical placement."

He paused, loving the intensity with which she listened to him.

"Think about it," he continued. "They get great seafood from the Mediterranean, which borders the southeast coast. To the west, the Pyrenees, where we're going, offers not only great cheese, but wild fowl. To the east, they have the vibrant gardens of Provence, and to the southwest is Catalonia and its Spanish influence." He reached out and touched her arm. A benign gesture. Nothing inappropriate, certainly not sexual. Yet, her whole being filled with wanting.

"No wonder the Languedoc region is gastronomically confused."

Yeah, but not as confused as she was.

Since the planes of Languedoc were largely dominated by vines, Carlos and Lindsay had to head for the town of Roquefort in the Midi-Pyrénées, into sheep and goat country, to find the famed cheese caves that were home to the famous blue cheese.

When they arrived, Carlos was surprised to find the subject of their interview, cheese maker Girard Martin decked out in a red shirt, suspenders and a Santa hat. The slight, petite man was not much older than he was, early forties at most. The getup, which Paula had to ask him to modify so that the spot could be timeless, gave him an elfin appearance.

Though Carlos might have been taken aback by Monsieur Martin's clownish appearance, he wasn't at all surprised by the way the man took an obvious shining to Lindsay.

As they walked the short distance to the caves, Martin offered Lindsay his arm—a gesture David liked—and fussed over her, making sure she watched her step, protectively steadying her at times. Carlos thought Girard's European disregard for personal space was excessive.

Obviously, he'd been away from Europe long enough to become accustomed to the American standard of keeping one's hands to oneself. Not that watching another man put his hands on Lindsay bothered him. It was simply that he knew how much she hated anyone making a fuss over her.

As they walked Girard droned on. And on. And on. "I was born in the beautiful town of Toulouse. You are staying there, yes?" He didn't pause long enough to let them answer. "I lived there until I was sixteen. Then I left to come here to work as an apprentice. In my early years, I never imagined I would become an *affineur,* that the cheese caves would be my destiny."

Caveman. The guy was a virtual Neanderthal the way he was pawing Lindsay.

"Ah, here we are," he said.

As they reached the entrance to the cave, Girard slid his hand up Lindsay's shoulder, kneaded it a couple of times, then slid his hand down her arm on his way to open the door. When he turned away, Lindsay took a step back and shot Carlos a look that said loud and clear she was a little bothered by Martin's attentiveness.

The moment he opened the door, the smell slammed into them like a wave of dirty socks. Or maybe it was baby spit-up. This was particularly ripe.

Girard inhaled a hearty breath through his nose, flaring his nostrils and closing his eyes. "Ah, smell that? Isn't it beautiful?"

As a chef, Carlos was used to various odors—delicious and foul—particularly after working in restaurant kitchens most of his life. Most smells—like the pungent cheese or the onions that had made Lindsay cry—didn't bother him. But not everyone had that sort of immunity to smells.

Martin droned on about himself and how the phenomenal cheeses he produced would be ordered by some of the top chefs in the world and would make their way into some of the world's best restaurants.

Carlos arched his brows at Lindsay, and she made a face at him, then smiled. Sam was right there to catch it all on camera.

Right. The camera.

This was good stuff for the show. Good chemistry—playing off each other's strengths and differences. Their dissimilarities amounted to combustible on-screen presence. They were good together that way. Their strengths and differences seemed to bring out the best in the other...on the job. And, of course, he'd already had a taste of how those ebbs and flows complemented each other when no one was watching.

As Sam jockied his way around Martin to get into position to film their exploration of the cave, Carlos noticed Lindsay looked a little green. Her eyes were wide and her mouth was pressed into a thin line. Obviously, she was doing her best to be a good sport, but she wasn't enjoying this.

Carlos turned his back to the camera and mouthed, *Are you okay?*

Her eyes flashed, but then she steeled herself.

Fine, she mouthed back.

By this time, Girard had produced a flashlight from inside the cave. With it, he motioned Carlos and Lindsay inside.

"Come in. Come in," Girard said. "Just shield your head should a bat decide to fly at you."

"Bats?" Lindsay stiffened. "There are bats in here?" She started backing up.

Martin threw his head back and laughed. "No, silly girl." He grabbed her hand and yanked her forward. "There are no bats in here. I am making fun with you."

Carlos smiled to himself. *Bet she loves that. Way to endear yourself.*

"Ah, Girard," Lindsay said. "You're just a funny guy, aren't you?" In the narrow cave entrance, Lindsay did a little sidestep around Carlos so that he was between her and Girard. As she brushed past him, she shot Carlos another conspiring look. This one wasn't for the camera.

It was just for him.

For the first time in a long while, they were connecting on more of a personal level.

Hmm…maybe ol' Girard wasn't so bad after all.

As they made their way into the cave, the Frenchman droned on. "My love of cheese began when I was a teenager. I was fortunate to meet people who would guide me to understand how the magnificent flavors and aromas of fine cheese enrich the senses."

Carlos glanced back and saw Lindsay rubbing her nose. Girard and Sam moved deeper into the cave. Lindsay moved up closer behind Carlos.

"Magnificent aromas?" she whispered in his ear. "That's debatable."

Sam and Girard moved ahead, taking the light source with them, leaving Carlos and Lindsay in the dark. Her voice washed over him in waves of ecstasy. Her sweet, hot breath in his ear warmed him from the inside out, tempting him to turn so that they'd be face-to-face, their lips a whisper a part.

She put her hand on his back, but they didn't move to catch up with the others. What the sound of her voice had started, her touch promised to finish.

Not a good idea, his head warned. Oh, but his body begged to differ. Awareness pumped through him, making him hyper conscious of the smell of her—honey and nectar with hints of something he couldn't quite define. He wanted to press his lips to hers and taste her and try to figure out the mystery ingredient.

"I hope he was right about this place being bat-free," she whispered again.

Before he could think better of it, he reached back and grabbed her hand so that her arm snaked around to the front of his waist. She didn't recoil, simply stood there, her curves flush against his back.

What had started between them that first night was still alive and well, pulsing between them, refusing to be ignored. The fact that she didn't pull away was proof that things weren't finished. And he intended to continue what they started—Carson Chandler and *The Diva Drives* be dammed.

"*Yoo-hoo!* Where are you?" Girard Martin's accented voice filled the air. "Did we lose you?"

Carlos gave her arm one last squeeze, pulling her in closer one last time—for now, Lindsay Bingham.

For now.

As they made their way deeper into the cellar, catching up with the others, Lindsay said, "So, Girard, who was the first brave soul to pick up one of these smelly hunks and decide to taste it?"

Frowning, Martin stared down his aquiline nose at her. "Smelly hunk?" He looked insulted. "I have no idea. However, once *I* was introduced to the world of cheese, my life was forever changed. *Pour moi,* life is a never-ending journey *du fromage* and no matter how many varieties are laid in front of me, my insatiable appetite shall never be satisfied."

"Yeah, I'll bet," Lindsay murmured.

Chapter Eleven

It was too dark to film on the drive back to the Leblanc Inn. So the production crew decided to call it a day. Carlos and Lindsay headed back in Bella.

It was a strange day. Strange flipping back and forth between the on-camera chemistry and the safe-distance platonic friendship, because suddenly keeping it platonic felt more like acting than the on-screen relationship.

Now that the sun was setting, it was hard to know how to act, what she should say to him about today in the cave or if she should say anything at all. But suddenly all she could think of was what it would feel like to be in his arms, kissing him, touching him. And that was much too dangerous.

She could still keep her distance behind this wall she'd erected. Staying cocooned away from him would only hurt a little, but if she let herself get in any deeper, there'd be too much at stake. Her job. Her heart.

"Quite a day, huh?" Carlos said.

Lindsay nodded. "I can't believe I was right here in Carcassonne and didn't get a chance to check out the upper city. I'll have to come back. Someday."

There was a beat of silence.

"Let's go there," he finally said. "Let's go now. We could go for dinner and a look-see."

"Are you serious?" Lindsay blinked. "No, Carlos. It's an hour outside of Toulouse—"

"It's only five-thirty. We'll be there before seven." He glanced at her. "That's plenty of time for a nice dinner and a walk."

Her mind skittered back to the last time they had a nice dinner and a walk. "I don't know if that's a good idea, Carlos."

"Why not?"

"You know *why not.*"

He looked at her blankly. "No, I'm afraid I don't. Is it me? Do you not want to have dinner with me?"

"No, it's not you...."

"Because if it's me, just say so, and I'll leave you alone. But something tells me that's not what you want."

She didn't say anything for a moment. She couldn't find her voice. Or at least the voice of reason that would say the right thing—the sensible thing. Something like, *No, I don't want your lips on mine, your hands on my body. I don't want you around me and certainly not in me....* The problem was, she wanted all those things.

He eased the car off the deserted road onto the gravel shoulder, and sat there for a moment with the engine idling, his hands clutching the steering wheel. They were in the middle of nowhere. No houses, no shops, only the rolling French countryside, over which the sun was setting and turning the field vivid shades of amber, orange and violet.

"The thing I hated most about working in television," he turned and looked her in the eyes, "was that sometimes it felt a bit like selling my soul to the devil. Suddenly they owned me. I was their puppet who danced when they said dance and sat quietly in a corner until they wanted me to perform. Only I didn't sit quietly. I caused way too much trouble, so they cut me loose."

"You sound so cynical."

"Maybe I am." He shrugged. "I almost turned down this job."

"But you didn't. How come?"

He laid his head back on the headrest and grinned at her. "Ever the inquisitive reporter, aren't you?"

She squirmed a little. *No.* She was so bad at it.

"I'll make a deal with you," she said. "Level with me and tell me your side of the story about why you lied about your credentials and I'll have dinner with you in Carcassonne."

He made a face, and blew out a forced breath between his lips. *Pfft.* And his dismissal of the question might have worked, except that she'd caught the look that flashed in his eyes before the wall went up.

"I lied. What more is there to say?"

"I don't believe you."

He laughed, but it was anything but humorous. "So you're saying I'm lying about lying?"

"Not exactly. I think there's more to the story than what you're telling me."

"And what if there is?"

She wanted to ask him how she was supposed to trust him if he wouldn't be straight with her.

"Carlos, I am not the enemy. We're on the same team now, remember? Why won't you trust me?"

"Why should I?"

What? Oh, for God's sake—

"Fine. Never mind. Let's go back to the inn."

Lindsay turned her head and stared out the window as she waited for him to ease the car back onto the road.

"I hadn't intended for everything to get so out of hand," he said.

Lindsay turned and looked at him.

"My ex, Donna, had huge social aspirations and worked hard to make the restaurant the hot spot in Miami, while I cooked. She did a good job, actually. Through her connections, I got guest judging spots on a few reality TV shows and eventually I landed *Piece of Me.* The only thing wrong was that Donna had padded my credentials. By the time it mattered, she'd already put these false claims out there and it was awkward to retract them. So against my better judgment, I let it ride because I never dreamed anyone would bother to research my background. God, I was stupid. I knew it was wrong, but once it got to the point where people were paying attention, it was too late to retract it. What was I supposed to do? Post a big sign that said, *I was too busy cooking to notice that my wife fabricated my résumé. I don't have a Grand Diplome from Le Cordon Bleu and I never worked at the Élysée Palace in Paris?*

"I was an idiot to let her do it. So I can't blame anyone but myself for the mistake. I knew that, and before I signed the contract with Food TV, I leveled with them. I told them the truth and how the false résumé came to be—and actually that was strike one against my marriage. Donna didn't want me to confess, but that's beside the point. When I laid it all out on the table with the network execs, I did it verbally. I didn't ask them to sign anything acknowledging the disclosure, because they said, 'Le Cordon Bleu and the Élysée Palace sound a lot sexier than saying you're self-taught. Let's just leave it as is.'"

He shook his head.

"I took them at their word. God, I was such a naive bastard. And of course, when the house of cards came tumbling down, they pretended to be just as surprised as everyone else. They wanted to distance themselves. So they suddenly had no recollection of that meeting."

Lindsay reached out and touched his arm. "I'm really sorry."

He pulled away. "Don't feel sorry for me. I was an idiot. The last thing I want or deserve is pity."

She shook her head. "Don't be ridiculous. I don't pity you. It's just not right."

For a moment, no one said anything.

"So, the paper started digging when you refused the Michelin rating, right?"

He nodded, a faraway look in his eyes.

"Yep. They took great pleasure in finding me out because originally they set out to prove that I'd refused the stars because I was trying to be different or difficult or I thought I was too good or some equally inane reason that had nothing to do with the real reason I turned down the honor."

Lindsay paused, hoping he'd tell her why. But he didn't. Not immediately.

"So why did you turn it down?"

"I was scared to death. That's why."

He looked away and she wanted to reach out and hold him.

"The television show had kept me away from Prima Bella Donna so much, I felt so out of touch. Because the kitchen, the food, that was my touchstone. That's why I left all the front-of-the-house business to Donna. She was good at schmoozing. I was good at cooking. They offered the award based on my kitchen, well, not entirely, but the quality of the food is a large part of it. But being away from the restaurant, I had no control over what was happening in the kitchen and the pressure to keep the rating was just too much and while I'm spilling my guts, refusing the rating was strike two against my marriage— Donna had a fit. But I held firm. Honestly, I never wanted to be *that* kind of chef in the first place. I sort of got caught up in the whirlwind of it all—and all this fame and fortune pleased my wife. My *ex-wife*. To her, the fame was great and the money was even better…but it was so far from who I wanted to be… God, I hate sounding like the victim. I hate sitting here and saying this all *happened* to me. I sold out. I should've had the balls to put my foot down before it spiraled out of control."

He shook his head as if he could erase the thought.

"Well, isn't that what you were doing when you refused the Michelin rating? It seems like it was the start of taking back control of your life."

He snorted. "It was the beginning of the end. Food TV suits fell all over themselves trying to disassociate themselves from me and they terminated my contract for falsification of credentials. Of course, it was my word against theirs. They lied and said no such meeting took place where I told them about the padded résumé."

Memories of her own failed attempt to take on the big boys crashed down.

"So, the long and short of it is that Donna filed for divorce and got her beloved Prima Bella Donna and the house. I didn't care. I just wanted to get the hell out of Miami. That's when I moved to Cedar Inlet."

He shook his head. "So there you have it. The undoing of Carlos Montigo. Happy now?"

Happy? "Well, no. Why would that make me happy?"

"That's why I don't like to talk about it. Why I didn't tell my side of the story, as you put it, to the press. The only thing it would change is it would amplify the fact that I was a jackass for not being more in control of my own life."

The way he was looking at her nearly broke her heart. She reached out and put a hand on his arm because she didn't know what to say or what else she could do.

"So, are you ready to explore Carcassonne?" he asked.

Chapter Twelve

With its cobblestone streets and medieval buildings all decked out for the holidays, the upper city of Carcassonne was indeed like something from a fairy tale.

Carlos half expected to spy Father Christmas and his team of reindeer flying through the inky sky. What he wouldn't give right now for Santa Claus to grant him a do over in the spirit of the holidays.

He hadn't intended to spill his guts and tell her the entire pathetic story. Beyond Max and Donna, who was long gone, no one knew the entire story. Not even the television bigwigs who'd cut him loose.

He felt exposed.

Lindsay must think him a moron for letting his life spin so far out of his own hands. Of course, she didn't act that way. In fact, she seemed more open now than she had in a long time.

As they roamed the walled city, he did his best to shake it off. It was his problem, and he needed to get over it. Or at least not let it spoil the evening.

Before they headed to Carcassonne, they called Paula to let her know they were making the stop. Lindsay had been uncomfortable with simply disappearing with the car—"It's a Ferrari, for God's sake. I think we'd better check in."

She was right. It was better to report in than to have them send out a search party. But checking in went against his grain.

They wandered the streets, peering in shop windows, *oohing* and *aahing* over the quaintness of the unique little city and its festive holiday mood. It had turned colder outside now that the sun had set. Though the high temperature had only reached the low fifties, Carlos was willing to bet it was dipping down into the forties.

Lindsay turned up the collar on her coat and rubbed her gloved hands together. He had the sudden urge to take her in his arms and warm her with his own body heat. Heat that was increasing as he thought of how it would feel to hold her again—and this time do it right.

When they turned from Rue Saint Louis onto Place Auguste-Pierre Pont, Carlos spied an elegant-looking restaurant called La Barbacane.

"How about this?" he suggested. "I'm in the mood for some good authentic food and I'll bet this place can serve it up."

It also happened to be the only restaurant in Carcassonne with a Michelin rating. One star. Just like the one he'd refused.

Maybe he was a glutton for punishment, but he

wanted to try it. To see how La Barbacane compared with Prima Bella Donna.

"It looks wonderful," said Lindsay.

He held the door open for her and they stepped into a wonderland of stained glass and rich paneled walls. A petite brunette greeted them, smiling warmly as they approached.

"Deux pour le dîner, s'il vous plaît," Carlos said.

"I have a very romantic table by the window over looking the rampart," she said.

They checked their coats and followed her to their table.

It really was a magnificent view of the gardens, the Citadel ramparts, with a glimpse of Carcassonne in the distance. But the menu, which was based on seasonal ingredients, looked even better. It boasted such mouthwatering offerings as green ravioli with *seiche,* a species of octopus, in a sauce of its own ink; crisp-fried cod with black olives; saltwater crayfish with strips of Bayonne ham. Simply from reading the descriptions, he could virtually taste the flavors. His mouth watered and his heart ached a little as he realized how much he missed being in the kitchen.

Lindsay ordered the Breton lobster with artichoke hearts and caviar. Carlos had the organic free-range guinea fowl rubbed with vanilla and stuffed with truffles.

It was heaven on a plate, but the food was nothing compared to the way Lindsay looked.

His gaze was riveted on her lips, and all he could think about was how she would taste. In the wake of all that he'd unloaded today, kissing her was probably not a good idea. Yet there was something about the way her eyes danced in the candlelight and the way she was smiling at him. Something sensual that hinted at possibilities and desire.

Something that whispered a promise of what was to come before the night was over. Suddenly good sense seemed highly overrated.

The confession that left him feeling raw and vulnerable obviously hadn't changed her mind about him. If anything, he felt closer to her.

He shifted forward and lightly stroked her hand with his fingers. It was just a light touch, meant to give her the opportunity to pull back if she wanted.

But she didn't.

Instead, she gently took his hand, turned it over, palm down, and studied it. "When was your divorce final?"

"Why?"

"Your ring finger doesn't show any signs of a wedding ring." She traced the place on his ring finger where a wedding band would've gone. Then shook her head and released his hand. "You're always so defensive."

It was true, he reflected as the busboy cleared the plates. Since losing the restaurant and his marriage, he'd always thought it was an emotion he couldn't help—aftershock of sorts.

The waiter offered them dessert. Lindsay declined, saying the lobster was delicious and rich, but she had no room for another bite.

Looking across the table at her, Carlos decided there was only one thing he wanted for dessert: a taste of her lips. Yet, her viewing him as defensive didn't exactly bode well for a chance to satisfy that craving.

He remembered what she said earlier: *Carlos, I am not the enemy. We're on the same team now. Why won't you trust me?* She was so earnest reaching out to him.

Was he really going to continue to let the past rob him

of happiness? There was only one way to make sure that didn't happen.

"It's been nearly three years now," he said. "That's more than enough time for any marks to fade."

"Except for here." Bracing her elbows on the table, she reached across the small table for two and put her right hand on his heart. The gesture took him by surprise. Instinctively, he put his hand over hers.

"No, that was the first part to heal."

She didn't pull away. "I don't believe you."

He started to ask if she was calling him a liar. But after today's confession, that did seem too defensive. Maybe there was hope for him after all.

"What makes you think that?"

"You're still holding on to the past."

He drew in a deep breath and counted to ten, until he could answer without an edge to his voice.

"The only reason it came up was because you asked," he said. Her hand was warm and small in his. And he ran his thumb over her smooth skin. "And I told you."

"But you almost let it cost you an opportunity. You said yourself that you almost didn't take the job because of all that happened."

"But I took the job. And here we are."

His words seemed to catch her off guard and for a moment she wavered, uncertainty shadowing her face.

"If you hate television work so much, why *did* you take the job, Carlos?"

He shifted his grip to lace his fingers through hers.

"There are two reasons. One is simple. The other is complicated. Which one would you like to hear?"

"Both."

He nodded. *Fair enough.*

"The simple answer is, I needed the money and I'll be honest, when Chandler offered the four-episode contract—future contracts to be negotiated after he had a chance to assess the first four—" he rolled his eyes and said the words in a mocking sing-song voice "—I sort of came into this with the idea of taking the money and running after I'd fulfilled the first contract."

Lindsay's eyes flashed.

He knew it sounded crass, but it was the truth and he had to lay the truth on the table so that she could see it plain and clear. He wanted her to know he had nothing to hide.

"Really, it hasn't been so bad. Not unbearable like my first go at television. But that's beside the point."

She pulled her hand away as utter panic washed over her face. "Carlos, if you don't come back, that could mean *I'm* out of a job, too."

"The reality is Chandler holds the strings here. We could both very well be out of jobs if the show doesn't suit him. Let's cross that bridge when we come to it, okay?"

She nodded, but her eyes still held a glint of wariness. "You're right. Please continue. You were saying…"

"Yes, I was saying…do you remember that first night at dinner when I mentioned this crazy dream of mine?"

He took her hand again. This time, he stroked her palm with his thumb. The silky softness made it very hard for him to concentrate, because his mind kept drifting to how her hands would feel on his naked body—touching and caressing, possessing.…

"Prima Bella Donna was never my vision. It was Donna's. Obviously, because of the name. She never wanted children so the restaurant was her legacy. She had no desire to have kids. They would've held her back, and with the restaurant *she* was the center of attention. She rubbed elbows with celebrities like Madonna and Lenny Kravitz and was essentially the toast of South Beach. The restaurant was her baby."

Lindsay quirked a brow. "Prima Bella Donna. I get it."

He stopped stroking her palm, and he sensed her pulling back a little. "Are you sure you want to hear this?"

She waited a beat. "Yes. I need to hear this, Carlos."

There was a heartrending tenderness in her gaze. Yet, in the next moment something intense flared between them.

"At first, it was a challenge. It seemed everything I created was well received." He nodded. "For a while it was exciting to be the king of my kitchen under those circumstances. But it didn't last long. It was never enough for Donna. She had to keep pushing upward, onward. When the television opportunities came along things began to change.

"You see, I loved the part of being able to cook what I wanted to cook, and when that changed, when the media dictated my every move, I wanted to retreat into my original dream."

She leaned forward again and squeezed his hand.

"What was that dream?"

He gave a nervous chuckle. He really was nervous sharing this with her. One look at the expression on her face and all discomfort evaporated.

"I always wanted to open a restaurant—nothing fancy—that offered kids who'd gotten into trouble a second chance."

Her eyes flashed with surprise. But it was good surprise. "Really?"

"Yeah." He took her hand in both of his. "My *abuela* did the best she could raising me, but like some kids with no solid male influence and too much free time out and about, I—how should I say this—had my share of run-ins with the authorities."

"So you were a bad kid, huh?"

He shrugged. "Relatively speaking. I never hurt anyone. It wasn't until I started cooking seriously that I found a true purpose. I thought about how food not only sustains, but can actually save a person's life. I'm living proof of that. I did a little research and discovered there aren't many places—and I'm talking quality places, fine dining—that offer wayward kids an opportunity to learn on the job and get their lives together.

"After the divorce, when I moved to Cedar Inlet, that's what I had in mind. To open a working restaurant that served as a training ground for troubled young adults. I want to call it Out of the Fire. It would be a teaching restaurant where the premise is you don't have to be formally trained at a hoity-toity culinary school. I'd love it if all the instructors were self-taught. The focus will be teaching these kids the basics, giving them a sense of self-worth, so that they can stand on their own two feet. But my preliminary efforts revealed two obstacles."

"What are they?"

"Zoning and, of course, money. So I put the restaurant on hold, wrote the cookbook and planned to tour until I had enough seed money to fulfill my dream. When Chandler offered me the show, the money was too good to turn down. I could accomplish in one month what it would take at least three years to rake in hawking my wares."

The waiter brought the check.

"Let me get it," Lindsay said.

He didn't even look up from the leather bill folder. "Don't be ridiculous. Besides, you picked up the last one."

Her belly did a curious spiral when she remembered what happened the last time after they'd had dinner together.

"Chandler picked up the last one," Lindsay protested, trying to keep her mind from getting carried away.

Carlos lifted his eyes and snared her gaze. "Yes, last time was business."

Oh, God. What did that mean?

She knew what it meant. People didn't hold hands across the table after a business dinner. There was absolutely nothing businesslike about this shared meal.

Unless you considered the unfinished business between them.

She'd started it earlier in the car, prodding until he opened up. Then a few minutes ago, when she'd traced the spot where his wedding ring had been; she'd known how long he'd been divorced. She'd learned about it in her initial research for *The Diva Dishes*.

She just had to make sure his head—and heart— were in the right place before…

"Come on," he said. "Let's get out of here."

He stood and helped her with her chair and coat once they got to the coat check stand.

Outside, the temperature had dropped dramatically and there were snow flurries. Lindsay shivered, and Carlos put his arm around her as they walked.

It was a fluid gesture. Natural. Not tentative or apologetic. It was as if they'd always shared this intimacy.

"So La Barbacane had a Michelin star," she said. "What did you think?"

He nodded his approval. "Delicious. Made me miss being in the kitchen, but not regret refusing the award. Cooking is my sanctuary. Having that award hanging over my head would be an albatross. It's subjective. Maybe the next year they wouldn't have understood what I was doing and they would have taken the star back. Maybe I shouldn't care."

He shook his head. "It seems pretty stupid of me, I suppose."

"No. Believe it or not, I do understand where you're coming from. Remember me telling you about my mother's recipe notebook? Baking is *my* sanctuary. When I'm stressed I bake, when I'm sad I bake. But there are no expectations. Reading my mother's writing always made me feel close to her. Even though I couldn't go to her. I mean, I never really knew her since I was so young when she died. Those recipes are a place where I can turn, without judgment. My sanctuary. I can't imagine having to strive for perfection every time I baked."

"Well, in a restaurant, the chef has an obligation to his customer. That's a given if he wants to stay in business—"

"Shh." Lindsay stopped and turned, pressing a gloved finger to Carlos's lips. "I get it. You don't have to explain."

Their faces were so close; his lips were right there. All she'd have to do is lean in a bit more… Instead, she laced her arm through his and walked on. Until Carlos stopped in front of a window with an animated display of Santa's workshop.

In the glow of the soft amber lights, she caught a glimpse of them—arm in arm, looking like a couple— in the storefront window and the sight took her breath away. Right then, she knew Chandler be dammed, they'd passed that point of question and were barreling head over heart toward the point of no return.

The only question left was, what next?

They lingered, watching the rosy-faced Santa raise and lower a "Naughty or Nice?" list as his elves busily hammered away at miniature workbenches in the background.

Carlos broke the silence. "Earlier, I mentioned there were two reasons I accepted Chandler's job offer, but I only told you one."

"What's the other reason?"

Gently, he took her by the shoulders and turned her toward him.

"The other reason was…you."

Me?

The way he gazed at her with those deep, smoldering eyes the color of dark jade turned her liquid with silken juices.

He looked at her in a way that no man had ever before. Just what did he see with that intense gaze?

When he shifted toward her and ran a finger along her jawline, suddenly it didn't matter what he saw. Because she knew he was going to kiss her. He hesitated, as if giving her a chance to pull away, but warm in his arms, the only place she wanted to be was right here.

She tilted her head and parted her lips slightly. A silent signal that she wanted him. He must have understood because he leaned in and kissed her, moving slowly at first, only brushing her lips with the most delicate of glances. He was a gentleman, no wandering hands. He simply rested one on her shoulder and the other on her arm, as if he waited for her to kiss him back.

Her heartbeat pounded in her rib cage, until slowly, almost cautiously, she leaned into the kiss. Her breath quickened as she surrendered to shivers of heat and need.

When she sucked at his bottom lip, it was as if she'd turned the burners on a gas range on high. Heat and need exploded and his body responded.

But as much as he burned to pull her against him, to explore her body with his hands until she turned to dough in his hands, as much as he wanted to sweep her up in his arms and into one of the Carcassonne hotels and take off her clothes and run his tongue over every inch of her supple body, he resisted. He stood there, steeling himself as he let her set the pace.

He didn't want either of them walking away with regrets this time.

When she nipped at his bottom lip, this time he angled his head to the side and parted his lips for her. As she slipped her tongue into his mouth, his body got hotter, harder, his need more intense. It was all he could do to keep his hands off her, to not take her by the hand and lead her into one of the alleyways and back her against the wall of one of these ancient buildings and make love to her then and there. Need consumed him, threatened to overwhelm him, but they were finally meeting on solid ground, mutual ground, and he was determined not to mess things up this time.

But when she deepened the kiss and sighed, it took every bit of self-control he had not to crush her to him. Instead he held his ground, kissing her back slowly, gently without unleashing the all-consuming passion that fired through his blood. And he waited for her to be the one to pull back first. When she did, gasping for breath, he steadied himself by cupping her face in his hands, touching her to make sure this kiss in this story-book city was real and not a dream.

It was real all right. The excruciating pleasure-pain of his rock-hard erection was proof of exactly how real.

As they made their way to the car, arm in arm, he felt scorching hot despite the cold. He tightened his grip on Lindsay, pulling her snug against his side, needing to feel her body against his. In time, the need to bury himself inside her would ease to a bearable level. His arousal would ease to a dull, aching throb until, in good time, they'd finish what they'd started.

And that *finish* would be the start of something brand-new.

When they reached the car, he bent down and kissed her again. The parking lot was dark and he was warm, and for a moment Lindsay got lost in the feel of his lips moving over hers.

Only for a moment. Because if it would've been more than a moment, she might have gotten completely lost and never found her way back.

"Carlos," she breathed, pulling away slightly from the kiss. "There are so many reasons why this is a bad idea."

He leaned in and found her lips again. "Bad idea…?" he said around the kiss.

"Mmm-hmm… We have to work together."

He ran his tongue over her lower lip.

"Work? Right now?"

She bit down lightly on his lower lip.

"No, silly, not right now. But tomorrow, and, I hope, many days after that."

She heard herself saying the words, but she couldn't find the strength to pull out of his arms. To focus directly on the conversation. Even though she knew she should.

"You know, talking is highly overrated. We do enough of that on camera. Right now it's just you and me and all this chemistry Chandler keeps talking about."

"Exactly. I don't want to mess this up…." Her voice shook.

He dropped his hands to her hips, and pulled her in close. Trailing his lips down her jawline to a place behind her ear, he kissed her in a way that made her lose her train of thought.

"I think we're far from messing this up. We're *so* good at this. I don't think we could mess up if we tried." He whispered this into her ear before sucking on her lobe, sending shivers of pleasure throughout her body.

"No, Carlos, really. It's happened to me before."

He flinched a little.

But there, she'd done it. He raised his head and squinted down at her.

"What's happened to you before?" He loosened his hold on her.

For a moment, she warred with herself. Why had she brought this up? No, she knew that answer. Knew she had to do it. This job was her chance to get on with her life. To make something of herself. To be the person her father always hoped she'd be. With all this at stake, why was she falling right back into the old trap again?

"Getting involved with a coworker and it turning out badly." The words made her cringe.

Especially when his body tightened and a strange,

confused half smile quirked up his lips. "Coworker? Is that that what we are, coworkers?"

His hands fell to his side.

Of course this wasn't going to be easy. Dredging up the past never was. But he'd had the guts to lay his past wide-open, she needed to do the same.

"Well, technically, yes. Because we do work together. The future of the show relies on us…and if we… And it doesn't work out…Chandler will—"

"I don't give a damn what Chandler thinks. When we're off the clock, what we do with our time is nobody's business but our own. That's the problem I had from the beginning."

"But you don't understand, I can't make that mistake again."

"I am not *that* mistake, Lindsay."

"You don't know what happened."

"No, I don't. There's no way I will unless you tell me." She sighed. "Let's get in the car."

And then she began. "When I was just out of college, I landed a reporting job at WKMO, a TV station in Charleston. I met and fell in love with a man who was one of their star reporters. He was vying for an anchor position. We eventually got engaged, but Derrick wanted to keep the engagement quiet. He seemed to think that he'd be more 'attractive' and promotable if he was unencumbered. In this business, family is seen as a liability—they want young, attractive free agents who are willing to move at the drop of a hat—or so he said. And yes, that was the air around the station. Movers and shakers who were all in a friendly competition to be the next one to climb up to the next rung. If a nose job made you more attractive, you had your nose done. If hiding your engagement made you more salable, you had a secret engagement. Boy, was I stupid...." She shook her head, embarrassed by how gullible she must seem.

"But of course, people knew Derrick and I were seeing each other. There was no law prohibiting interoffice romance. In fact, the pairings often shifted depending on who was coming and going. So since we weren't very private about our romantic relationship, my boss decided I must have been a player and decided to test me to see how badly I wanted to move up. I was young and stupid and thought I was in love. So basically, I told him to keep his hands off me and when it was clear he wouldn't take me seriously, I lodged a sexual harassment complaint against him.

"Long story short, because I was 'sleeping with' Derrick, as he put it, he made me out to be the station tramp. He even got others to lie and say I'd slept with them, which was totally false. Lies. I was in love. I was going to get married....

"But when it came down to it, Derrick distanced himself. You see it was the promotion or me. And suddenly I was a pariah. He broke the engagement, and then—surprise, surprise—my contract wasn't renewed the following year.

"Lies cost me my job and my fiancé. Go ahead and say it. I'm sure you're wondering how I could've been so blind. So stupid not to have seen it coming. How do you find yourself engaged to a man who, in the end, you didn't even know? Believe me, I've asked myself that same question every single day over the past seven years. How could I have been so blind? It's caused me to question my judgment and every single man I meet."

Carlos held up both hands. "I am the last person who would ever judge you. Yeah, me, the jester of Prima Bella Donna's court."

They were quiet for a moment. The stillness was vibrant with confession.

"But think about it," he finally said. "Aren't you glad you didn't marry him? I know you went through hell, but it sounds like the situation may have saved you from a bad marriage."

She frowned, not quite on the same page as Carlos. "Yeah, but it was a pretty high price to pay. Don't you think?"

"And a bad marriage is no picnic, either. Take it from someone who knows. And just so you're clear with it, I think it's abominable that he threw you over like that. What kind of a man won't stand up for his fiancée? I'm not Derrick."

No, he wasn't. He couldn't be further apart from Derrick. She'd known him such a short period of time and already she felt as if she knew more about Carlos than she'd known about a man to whom she was ready to pledge the rest of her life.

Bad judgment.

"There does come a time when you have to stop blaming yourself," he said. "I've been through it. So I know."

He started the car and turned on the radio. On the long drive back to Toulouse, neither of them said much. Instead, they listened to the plaintive French tunes that emanated from the speakers. She didn't understand most of what they sang, but the songs filled the silence and gave her time to think.

Now that everything was out on the table, the similarity of their situations was a little eerie. Both of them had been burned by people they'd loved and trusted. Both had lived through the decimation of their careers and were just starting to come out on the other side. Now here they were, two broken, battered souls, trying to make their way the best they knew how.

Brutal honesty was one way to kill a budding romance. But at least she'd saved her job this time.

Regret—for having said too much, for having chased him off—sat like a rock in the pit of her stomach. She felt a little shaky as she tried to convince herself that having shared so much with him was for the best. It was sort of like she'd run an emotional marathon. She hurt now, but in the days to come she'd feel stronger and better for having done it.

Only right now the voice inside her screamed, *What the hell were you thinking?*

They pulled into the Leblanc Inn parking lot about an hour later.

"Here we are." He killed the engine and turned to her. "It's been…quite a day."

She nodded, completely drained of words.

"You know," he said, "they only win if we let them."

So easy to say. So much harder to do.

"After tomorrow's shoot, we're off until after the new year. Why don't we prove to ourselves how far we've come? Lindsay, come to Paris with me. Let's spend the holidays together."

Her first instinct was to leave. Fast. But it was too late. She'd already let him in.

Chapter Thirteen

Paris for the holidays. How could she resist?

Her first reaction had been to say no.

But along with the romantic notion came a whole host of questions. It sounded too ridiculous to ask what his intentions were—the guy had nearly kissed her pants off in public. She'd managed to exercise good judgment and get to her room—alone—that night, but if she spent ten days alone with him in Paris, she wasn't sure she'd be so strong. She wasn't sure she wanted to because all logic had been completely undone by the memory of Carlos's kiss and the pull of a feeling that simply wouldn't go away—no matter how she tried to distance herself from him.

A feeling that she was quite possibly falling in love with him. That she'd already fallen.

The realization hit her hard. She didn't know when

it had manifested—during the kiss or the first moment their eyes met at the wedding.

It simply was. As if it had been rooted inside her always, lying dormant until now.

It was a timeless feeling, as primal and organic as the earth and the oceans and the sky.

This was different than anything she'd experienced before and she had no idea what she was going to do about it. Except that the best place to try and find out was in Paris.

The left-bank apartment belonged to Carlos's friend, Paul, whose job had taken him to Istanbul for three months. When Carlos called to tell him he'd be in Paris for the holidays, Paul had insisted he stay there.

"I'll leave word with the concierge," Paul had said. "He'll have a key for you."

Situated on a charming cobblestone street in Paris's Latin Quarter, it was a welcome change from the hotels Carlos had been living in since Max had arranged the book tour.

As Carlos took their bags out of the tiny, mirrored lift, which was barely large enough for the two of them and their luggage, he caught a glimpse of Lindsay's reflection. Her long, blond hair hung in loose curls around her shoulders. It looked like spun gold contrasted with her black knit beret and wool coat. Her cheeks were blushed pink from the cold night and her brown eyes looked dark and seductive in the half-light of the elevator.

Her beauty astounded him, or maybe it was the fact that they were here together in Paris.

Her gaze snared his in the mirror. "Is this our stop?"

"It is." He cleared his throat, inexplicably nervous. *Did someone just turn up the heat?*

They found unit 294. He unlocked the door, then held it open for her to enter first. As she moved past him, he breathed in her scent, an action that had become almost reflexive when she was near—breathing her in, wanting to experience as much of her as possible. One hand on the doorknob, he shoved the other in his coat pocket to keep himself from reaching out and pulling her into his arms.

With its tall, beamed ceilings and rough-hewn plank floors, the apartment was gorgeous. A door at the end of a small hallway opened into a bathroom. The other two doors were bedrooms.

Two bedrooms.

Carlos simply set both bags in the hallway.

"Look at this," Lindsay called from the living room.

She was standing at one of the large windows looking out. "You can see the Seine from here. Let's go take a walk."

It was just a short walk, less than five minutes, from the apartment to the river. They both remained silent, listening to the cars whir past and the sounds of Paris after dark.

The cold night air was invigorating. The City of Love was all around her and Carlos was next to her, reaching for her hand.

Why she was so anxious? It was too late to change her mind, she thought as he laced his fingers through hers. Well, it was never too late to decide *not* to sleep with a man. It was every woman's prerogative to say no right up to the last second.

The problem wasn't that she didn't want him. In fact, it was her feelings that made this situation so impossible. She also wanted her job. She needed her job. She was just getting her life on the right track and then she had to go and fall in love.

He led her down the steps of the quay, and there they were—standing along the Seine River. Water lapped against the embankment and lights danced across the rippled surface like a moody Impressionist painting come to life before her very eyes.

What if things didn't work out? What if he changed his mind about how he felt about her? They'd still have to work together. Memories of Derrick flashed through her mind.

She'd thought she'd had it all then, too. The perfect job, the perfect man...then one day she woke up and it was all gone.

It had changed the direction of her life. Yet she'd let herself get swept away again. This wasn't a vacation romance.

"Are you okay?" Carlos dropped her hand and slid his arm around her, pulling her in close. "Is it too cold for you?"

She shivered a little, but shook her head.

The power of suggestion.

"*Nah,* just tired, I think."

There was nothing like an open-air Parisian market. The array of fresh baked bread, vegetables, meats, cheeses and wine was a chef's dream. Succulent white asparagus. Ripe blueberries, strawberries, blackberries and raspberries. Artichokes so fat and healthy Carlos could almost taste them...mmm...served with lemon-garlic aioli.

It was more than a dream.

It was nirvana.

He'd gotten the fixings for coq au vin. With mashed garlic-leek potatoes and green beans, it was the ultimate comfort food.

Just what Lindsay needed.

Earlier, she'd baked her mom's Ultimate Cookies for dessert.

They were the most incredible and delicious of any sweet he'd ever tasted. When he first bit into the chewy goodness, he had visions of living happily with just Lindsay, a bed and an endless supply of her Ultimate Cookies.

They were an absolute aphrodisiac.

But then again, it was the first time they'd cooked together. There was something sexy about the process of working side-by-side in the kitchen. He wished they could simply ditch the rest of the show and live in this private culinary bubble from now on.

But…he would honor his commitment.

The press might say a lot of bad things about him, but one thing he prided himself in was upholding his commitments.

He uncorked a bottle of Volnay and poured two glasses, one of which he handed to Lindsay. After they clinked goblets, he lifted his and savored its bouquet of red berries and violet. It would be delicious with the chicken. It was great to be in the kitchen again. He missed moments like this, shopping for and cooking a good meal; pairing just the right wine to go with the dish. To him these were life's simplest pleasures.

Lindsay sat at the bar that divided the kitchen and living room. "I've always wondered how to make coq au vin."

Carlos furrowed his brow. "Oh, it's terribly difficult."

"Really?"

He pulled several sprigs of the fresh thyme he'd purchased, then held them under cool running water.

"No, actually it's quite simple. The secret to a good coq au vin is to use good wine and let it take its time cooking so that all the ingredients have a chance to meld."

He put butter in a sauté pan and turned on the stove's burner. The flame ignited with a *poof,* and immediately the butter began to sizzle and slide around the pan.

"Let me teach you how," he said. "That way you'll have a wonderful dinner to add to your repertoire."

"I guess a repertoire has to start with a first recipe."

He did a double take. "What? You don't cook for yourself?"

She shook her head. "I bake. I didn't make any claims about cooking."

"How do you subsist?"

She shrugged. "I manage, I guess."

"Come in here," he said. "I want to teach you how to make this."

"How can I resist a private lesson?" She slid off the stool and appeared in the kitchen. The overhead light brought out the gold in her hair. Yet her porcelain skin seemed to glow from within. She stood so close to him, if his hands hadn't been full of pearl onions, he would've reached out and taken her into his arms. He did the second best thing; he listed to the right until their shoulders touched.

"First, we're going to blanch the onions in boiling water," he said. "That'll help the skin to slide right off."

She reached out and took one of the small bulbs from his hand, and her pinkie trailed along his palm. She looked up snared his gaze.

"Onions, huh? I don't want to cry again."

He set down the onions and took her face in his hands.

"I promise you, I won't make you cry, Lindsay. I am not Derrick."

They stared at each other as the truth of the moment closed in around them. They'd set aside the posturing and their guards had fallen, letting in an intimacy that was so deep, so intense, it stung.

They'd shared their most personal secrets. They knew the worst and the best of each other. Even though it scared him to think of caring for someone that much, he'd already passed the point of no return. There was no denying the truth. He'd fallen for her...hard.

The only question was, where did they go from here?

She must have read the question on his face, because she answered it by turning off the stove burners, then leaning in and kissing him. He responded by pulling her in closer and wrapping his arms around her as if he'd never let her go.

Every inch of her body was pressed against his. He lost himself in the heated tenderness of their embrace.

He knew instinctively that she'd be a decisive lover. The way her hands explored his body—his shoulders, his back, his waist. Her touch excited him and promised that she'd claim him with a need that just might leave him even more defenseless than he was now. If that was possible.

In response, he wanted to show her how much he ached for her, how he'd longed for this moment since the night he'd first laid eyes on her. Rather than using words, he conveyed his feelings as his lips claimed hers in a kiss meant to sear her soul.

Desire grew as he held her and tasted her. In response his own body swelled and hardened. He loved the feel of her curves, supple to his touch. When he dropped his hands to her hips and pulled her closer, she arched against him, fueling the hardness of his desire.

"I want you," she murmured breathlessly.

He raised his hands to her breasts, cupping them, memorizing her curves before teasing her hard nipples. She gasped. Her head dropped back and she seemed to lose herself in his touch.

Then it was his turn. She slid her hand down the front of his jeans and claimed his erection. Over and over she teased him, rubbing and stroking his desire through the layers of his jeans and briefs. The sensation was almost too much to bear. So he backed away a little, leaning in to kiss the side of her neck, playfully biting down on her earlobe.

In anticipation of their lovemaking, a shudder racked his whole body. Suddenly he needed her naked so that he could bury himself inside of her.

She must have wanted the same thing, because in one swift move, she began to unbuckle the button on his jeans, slid down the zipper and pushed his briefs to the floor. He stepped out of both, and shrugged off his shirt, unashamed of his nakedness.

Wanting to permanently imprint her on his senses, he deliberately slowed down and undid each button on her shirt. Pushing it away, he unhooked the front clasp on her bra. As he freed her breasts, he lowered his head and, in turn, took each one into his mouth, suckling them until she cried out in pleasure. Then, when he was sure she was ready, he tugged down her trousers and panties.

As they stood together naked, despite the need

driving him to the edge of madness, again, he purposely slowed down, taking a moment to commit to memory the way her beautiful body looked.

And then they were reaching for each other and touching everywhere, a tangle of arms and legs.

"Let's go into the bedroom," she murmured.

He kissed her deeply as he backed her down the hall—tongues thrusting, hands exploring, teeth nipping. A sensual *pas de deux* that led them to a bedroom. He wasn't really cognizant of which one, but was only aware of laying her down on the bed.

"Now," she said. And he buried himself inside her.

Their vacation in Paris was what Lindsay liked to call a *snow globe moment*: a picture-perfect vignette suspended in time.

Oh, how she wished she really could stop time so that she and Carlos could live inside that bubble forever. It was the most romantic ten days of her life, and their time together went by as quickly as the snow settled in a shaken snow globe.

They spent a romantic Christmas together cooking a traditional stuffed goose. They'd even purchased a small tree at the open-air market on the rue Cler, which they decorated and lit on Christmas Eve before they'd eaten and exchanged gifts.

Carlos surprised her with a hand-tooled leather journal. "Your mother's book has meant so much to you. Now, it's time you started your own."

The gesture brought tears to her eyes. For a moment, she thought she'd come undone. Never had such a simple gift held such meaning and possibility. It made the vintage brass bowl she'd found for him at one of the open-air markets seem insignificant in comparison. But he made it seem as if the gift was perfect.

They rang in the new year drinking champagne and making love until dawn. Lindsay would've been perfectly happy to stay naked in his arms for the rest of the year. Alas, soon enough reality came calling, shattering their snow globe existence and forcing them back into the real world: they had to go back to work.

Except for Max, none of the cast and crew knew that Lindsay and Carlos had spent the holidays together. They'd decided it would probably be best if they kept their relationship a secret.

At least until after they negotiated the new contract with Chandler.

That seemed like the smart thing to do. Especially when, on the first day back, Chandler called a breakfast meeting with the two of them in his hotel suite.

He'd ordered in a variety of pastries and fruit, coffee and tea. They expected the reason for the meeting was to talk about their contracts since the Paris shoot was the fourth and final shoot on the current contract.

As they settled in with their plates, he asked, "Did you have a nice Christmas?"

"Yes." Lindsay sipped her coffee. Her mind raced to come up with a plausible explanation as to how she'd spent the holidays, if he asked. A natural overview, without giving away too much—and without lying to Chandler.

"How about you, Carlos?"

Carlos bit into his pastry. He nodded furiously, pointing to his mouth, playing the old can't-talk-with-food-in-my-mouth card.

Chandler looked back and forth between them. "Well, it looks to me like you had quite a romantic time."

He took a folder off the end table next to his chair and began to flip through a stack of eight-by-ten photographs.

"I see you made it to the Eiffel Tower."

What? Lindsay sat frozen, afraid to even glance at Carlos.

"And the Louvre." He held up another of them embracing on the rue du Rivoli, the street that ran along the north wing of the museum. "Did you happen to make it to the Musée Marmottan? It always seems to live in the shadow of the larger, better-known Parisian museums. But your walk along the Seine looked particularly romantic."

Lindsay's chest tightened as he held up photo after photo chronicling their holiday.

"In the future, you might want to be more aware of who's following you. Now that you're on television, there are always cameras about. Paparazzi looking to make a buck."

But the show hadn't even aired yet.

"What we do on our own time is our business." Carlos spat the words.

"Your business and anyone who cares to look at CelebrityLoveFest.com. That's where these came from."

Chandler tossed the photos onto the coffee table and they scattered in different directions.

She and Carlos each grabbed a photo off the table. The caption on the one Lindsay held said, *Former Food TV bad boy Carlos Montigo has signed on with a new network to host a brand-new show called* The Diva Drives. *He and his Diva cohost, Lindsay Bingham, were spotted together heating up Paris. Maybe Montigo is no longer yesterday's leftovers.*

Lindsay's blood pounded and her face grew hot with humiliation. Especially when Carlos flung the photo he'd been looking at back onto the table.

"You can't dictate what we do when we're not filming, Chandler." There was an edge to Carlos's voice. Lindsay slanted a glance at him. His expression matched his tone.

Chandler's face darkened. "The only reason I'm not arguing that point is because this isn't bad publicity for the show."

He and Carlos stared at each other. Two alpha males in a standoff.

"Everybody loves a love affair. So, as long as this generates good publicity for the show, I have no problem with it. But the minute it starts interfering it'll be a different story."

Carlos stiffened.

"Nowhere in the contract does it mention anything about you dictating our personal lives."

Chandler folded his hands in his lap. "That's covered by the morals clause. Believe me, Mr. Montigo, when it comes to business, I leave nothing to chance."

Chapter Fourteen

There were few things that Carlos hated more than feeling owned. In fact, right about now, he couldn't think of a single thing that irked him more.

Except, perhaps, Chandler using Carlos's and Lindsay's relationship to further his business interests. Sure, common sense dictated that in this case Chandler's business interests benefited Carlos. They were banking on the show getting off on the right foot so that Chandler would extend the contract.

However, even that was up in the air for the time being. Chandler said the fate of the full season was still in limbo because he was still negotiating with sponsors. Something about it sounded like a flimsy excuse. They were in their last week of the pilot, and surely Chandler would've known by now if he was going to continue with the show.

Max had ensured him there was no need to worry. He'd make sure these *negotiations* didn't drag on too long. Right now, Carlos didn't know if he wanted to sign his life away for a full season. The money from the pilot was enough seed money to go back to Cedar Inlet and open his restaurant. After this week's shoot, he would've fulfilled his contractual obligation to Chandler. Then he'd be free to tell him what he could do with his morals clause. The only thing stopping him was Lindsay.

Carlos's walking away would affect her, too. He didn't know what he was going to do about the situation. But Chandler hadn't yet put the new contracts on the table, so there was no sense in worrying about it until he had to commit to signing his life away.

In the meantime, it was more important to him to prove to Lindsay that despite how much he hated the prying media and Chandler's assertions of ownership, the bad situation had not changed his feelings for her one bit.

That's why he'd worked with Paula to arrange an on-camera surprise for Lindsay on their third day of shooting.

"Here, put this on." The cameras were rolling as Carlos and Lindsay sat in Bella. He handed her a red silk scarf.

She laughed. "What is this, a scarf-tying test? Just because we're in Paris does not automatically mean I've become scarf-savvy. Even if this is an Hermès scarf. *Ooh,* this is nice—"

"It's a nice blindfold." He took the silk fabric from her hands. "I want you to put it on because I have a surprise for you."

Thoughts of the things they could do with a silk scarf and a four-poster bed flashed through his head and blood rushed south and pooled in his groin.

He shifted. It wasn't the time for that. Reaching over, he gently tied the scarf over her eyes.

"Carlos, are you sure this is absolutely necessary?"

"Absolutely." He gave the camera his most devastating grin before he steered Bella out of the parking space.

"Where are you taking me?"

"If I told you, it wouldn't be a surprise, would it?"

She looked sexy with the silk tied over her eyes, the wind tousling the ends of her blond hair about her shoulders.

He only had a short distance to drive and a few minutes later Carlos stopped in front of a small bakery.

"Stay right here," he said. "I'll be around to help you out of the car. And don't peek."

A small crowd gathered outside as the cameras filmed Carlos helping Lindsay from the car and into the bakery.

"Okay," he said. "You can remove the blindfold."

Even with her eyes covered, the first thing that hit Lindsay once she stepped inside out of the cold was a luscious mélange of sweet aromas—fresh-baked bread, almond paste, chocolate and strong-brewed coffee.

Her mouth watered. *Mmm…* Her favorite smells. Maybe this segment was a pastry tasting…or a spot on the best boulangeries in Paris? But why the blindfold? Well, whatever it was, if it involved French pastry she wanted in.

She pulled the scarf from her eyes and blinked as she looked around a stunning Art Deco-style pâtisserie, complete with starburst light fixtures, 1930s-era mirrors, marble counter tops and a curved brass and glass display case.

It was gorgeous. If she ever opened a place of her own this is what it would look like.

The cameras were rolling as Carlos and a rotund man in a crisp white apron stood next to her, smiling as if they knew the punch line to a joke Lindsay wasn't yet aware of. Though she had a feeling they'd enlighten her soon enough.

"It's a tightly kept secret that one of Lindsay's passions is baking," Carlos winked at the camera. "But I happen to believe she makes the best cookies *anyone* has ever tasted. Today we wanted to put that to the test and surprise her by introducing her to the man who was voted Paris's best pastry chef, Rene Delanoë."

Lindsay stood blank, amazed and not quite sure how she felt about her secret love of baking being revealed to the world. It had always been private, something she turned to when she was sad or lonely or otherwise needed cheering up. Something that connected her to her mother.

But, wow. Rene Delanoë. She'd heard of him and his world-famous Pâtisserie Delanoë.

Had Carlos arranged this for her?

Sure, it was for the show. What was a trip to Paris without a sweet treat? But he could've just set it up in the same way they set up all the segments.

He'd obviously gone to a lot of trouble to make this a surprise. And that warmed her from the inside out.

"A *pâtisserie* is a French bakery that specializes in pastries and sweets," Carlos said. "In France, it is an official title that only bakeries employing a *maître pâtissier*—or master pastry chef—may use. The Pâtisserie Delanoë is actually both a *pâtisserie* and a *boulangerie,* right?"

It was awkward standing there mute. Even though she hadn't had the benefit of preparing for the segment, Lindsay decided it was better to jump in than say nothing. "What's the difference between the two, chef?"

"A *boulangerie* specializes in bread," said Delanoë in heavily accented English. "A *pâtisserie* is about the sweets."

"While we're here, Chef Delanoë is going to show us how he makes his world-famous madeleines," said Carlos. "We'll try to wrangle the secret recipe out of him. And speaking of secret recipes, I'm going to see if I can't convince Lindsay to treat us all to the incomparable treat of her Ultimate Cookies. What do you say, Linds?"

She knew the recipe by heart. But she'd never really put it to the test.

"Hmm…" she stalled. "Well, this is quite a surprise. Why do I get the feeling if I say anything other than yes that you'll tie me to a chair with that scarf until I agree?"

The thought sent butterflies swooping in her stomach, but that was nothing compared to the way her body reacted when he quirked his brow and flashed that devastating smile of his.

"Now there's an idea. But before we get too distracted, Rene is going to give us a tour of the pastry case over here."

Lindsay trailed behind Carlos, following the siren song of his broad shoulders over to the glass case.

"Who needs any other enticement?" she said wistfully.

Reluctantly, she tore her gaze away and focused on the artful array of sweet decadence in front of her: tarts in nearly any flavor one could name—even chestnut; rustic, free-form fruit tarts that begged to be tasted; cakes of all shapes and sizes that looked more like works of art than sugary confections: Napoleon, chocolate *rhum* and something called a Hippodrome, which was decorated with meringue, almonds and apricot glaze. *Ooh...*then there were the chocolate éclairs, the Choux Chantilly and Praline Riviera....

"Could I have one of each, please?"

"But of course." With a wave of his hand, Delanoë's assistant began assembling a sampler platter, as the chef moved on to introduce a range of specialty breads: baguettes, boules, ficelles and fougasse, which Delanoë explained was a ladder-shaped loaf doused with olive oil and baked with fillings that changed daily—black olives one day, chèvre and tomatoes the next. Then there were the croissants, decadently plump, with a golden exterior that looked as if it would flake at the slightest touch.

"And over here we have the ever popular *pain au chocolat,*" said Delanoë. "It is sort of, how you say, a bridge between the bread and the sweets. We use the best possible chocolate. Good quality is a must. We will not settle for less.

"You see, not all *chocolat* is created equal. True, it is all made from cacao beans, which are from the Theobroma tree. Did you know that *Theobroma* translates to 'Food of the Gods'? That's probably because of its great aphrodisiac qualities." He wiggled his bushy gray brows at Lindsay.

Paula called, "Cut. That's a perfect note to end on. Because we'd planned on giving some details on where chocolate comes from. We were going to do this in a chocolate shop, but it looks like the shooting schedule will be a little tight. I think we'll cut that and expand on the patisserie. Lindsay, you'll do a voice-over, which we'll dub as we transition from the front of the house into the kitchen. Why don't you do a quick read-through of what's on the cue cards?"

"Sure."

Paula held up the cards and Lindsay recited:

"The type and blend of cacao beans and where they are grown all contribute to the final quality and taste of the chocolate. Other factors are how the beans are grown and ultimately roasted, and how they're processed.

"Here's a bit of trivia for you. Did you know there are three types of cacao beans? The forastero, criollo and trinitario.

"The most important point to consider when choosing the chocolate with which you will bake is whether you like the taste of the chocolate when you eat it in its unmelted form. Come on, let's go into the kitchen and see what the chef has cooking."

Despite the freezing temperatures and one rainy day, the Paris shoot went by nearly seamlessly.

Lindsay prepared her mother's cookie recipe for Chef Delanoë, and he proclaimed it "magnifique," with a quiet reverence that spoke volumes. He even asked her to share her recipe. She wouldn't, because it was an old family recipe. Even so, he said she had a job working with him at Pâtisserie Delanoë if she ever wanted a career change.

"That's very nice of you," she said.

"No, no, no," he said. "Make no mistake. I am never simply *nice.* Not when it comes to business. When I say you have talent, I mean it. You seem to have a knack for taking ordinary ingredients that when mixed together are," he scrunched up his face and waved his hand in a circular motion, "they are usually fine, but your seem to possess a special sensibility that allows you to make magic."

He was right about that, Carlos thought. Lindsay Bingham's touch was magic. In more ways than one.

"Maybe it's my mother baking through me?" She'd laughed it off. "Nah, baking is something I enjoy. I've been experimenting with it for so long, it's second nature."

"Well, you have a standing job offer at my patisserie."

At that moment, the irony of Delanoë's offer escaped them. It would be three days later, on their last day of shooting, when Max dropped the bomb.

They were taping the final segment for the last *Diva* episode—a nighttime picnic on the Champ de Mars, the lawn that stretches between the Eiffel Tower and École Militaire—in the freezing cold, but since the spot had to be timeless, they had to pretend like the weather was bearable.

The Eiffel Tower light show was in full flash in the background, Lindsay and Carlos were enjoying a baguette, cheese and some wine on a blue-and-white checked picnic blanket.

"The perfect ending to a perfect visit to Paris," Lindsay said as they clinked glasses. "See you next time on *The Diva Drives*."

"Cut!" said Chandler. "We got it. Good show. That's a wrap, everyone! I'll see everyone at Jules Verne, the restaurant on the second level of the Eiffel Tower at ten."

The sixteen-member crew murmured good words and milled about, gathering up cords and equipment.

"I'm going to go back to the hotel and freshen up before the party," said Lindsay. "I'll meet you there."

"I'll ride back with you," Carlos said.

As he started to walk with her to the car, Chandler put a hand on Carlos's shoulder. "Actually, I was hoping you had a minute. I need to talk to you about something."

When Max walked up, Carlos figured it must have something to do with the new contract.

"Sure," he said to Chandler. "Lindsay, I'll walk you to the car."

"You don't have to do that. In fact, I think Paula's going that way. I'll walk with her. See you later."

Carlos squeezed her hand and watched her walk away before turning back to Chandler and Max.

"So, what's up?"

Max and Chandler exchanged a look that didn't bode well.

"What?" Carlos insisted.

"I hate to put a damper on things." Max raked a hand through his hair, a familiar nervous tic. "But I got a call from a writer for a small tabloid out of Barcelona. It seems they're working on a story."

Every muscle in Carlos's body tensed. Judging by the look on Max's face, it wasn't positive.

"Good press?" he said sarcastically.

Max scowled. "That depends on your definition of *good*. Some diehards believe *any* press is good press."

Carlos uttered an oath.

Max held up a hand. "Now wait, before you jump to conclusions, let's put it in perspective."

"Put *what* into perspective?" Carlos glanced at Chandler, who was standing there so silently it was creeping him out. Carlos fisted his hands. "What kind of muck are the scumbags raking now?"

"It's just an insignificant tabloid," Max continued as if he hadn't heard him. "A minor player in Spanish gossip."

Carlos leveled him with a glare. "Quit beating around the damn bush and tell me."

Max sucked in a breath and blew it out noisily. "They've been doing some digging into your past. They're making an issue out of an old arrest record."

For a moment, Carlos didn't know whether to laugh or put his fist through a wall. Thank God there wasn't a wall nearby. He settled for gritting his teeth and closing his eyes against the white-hot anger surging through his veins.

"You've got to be *kidding me*," he hissed. "I was fourteen years old when it happened."

"What did you...*do* to warrant assault charges?" Chandler looked like he was sucking on a lemon. Of course. He was worried he'd made a mistake and hired a felon. Surely guys like Chandler did background checks before they invested in an employee. Then again, this probably wouldn't have come up in a background check since Carlos was so young when it happened...and the charges were bogus.

"I was caught driving a delivery truck without a license. I lived in a small village and the cop who caught me had an ax to grind with my mother." He shrugged. "When she was alive, she seemed to have that affect on men, but that's another story."

He hadn't counted on the rush of emotion that accompanied this unexpected trip down memory lane. He cleared his throat, hoping to clear the knot that had lodged there. Poker faced, Chandler stared at him, while Max shifted uncomfortably.

"I'll level with you, man. The scumbag is asking questions about your mother's drinking and your childhood. Look, we don't have to get into this here." Max gestured to the people—some crew, some tourists—milling about. "This is a delicate subject. Why don't we go back to the hotel where we can discuss this privately?"

Carlos shook his head. "There's not that much left to say. We might as well finish it here."

"Well, if you'd rather go somewhere else—" Chandler said, glancing around.

"No, I said this was fine. It'll be out soon enough. The long and short of it is, when the cop saw it was me, he tried to rough me up a bit and suddenly the driving-without-a-license charge morphed into assault and resisting arrest charges. It was all bogus. Everything was eventually dropped, but somehow money-hungry reporters can always dig up those sensational headlines, can't they."

Max looked away and cleared his throat.

"He's suggesting that maybe your rough past is a contributing factor to why you lied about your culinary background. Basically, the gist of the article seems to be that's what is at the root of your psyche."

White-hot anger simmered in his gut. He was a pressure cooker ready to blow. "So now they're trying to expose my psyche? Saying I covered up my past to avoid exposing the fact that I was raised by an abusive drunk of a mother?"

As if putting his private life on trial in the tabloids wasn't entertainment enough, now they wanted his soul. Again. Leaving him obliged to defend himself.

He watched all the people walking by, going about their happy, anonymous lives because no one gave a damn what they did when they were fourteen or thirty-four; whether they punched a crooked cop who said foul things about their mother or refused a restaurant rating.

He envied them and their anonymity. He wouldn't wish life in the public eye on his worst enemy.

"Well, I'm sure Max can handle the reporter," Chandler was saying, but Carlos could barely hear him over the blood rushing in his ears.

"Listen, I have to go."

"Are you okay?" Max asked.

"We'll see you later at the party?" Chandler said.

Carlos just turned and walked away.

When Max relayed the situation with the tabloid, Lindsay's first thought was that Carlos simply needed a some time alone to process everything, but when the dinner plates were cleared and there was still no sign of him, she started to worry. As the restaurant staff served dessert, she excused herself to go call him. She ran into him in the lobby.

"Carlos, are you okay? You missed dinner."

He looked dark and drawn. There was a long pause before he said, "Yeah, I'm not in a very festive mood tonight. I probably shouldn't have come. I'm sure Max told you what's going on?"

She nodded and touched his arm. "I'm sorry."

He stiffened and pulled back. It was an almost imperceptible flinch, but it happened, and his withdrawal stung.

"Yeah, well, I guess that's how it goes in this business," he said.

"Do you want to talk about it?" She shifted her weight from one foot to another. She'd worn the Jimmy Choo heels for the last day of the shoot, and after a sixteen-hour day her feet hated her for it, but that was nothing compared to the way her heart ached seeing him like this.

He crossed his arms and his face shuttered. "Not really."

"Come on, let's go for a walk anyway." Despite her aching feet, the best thing they could do was go somewhere so they could be alone and they could talk this out.

He hesitated, drawing in a deep breath as if preparing to protest.

"The mood you're in, do you really want to go in there?" she asked.

He smiled, but there was no humor in his eyes.

"Let me get my coat," she said, "and then let's get out of here."

When she returned, he was standing at the bank of elevators. He'd already pushed the call button.

It was just the two of them alone in the elevator. The silence was deafening. She'd never seen Carlos like this—not even earlier in the week when Chandler told them about the photographs. She'd caught glimpses of his stoic media animosity when she'd asked questions during their initial interview and when he finally opened up about the past, but it paled in comparison to this silent simmering anger.

Common sense told her his mood wasn't directed at her, but it was hard not to take it a little personally. Even so…maybe if she could just get him talking about it—

"We haven't even talked about what happens next?" His question surprised her.

Next? As in them? Together?

Or as in them as coworkers?

"I don't know, Carlos. I was sort of banking on the transition from one contract to another being seamless," she said. "I wasn't counting on much downtime, especially after having the time off at Christmas. But it looks like it may be a while before Chandler makes up his mind."

Saying the words aloud made her gut clench. All the uncertainty and fear she'd tamped down since Chandler announced he was temporarily putting the project on hold surged to the forefront.

He nodded. "That's what I want to talk to you about."

But then the elevator stopped and they had to dodge a gaggle of tourists as they stepped outside into the chill night. The cold January air was like a reality slap. Despite how Carlos put his arm around her as they walked, she had a bad feeling about what he'd come to say. A sense of foreboding hung in the air like an invisible fog, but when she glanced up, all that loomed above them was the Eiffel Tower, a giant decked out in lacy black steel silhouetted against the inky midnight sky.

They walked across the Champ de Mars lawn in the direction of the hotel, and for a long time neither of them said anything. She was determined to let him be the first to speak. Because in the meantime, they could simply walk arm in arm, through the lamp-lit streets of Paris and everything would be fine.

"I don't know how else to say this, Lindsay, other than to…just say it." His voice was thick with emotion. "I can't do this anymore."

There it was. The clock striking midnight, her coach morphing back into a pumpkin.

"Do what anymore? This?" She gestured back and forth between the two of them. "Do you mean *us?* Or—"

Her breath caught in her throat as if stopping her words. Good thing, too, because she hated the sarcasm in her voice, and the way her heart hammered at such a furious rate as if it were nailing her windpipe shut so that another word couldn't escape. Her hand fluttered to her neck. He reached out and grabbed her hand, lacing his fingers through hers.

"This has nothing to do with *us*." The way he looked at her, his eyes so dark and full of raw sorrow, made her want to lean into him and wrap her arms around him. That, in turn, made her want to run. But she couldn't because of the firm grip he had on her hand.

"I realized today, I can't live my life in the public eye anymore. I'm just not cut out for it. And because of that, I would be holding you back."

"That's not true." Her voice was a hoarse whisper. "The show is going great. How can you just walk away from it now?"

With eyes full of torment, he searched her face, then ran a finger along her jawline. Her body responded to his touch and she hated herself for it. For God's sake, he was breaking up with her. How could she be so weak? But then again, weakness was what got her into this mess in the first place.

"You'll be fine. Chandler found you first. He'll simply revert back to the single-host *Diva Dishes* format, or there's no reason you can't drive the show yourself. Your talent is not dependent on me."

I'll be fine?

"So, if you're not re-signing for the show, what are you going to do?" she asked.

"I'm going back to Cedar Inlet and opening my restaurant."

It sounded like he had his mind made up.

"Great," she said. "I'll be on the road and you'll be in Florida. That doesn't sound very conducive to a relationship."

"It's the only way both of us will be happy, Lindsay."

She started backing up, trying to get away from him.

"So being apart will make you happy? That's certainly not the effect it'll have on me."

He shook his head. "I don't know what else to do," he said. "I can't stay, and I won't ask you to leave. It's killing me to do this, but I can't expect you to give up the show and follow me back to Cedar Inlet, to a restaurant that's still only the germ of an idea."

Through the tangle of emotions, she remembered what he'd said that night at dinner in Carcassonne; that he'd accepted the initial contract fully intending to take the money and run after he'd fulfilled his contractual obligation. She was the idiot for not seeing this coming—for blurring the lines between her professional and personal lives.

Fooled once, shame on the other guy; fooled twice…

Well, she was the fool.

"Just stop." She jerked her hand from his and took a big step back. When she did, her foot wobbled and she felt the slight drop of stepping onto an unsteady surface. But she righted herself without accepting his outstretched hand.

She glanced down and saw her right foot was on a sewer grate.

"You don't have to give me a sad, sad song and dance, Carlos." As she talked, she tried, as inconspicuously as possible, to free her heel from the grid. "All you have to say is, 'It's been fun, but I'm done here.' You're taking the money and running like you told me you were going to do."

"No, that's not—"

"Just stop! I don't want your reasons and excuses."

She wiggled her foot some more. To no avail. The damn thing was stuck.

Oh, God.

Why?

Why this? Why now?

She was such an idiot.

Tears welled in her eyes. All she wanted to do was leave. To get as far away from him as possible. "You don't have to pretend like it was anything more than it was—" She choked on her words.

As the first tear crested and fell, she curled her toes in her shoes and pulled with her right leg as hard as she could. The force sent her stumbling backward, but she was finally free.

Only when she started to run did she realize she'd broken the heel of her shoe.

Jimmy Choos be damned, there was no way she was going to turn around and get down on her hands and knees to pry the heel of her shoe out of a sewer grate. She'd suffered enough humiliation.

She just kept running.

Because there was no looking back now.

Chapter Fifteen

A week later, Lindsay sat at the kitchen table in her house in Trevard, North Carolina, talking to Ida May Higgins and spooning out chocolate chip cookie dough onto a baking sheet.

"It's nearly noon," said Ida May. "You know what you need, darlin'? You need to get yourself upstairs and take a good long shower, fix your hair and put on some color. Nothin' like a little color to perk up the mood."

She couldn't shower now. They were doing a taste test. Her mom's original recipe versus a variation that a well-known baking guru claimed was the best recipe *ever*. Ida had insisted on the taste test—immediately— despite how Lindsay suggested they do it another day. The last thing she needed was more sweets. She'd been trying to bake away her heartache since she'd been home, but it wasn't working.

First, she thought the brioche would do the trick, but that only reminded her of being with Carlos at the Leblanc Inn. She'd skipped her mom's Ultimate Cookie recipe because it would always and forever remind her of how he'd surprised her at Pâtisserie Delanoë. Instead, she made her mom's red velvet cake, three different kinds of pies and a double batch of coconut macaroons.

None of it worked.

"Of course not," Ida May had insisted. "Everyone knows *chocolate* is the cure for a broken heart, honey. You need chocolate chip cookies and you need them *now*. Because what's better for a broken heart than warm cookies with all that gooey, melty chocolate?"

As Ida May scraped dough from the sides of the bowl, she slanted a sidelong glance at Lindsay. "Have you heard anything from him, darlin'?"

Lindsay shook her head and tried to push the thought of Carlos from her mind. All week he'd been trying *not* to think of him.

She didn't blame him for not wanting to continue with the show. She wasn't even sure it was what she wanted anymore.

There was no job security in television. That had never been so clear as it was now, with Chandler holding up the show—and her life—while he tried to decide whether he wanted to take *The Diva Drives* to a full season.

He was hashing it out with sponsors, trying to *work out a deal*. Lindsay suspected he was buying time to see if he really wanted to move forward with her as the sole host of *Diva Drives,* or *Diva Dishes,* or…*ha ha Diva Dashes*.

Max told her Chandler hadn't been thrilled when she'd left Paris in the middle of the night—without saying goodbye. She'd called to apologize, but it had been a week and he'd yet to return her call.

It didn't bode well.

Sure, he was a busy man, but he was also very prone to changing his mind, especially if a venture didn't seem to be profitable.

Even more, common sense dictated that even if the *Diva* went to a full season, there would come a time when Carson Chandler turned his sights to newer, fresher…programming.

She supposed if her heart were really in the job, she'd fight for what she wanted, but Chandler's hemming and hawing over the show—keeping her future in limbo— reminded her that she really didn't *love* the television business, and how she hated putting her fate in someone else's hands. It had bothered her before when she'd reported for WKMO. But the *Diva* spot was a different format than dry news reporting. She'd thought it was a chance to be creative.

But really, the heart of the matter was that she wasn't in love with the job itself.

What she'd loved about it was working with Carlos. Spending time with him, getting to know him.

Falling in love with him.

She had enough money to tide her over for the time being, but she needed to have "Plan B" in the works so that she could invest her money rather than burn through it.

She sighed and looked up into the sweet, dark, wrinkled face of the woman who'd been the closest thing to a mother Lindsay had ever known. Ida May had helped her pick out prom dresses and held Lindsay's hand as she picked out the casket in which she buried her father.

When she'd gone over for Sophie's wedding Ida May had gladly watched the house. Then she extended the house-sitting for six weeks, insisting Lindsay accept Chandler's job offer.

And it was Ida May's shoulder she cried on for the first two days that she was back. She'd cried over Carlos; over the uncertainty of the show's future; over her future's murky forecast.

"That was a heavy sigh, darlin'," Ida May said as she reclaimed her chair at the table. "What are ya thinking?"

"That I missed you while I was gone."

The old woman reached out and took Lindsay's hand in hers. "I missed you, too, honey. But I can tell from looking at you that's not all that's on your mind."

Ida May knew her so well. It was comforting, but it also meant there was no place to hide when they were together.

"I'm twenty-nine years old, and I just can't seem to get it right."

The woman narrowed her eyes at Lindsay and cocked her head.

"I guess what I'm trying to say is if I have one regret in my life it's how I disappointed my father. I couldn't get my life together when he was alive. And I still haven't."

Ida May frowned and pulled herself up straight, a posture Lindsay knew meant the older woman was getting ready to speak, and she'd better listen.

"I have no idea what nonsense you're spouting. Aside from your mama, you were the love of your daddy's life. How is it you think you disappointed him?"

Lindsay closed her eyes for a moment, fighting off a sudden swell of tears, unexpected because she thought she'd cried herself dry earlier this week. But there was no mistaking the burning sensation stinging the backs of her lids.

Still, she took a deep breath and opened her eyes. "He always had such high hopes for me, and I let him down. I never lived up to his expectations. The only time I came halfway close was when I had the job with WKMO. I know it's crazy, he's been gone for four years now, but taking this job somehow felt like I was finally making good on all those years I let him down. But I couldn't sustain it."

God. She sounded pathetic. If there was one thing she hated it was playing the victim—a woman incapable of taking care of herself. She was just about to retract her pitiful dumping when Ida May said, "I assure you, your father was very proud of you. Lord, child, his only concern was that his daughter grew up to be a strong, independent woman. Someone who could take care of herself. I assure you if he could sit here at this table with us today, he'd be mighty proud of the woman you've become. The only way you could disappoint him is if you let yourself down."

There was a long stretch where neither of them said anything. Lindsay mulled over Ida's words.

Enough of this maudlin self-pity. It was time to put on her big-girl pants and figure out what was next—whether she should call Chandler again or have Max call Chandler to work his agenting magic. It seemed like what she *should* do. It was an opportunity that most people would die for.

But the thought of being away from home for months on end made her heart heavy. She didn't realize what a homebody she was until this week—being home, cooking in her own kitchen, sleeping in her own bed, sitting at her own table, talking to Ida May.

"Honey, if I can be honest with you, I think the only reason your daddy disliked you working as a reception-ist was that he knew you weren't truly happy. Were you?"

Lindsay shook her head.

"What I think you need to do is search your soul and figure out your heart's desire. If it's being a television star then you need to get your butt on up to wherever Chandler is and demand that job—"

"That's the problem. I don't want it that bad. I really hated being away from home. This is where my heart is, and even if I don't quite know what the next step is, I'm fairly certain that's not it."

A smile spread across Ida May's face.

"You need to cross that one off the list. I think you need to give yourself a little credit for taking the leap of faith and trying it out. I hope you'll stay open-minded and take that leap again. 'Cause the only way you'll be a failure is if you close yourself off." She glanced at her watch again. "In the meantime, why don't you get yourself upstairs and fix yourself up like I suggested? I'll finish up here."

A shower would do her some good. She'd been lazy since she'd been home, sometimes staying in her paja-mas until noon.

She put her arms around the old woman's beefy shoulders, breathing in the sweet scent of cookie dough, baby powder and sweat. "Ida May, have I told you how much I love you?"

The old woman squeezed Lindsay's hand. "Child, I love you, too. Now get yourself upstairs and tend to yours."

A dull, aching sadness settled in the pit of Lindsay's stomach. As she started toward the stairs, she counted her blessings, beginning with Ida May.

But before she could set foot on the first step, some-one knocked on the front door.

"Oh, Lordy!" Ida May exclaimed from the kitchen. "I knew I should've hurried her up," the older woman murmured as she rushed into the living room.

When Lindsay turned to head back upstairs, Ida May said, "I suspect you'll want to get that."

Lindsay's hand was on the banister. "Well, I was just going to head back up—"

Ida May gave her head a quick shake. "No, ma'am. You'll definitely want to get this."

Puzzled, Lindsay studied the woman's wrinkled brown face as she walked toward the door. "What's going on, Ida May?"

Taking off her apron, the elder woman shrugged. "I reckon you ought to open the door and find out for yourself."

There was something in Ida May's eyes, which she quickly averted, that made Lindsay's heart quicken.

She opened the door and there was Carlos.

"Hello, I understand there's a woman here who lost a heel to a rather expensive pair of shoes. I've come to return it."

He pulled the heel to her Jimmy Choos out of his pocket and stood there holding it like a mini scepter.

"I would've been here sooner, but this thing was the devil to get loose from that storm drain. I hope you didn't throw the shoes out. I hope I'm not…too late? Am I?"

Lindsay threw her arms around him and held him as if she'd never let him go.

"Child, I tried to tell you to get yourself upstairs and get washed up," Ida May groused. "I told her to change clothes and put on some color. Never listens. Mmm-hmm. Never has from the time she was a tiny thing."

Lindsay turned and looked at Ida May. "You knew he was coming, didn't you?"

Ida May and Carlos smiled conspiratorially.

"Baby, you know how the story goes. Prince Charming always delivers the shoe. Well, in this case it was just the heel, but you'd have gotten no good out of those shoes without it."

Lindsay turned back to Carlos. "But how…? You two…?"

"I was afraid you wouldn't see me if I asked you if I could come," he said. "So, when I called the other day and got Ida May on the phone… Well, here I am. This time I don't intend to leave."

A sense of utter joy flooded through Lindsay. "But what about the restaurant?"

"I'm going to open it here."

Lindsay blinked. "Here in Trevard?"

He nodded. "I've spent the last week looking into business licenses and permits and facilities. Oh, and I heard there's a fabulous pastry chef in Trevard. She's sort of a diva, but I think the fact that she's self-taught fits right in with the concept of Out of the Fire. I've come to make her a partner. Do you think she'll accept?"

Epilogue

Four months later, Carlos and Lindsay opened the doors to Out of the Fire, a training restaurant for teens and young adults who'd gotten into trouble and needed a second chance.

A new direction.

A fresh start in life.

The rules for the on-the-job training program were rigid, but if a kid was willing to walk the straight-and-narrow and give one hundred-and-fifty percent, they just might qualify for one of twenty-five spots in the program.

Carlos fought off the nervous energy that was causing his heart to beat so furiously it was a wonder it didn't echo in the cavernous warehouse that they'd converted into a chic, ultramodern spot. Tonight was their first official test: prepare samples from the seasonal menu for the one hundred invited guests. Chandler, Max, Paula,

Sam and the whole *Diva* crew joined local dignitaries and regional food writers. Even Sophie, Luc and her daughter, Princess Savannah, flew in for the soft opening.

The Out of the Fire staff had worked nearly through the night prepping and planning so that the soft opening would wow the impressive guest list.

Carlos smoothed his moist palms on his black-and-white chef's pants as he watched a tall, slender boy who looked like he couldn't be more than sixteen or seventeen carry a tray full of Lindsay's desserts—everything from shortbread and chocolate chip cookies (her mother's recipe, of course), to fancy petits fours, cakes and tarts—toward the dessert tables.

The extensive work was paying off. The guests seemed to be enjoying themselves, and the night had all the signs of a successful soirée.

It was time for introductions of the kitchen staff and a champagne toast to christen their new venture. That meant Carlos faced just one more task. It was a pass or fail situation. He was sticking his neck out, taking a chance that quite frankly would either make him or break him.

He drew in a deep breath and pulled himself up to his full six-foot-four-inches, then gave Max the signal.

Max picked up a knife off an adjacent table and gently tapped it against his champagne flute.

"Could I have everyone's attention, please?"

The crowd quieted down in short order.

"Chef Carlos Montigo and I go way back. We've been through a lot together. That's why I'm honored to lift a glass in celebration tonight and toast the realization of my good friend's dream. This restaurant, the food you're eating tonight and the program that you all will find outlined in the brochures at your tables represents hard work, perseverance and frankly the investment of the chef's soul. However, even he didn't realize that in achieving all this—" Max gestured around the restaurant "—there would still be something missing. But I think he's figured out how to have it all. Before we introduce the kitchen staff, I'm going to turn the floor over to Carlos so he can tell you about that missing link. Chef?"

Hmm, this was a little different from what they'd discussed, Lindsay mused as she racked her brain for the missing link that Max spoke of. Maybe he'd found an investor for the program? It had to be something big to cause him to stray from the agenda.

Lost in thought she was suddenly aware that most every gaze in the room was riveted to her.

"Lindsay, would you join me over here?" Carlos repeated. "I promise I won't bite."

Waves of appreciative laughter rippled through the room.

Lindsay inclined her head to the side in a mock *I'm-not-so-sure* gesture.

As a partner in the restaurant, she wasn't surprised he wanted to introduce her. It's just that the evening's program was a bit out of order.

What did surprise her—in fact, it nearly knocked the wind out of her—was when Carlos took her hand and said, "I thought my dream would be realized when I finally opened the doors to Out of the Fire, but now that that has happened, I realized there is still a gaping hole right here."

He gestured to his heart. Then, as if in slow motion, Carlos reached into his pocket, pulled out a small black box, and knelt to the ground. "Even my life's work will not make me feel whole. The only way that will happen is if you will agree to be my wife."

Amidst the guests' gasps and sighs, Lindsay's head began to swim. For a moment all she could feel was the slow burning heat creeping up the back of her neck, making its way across her cheekbones. Carlos opened the box and held it out to her.

Her gaze was transfixed on the gorgeous diamond that seemed to light up the room.

"Will you do me the honor of being my wife?"

A slow scream of joy tried to bubble up her windpipe, but all she managed was a frantic nod and slightly guttural sound, which, at least, Carlos recognized as the yes she'd intended.

The crowd cheered as he slipped the ring on her finger.

Funny thing was, at that moment, the lyrics to "When You Wish upon a Star" drifted through her mind as if someone had turned on a radio. It was that part about the bolt from the blue pulling you through and how if you believe, your dreams really will come true. Well, she thought of that and how much she loved the man who was taking her into his arms.

In a moment, after the hysteria from the engagement celebration settled to a dull roar, Carson Chandler caught Lindsay's eye.

"I've just had a brilliant idea," he said. "How about a reality television show taped right here in your restaurant? Think about it…it'll be a natural winner…"

Lindsay smiled at him and turned back to her fiancé. This was all the reality she wanted. Right here in Carlos's arms.

* * * * *